Anim

Enid Blyton

Six Cousins at Mistletoe Farm

Six Cousins Again

MULBERRY EDITIONS

This edition published exclusively for Mulberry Editions
by HarperCollins Children's Books 1992

A division of HarperCollins Publishers Ltd,
77–85 Fulham Palace Road, Hammersmith,
London W6 8JB

Printed in England by Clays Ltd, St Ives plc

Contents

Six Cousins at Mistletoe Farm

First published in a single volume in hardback in 1948 by
Evans Brothers Ltd, London.
First published in paperback in 1967 in Armada

The author asserts the moral right to be identified as
the author of the work

CHAPTER ONE

The Telephone Call

It was half-past five one April evening at Mistletoe Farm. In the big sitting-room sat five people, finishing high tea.

Three children sat at the table with their father and mother. There were the twins of fifteen years old, Jane and Jack. There was eleven-year-old Susan, with Crackers the black spaniel sitting as close to her as he could. Susan passed him everything she didn't want to eat, and he gulped it down.

Mr Longfield, their father, was a big, burly farmer. He sat at the head of the table, eating quickly, and frowning as he thought of all the work to be done in the next week. Springtime was always so busy – never a minute to spare for anything.

Mrs Longfield sat at the other end of the table. She was plump and short, with soft curling hair, and eyes that twinkled. They didn't always twinkle, though. They could look hard and cold and stern when she didn't approve of something.

She was half-smiling now as she looked at her family sitting round the table, eating the things she had cooked. She looked at the twins – nobody would ever think they were twins! Jack had curly hair, Jane had straight hair. Jack was tall, Jane was short. Jane was quick, talkative and impatient, and Jack was slow and silent – but what a temper he had!

Mrs Longfield looked at Susan, who was stolidly eating an enormous slice of cold pudding. Susan stared back at her mother solemnly, then smiled the sudden smile that made her plain face quite pretty.

"Well, Solemn Sue," said her mother. "You haven't said a word all through the meal."

"I hadn't anything to say," said Susan. "I was thinking."

"And feeding Crackers!" said Jane. "You shouldn't, Susan. He's getting so fat. I hate a fat spaniel."

9

"*Oh*! How could you *possibly* hate Crackers?" said Susan in a horrified voice. "Our own dog that we've had since he was so small he couldn't even bark!"

"Of course Jane would never hate Crackers," said Mrs Longfield. "But I agree with her that fat dogs are dreadful. Crackers really is too fat now."

"I've said before that the dogs are *not* to be fed at table," said Mr Longfield suddenly, entering into the conversation unexpectedly. "Do you hear, Susan?"

"Yes, Daddy," said Susan, alarmed. Her father so rarely said anything at mealtimes that it was quite a shock to hear his deep voice. He had the same sudden hot temper that Jack had – and the same kind heart and the same love for every animal and bird on the farm and in the countryside.

Silence fell on the table again. Crackers gave one of his heavy sighs, and Susan put down her hand to comfort him, feeling certain that he had understood what her father had said. He licked her fingers.

Mrs Longfield poured Susan another cup of milk. She liked this time of the day best of all, when she had the whole of her family there together in peace. Life at Mistletoe Farm was good – plenty of work to be done, and plenty of happiness in the doing of it. She ran the farmhouse in her own way, just as her husband ran the farm the way he liked. Nobody interfered, nothing upset the happy routine of the year.

Then the telephone bell rang out in the hall. It made everyone jump. Crackers leapt to his feet and barked madly. He never could learn that the bell was nothing to worry about.

Nobody moved. Mrs Longfield looked at her husband. "Telephone," he said, with a frown. "Isn't anyone going to answer it? One of you children go."

The three children gave Jane a nudge. "Your turn to," he said. "Go on, Jane, before it rings again."

It rang again, shrill and loud, sounding very impatient.

"Who can it be?" said Mrs Longfield. "Do go and answer it, Jane."

Jane got up and went into the hall. The others listened as she picked up the receiver.

"Hello! This is Mistletoe Farm."

Somebody spoke sharply and quickly the other end. Jane listened, her eyes opening wide. "What did you say? Who is it speaking? Oh – Uncle *David*!"

The voice in the telephone spoke again, urgently, and Jane listened, her eyes almost popping out of her head.

"Who is it? Uncle *David*? Whatever does he want?" said Mrs Longfield.

"Oh Uncle – how dreadful! Oh, I'm so sorry! All burnt down – oh, *Uncle*!" she heard Jane's voice from the hall.

"I'll fetch Daddy."

Jane put down the receiver and came running back from the hall, almost bumping into her mother and father, who were both on the way to the telephone.

"Mummy! Daddy! It's Uncle David. Their house has been burnt down – and Auntie Rose is in hospital – and . . ."

But her father had snatched up the receiver and was listening intently to his brother's voice. He motioned impatiently to Jane to stop talking. By now Jack and Susan and Crackers were all in the hall, and their mother was trying to gather what was being said over the telephone.

"David, I'm horrified – I'm terribly sorry for you," said Mr Longfield. "Poor Rose – she wasn't burnt, was she? Oh – just badly shocked. What about the children – are they all right?"

The talk went on and on. Then Mr Longfield turned to his wife. "You speak to David," he said. "He wants to know if he can bring the children over to stay with us till he can arrange for somewhere else to live – and till Rose is better. He's at his wit's end, poor boy."

Jane glanced at Jack and made a face. Susan screwed up her nose, as she always did when she didn't like the idea of something. But they didn't say a word to one another.

At last their mother put down the telephone receiver. She led the way back into the sitting-room. Nobody felt like having any more to eat.

11

"Well, what a shock!" said Mrs Longfield, sinking down into her rocking-chair. "Oh Peter – poor things – all their lovely house gone – hardly anything saved."

"Mummy, what's happened? Tell me!" demanded Susan "Has Three Towers been burnt down?"

"Yes – your uncle's beautiful house is nothing but a shell now," said her mother. "Nobody seems to know how it happened – but the flames got such a hold almost at once that there was no saving it. All their lovely furniture – and all Rose's clothes – those fur coats too! The children's clothes were saved, but not much else."

"And, of course, Rose *would* be taken off to hospital with shock," said Mr Longfield. "She always retires to bed when anything happens to her family."

"Oh, don't be unkind," said his wife. "It would be a terrible shock to me if Mistletoe Farm was burnt down."

"Oh, I dare say," said Mr Longfield, "but I can't see you retiring to bed and leaving me to cope with everything, Linnie – and leaving the children, poor things."

"Well, never mind about that," said Mrs Longfield. "We've got to help. The children are staying at neighbours' houses tonight, and David will bring them tomorrow."

"Mummy," said Jane, "how long will they stay?"

"Oh, till they go back to their schools, I expect," said her mother. "About a week or two."

"Oh," said Jane, looking relieved. "I'm awfully sorry for them all – but I don't think I could bear to put up with Melisande and the others for very long."

Jane, Jack and Susan went out of the room into the garden. It was a warm and sunny April evening, with primroses lining the garden path, and a blackbird singing in a clear, cool voice from an apple tree.

They all went to the apple tree. It was very old and had a curious low branch, broad and flat, that made a fine seat. Their father had sat there as a boy, and so had their grandfather. Now all the children squeezed on it together, and looked gloomily at one another.

The blackbird stopped singing and flew into a pear tree.

He began his fluting song again. Crackers tried to get on to Susan's knee and was pushed off. He sat against her legs, listening to the talk that went on above his head.

"Gosh! Fancy having your house burnt down like that! It's pretty awful," said Jane.

"Yes – and it's pretty awful having Melisande, Cyril and Roderick here," said Jack. "Awful snobs - turning up their noses at everything – calling us country clods behind our backs, and sniggering because our riding breeches are dirty."

"Frightful names they have too," said Jane. "Melisande! What a name!"

"Oh – is it *Meli*sande?" said Susan, sounding astonished. "I always thought it was *Smelli*sande – and I thought it was such a good name for her, because she always does smell of powder and soap and things."

Jane and Jack chuckled. "You're always making mistakes like that," said Jane. "That's pretty good – Smellisande! Don't you go calling her that now! You never did before, or I'd have noticed it."

"Susan never opened her mouth when they came here last year," said Jack. "Anyway, Melisande is a better name than Cyril – though I really must say Cyril's name suits him."

They sat and pictured Cyril. He was almost sixteen, a tall, white-faced boy, with wavy hair that he wore too long, and an affected, slow way of talking that exasperated Jane and Jack unbearably. He was very fond of poetry and music, and had quite made up his mind to be a writer of some kind.

"Roderick's the best of the three," said Jane. "Though he's a frightful little coward, and an awful ninny. Darling mother's boy! Why is Aunt Rose so silly?"

Nobody could answer that question. Aunt Rose was beautiful. She dressed beautifully, she smelt lovely; she was a year older than Mrs Longfield, but looked ten years younger – and oh, how silly she was!

She fussed, she pouted, she squealed, she simpered – and she spoke to all the children, her own as well, as if they were about five years old. No wonder Melisande, Cyril and Roderick were peculiar, with such an odd mother!

"Well – they'll all be here tomorrow – and we shall have to put up with them. After all, it must have been a frightful shock when their house went up in flames," said Jane. "We'll have to be as nice as we can."

"It would be easy if they were nice to us," said Susan. "But they never are. Are they, Crackers?"

"I suppose I'll have to give up my room to Melisande and sleep with you, Susan," said Jane thoughtfully. "I hate sleeping with you. You kick about so at night."

"Gosh! And I'll have to share my room with Cyril, I suppose," said Jack. "There's hardly enough room in it for me. I have to keep my things as tidy as I can or I'd never have room to do anything – and I bet Cyril's as messy as a girl."

"Thank you!" said Jane indignantly. "You take that back!"

"Well – your bedroom's always in an awful mess," said Jack. "Go on, be honest, Jane. You're frightfully untidy, you know you are. I can't think what Melisande would do if she had to share *your* room!"

"Where will Roderick sleep?" said Susan. "In the boxroom, I suppose! That's the only room left!"

The farmhouse was old and rambling. Its ceiling slanted in odd ways. The passages were uneven, and odd little steps up and down made it dangerous for a stranger to go along without a light. There was only one bathroom, and that had cold water, but not hot. The hot water had to be carried up the backstairs each night when anyone wanted a bath.

The children were used to cold baths. They all hated carrying the pails of hot water up the narrow backstairs for hot baths. Susan grinned suddenly when she thought of her three cousins being offered a cold bath. She couldn't imagine any of them saying "Yes."

Mistletoe Farm looked peaceful and lovely that evening. It was built in the shape of an L, and there was an

14

old paved courtyard in the crook of the L, with a pond full of fat goldfish. Behind was a kitchen garden and orchard. All around lay undulating fields, now green with the growing corn and other crops.

The three Longfield children loved their home. It didn't matter that there was no hot water, that they had to use oil lamps, and that the floors were uneven. They would rather put up with all those things and live at Mistletoe Farm surrounded by their horses and dogs and cows and sheep, than live at a wonderful place like Aunt Rose's. Three Towers seemed almost like a palace to them.

"And yet Three Towers isn't a home, really," said Susan, thinking her thoughts out loud, in the way she sometimes did. "It's just a beautiful house. I mean it *was*. I forgot it was burnt down, for a minute. Jack, wouldn't you hate to live in a big town always, like our cousins? No field for miles – and not even their own horses to ride!"

"Well, they had three cars," said Jack. "They wouldn't need horses. Horses are just things to ride at a riding school to Melisande and the others. They just wouldn't understand how we think about our own ponies. I mean – unless you saddle and bridle and groom your own horse, it isn't a real horse!"

Jane and Susan knew quite well what this peculiar statement meant. All three Longfield children had their own ponies. Jane had Merrylegs; Jack had Darkie; and Susan had a strange little barrel of a pony called Boodi. He was an Iceland pony, sturdy, full of character, and not at all good-tempered. But Susan loved him passionately.

Somebody came out of the farmhouse and beckoned and called. "That's Mummy," said Jane, getting up. "She wants me to feed the hens. I expect. She'll be busy getting ready for the others tomorrow. Susan, come and give me a hand with the corn."

They left the apple tree, and the blackbird flew back to it. It was the particular tree he liked to sing from in the evening-time. Crackers watched him flutter into the boughs, and then followed the children sedately, his long silky ears swinging as he went. He was their faithful black shadow.

15

CHAPTER TWO

Getting Ready for the Visitors

The next morning everyone was very busy getting ready for the arrival of the three cousins. Jane heard to her horror that she was not to go into Susan's room; she was to share her own room with Melisande.

"But, Mummy! You know how I'd hate that," objected Jane at once. "I couldn't *bear* to have Melisande sharing a room with me."

"Well, you hate sleeping in Susan's double-bed with her, because she kicks about so," said her mother. "I thought it would be the lesser of two evils if you share with Melisande. And, anyway, it does mean we don't have to move all your things. I do wish you'd be more tidy, Jane. Your bedroom is an absolute disgrace."

"*I'll* take all my things out, and put them into Susan's room," said Jane. "It won't be any bother, Mummy."

"No. I've settled the matter now," said her mother firmly. "You'll share your room with Melisande – and maybe you'll be ashamed to be so messy and untidy when you've got her in the same room."

"But, *Mummy*," began poor Jane again, but her mother simply didn't seem to hear. She swept about from this room to that, efficient, quick and commanding. Jane was to share with Melisande. Jack was to share with Cyril. Roderick was to have the little boxroom, and Jack and Jane were to go up there at once and clear it of its boxes and trunks.

"Why can't *I* have the little boxroom, and let Cyril and Roderick share *my* room together?" said Jack, annoyed.

"Because we haven't got time to remove everything from your room, or from Jane's either," said his mother, exasperated. "Good gracious me! Anyone would think they were coming to *live* with us, not stay with us, the fuss you're making! Can't you be a little bit helpful when I'm in such a rush?"

Jane and Jack went up to clear the little boxroom. Jane was furious and talked nineteen to the dozen. Jack was also furious, but didn't say a word. Soon they had the room clear of the boxes and trunks, which they put in the cistern room – and their father brought up a camp-bed for Roderick to sleep on.

"I wish I could sleep on that," said Susan, longingly. "Roderick is lucky."

"Well *you're* the only lucky one of us three," said Jane, sharply. "You're keeping your room to yourself. Jack and I are not. Thank goodness there are two beds in my room. I simply couldn't bear to sleep in the same bed with Melisande. She smells like a scent-bottle all the time."

"Dear old Smellisande," said Susan with a giggle. "I do hope I don't suddenly forget and call her that."

At last the three rooms were ready for the unexpected visitors. Jane had tidied her room and put everything away in drawers – not neatly, alas! but crammed in anyhow. Jack had not been able to make much more room in his bedroom, because he was already very tidy, but he had moved out the cupboard in which he kept most of his treasures, and that did make a bit more space for Cyril's belongings.

Susan had nothing to do to her own bedroom, so she helped her mother to arrange Roderick's little room. They talked together as they made the camp-bed, and put out towels and soap and tooth-mug.

"I hope you and the others will be very nice to your cousins," said Susan's mother. "I know they are not a bit like any of you – they have been brought up so very differently – but they have had a dreadful shock and they will need kindness."

"Yes, Mummy," said Susan. "But how long have we got to go on being as kind as all that?"

"Oh, Susan! Is it such an effort?" said her mother. "You make me ashamed of you. Now go downstairs and ask Dorcas if she wants you to go and fetch anything from the shops. It's my shopping morning, but I'm too busy to go."

Susan sped downstairs to Dorcas, who was in the kitchen, making a big sponge pudding. She was a fat, elderly woman with a bright red face, untidy hair, tidy knob of a nose and a pursed-up mouth. She wore an enormous white apron, and moved about surprisingly briskly for such a big woman. She was humming one of her favourite hymns when Susan came flying into the kitchen.

"Ah, here comes Susan Headlong again," she said. "What do you want? To scrape out the pudding basin, I suppose."

"Well, Dorkie, I wouldn't mind," said Susan. "But really I've come to see if you want any shopping done, Mummy's too busy."

"Yes, that she is," said Dorcas, stirring the pudding mixture hard. "With three more to do for, she's going to be busier than ever. Yes, and you mark my words, Miss Susan – them cousins of yours will be here for good!"

"Whatever do you mean?" said Susan, alarmed.

"I mean what I say," said Dorcas. "Your Auntie Rose is in hospital, and your uncle's got no house for the children, and not likely to get one either, these days – and your Ma will be landed with them for good."

"Oh no!" said Susan. "You're just silly, Dorcas! You know we couldn't have them here for long. There isn't room. Besides, Mummy would have too much to do. And Auntie Rose will soon be out of hospital and Uncle will find a house, and they'll all be together again."

"Well, you'll see," said Dorcas, darkly. "Take your finger out of my basin, now, Miss Susan, or I'll rap it with my wooden spoon. And if you want to be useful, get down the old shopping bag, find my shopping list on the dresser, and go and get the things I want."

"I'll go on Boodi," said Susan. "He likes shopping."

"Well, you see you shut him up properly when you come back," said Dorcas. "Last time you let him wander around, and he stuck his wicked head in my kitchen window and licked all over the bar of salt I'd left on the table nearby."

18

"Yes, I know. You told me before. It made him terribly thirsty afterwards," said Susan, getting down the shopping bag. "He's a darling. Don't you really think so Dorcas?"

"Indeed I don't," said Dorcas, pouring a little milk into her basin. "He's a pest if ever there was one, that pony of yours. I don't like that wicked look in his eye, either. Now off you go, or I'll not get the things I want today!"

Susan ran off to the stables. Boodi, the Iceland pony, was there, his head over the door, waiting for her. He was brown all over, with a short thick mane and a long, thick tail. His eyes were beautiful – dark and clear, with sweeping eyelashes that curled up just like Susan's own.

"Boodi! Have you been waiting for me to come? I've been busy," said Susan as she saddled him. "Boodi, Dorkie says you're a pest and that you've got a wicked look in your eye. And I do believe you have!"

Boodi certainly had. He was a queer character. Mr Longfield often said he would never have bought him if he had been the last horse in the world. He had had to take him in payment of a bad debt, and had brought him home one night.

Susan had met him riding Boodi, and stood still in delight. At that time she had no pony of her own, and she quite thought her father had been to buy one for her – and she thought it might be Boodi!

"Daddy! Is he mine? Have you bought me a pony at last?" she cried, and she had been bitterly disappointed when she knew that Boodi was not for her.

"He's vicious," said her father. "Do you know what he does? He suddenly goes into the hedge and squeezes himself alongside to squash your leg and make you get off! He tried it once with me, but he won't again!"

Boodie looked at Susan under his long eyelashes and she looked back at him. He blinked. Susan rubbed his soft nose.

"You winked at me," she said softly. "I saw you! Daddy, I'm going to *pretend* that he's mine."

And so she had pretended, though for some time her

father would not let her attempt to ride the Iceland pony. "He's too fat for your short little legs," he said. "And I don't trust him."

"But *I* do," said Susan, earnestly. "He's queer in lots of ways, Daddy, but he's all right with *me*. Really he is. I've found out that he won't go if you say, 'Gee-up.' You have to say 'Woa!' And he won't stop unless you whistle to him. As soon as I whistle he pulls up at once."

"I expect, being brought up in Iceland, the ways there are different from here," said her father. "He's an odd fellow."

"He thinks for himself," said Susan. And it was quite true. Boodi did think for himself. He had an intense curiosity, and if he saw anything that puzzled him he had to go up and look at it closely. He had an incurable habit of licking things too, and an even worse one of nibbling the tail of any horse that happened to be standing in front of him.

He soon became known as Susan's pony, and when he had been there a year he followed Susan about rather like Crackers did, Mr Longfield still would not let Susan ride him, much to the little girl's grief, because he felt convinced that Boodi was not trustworthy, and he had visions of Susan being flung from his back, her foot still caught in a stirrup, and being dragged home at Boodi's heels.

"Well, let me try him without stirrups then," begged Susan one day. "I can't come to any harm then. I've taken tosses from Merrylegs and Darkie and come to no harm. If I ride Boodi without stirrups I can't possibly have a real accident."

And so she had first been allowed to ride Boodi without stirrups, and had gone gaily along the lanes, slipping and sliding about on his back. Never once had Boodi tried to get her off by his trick of squeezing her leg close against a hedge.

Now she was allowed to ride him properly, with stirrups, and he was as good as gold with her, but neither of the twins was keen on getting on his back. They couldn't imagine why Susan was so fond of Boodi, when there were lovely ponies like Merrylegs and Darkie to rave over.

Susan rode off on Boodi, cantering down the lane that led from Mistletoe Farm to the little village in the valley below. Boodi was in a happy mood, and tossed his head up and down as he went. Susan sang in her high clear voice, and forgot all about the coming of the three cousins.

She did the shopping and mounted Boodi again, turning his head homewards. She suddenly remembered that Melisande, Cyril and Roderick were arriving that day, and her heart sank. They would turn their noses up at everything, including Boodi. They would expect to be waited on. Melisande would probably weep all the time, and keep telling them about the fire.

"I must be kind. I really must," said Susan to herself. "It's awful for them. And I don't expect they want to come and stay with us any more than we want them to! I expect they're miserable too. I shall be kind. I shall offer to carry up hot water for . . ."

A car came up the narrow lane behind Boodi. Susan got as close to the left side as she could. The car hooted loudly, and Boodi reared in fright, almost throwing Susan off.

"What did you do that for?" shouted Susan in anger. "You idiots! Quiet, Boodi! Get down. It's all right, Boodi, I tell you."

The car swept by, and Susan glared at the people inside. "Beasts!" she yelled, quite beside herself with fury at their stupidity.

And then she saw that it was her cousins! Her Uncle David was driving the car, and Melisande was sitting beside him. It must have been she who had hooted to attract Susan's attention. Cyril and Roderick were sitting behind.

Susan could not smile. The four driving by saw an angry little red face, and then the car swept on up the lane and disappeared round a corner.

Boodi was still rather unmanageable. He hated sudden

21

. . . and Boodi reared in fright . . .

noises, and had once run for miles when a traction engine had met him unexpectedly, hissing out steam. Susan slid off his back and went to his nose to calm him down.

"Aren't they stupid, Boodi?" she said. "Just the kind of thing they *would* do! How can I smile and say nice things to people like that? And just look at all my shopping! I must have dropped the bag when you reared up like that. Now stand whilst I pick everything up."

She began to whistle softly. Boodi liked that. Whistling always soothed him. He stood almost still whilst Susan picked up the things that had fallen out of the bag. She couldn't find the tin of golden syrup anywhere.

"Blow! It must have rolled right down the hill," she said. "Come and look, Boodi."

It had rolled down the lane and into the ditch round the

corner. Susan fished it out, wiped it and put it back into the bag. Then, still feeling exasperated, she mounted Boodi again. "Woa!" she cried. "Woa!" and Boodi, contrary as ever, set off up the hill just as if she had clicked to him to gee up!

"So they've arrived," thought Susan as they jogged along. "Oh, I do hope Dorkie isn't right. I do hope they haven't really come for good!"

CHAPTER THREE

The Cousins Arrive

Jack and Jane saw the car coming as they looked out from the sitting-room window. It swept into the drive and stopped. Jack yelled to his mother:

"They're here! Quick, Mummy!"

Mrs Longfield hurried down, the two children following her to the door. Uncle David was getting out, looking tired and grave and old, though he was younger than his brother, the farmer. Melisande got out, helped by Cyril, who was always very gallant and well-mannered.

"You poor things!" said Mrs Longfield in her warm, kind voice. Melisande fell into her arms and burst into tears. Cyril looked as if he was about to weep too. Roderick stared stolidly in front of him, a pretty, girlish boy, too plump, and with a rather stupid look on his pale face.

Jane and Jack felt and looked most uncomfortable. They wished Melisande would stop crying. They didn't know what to say to their uncle. They were even afraid of shaking hands with Cyril in case he too began to cry. So they looked at Roderick.

"Hello, Roderick," said Jack, and then felt that his voice was much too cheerful. He lowered it a little. "Er – hand me out those cases. I'll take them in."

23

Cyril began to help. Melisande was being taken indoors by Mrs Longfield, who was trying to comfort her. Jane noticed that Melisande was dressed in a pale blue tailor-made suit, very pretty and smart. "It makes her look almost grown-up," she thought, "and yet she's hardly fifteen. And her hair is a mass of waves – just as if she's spent hours over it this morning. And she's even found time to put on a brooch. I bet if my house had burnt down yesterday, I wouldn't have cared how I was dressed!"

Cyril too looked as if he had taken a lot of trouble with his clothes – much too much, Jack thought. And yet he looked sloppy, though probably he meant to look artistic. His tie was a floppy bow. His shirt was a peculiar colour. He wore sandals!

"*Sandals*!" thought Jack. "*Gosh*! Well, I suppose his shoes were lost in the fire. I'll have to lend him a pair of mine – but my feet are twice his size."

They all went indoors with the luggage. Jane wondered where Susan was. "Just like Susan to get out of welcoming them!" she thought, not knowing that Susan had gone out shopping, and was even then riding up the lane homewards.

Melisande had been taken upstairs to Jane's room. Mrs Longfield was trying to persuade her to go to bed.

"It must have been a terrible time for you," she said gently. "And I don't expect you slept much last night. I'll help you undress, dear, and then you stay in bed today. You'll feel better tomorrow."

"It was dreadful," wept Melisande. "I shall never forget it, never. No, don't make me go to bed, please. I shan't rest or sleep for ages."

"How is your mother?" asked Mrs Longfield, and immediately regretted asking the question, because it brought a fresh flood of tears at once.

"Poor Mummy! She had to be taken to hospital. She simply collapsed," wept Melisande.

Mrs Longfield sighed. She patted her niece and told her to wash, and dry her eyes, and come down to lunch if she really wouldn't stay in bed.

"I couldn't eat a thing," said Melisande.

"Well, you shall do just what you like, dear," said Mrs Longfield. "I must go and see to Cyril and Roderick now. I'll see you later. Shall I send Jane up to help you unpack?"

"Yes, please," said Melisande. She began to cry afresh. "Not that there's much left to unpack. We only saved a few of our clothes."

Mrs Longfield thought of the many cases and bags in the car. Half of them would be enough to pack the clothes of all five Longfields in! She gave Melisande another pat and went out of the room.

Cyril was unpacking in Jack's room, and there was literally not enough room to stand up in. Jack sat on the windowsill, looking miserable. Whatever would his room be like when Cyril had finished?

Mrs Longfield looked at Cyril. Well, thank goodness *he* wasn't crying! He looked grave and rather important.

"Managing all right, Cyril?" she asked. "Aren't you helping him, Jack?"

Jack got up unwillingly and tried to find a place to stand and help, but he couldn't without treading on Cyril's belongings.

"There are plenty of empty drawers, Cyril," said Mrs Longfield. "Put what you've unpacked into the drawers, and then you'll be able to find room to unpack the rest."

"Well, it's only books that are left, and my papers," said Cyril. "I simply don't know *where* I'm going to put my books."

"There's plenty of room downstairs in the bookcase," said Jack.

"Oh, I *must* have them up here," said Cyril in his rather affected voice.

"I don't see why," said Jack, ready to argue. His mother frowned at him, and he stopped.

"Put them all at the bottom of the big cupboard for now," she said to Cyril. "Then we'll see what we can find for you to put them in later on."

Roderick was upstairs with Susan, who had now

arrived. She was still feeling rather sulky about the stupid hooting that had made Boodi rear, but she was really trying hard to be nice.

She had peeped into Melisande's room, and retreated hurriedly when she saw Melisande dabbing her eyes and sniffing dolefully. She had then peeped into Cyril's room, and looked in horror at the masses of clothes on the floor and on the two beds. She saw Jack sitting scowling on the window-sill, and decided to go away. She climbed up to the little boxroom and found Roderick there, looking very glum.

"Am I to sleep here?" he said to Susan, before she had even had time to say, "Hello."

"Yes. On this camp-bed. Aren't you lucky to have a camp-bed to sleep on?" said Susan. "I've only got an enormous old double-bed."

Roderick didn't look as if he felt it was at all lucky to sleep on a camp-bed. He looked round the little room as if he thought it was a dreadful little hole.

"I don't think much of this," he said. Susan forgot all her good resolutions at once.

"What's the matter with it?" she demanded.

"Well – it's so small – and dark," said Roderick. "And I've already heard peculiar noises up here."

"Oh – that's only the cistern," said Susan. "It gurgles. Once I slept up here for a week, and I liked it when the cistern gurgled. It sounded sort of friendly."

There was a pause. Susan heard a pattering of feet up the uncarpeted attic stairs, and in came Crackers the spaniel. He ran straight at Roderick and sniffed his legs. Roderick pushed him away.

"That's Crackers," said Susan. "We called him Crackers when he was tiny because he did such mad things. He really was crackers. I say – tell me about the fire. Did it burn everything in great hot flames?"

To Susan's alarm, Roderick put his hands in front of his eyes and cried out loudly: "Don't! Don't ask me about it! I shall scream if you do."

"But, Roderick – I only wanted to know," said Susan. "Was it – was it so dreadful? Did you see the house burn?"

26

Roderick screamed. Crackers growled, and Susan jumped in surprise. Her mother came running up the stairs.

"What's the matter with Roderick?" she asked Susan.

"I just asked him to tell me about the fire, and he screamed and said I wasn't to ask him," said Susan. She was puzzled. Roderick was shaking all over, and his hands were in front of his face.

"It looks as if *he's* the shocked one!" said her mother in a curiously gentle voice. "Poor old Roderick! Susan, would you like to take a picnic dinner out with Roderick, and show him the three tame lambs up on the hill?"

"Not have dinner properly downstairs?" said Susan, delighted, though she would much rather have gone alone on a picnic than with this strange, shivering Roderick. Her mother had her arms round him now, and he was clinging to her as if he was a baby.

She spoke to him in a firm, kind voice. "Everything is all right now, Roderick. It's all over. You'll soon forget it. Look, I'm going to take off this nice suit of yours, and get you to put on a jersey and shorts. Those will be best for a picnic. You'll like to see the pet lambs. We brought them up on the milk bottles, you know. Susan fed them every day."

"And they still know me," said Susan. "They come running when I call them. Mummy, shall I go down and ask Dorkie for sandwiches?"

"Yes. You go," said her mother, who was really worried over Roderick. It was quite clear that he had had a terrible shock, and because everyone had been too busy to take much notice of him, no one had known that the fire had affected Roderick most of all.

Susan sped downstairs, pleased at her mother's suggestion. She looked in on Jane on the way.

"I'm going picnicking with Roderick," she said.

"Who said so?" said Jane, at once.

"Mummy!" said Susan, and disappeared, leaving Jane to wish that she too was going to escape the family lunch with a weeping Melisande, a solemn Cyril and a sad, old-looking uncle.

Dorcas soon produced sandwiches and slices of cake and a

bottle of creamy milk. Roderick came down with his aunt, looking a little better. He was now in jersey and shorts, and was no longer howling.

"Come on," said Susan. "I'll take you to the hill where the lambs are. I won't ask you about the fire, I promise. We'll see old Hazel, the shepherd. He's got plenty of good stories to tell. Come on!"

CHAPTER FOUR

Plans – and a Shock for the Cousins

The first two days were rather difficult. Melisande seemed determined to weep at the slightest encouragement, and talked about "Poor dear Mummy" till Jane could have screamed as loudly as Roderick.

Cyril still kept up his grave, grown-up pose, which eventually made Jack retire into himself, and not say a word. Uncle David looked terribly worried. The children soon discovered why.

"I say! Did you know that Three Towers wasn't insured?" said Jack to Jane the second night. "Apparently Uncle David let the insurance lapse – didn't bother to pay it when it was overdue."

Jane whistled. "My goodness! Does that mean he won't get any money to buy another house and furniture?"

"Yes. It does mean that," said Jack. "I heard Daddy telling Mummy. And he said, 'It's so like David. He always was irresponsible. And Rose is a butterfly, so what can you expect?'

"Did he really say that?" said Jane. "Well – if he can't get the money to buy another house, what's going to happen? Oh Jack – surely, surely they won't expect Daddy to keep Melisande and the others here?"

Uncle's got other money," said Jack. "But not much. It

won't buy a house like Three Towers. He's going to look for somewhere, and make a home for Aunt Rose when she comes out of hospital. Anyway, Cyril will have to go back to his public school in two weeks' time, so we'll get rid of *him*. He's an awful ass, isn't he, Jane?"

"He's so *pompous*," said Jane. "That's the right word for him. And I'm sure he's going to spout poetry at me sooner or later. I shall scream if he does."

"Does Roderick go to boarding school?" said Jack, trying to remember. "I bet he doesn't. He's a real mother's boy. I always thought Susan was pretty young for her age, but, honestly, Roderick's worse."

"Well, if he doesn't go to boarding school, he'll stay here and go to school with you, I expect," said Jane gloomily. "And I know Melisande had a private governess, and just went to dancing classes and painting classes and things like that. So she'll be parked on us too, if Uncle David can't get a house."

This was a very gloomy prospect. Mistletoe Farm didn't seem the same place with three townspeople in it. You couldn't count Uncle David as a town person, because he and Daddy had been brought up together at Mistletoe Farm.

Roderick seemed to have forgotten about the fire by the time he had been at the farm for two days. Melisande was still inclined to weep and loll about, but was thinking better of her repeated statement that she "couldn't eat a thing." She had begun to eat very heartily, to Mrs Longfield's secret amusement.

Cyril was really the greatest trial. He seemed to consider that he was on a level with the three grown-ups, and would listen to their conversation with a grave and wise expression that really infuriated his Uncle Peter. His father seemed too unhappy and weary to notice his behaviour. Jane privately wondered how long it would be before her father showed Cyril the rough side of his tongue. He could not bear posing of any kind.

He was good to his brother, and tried to help him with advice. But, as he said to his wife afterwards, "David

29

never would take advice even as a boy – he just listens, and nods, and promises – and that's all. He'll never get a house with all those large ideas of his – and if he happens to find a small one, Rose will never consent to move in."

"Well, what will happen then?" asked Mrs Longfield. "We really cannot house the whole family – for one thing, there isn't room. And for another thing, we couldn't afford it. We have a pretty tight squeeze for money as it is."

"Farmers always do," said her husband. "Well, Linnie, we can't turn them out, that's certain. Rose has money of her own. Perhaps she'll think of something. Maybe she's not such a silly butterfly as we imagine."

But, as the days went on, it became quite clear that Uncle David was quite helpless at managing his affairs, now that he hadn't endless money to draw on. He had lost thousands of pounds of property in the fire, and could not claim one penny in insurance. Worse still, a lot of the money in the property belonged to Aunt Rose.

Her husband saw her often at the nursing-home to which she had now gone. She cried, and begged him to do impossible things. She wanted another Three Towers. She wanted her lost fur coats and her beautiful dresses. But they were gone, and there was not the money to throw away on things like that again. Uncle David, charming as ever, but weak as water, promised her everything "some day soon." And when he told her about a little house he had at last found not far from Mistletoe Farm, she cried with rage and grief.

"How could you expect *me* to live there!" she stormed. "After the life we've had, David. And the poor children, too. I couldn't think of it."

One day her sister-in-law, Mrs Longfield, went to see her. It was difficult to leave Mistletoe Farm, now that there were six children to see to, but she managed it. When she saw the dainty, beautiful Rose lying in bed, looking perfectly well, Mrs Longfield felt angry.

"When are you going to get up, Rose?" she said bluntly. "David needs you. And the children need you too."

"When David has found a nice house, we'll all be together again," said Rose in a feeble voice.

"He won't find a nice house," said Mrs Longfield. "How can he? You should be up and about, helping him to find some place to make a home."

"Oh, Linnie – are you trying to tell me that my children are a nuisance to you?" said Rose in a tearful voice, and two tears rolled down her cheek. They made Mrs Longfield think of Melisande and her easy tears. "My poor children! It wasn't *their* fault that the house got burnt. I blame David bitterly for letting the insurance lapse. I shall never forgive him for that. After all, the man of the family should at least be a responsible person."

"I agree," said Mrs Longfield. "But the wife should also be a responsible woman, Rose. And you are not. You won't take up your responsibilities. You don't help at all. You are trying to escape all the tough things of life."

"Oh, Linnie – you have such a lovely life," said Rose, weeping again. "That lovely old farmhouse – your nice husband – and glorious farm."

"Rose, don't be such a hypocrite," said Mrs Longfield, wishing she could shake her hard. "You know you'd hate to live in a farmhouse and manage hens and ducks, and make butter and cook. You'd hate to have a husband who came in every day smelling of cow-dirt and of the pigsty. You wouldn't like to be without constant hot water. You'd hate oil-lamps. So don't talk like that to me, as if you envied me."

"You're very hard and cruel," said Rose, and she turned her face away.

"No, I'm not," said Mrs Longfield. "I'm trying to make you be sensible. You've a husband who needs help. You've three children to see to. You should get up from this bed and dress and go to your duties."

She stood up, half sorry she had said so much, and half glad to get it off her chest.

"*I'm* having to take on your duties, Rose," said Mrs Longfield as she pulled on her gloves. "I'm cooking for your children, and seeing to them, doing all kinds of extra work for a family that has doubled in number. I don't mind a bit – but they're *your* duties, not mine. You'll be very sorry. You're trying to escape from your difficulties, and there never *is* any escape from difficulties, never. They have to be faced and fought. Goodbye, Rose."

She went out, and left Rose alone. What was she thinking? Would she get up and face things? Would she take the children and see to them, and help David?

Mrs Longfield didn't think so. She went home very thoughtfully indeed. What was to happen to Melisande, Cyril and Roderick?

Jane, Jack and Susan wanted to know this too! The time was going by, and school would be starting again soon. Jack went to an old and famous public school in the next town that took day-boys as well as boarders. Jane and Susan went to a girls' private school not far from Jack's school. They all rode in on their ponies each morning, and back again at tea-time.

If their cousins were staying on at Mistletoe Farm, what was to happen to their schooling? Could Uncle David afford to go on paying for Cyril at his expensive public boarding-school? What would happen to Melisande, who had never been to school? And what about poor Roderick, the mother's boy, who had been so coddled?

Jane asked her mother what was going to happen. "Aren't they going away yet?" she said, anxiously. "I do so want my bedroom to myself, Mummy. I just hate to keep on and on having to tidy it up for Melisande's sake."

"Well, that's very good for you!" her mother said. "For once in a way you've had to learn to ber really neat. I can't tell you yet what's to happen to your cousins. Daddy, Uncle David and I are having a sort of family council about it tonight."

The council was held. It was quite clear from the first what was going to happen. Rose was not going to leave her comfortable nursing-home and face any difficulties. David hadn't found a house. He hadn't enough money to send Cyril to an expensive school any longer. But he had enough to pay for the three children's board and lodging and clothes and ordinary day-school fees, if his brother would let them stay on at Mistletoe Farm.

"Linnie, I know it's asking a lot of you," he said. "But I do admire you so, and the way you've brought up your three children – I know you'd be awfully good for mine. I've had a good job offered me in Scotland. I want to go up there and try it, and see if I can make some money. Will you take my children on till Christmas-time this year? By that time I ought to have my job going well, Rose will be with me and can find a home for the children, and we'll hope to be all together by Christmas."

"What's this job?" asked his brother.

"Farming," said David. "Oh, I know Rose won't like the idea of that, but after all, it's the thing I know best. You and I were brought up on this farm, Peter – and you know that I have always loved the country. It was just that Rose wanted a town life – and she had so much money, I hadn't the heart to say she was to go my way and not hers."

"This sounds, David, as if you've set about settling your affairs properly at last," said his brother, pleased. "Well, Linnie must decide about the children. That's her job, and she'll have to bear the brunt of that."

"I'll take them on," said Mrs Longfield in her warm, quiet voice. "You needn't worry. But I must have a free hand with them, David. They haven't been brought up well, you know. They've a lot to learn. And I think they can teach *my* children a few things too. My two girls are such tomboys, and dear old Jack hasn't very good manners. I've no doubt they'll all shake down together, and be very good for one another."

"It's kind of you to say all those comforting things," said David. "Of course you can have a free hand. Do whatever you like! Cyril can go to Jack's school, can't he? And Roderick can go too. And Melisande can go with Jane."

"Right," said his brother. "That's all settled, then. We wish you the best of luck in this new job, David."

"I'll make a success of it," said David. "I'm up against things now. Do you remember what our mother used to

33

say to us, Peter? When obstacles crop up, just use them as stepping-stones, my boy, and you'll get somewhere!"

"I hope the children will be happy – your children, I mean, David," said Mr Longfield. "It's such a very different life for them. Up till now they've just been visitors – but from now on they'll be family. And that's very different. I'm afraid there will be squabbles and fights and jealousies and calling of names!"

"Let there be," said Mrs Longfield. "There always is in families as big as ours will be! They'll shake down and rub each other's corners off. You can have the job of telling them all, Linnie. I fight shy of that."

It was not an easy job to break the news to six dismayed children. Melisande, Cyril and Roderick could hardly believe that they were not to go back to some life like the one they had known. And their cousins viewed with the utmost dismay the long weeks ahead of them that would be shared – and spoilt – by Melisande and the others.

"I've never *been* to school!" wailed Melisande. "It's too bad. Why can't I have a governess?"

"What! Go to Jack's day-school?" said Cyril in such horror that Jack stared at him in angry astonishment.

"Mummy! Am I to go on sharing my bedroom with Melisande?" said Jane, almost in tears.

"What about Cyril?" demanded Jack. "I can't pig it with him in my room any more. I want my room to myself."

"We – we haven't got to share our ponies with them, have we?" said Susan's small voice.

"I want to go and live with my mother," wailed Roderick, his whole world falling to pieces at the idea of having to live with his noisy and rather alarming cousins. He looked as if he was going to howl.

"Mother's boy!" said Susan scornfully. And then Roderick did howl! But this time his aunt didn't put her arms round him and comfort him. She looked at him sternly.

"Roderick! Behave yourself! You'll have a dreadful time at Jack's school if you act like this. Don't be a baby."

Nobody had ever spoken like this to Roderick before. He looked quite shocked, and stopped howling at once. Crackers watched him in interest, his head on one side. He wouldn't make friends with Roderick, and would never come when the boy called him. He had not forgiven him for pushing him away when he had first arrived.

"Now listen to me, all of you," said Mrs Longfield. "It isn't going to be easy for any of us. I have much more work to do, and so has Dorcas, looking after six children instead of three. Melisande, you and the others will find life harder here than at home and not nearly so comfortable. Jane, Jack and you too, Susan, will find it difficult to share your home with three cousins so unlike yourselves."

She paused and looked hard at all of them. "But," she said, firmly, "it's got to be done, and done as happily as possible, and we'll do it. There's going to be no argument about it, no whining or grumbling from *any* of you – so it's no good getting out your hanky, Melisande! It's all decided, and you're all going to help me as much as you possibly can. Will you?"

"Yes," said everyone, even Melisande, and nobody said any more. Mrs Longfield smiled at them all and went out of the room.

"*Well*!" said Jane, letting out a big breath. "So that – is – THAT!"

CHAPTER FIVE

School Begins Again

Jane, Jack and Susan, with Crackers listening nearby, got together to talk over the news as soon as they could. They were horrified to think they were to have their three cousins with them for so long.

"Dorkie said this would happen," said Susan, fondling Crackers' silky ears. "I bet she isn't pleased about this either."

"She'll back Mummy up, though," said Jane. "She always does. Anyway, she doesn't like Melisande or Cyril. She doesn't mind Roderick so much. Oh dear – I do think it's all frightful. I wish I could have my room to myself. That's what I mind most of all."

"I'm going to hate telling everyone at school that Cyril's my cousin," said Jack gloomily. "He's such an ass."

The other three cousins were also having a meeting about this dreadful idea. Melisande was sniffing as usual, and Roderick looked scared and miserable.

"Why doesn't Mummy come to us?" he kept saying. "Is she really ill? Why can't she come here and help to look after us all? I want her back."

"Don't be such a baby," said Melisande. "Susan's right when she calls you a mother's boy! I don't wonder they all think you're too silly for words."

Roderick felt worse than ever. It was bad enough to have his cousins looking at him scornfully, but it was worse still having his own brother and sister unkind to him too.

"I must say I don't like being here," said Cyril rather pompously. "So primitive! I do like a hot bath every day – but it's such a business carrying those pails of water up each time. We shall soon be like Jack and the others if this goes on – real farm-clods!"

"It's awful sharing a bedroom with Jane," said Melisande. "She's no idea of being neat and tidy. I hate having to step over all her things when she throws them about on the floor. I can't think why her mother allows it. And she grumbles so when I object. But I'm jolly well not going to tidy up her things for her!"

"I should think not," said Cyril. "One of the things *I* hate is not being able to read in bed at night unless I take up my torch. Who can read by candlelight? Fancy having candles these days! How can Aunt Linnie and Uncle Peter live like this?"

"I don't know! And how can Uncle Peter stand seeing Aunt Linnie looking so flustered and red-faced as she rushes about?" said Melisande. "Our mother never looked like that! I must say that Aunt Linnie seems to me to look a lot like old Dorcas sometimes!"

"But she's nice," said Roderick suddenly. "I do like her. And she's got a lot to do now."

The others took no notice of this. "*How* Aunt Linnie can allow Uncle Peter to come in out of the farmyard smelling of cows like he does, I don't know!" went on Melisande. "I can hardly bear it sometimes. I know I shall hold my nose and go out of the sitting-room one day!"

"Gosh! You'd better not!" said Cyril in alarm. "Uncle Peter's got a frightful temper. You should have heard him flare out at me the other day when I wanted to put the wireless on for something. Just because he was reading his newspaper!"

"I think I shall tell Jane she ought not to come into meals wearing those smelly old jodhpurs of hers," said Melisande. "If she does, I shan't sit next to her."

The three looked at one another. They were all cross and miserable. Oh, for life at Three Towers again, with a beautiful, easy-going mother, and a charming father who never said "No" to anything!

"Well, we've got to put up with things, I suppose," said Cyril.

"We needn't put up with them too much," said Melisande spitefully. "You can bet the others won't try to make things easy for us – so I don't see why we should make things easy for *them*!"

"I'd rather be friends with them, really," said Roderick timidly.

"Oh you! You're always so afraid of everyone and everything!" said Melisande, scornfully. "You'll be sucking up to them before you know where you are! See what they say to that! They'll see through that all right and laugh at you just the same."

"I wish I didn't sleep alone," said Roderick suddenly. "I keep having awful dreams about the fire, and when I wake

37

up I feel awfully afraid. Couldn't you ask if I could sleep in Jack's room instead of you, Cyril – and you could come up to the box-room?"

"No thanks! Catch me sleeping next door to a cistern that warbles all night!" said Cyril. "You're a dreadful ninny, Roderick. No wonder people laugh at you."

Roderick said no more. He really did have terrifying dreams about flames and fire, and when he woke up he was trembling with fright. And there was nothing and nobody to turn to for comfort – not even a light-switch to put on. He didn't dare to strike a match and light his candle, because he was afraid his shaking hands would drop the match – and then up would come those terrifying flames again, this time real, and not a dream!

It was just no use the six cousins grumbling and grousing. They had got to put up with one another. It was a great pity they were not more alike and friendly, because they could have had plenty of games and fun. As it was, the trios kept apart as much as possible.

The next excitement, of course, was going back to school. Jane, Jack and Susan loved school, though they always groaned when the holidays were over and their nice long days on the farm were finished. Still, they had Saturdays and Sundays, so that was something.

Cyril was secretly rather scared of going to school with Jack. He was no good at games, and he had never been very popular with other boys. Melisande was very frightened indeed of going to school, but that was understandable, because she had never been before.

Roderick was already so miserable that he felt it wasn't worthwhile worrying about school. He knew he would do everything wrong. The school he had been to before was very small and select. Jack's school was large, and Roderick was afraid of the boys that they sometimes met, who yelled out to Jack and exchanged their news.

"How are we going to get to school?" asked Melisande the day before. "We can all ride, you know. Has Uncle Peter any horses he can lend us?"

Her three cousins stared at her. "You've been here two

weeks already — and yet you don't know what horses we've got!" said Jane scornfully.

"Perhaps Melisande would like to ride Clip or Clop," said Susan with a giggle.

Jane roared. Clip and Clop were the two large shire horses used for farm work. They were well-matched bays, with lovely shaggy hooves. Roderick grinned too. He knew Clip and Clop, because Susan had told him about them.

"One of your feeble jokes, I suppose, as usual," said Melisande.

Jane backed up Susan. "A joke all right, but not feeble," she said. She turned to Susan. "Do you suppose Daddy would lend dear Melisande his grey cob?" she asked solemnly, winking at her little sister.

Susan looked solemnly back. "What, Sultan, do you mean?" she said. "Melisande could ask Daddy and see."

Melisande fell straight into the trap, and actually did ask her uncle. "Uncle Peter, may I have Sultan to ride to school on?" she said. "I'm sure I could ride him all right."

Uncle Peter exploded. "Have *Sultan*? The horse I use to ride round the farm every day! Lend him to you to take off to school all day long! Are you mad?"

Melisande retreated hurriedly in alarm. She saw her three cousins bursting with suppressed laughter, and she was very angry indeed.

"Sorry, Uncle," she said, scarlet with anger at having fallen into such a silly trap.

"I should think so. Where's your common-sense?" boomed her uncle. "Asking for the farm-cob to take your lazy bones to school! What should *I* ride, I should like to know? I never in my life . . ."

"It's all right, Peter. Melisande didn't understand," said Mrs Longfield soothingly. She sensed that her three had been up to something. Melisande went out of the room, angry and humiliated. She would pay her cousins out for that!

It was decided that the three cousins should walk to the bottom of the hill and catch the bus that passed fairly near

Clip and Clop were the two large shire horses. . . .

the schools. Jane and her brother and sister would ride their ponies as usual.

"I'm not going to offer to give that lazy Melisande a loan of Merrylegs *ever*," said Jane.

"And I wouldn't dream of letting that fathead of a Cyril handle Darkie," said Jack. "He's always dreaming. You've got to be alert if you're going to handle a horse like Darkie in the town."

"Nobody but me can ride Boodi," said Susan, exultantly. "So I'm safe! Boodi would just love to play one of his tricks on Melisande or Cyril. He'd stop suddenly and throw them off. He'd scrape their legs along the hedge. He'd stand still and refuse to budge. He'd . . ."

"I don't know why you like Boodi so much," said Jane. "Fat little barrel! I wish he wouldn't nibble other horses' tails. Merrylegs just hates it when Boodi gets behind him. It makes him fidgety and cross."

"I love Boodi best of all our horses," said Susan obstinately. "And I'm very glad nobody else wants to ride him."

Mrs Longfield heaved a sigh of relief when school began. She would get rid of the six children for five whole days every week! No big dinner to prepare in the middle of the day now, except on Saturday and Sunday. What a relief!

Dorcas was glad too. She had taken as much of the load from her mistress's shoulders as she could, and had been on her feet from six o'clock in the morning till ten o'clock at night. She was fond of all the children except Cyril and Melisande. Susan was her favourite. She was sorriest for Roderick, and wondered why all the good farm food and open air did not bring a little colour into his chalk-white face.

"Misses his mother, I expect," she said to Mrs Longfield. "Though what a boy of ten or eleven is doing missing his mother like that beats me! He should have left her apron-strings long ago."

"Of course he should," said Mrs Longfield. "Oh, Dorcas, what peace in the house today! All of them off to

41

school. Poor old Crackers looks so terribly miserable, doesn't he?"

So he did. He sat at the garden door, his ears drooping almost to the ground, his soft spaniel eyes sad and sorrowful. He could never understand this school business. He would sit there patiently nearly all day, waiting till he heard the first clip-clop of hooves up the lane. Then off he would dart madly, barking at the top of his voice, his tail wagging like a black feather.

"It certainly is peaceful," Dorcas agreed. "Always bickering with one another, aren't they? And that Melisande, she does turn on the tap easily! Cries if she so much as has to carry up a pail of hot water!"

"They'll go on bickering till they all shake down," said Mrs Longfield. "If they ever do!"

That first day at school was terrible for Melisande and her brothers. Melisande had decided to be rather scornful and aloof. She was certain that she knew far, far more than the other girls of her age. She was put into Jane's class, and was rather thankful to have her there to ask what to do.

Jane had plenty of friends. They chattered and laughed and exchanged news, whilst Melisande looked on rather coldly. What awful loud-voiced girls! And no manners at all. Well, certainly Melisande did not want to mix with *them*!

The other girls, having been introduced to Melisande, were quite prepared to be nice to her for Jane's sake. They talked to her and tried to draw her into their conversations. But Melisande soon froze them.

"Stuck up, isn't she?" whispered one girl to another. "Leave her alone! She's not a bit like Jane."

So they left Melisande severely alone after a bit, and she didn't like that either!

Cyril was not getting on much better. The boys nudged each other and giggled when they saw his long hair and languid ways. Jack had warned him not to say what his Christian name was. He was afraid that the joint effect of the name and Cyril's appearance would be too much for

42

the boys. He was to give his second name, if he was asked. This was Graham.

"What's the matter with my first name?" asked Cyril indignantly. "I'm not the only fellow that ever had that name! You can't tell me there's nobody else with that name in your school, Jack!"

"I'm not telling you that. I'm only saying that if you're called Cyril you shouldn't *look* like a Cyril, or you won't carry it off," said Jack impatiently.

"And what does a Cyril look like, if you'll be good enough to tell me?" inquired Cyril coldly. "I can't help my name, can I? And, personally, I can't see anything wrong with it."

"No. That's just the trouble," said Jack. "If you could, you'd jolly well get your hair cut as short as possible, you'd talk properly instead of in that namby-pamby fashion, and you wouldn't wear floppy bows and spout poetry!"

This was a long speech from Jack, and he probably would never have made it if he hadn't been afraid that the boys would tease him about Cyril's looks and ways.

Cyril was very obstinate and very touchy. He went white with rage and walked off, determined that nothing on earth would make him have his hair cut as short as Jack's, or talk any differently. Neither would he hide the fact that his name was Cyril. Anyway, he would be called Longfield at school, and it was probably all Jack's make-up that anyone would ever snigger at his name or ways.

He soon found that, unlike his other school, there was no little clique of boys like himself – no little band of would-be poets and painters and musicians – no easy rules that let out those who didn't want to play games every day. He was one on his own, and that wasn't easy to bear. At first, as in Melisande's case, the class had been willing to welcome Cyril because he had a cousin to vouch for him. But it wasn't long before Cyril found himself ignored, or, more unpleasant still, hauled into the limelight and well and truly criticized.

Roderick fared the best of the three cousins. He didn't pose and think a lot of himself, like his brother and sister.

He only wanted to remain unnoticed, and to try to feel his feet before any great catastrophe overwhelmed him. Fortunately for him, there were three other new boys in his class, all a little scared and eager to keep together until they knew a bit more about the ways of the school.

Roderick stuttered with fright when a master asked him a question – but then so did the other new boys. Nobody took much notice of that. The master was a young and kindly fellow, and he left the new boys to find their feet. Roderick found to his great relief that the work was about his standard, and that he hadn't got into any trouble at all in his first week.

"How are you all getting on at school?" asked Mrs Longfield on Friday evening. "You've had three days – time enough to know!"

"All right," said Melisande, Cyril and Roderick cautiously, trying not to look at their cousins. And that was all that their aunt could get out of them, though she knew there was quite a lot more to be said!

CHAPTER SIX

Jane and Melisande

The three cousins who had come to stay at Mistletoe Farm soon found that it was one thing to be visitors, but quite another to be "family"! Nobody offered to do anything for them any more. Instead, they had to run about at other people's command!

Cyril was taken from his books and sent to fetch the cob Sultan many times for his uncle. Melisande was told to go and give Dorcas a hand with the washing-up. Roderick had to clean his own shoes, and made a terrible mess, which he had to clear up himself, with Dorcas standing over him, scolding.

44

"Well, I've never cleaned shoes before!" he protested to Dorcas, knowing that her scolding was not quite so fierce as it sounded.

"No, I dare say not! Funny sort of upbringing you've had! said Dorcas. "Can't even go and feed the hens either without leaving the garden gate open for the cows to get in!"

Roderick went red. Dorcas was a dreadful one for remembering misdeeds. He said nothing.

"And turning up your nose at all the little jobs a boy ought to know how to do!" went on Dorcas. "Saying you didn't know how to wash eggs and grade them into sizes . . . and . . ."

"Dorcas, I *don't* turn up my nose at things," said Roderick earnestly. "I *like* washing the eggs now and sorting them out – yes, and I like cleaning my shoes too. I do really. It's a change from lessons. Susan likes things like that too."

"Oh, Susan – she's been brought up right," said Dorcas. "Now, that sister of yours, she wants a good shaking up, it seems to me. Puts the glasses into the same greasy water as the bacon dishes. I never did know of such a thing!"

Susan came running into the kitchen. "Roderick! Where are you? We've got to go and feed the calves."

Roderick was pleased. He was frightened of cows, but he liked the calves. He liked carrying out the pails of skimmed milk, and seeing the calves plunge their pretty heads in to drink. He had learnt to talk to them now just as Susan did. Cyril laughed at him when he saw him doing jobs like this, and called him a boor and a clod.

"Well, but you do jobs on the farm, too," retorted Roderick. "I saw you in the stables yesterday."

"Yes. But I do them because I've jolly well got to, but you're doing them because you like to!" said Cyril. "That's very different."

Roderick stared at him. He didn't like arguing with his elder brother, because he was so much older and cleverer. But it did seem to Roderick as if there was something wrong with his reasoning.

"Well," he said at last, "isn't it better to do jobs and like doing them than to do them without liking to?"

"You don't know what you're talking about," said Cyril loftily, and stalked off. Roderick watched him go, and felt puzzled. Cyril must be right, because he was old and clever. "Well, I'd rather think what I do think and be wrong," decided Roderick. "I can't help liking to feed the calves and giving the hens fresh water, and feeling them peck corn out of my hands."

Jane was very careful to see that Melisande was made to do her fair share of whatever household or farm jobs there were going. Melisande resented this very much. After all, she thought, Jane had been used to this kind of life all her days – but she, Melisande, hadn't. She took a pride in keeping her hands nice and her nails clean. Jane's hands were always dirty, and she bit her nails.

"Disgusting!" thought Melisande with a shiver. "Her horrid, short nails – so dirty too! She ought to have been a boy, I do *wish* I hadn't got to share a room with a girl like Jane."

She objected to Jane hanging her riding things up in the bedroom.

"They smell so," she said. "Hang them in the cupboard on the landing, for goodness sake, Jane."

Jane glared. "Whose room is this, yours or mine, I should like to know?"

"It belongs to both of us, unfortunately," said Melisande, nose in air. "I only wish I could draw a line exactly down the middle of it and say, 'Keep your dirty, smelly, untidy things over there, and I'll keep mine here!' I've a good mind to ask your mother if I can."

"Ask her," said Jane dangerously. "Just ask her! I'll soon tell her you keep lipstick in your top drawer! *Lipstick* – and you're not fifteen yet. You might be a silly little shop girl, just left school, and thinking she's grown-up enough to use powder and lipstick and all those idiotic things."

"So you've been prying in my drawers, have you!" cried Melisande angrily. "And yet you make yourself out to be

46

so straight and truthful! I won't put up with it, Jane. After my lovely, flowery bedroom at home, twice as large as this – and all my own – to have to share a *pigsty* with you – yes a *pigsty* . . ."

Melisande began to cry. She felt very sorry for herself indeed as she remembered the charming bedroom she had had at Three Towers, so pretty, gay and sweet-smelling.

"That's right. Turn on the tap again," said Jane contemptuously. "You can always do that, can't you, Melisande?"

She took off her boots and threw them on the floor. She didn't attempt to put them away, or take them down to clean. Let Melisande fall over them if she wanted to.

"I'm *not* going to take my riding things out on to the landing," she told her cousin. "And I'm not even going to hang them up if I don't want to. You'll be lucky if I don't throw them on your bed."

"You'll be lucky if I don't throw them out of the window!" shouted Melisande, forgetting to cry in her rage. "Ugh! They smell horrible! They smell of that awful horse of yours!"

She caught up a scent-bottle from the dressing table, and sprinkled the air with it. At once a sweet, sickly smell of jasmine rose up. Jane almost choked.

"Melisande! How can you? For pity's sake stop that!"

"It's better than your horsy smell," said Melisande, delighted with her cousin's look of disgusted rage. She sprinkled a few drops more, and some went on to Jane's bed.

Jane retaliated by taking her filthy jodhpurs and rubbing them over Melisande's bed-cover. There would have been a real struggle if Mrs Longfield hadn't put her head in at that moment.

"Jane! Melisande! I'm ashamed of you both, quarrelling at the tops of your voices like this!"

"Mummy, listen!" shouted Jane. "She . . ."

"Aunt Linnie, she . . ." began Melisande.

But Mrs Longfield wasn't going to listen. "I don't want to know what your silly babyish quarrelling is about," she said in a disgusted voice, and she walked out and shut the door.

"Sucks to you," said Melisande at once.

Jane said nothing. She didn't like it when her mother spoke to her like that. She pursed up her lips and took her jodhpurs off Melisande's bed. She hung them up in her cupboard, and left the door open for the smell to come out. She honestly did not understand anyone objecting to the horsy smell. She thought it was lovely.

She went downstairs. Melisande sat at the window, feeling spiteful and angry She didn't dare to do what she had threatened to do, and throw the offending clothes out of the window. But she had to do something to show she objected strongly to Jane's horsy smell.

She took up her scent bottle again and liberally sprinkled herself with the sweet, sickly perfume. It was a very good and expensive perfume, which her mother had given her from her own store, but it was certainly rather sickly.

Not content with that, Melisande powdered her arms and legs and neck as thickly as she could with her sweet-scented toilet powder. Then she took her bottle of hand lotion and tipped some into her palms. She rubbed her hands briskly together, till the oily lotion had softened her pretty hands and made them smell like flowers.

"That's better!" said Melisande, pleased. "Now perhaps I shall only smell my own smell and not Jane's. It isn't only her clothes that smell – *she* smells of horses too. I don't believe she ever really washes the horsy smell off her dirty hands."

She went down to high tea, a meal she was now quite used to, and liked very much. She remembered the dainty teas her mother had had at Three Towers, and somehow she no longer thought of those with regret. Aunt Linnie's high teas really were what that silly little Susan called "smashing".

Melisande went downstairs slowly and gracefully, imagining that she was some gracious lady descending to see her visitors. She went into the sitting-room, where everyone was now at the table.

"Hurry up, Melisande," said her aunt. "What a time you've been!"

"Sorry, Aunt Linnie," said Melisande, and sat down. Susan was next to her, and got a good waft of the perfume all over her.

"Pooh!" she said. "What's that smell?"

"What smell?" asked her mother. "Has Crackers been into the pigsty again? If it's he who is smelling, he must go out."

"It *isn't* Crackers," said Susan indignantly. "He always smells lovely. Oooh – it's *you*, Melisande!"

"Don't make such personal remarks," said Melisande coldly.

"What *are* personal remarks?" asked Susan. "Mummy, can I come and sit next to you? I don't like Melisande's smell. It makes me feel sick."

Everyone was now looking at Melisande in astonishment, even Mr Longfield. Her uncle sniffed the air.

"Well, even *I* smell something," he said. "What is it?"

"If you want to know," said Melisande, trying to speak coolly and contemptuously, "it's merely that I have put on a little of my mother's perfume to try and get Jane's horrible horsy smell out of my nose."

There was an astounded silence. Then, to Melisande's astonishment, her uncle threw back his big head, and guffawed so loudly that he made everyone else laugh too.

"Well, well, well!" he said at last, wiping his eyes with an enormous red handkerchief. "I didn't think you'd got it in you, Melisande, to try and go one better than Jane. Did *you*, Linnie?"

Mrs Longfield was laughing too. She looked at Jane, who had been unable to stop herself from laughing when she heard her father's great guffaws, but who was now looking down her nose at Melisande.

"Oh, Jane! It's your smell against Melisande's now," said her mother. "I have often told you you shouldn't wear your jodhpurs so long. You've got another pair, and you can easily get your dirty ones cleaned. And your riding mack almost smells the house out."

Jane looked surprised at this attack. "Mummy, we're all

49

used to horses, and they smell very nice," she said. "But you *can't* let Melisande smell like that! It's frightful."

"Well, if you like one smell and Melisande likes the other, and neither of you will give way, we'll just have to put up with both of you," said her mother cheerfully.

"I prefer Jane's smell," said Susan, dragging her chair round the table to Jane. "Oooh! *Smelli*sande!"

There was another roar of laughter. Susan was pleased. It wasn't often that a joke of hers was so much appreciated.

"I always thought her name *was* Smellisande," explained Susan. "When I was little, I mean. It suits her now."

And, to Melisande's rage, her three cousins addressed her as Smellisande the whole of the evening, till she could have wept with fury. Jack and Jane dropped it the next day, but Susan persisted in it, and even shortened it to Smellie.

"*Will* you stop it, you little pest?" cried the exasperated Melisande. "Rude, impertinent little beast!"

"Well, you stop sprinkling yourself with that awful scent, then," said Susan. "If you're not smelly, I won't call you Smellie, but if you are, I shall."

"You want your ears boxing," said Melisande, her face scarlet with annoyance. But, really afraid that Susan might start calling her Smellisande at school, she did stop using her scents and lotions, and was soon quite inoffensive even to Susan's sensitive nose.

Jane's jodhpurs went to the cleaner's, and she wore her other pair. She took her riding mack down to the kitchen and scrubbed it for half an hour on the kitchen table. It smelt strongly of carbolic soap after that, and nearly made poor Melisande sick, but she didn't say a word. After all, anything was better than that strong horsy smell.

Cyril had to do his share of household jobs too. He didn't complain much, though he certainly didn't like them. He had to clean his own shoes, and, much to Jack's surprise, he cleaned Melisande's too. One night Jack even discovered him carrying up the hot water for his sister's bath.

Jack stared in wonder. "What are you doing that for, Cyril? Melisande is lazy enough without you making her lazier!"

"I'm not doing it to make her lazier," said Cyril with dignity. "I'm doing it because she's my sister, and boys ought to do certain things for girls, just as my father always did certain things for my mother. It's – well, I suppose it's a question of good manners."

Jack whistled. "Well, my goodness, don't let Jane see you doing that, or she'll expect me to wait on her too. And I'm not going to, good manners or no good manners."

"She wouldn't expect you to," said Cyril. "And nobody knowing *you* would expect you to, either. But I've often thought you could carry up your mother's hot water for her, even if you don't carry anyone else's! Not out of good manners, if you can't bear the thought of them – but just because she's your mother. I'd do it for mine."

He went up the stairs with the heavy bucket, leaving Jack staring after him. Good gracious! That ass Cyril had a lot more in him than Jack had thought. His idea would certainly bear thinking about!

CHAPTER SEVEN

Susan, Roderick – and Crackers

The weeks went on. School filled up most of the time, and the weekends simply flew by. Roderick was getting on quite well. In fact, it if hadn't been for two things, he would have been fairly happy.

One thing was his nightmares. He still had these, and dreamt of the great flames that had swept his home from top to bottom. In his dreams he heard the crackling noise they made, and he even smelt the strong, choking smell. He awoke night after night, trembling and perspiring, not daring to strike a match. Sometimes he tried deliberately to lie awake for hours so as to keep away the nightmare as long as possible, but in the end his eyes always closed, and the flames rose up.

The other thing that made him unhappy was the fact that Crackers wouldn't be friends with him. Roderick had got very fond indeed of the little black spaniel with the melting brown eyes. He hadn't had anything to do with dogs before, except his mother's little Peke.

"But somehow that Peke didn't seem like a *real* dog," he told Susan. "It was awfully yappy too. Not like Crackers, who has a real, proper, doggy bark, and barks as if he meant it."

"Yes. Crackers has a lovely bark," said Susan. "I'm sorry he won't be friends with you, Roderick. I really am. You shouldn't have pushed him away that first time."

"I know. I didn't really mean to," said Roderick. "I just hate the way Crackers always sits with his back to me, Susan. It's really rude, you know."

"Well, I've told him about it all I can," said Susan. "He's like Boodi - a real character. He thinks for himself, and he's made up his mind he doesn't like you, and so he just pretends you're not there."

They were going up to the stables to see the three ponies. Jack had actually said that Roderick could go for a ride on Darkie if he liked, if Susan went with him on Boodi. Roderick had ridden before, but only with a riding-master.

They stopped in front of the stables. The three ponies belonging to the children all had their heads out over their doors, waiting. Boodi stamped impatiently, and whinnied.

"Which do you think looks the nicest?" said Susan hopefully, looking at Boodi with adoration in her eyes. Roderick considered them very carefully.

First Merrylegs – a New Forest pony, bright chestnut, with a long mane and tail. He had a white star on his forehead, and white socks.

Then Darkie, a dark bay with a black mane and tail. He came from Dartmoor, and was a fine little pony.

"See the blaze down his face," said Susan. She meant the white mark that ran all the way down the horse's face, and which was named the "blaze".

Roderick gave Susan a surprise. He turned to her with a frightened look. "Blaze?" he said. "What do you mean? I can't see a blaze."

Susan stared at him in astonishment. He had gone quite white. "What's the matter?" she said. "Don't you know what a horse's blaze is? It's that white mark down Darkie's face. What is there to be frightened about?"

"It's a horrid word – blaze," said Roderick in a strange voice. "I don't like Darkie as much as Boodi, because he's got a – a – blaze."

"You're potty," said Susan. "Come on. Get Darkie out and I'll get Boodi."

In silence, Roderick got ready the Dartmoor pony. Susan glanced at him, puzzled. When they were galloping over the hills she looked at him again. He had got his colour back again, though he was still silent.

The sun was going down. Susan looked at the brilliant sky, and had a sudden thought. She turned to Roderick and shouted: "Look at that BLAZE of colour! What a FLAMING sky!"

"Don't," said Roderick. "Don't spoil this ride."

Susan reined Boodi to a stop. Darkie stopped too. "Roderick," said Susan, "is it because of the fire? I notice you never go near the kitchen fire – and when you came round the corner and saw the bonfire the cowman had made the other day, you ran for your life. Tell me."

"No," said Roderick. "You'll tell the others, and they'll laugh. I couldn't bear *that* – to be laughed at, Susan."

"Once I fell off Merrylegs, and got an awful shock, and I dreamt about it for ages," said Susan. "Do you dream about the fire, Roderick?"

"Let's ride again," said Roderick. "I'll tell you if you'll promise not to tell the others."

"You know I won't," said Susan. "Come on."

They rode on again, and Roderick poured out all that

They stopped in front of the stables

he remembered about the terrible night of the fire. He told Susan of his continual nightmares too.

"Why don't you light your candle?" asked Susan at once. "Nightmares go when you have a light."

Roderick told her why. "I'm even afraid of lighting a match!" he said mournfully. "I'm a coward."

"You'd better tell my mother," said Susan after a pause. She understood Roderick's fears very well indeed.

"No. I can't possibly tell anyone," said Roderick. "I almost wish I hadn't told *you* now."

"Well, you have," said Susan. "I know what we'll do. Roderick. My bedroom is just under yours. When you wake up out of a nightmare, just tap on the floor and I'll come up and light your candle. Then you'll be all right."

"Oh – would you really do that?" said Roderick, hardly believing his ears. "I wouldn't mind nearly so much then."

So, that night, when Susan awoke to hear a tap-tap-tap on the ceiling of her room, which was the floor of the box-room above, the little girl crept quietly upstairs and slid into the room. She had her own box of matches in her hand, and Roderick's candle was soon alight. His white face stared at her out of the jumping shadows.

"Hello," she said. "I heard you. Did you have it again?"

"Yes. It's all right now you've come, though," said Roderick. "Just wait a minute or two, then you can go down again, and leave my candle alight. I can blow it out when the feeling has gone."

For three nights Susan heard the tap-tap-tap from Roderick, beset by his frightening nightmares of flame and smoke. Then, alas! deep in sleep, she heard it no more. On the fourth night when the tap-tap-tap came, only Crackers heard it. He slept at the end of Susan's bed, and had watched, puzzled, when Susan had crept out each night to go up the stairs to the box-room. She hadn't let him come with her.

He heard the tapping and cocked his ears. He waited for Susan to get up and go. But she didn't. Crackers sat there, listening for another tap. It came, more urgently this time.

55

Well, well, if Susan wasn't going, Crackers had better go and investigate himself! The black spaniel jumped off Susan's big double bed and went to the door. It was ajar. He pushed it open wider with his nose and went out on the big landing. He trotted up the uncarpeted stairs, his nails clicking as he went.

Roderick had had a very bad nightmare indeed, full of roaring flames and smoke. He awoke trembling, wet with perspiration. He tapped at once.

Susan didn't come – but what was this noise on the stairs? It sounded like Crackers! But it couldn't be! Crackers wasn't friends with him.

A wet nose was pushed against his face, and Crackers snuffled as if to say, "Well, what is it you want? I'm here!"

"Oh *Crackers*! Nicest dog! Best dog!" said Roderick, happily, holding the long silky ears just like Susan did.

Crackers wagged his plumy tail, and Roderick heard it striking against a chair-leg, bump, bump, bump. He put his arms round the dog.

"You're friends with me," he said. "You knew I was afraid, didn't you? I suppose Susan was asleep and didn't hear. But you did."

Crackers licked his nose. He knew quite well that Roderick had been frightened. He sensed it clearly. He was pleased with his welcome. This boy was quite nice after all!

He climbed on to the camp-bed and settled down with Roderick. The boy could hardly believe it. "I shan't have a single nightmare whilst you're with me!" he said. "I'm not a bit afraid to go to sleep now! Oh, Crackers, whatever will Susan say in the morning?"

Susan was astonished, and at first inclined to be cross with Crackers for deserting her and going to Roderick. "Well, I won't bother to keep waking up at nights for you now," she said. "Crackers can come instead. Didn't I tell you that he thought things out for himself? He's as clever as Boodi."

Crackers often went up to spend the night with Roderick after that, whether he had nightmares or not –

and gradually the terrifying dreams became fewer and fewer till he had none at all. He felt safe with Crackers there.

The others were astonished to see that the spaniel had made such friends with Roderick after all. Jane and Jack had always been rather pleased that Crackers had shown such a dislike. "Even Crackers knows how awful they are," they said to one another. But now it actually seemed as if Crackers had accepted Roderick as one of themselves.

Cyril and Melisande noticed the changeover too. "Roderick's going over to the enemy," said Melisande maliciously. "He's even got into Crackers' good books now!"

Cyril had had his hair cut. The boys had called him "Barber's Joy," and even he could not put up with that, for all his obstinacy. So he appeared at tea-time one day with his long hair gone, and looked quite different.

"Good gracious! Can this be Cyril?" said Jane in pretended astonishment. "He's quite good-looking now we can see his face!"

"Time he did get a haircut," growled Mr Longfield. "I was thinking of taking the shears to it soon."

"Perhaps he'll stop wearing sandals in the weekend too, now that he's taking a turn for the better," said Jane, enjoying a dig at her la-di-da cousin.

"Don't tease him so," said her mother. "You're always so very personal, Jane. I could say a few things myself – very personal ones too - about you. But I don't."

"Let me say them for you," said Cyril in his drawling voice. "Dirty hands – dirty neck – dirty nails . . ."

"Shut up," said Jane fiercely.

"Well, you rather ask for it," said Cyril.

"She does," said Melisande. "Anyway, *I'm* the expert on Jane's personal habits. Let me see, Jane, when did you last . . .?"

"Who got put down to the class below me last week?" demanded Jane in a dangerous voice, glaring at Melisande. Her cousin went red. It was a continual annoyance to her that Jane's place in school was so much higher than hers. Poor Melisande was finding it very difficult to settle down properly, after having had a private governess for so many years.

"That's enough," said Mr Longfield's deep voice. "Lot of puppies and kittens biting and scratching! Only ones who behave in a decent way to one another are Sue and Roderick. Another squabble, and you'll all leave the table and let me have a bit of peace!"

CHAPTER EIGHT

Shearing Time. Mr Twigg and Mr Potts

The term went on, flying more and more quickly each week. The early summer days passed with the hawthorn blossom. Then the sheep-shearers arrived and all six children spent the whole of Saturday watching the men in the shearing sheds. Mr Longfield hadn't enough sheep to bother about shearing machines, and his shearing was done by hand.

"I hope your tame lambs, the ones you fed from a bottle, won't be sheared," said Roderick anxiously. He and Crackers and Susan had been first in the shearing shed, up early before anyone else.

"No. Of course they won't," said Susan. "Didn't you know that first-year lambs are never shorn?"

"No, I didn't," said Roderick. "I'm glad. I wish I knew as much about the country and the farm as you do, Susan. Still, I'm learning."

"Yes, you *are* learning a bit," said Susan critically. "You already know miles more than Melisande and Cyril. Still, they just don't try to learn. But you do. Doesn't he, Crackers?"

"Wuff," said Crackers. He was looking forward to this

shearing business. He remembered it from the year before, when he had been most astonished to see the sheep
looking so very different from their appearance the day
before. He meant this year to find out all that happend.

"You'd better keep away from the shearers, Crackers,"
said Susan. "Or they'll have your beautiful silky coat off,
and before you know where you are, somebody will be
wearing it for a fur!"

"Wuff," said Crackers politely, but disbelievingly.

The shearers arrived. Jane and Jack arrived. The sheep

. . . his shearing was done by hand.

arrived, driven, lamenting loudly, by Hazel, the old shepherd. And, much later, Melisande and Cyril came, looking rather self-conscious over their interest in this farm procedure.

Cyril, especially, found himself taking more and more interest in the farm and in the countryside. He began to see that the poetry he loved wasn't just a string of beautiful words, but that it meant something real.

He stood near the shearing shed and looked round him. It was a beautiful, sunny morning. The sky was not the deep blue it soon would be; it was a harebell blue, Cyril thought. . .

Hazel, the old shepherd, was sitting under the hawthorn hedge, talking to Roderick and Susan, who were petting the three little bottle-fed lambs. Dorcas was going back to the farmhouse swinging a milk-pail and humming loudly, as she so often did. Up in the barn someone was sharpening a scythe, and the sound came clearly through the still morning air.

Something stirred in Cyril's mind, and four or five lines of poetry came surging out, ones he had said many times before without thinking:

> "And the milkmaid singeth blithe,
> And the mower whets his scythe,
> And every shepherd tells his tale
> Under the hawthorn in the dale . . ."

"Oh!" thought Cyril, "it's the first time I ever felt that poetry meant something *real*! I've just been posing up to now – pretending I loved it and thought it wonderful. I never thought it meant anything real, but it does."

He began to say the lines out loud:

> "And the milkmaid singeth blithe,
> And the mower whets his scythe,
> And every shepherd tells his tale
> Under the hawthorn in the dale . . ."

"What are you spouting about?" said Jack's blunt voice. "Not your everlasting poetry again! You're crazy!"

Cyril felt as if some cold and dirty water had been flung all over him. He turned away, humiliated to have been heard by the practical Jack, all his pleasure gone.

But a voice behind him took up the verse:

"Straight mine eye hath caught new pleasures,
    Whilst the landscape round it measures;
    Russet lawns and fallows grey
    Where the nibbling flocks do stray. . .

but, of course, the nibbling flocks are in the shearing shed at the moment, aren't they, Cyril?"

In astonishment, Cyril turned and saw his aunt smiling at him. "Why, Aunt Linnie," he stammered. "Did you hear me too – and you know that verse so well!"

"I know a lot of poetry!" said his aunt. "I love it. But it's rather gone from me now, Cyril, with so much to do and think of. You've just got hold of the very verse that suits this particular morning, haven't you? I was so pleased to hear you say it."

Jack was standing by, listening in astonishment. "I didn't even *know* you liked poetry!" he said, looking as if it was something rather to be ashamed of. "You never told me!"

"Well, it isn't a thing you go about telling people, usually," said his mother.

"Cyril does." said Jack.

"Well – he'll grow out of that soon as he grows up a bit." said Mrs Longfield. "You go and take this jug to the shearers, Jack. It's their morning tea."

Jack went. Cyril looked at his aunt. "I'm glad you didn't laugh at me too," he said. "Do you know, Aunt Linnie, it was the very first time I ever saw anything real in poetry this morning? I think it was old Hazel over there, sitting under the hawthorn, talking to young Susan and Roderick, that made it come alive, if you know what I mean."

61

"Yes, I know what you mean," said his aunt. "Well, this shall be a little secret shared between us. And you'll find, Cyril, that the more you know the country, and find out about it, the more will poetry come alive to you. But not if you pose and pretend."

"Linnie! LINNIE! Do come here!" called her husband. "Can you get me some sandwiches quickly?"

His aunt gave Cyril a quick humorous look, and turned away from him. He felt warmly towards her. It was almost as if she had said, "Well, there now. You can see quite well, Cyril, why poetry hasn't much place in my life. But it's there all the same."

"Cyril! What on earth are you gaping at?" said Jane, coming up to him. "Do come and watch the shearing. It's begun."

Cyril went off with Jane, and watched in real admiration and pleasure the neat, deft way in which the two shearers "peeled" the sheep, as Susan called it. "The wool comes away from the sheep like the skin comes off a banana," she said to Roderick, who gave one of his sudden laughs.

The sheared sheep, looking ridiculously surprised at themselves, and feeling very strange and light, went out to join the rest of the flock. Crackers went with them, most interested in their new appearance.

He suddenly gave a loud series of barks, and the children ran out of the shed to see what was the matter. They saw a peculiar-looking fellow, in a very baggy coat, with leather patches at the elbows and leather edgings to the cuffs. He had a brown, wrinkled face, screwed-up eyes, and tufts of black eyebrows that gave his face a very humorous expression.

"Oh, it's Twigg!" cried Jack. "Hello, Twigg. Where have you been so long? I haven't seen you for ages."

"Better not inquire," said Hazel, the old shepherd, from his seat under the hawthorn hedge.

"Why? Have you been to prison for poaching again, Twigg?" asked Susan.

"Poaching! That's a nice thing to say to an honest feller

like me," protested the little man in the baggy coat. He wore leather gaiters, and his feet were astonishingly small, sticking out at the end of them. When he walked he limped a little, and Cyril saw that one leg was shorter than the other. He gazed at the curious-looking fellow with interest.

"Where's Mr Potts?" asked Susan suddenly. "Didn't you bring him?"

"He's somewhere around," said Twigg. "Gone to visit Dorcas, I don't doubt! She've got a soft spot for Mr Potts. He'll get a nice juicy bone from her, maybe."

This sounded very extraordinary to Melisande, Cyril and Roderick. Jack saw their faces and laughed.

"Get Mr Potts here," he said to Twigg. "Whistle him. Let the others meet him, Twigg."

Twigg put two fingers to his mouth and gave such a shrill whistle that Melisande jumped. Out from the kitchen door came a red-gold streak at top speed.

"Why! It's a golden spaniel!" said Roderick in delight. So it was – very like Crackers, except that he was a different colour. Crackers tore to meet him, and the two dogs collided and rolled over and over madly.

"Here, Mr Potts," called Twigg. "Stop your fooling, and come and say how do you do?"

The golden spaniel trotted up, his long ears swinging. His mouth hung open, and Roderick thought he looked exactly as if he was grinning.

Everyone petted him, even Melisande, who usually wouldn't touch strange dogs; but Mr Potts was too lovely for words, and his coat shone as if it had been brushed as many times as Melisande brushed her hair.

"Why do you call him Mr Potts?" she said. "It seems an extraordinary name for a dog."

Twigg gave a curious grunt, but said nothing. Hazel the shepherd grunted too, and his eyes twinkled.

Melisande glanced up, wondering why Twigg hadn't answered her. She saw Jack, Jane and Susan grinning at one another.

"Have I said anything silly?" she asked rather

indignantly. "I just wanted to know why this lovely spaniel had such an odd name."

"I'll tell her," said Jack. "He's named after the village bobby, Mr Potts. P.C. Potts, Melisande."

"But why?" said Melisande. "Why call a dog after a policeman?"

Susan giggled. "Twigg did it for a joke, didn't you, Twigg? You see, Melisande, Mr Potts is always after poor Twigg for something or other, and whenever he sees him at night with anything in his pockets, he calls, 'Twigg! Hey, Twigg! Come here, you!' And Twigg can't ever call Mr Potts like that, in that sort of haughty voice. So he called his dog Mr Potts, and whenever he sees the policeman coming, he shouts to his dog."

"Yes. He yells, 'Mr Potts! Hey, Potts! Come here, you!'" said Jack, with a sudden gust of laughter. This struck all the children as such a huge joke that they all went into fits of laughter, in which Twigg and the shepherd joined heartily.

"But the *cream* of the joke is that after he's yelled out 'Come here, Potts!' to his dog, he pats him and fusses him and says, 'Good dog, Potty! Good dog!'" said Jane.

"What does the policeman say?" asked Roderick with great interest.

"He don't say nothing," said Twigg, chuckling. "Potts by name and Potty by nature, I say."

"Gosh! Wouldn't I love to be there when you run up against Potts some time, and call your dog!" said Cyril.

"Mebbe we can arrange summat," said Twigg. He twinkled at the children. "Enjoy that, wouldn't you?"

"Oh *yes*," said everyone.

"Daddy says Mr Potts is an ass," said Susan. "And he says you're a . . ."

"Shut up, Susan," said Jack. "You know you're not supposed to repeat things you hear."

Mr Potts ran off with Crackers. Roderick began to laugh. "Look – there go Crackers and Potty!" he cried. "Jolly good pair of dogs, Crackers and Potty!"

Twigg went to pass the time of day with the shearers.

The children went to have a snack in the kitchen, accompanied by Crackers and Mr Potts.

Cyril found himself suddenly feeling very contented. He was astonished. Contented! "Look out, Cyril! You'll turn into a farm-clod before you know where you are," he told himself sternly. "This won't do, old man. This won't do!"

CHAPTER NINE

Preparing for Aunt Rose

In the month of June everyone enjoyed the haymaking. Even Melisande so far forgot herself as to get thoroughly hot and untidy, as she threw the hay into the air and squealed with laughter.

"It smells good," she said, sniffing hard.

Susan looked at her.

"I didn't think you liked any farm smells," she said in surprise. "You always turn up your nose at them."

"Oh, don't keep reminding me of all the things I say and do," said Melisande, who found Susan's blunt tongue very trying at times. "There *are* some farm smells I like very much – the smell of the warm fresh milk, for instance, and this new-mown hay. Heavenly!"

"Would you like scent made of the smell of hay?" asked Susan, who never could understand Melisande's liking for perfume. "Now, I shouldn't mind at all having a bottle of hay perfume. I'd put some on my hanky all the year round to remind me of haymaking time."

Roderick crept up behind her with a great armful of hay. He flung it over her, and pushed her down on a haycock, smothering her with the tickly hay.

She squealed, and the two began to fight like puppies. Melisande didn't turn up her nose at them as she would have done two months ago. She smiled at the two little idiots and even considered flinging a little more hay on top. Crackers rushed up to join in the fray, and what with yelps and squeals and yells, nobody heard Jane coming up with iced lemonade to drink.

She wasn't so prim as Melisande. She set down the big stone jug and entered into the battle. She flung herself on the madly yelling three, and soon she and Roderick had got Susan completely buried in the hay. Then they turned on Melisande, and she went down under their combined attack.

Five minutes later they were all sitting down, panting, drinking the delicious iced drink. Melisande had hay in her tangled hair, and drops of perspiration rolled down her scarlet cheeks. She wriggled.

"I've got hay down my back," she said. "It tickles. Still, I forgive you for your attack, Jane, because of this wizard drink."

"Smashing, isn't it?" said Susan.

"What a word!" said Melisande.

"Well, you said 'wizard' just now. It means exactly the same as 'smashing'," said Roderick.

"Now don't *you* start being cheeky! said Melisande, surprised. Roderick wasn't nearly as meek as he had been. Now that he had lost his nightmares, and was sleeping like a top, he looked and was a different boy. He could stand up for himself, and Cyril and Melisande thought he really was getting too cheeky for words.

It was too lovely a day to quarrel. Melisande lay on her back and looked up at the blue sky above. It seemed to shimmer as she looked at it. Tiny white clouds floated across very slowly.

"They're like puffs of cotton wool," said Susan. She had quite an uncanny way of saying what things were exactly like.

"Not very poetical, but most apt," said Melisande. "Isn't it, Jane?"

"Isn't what?" said Jane. "Get off me, Crackers. Why do you always choose the very hottest day to come and lie on my tummy? Susan, he's getting awfully fat."

"He is *not*," said Susan. "I weighed him on the bathroom scales yesterday, and he's exactly the same weight as last month."

"Gosh! Do you really sit him on those scales?" said Jane. "Melisande will never use them again!"

Melisande didn't rise to the bait. It really was too hot to argue, besides being too lovely. It was a Saturday, and the whole weekend would be spent in haymaking. Melisande decided that living on a farm had some compensations. It needed them too! She remembered the miserable hot baths, with only about five inches of water, and the constant nuisance of cleaning the oil-lamps, and only having a candle in the bedroom.

That day, when they got back to a high tea, ravenously hungry, Mrs Longfield had some news for Melisande, Cyril and Roderick.

"Melisande, I'm sure you will be very delighted to know that your mother is coming for the day tomorrow," she said. "She is arriving about ten o'clock."

The three looked amazed. They had had letters each week from their mother, addressed from the nursing home, and they hadn't thought for a moment she would be well enough to come and see them.

Roderick's face lighted up. "Is she *really* coming?" he said eagerly. "I haven't seen her since we came here."

"Well, the nursing home was so far away," said Mrs Longfield. "I went once, you know, and it took me a whole day to get there and back. I would have taken you three with me, but I thought your mother was too ill to stand such a lot of us. As it was, I think she could quite well have seen you all."

Melisande thought of her pretty, charmingly dressed mother. She looked at her Aunt Linnie. She was neatly dressed in a flowered overall with a belt, but it was rather shapeless. Her hair looked untidy, but then it was so curly that it would go its own way, and somehow the untidiness didn't matter. It suited Aunt Linnie.

"Aunt Linnie will show up badly beside Mother!" thought Melisande. "I hope Mother wears that lovely frock she had last year. Oh no, of course she won't. It would have been lost in the fire. What shall *I* wear? I'll get out that lovely blue frock I had for my party. I expect Jane will have on those awful shorts and that dirty cotton shirt as usual. I hope she does! Perhaps Aunt Linnie and Uncle Peter will be ashamed of her when they see her beside me."

"Isn't Mother staying the night?" asked Roderick. "I'd like her to."

"She didn't say she would, though I did ask her," said his aunt. "*You* can ask her, Roderick. I'm sure she would stay for you! It's very uncomfortable for her here, that's the only thing. She would have to sleep in your uncle's dressing-room."

Jane, Jack and Susan didn't much welcome the idea of Aunt Rose coming. "Still, it's only for a day," said Susan. "And we can go out into the hay fields and leave her. We can't stop haymaking just because Aunt Rose is coming."

She didn't say this to Roderick, of course, who was wild with delight to think he was going to see his mother again. "We'll take her to see Merrylegs, Darkie and Boodi, won't we?" he said to Susan. "And she simply *must* see the calves, though they're pretty well grown-up now."

"Do you think she'll want to?" said Susan doubtfully. From what she remembered of her aunt, she couldn't imagine her wanting to visit ponies or calves.

"And I do hope Crackers makes friends with her at once," went on Roderick, taking no notice of the doubt in Susan's voice.

"Well, he didn't last time she came," said Susan. "Perhaps you don't remember, because you didn't seem to take any notice of anything much, Roderick – not even when I took you to see all the new week-old chicks running about."

"I must have been potty," said Roderick, looking back at himself in surprise.

"Well, actually I did think you were potty," said Susan honestly. "I thought you were mother's pet lamb, and ought to be fed out of a baby's milk bottle, like I feed the motherless lambs with."

"You say awful things, but they sound so funny you make me laugh," said Roderick with a sudden squeal. "I feel sort of half-cross with you and then I laugh. I say, do you think Mother will come into the hay field and help us hay-make? I'd hate to miss a day's haymaking just now – and it's very, very important to get on with it now the weather's right, isn't it?"

"Goodness, yes," said Susan. She considered the question. "Well, honestly, I don't think your mother would *dream* of haymaking, Roderick," she said. "I don't believe she would even want to watch *us* messing about with the hay, either. I expect you'll have to sit with her all the day, and not go to the fields at all."

Roderick looked dismayed. "I *must* help," he said. "Your father said I was jolly good with the hay-tossing."

The next day was Sunday. The whole of the family got up early and went to church in the cool of the morning. It wasn't really early to them, because they were so used to being up and about. Even Melisande and Cyril were used to it now, and as for Roderick, he liked to get up as soon as he was awake, and go out to see how things were getting on. He and Susan were alike in that. Sometimes Jack would tell him he could take Darkie for an early morning gallop, and then Roderick and Susan would go off in delight.

Breakfast was over by nine o'clock. Melisande sped out to help with the washing-up. "I'll do your share today," said Jane. "I know you'll want to titivate yourself for your mother. You go on upstairs. I suppose you'll want me to do my nails, and brush my hair a hundred times, like you do, because Aunt Rose is coming, Melisande!"

"Of course not," said Melisande in surprise. "If you don't do those things for your own mother, why should I expect you to do them for mine? Aunt Linnie is always asking you to stop biting your nails, and to brush your hair more – but you don't! I shan't expect you to be any different just because *my* mother is coming! Thanks for offering to do the washing-up, Jane. Jolly decent of you."

She sped upstairs. Jane put the things into the hot water

rather thoughtfully. She had honestly meant to clean her nails and scrub her dirt-roughened fingers, and tidy up her hair because Aunt Rose was coming. She hadn't thought that she never did these things for her own mother's sake, unless she was badgered into it. She felt rather mean.

She thought of Jack, who now always carried up the hot water for his mother's bath, a thing that had surprised Jane and Susan very much indeed. It had surprised their mother even more. She had been very touched by Jack's offer.

"Thank you, Jack," she said. "I do often feel tired at the end of the day. I'd like you to take up the water for me very much."

"I'd have done it for you myself," said her husband's voice from behind a farming paper. "Why didn't you ask me?"

"Oh Peter – you've so much to do. I wouldn't dream of making you get up out of your chair at the end of a hard day's work," said his wife. "But Jack can easily do it. He doesn't have a hard day like you."

Jack looked at his mother in silence. He knew that she had a hard day too. She was always doing something in the house, or in the dairy, or with the hens and ducks. She was cross sometimes, but she was always so cheerful and kind and ready to laugh. And it had needed that ass of a Cyril to put it into his head to do a simple thing like carrying a heavy bucket of hot water for his mother's bath!

Jack really felt ashamed of himself. "I *could* have thought of it," he said to himself. "I'm blind! I *am* a clod, just like Cyril often says. I'm pretty dumb too – I never can think what to say – not like Jane who can chatter nineteen to the dozen."

He carried the hot water up every time his mother needed it after that. He couldn't bring himself to take up Jane's or Susan's. For one thing, he was sure they would laugh at the idea, and for another thing, he couldn't see why the girls shouldn't do it themselves. But his mother was different.

And now Jane too had been forced to think along the

70

same lines as Jack, because of what Melisande had so lightly said a few minutes since. "If you don't do these things for your own mother, why should I expect you to do them for mine?"

"Well," decided Jane, "I shan't do them for Aunt Rose today. But I might start doing them for Mummy some time soon – and then if Aunt Rose comes again, my hands and hair will be decent, anyhow. But I can't possibly spend hours over myself like Melisande does."

She dried the dishes carefully, under the keen eye of Dorcas, who would never let a job be done badly. "If a job's worth doing at all, it's worth doing well," she had said a thousand times. She had said it so often that the children didn't even hear it now – but they knew well enough that they had to work hard if they did anything for Dorcas!

It was five minutes to ten. Mrs Longfield put her head in at the kitchen door. "Have you finished, Jane dear? Good! Then you'd better go up and make yourself tidy. Aunt Rose will be here soon. And just see that Susan is at least *clean*, will you? I'll see to Roderick."

She disappeared, and Jane went upstairs. She put on a pair of flannel shorts and a clean blue cotton shirt. She ran a comb through her hair. That would do! She went to look for Susan.

A cry went up from downstairs. It was Roderick's voice: "Melisande! Cyril! Here's the car! Mother's here!"

CHAPTER TEN

Aunt Rose Arrives

Roderick was first at the car. He opened it before the driver could get down, and flung himself on his mother.

"Mother! You've come! Are you well again?"

A pair of soft, silk–clad arms held him close. "Darling Roderick!" said his mother's soft voice. "Mother's own boy! How I have missed you!"

Then came Cyril and Melisande. Cyril looked his most flowing and artistic today. He knew that his mother liked him like that, though he felt a little self-conscious about it now. Melisande was looking self-conscious too, but for a different reason!

She had grown plump with all the good farm food, the fresh air and the healthy life – and her lovely blue frock no longer fitted her properly. Poor Melisande had tried on her other pretty frocks, but the same thing had happened with all of them! They were much too small. Only her everyday things fitted her now – her school blouses and skirts, which Aunt Linnie had bought for her when she went to Jane's school and had to have the usual uniform.

She couldn't bear her school uniform, and she certainly wasn't going to put it on when her mother came. There was no time to alter any of the frocks, so she just had to put on the blue one and hope that it wouldn't split anywhere. Melisande felt uneasily that it certainly would before long.

She hugged her mother joyfully. Then Cyril put his arm round her and helped her from the car. She leaned on him.

"Are you quite well again now, Mother?" asked Cyril. "You've been such a long time in the nursing-home."

"Not *quite* well," said his mother, who looked the picture of health and prettiness as she walked up to the farmhouse door on his arm. "But much, much better. It was such a *terrible* shock, you know, and I've never been very strong. Oh, it's wonderful to be with my big boy again, and my pretty girl, and my baby!"

Roderick didn't much like being called her baby, though he had never minded it before. He hoped fervently that Susan hadn't heard. Crackers came rushing out with joyful barks.

"Oh – that dreadful dog! I hope he won't ruin my stockings!" said Aunt Rose to Jack, as he came out to meet his aunt. "Do put him away somewhere. I can't bear dogs."

Jack kissed his aunt politely. She smelled very sweet, and he thought she looked beautiful. Crackers ran round her, still barking.

"Quiet!" said Cyril. "Susan, take Crackers away."

Susan appeared, looking so tidy and clean that Jack hardly knew her. She picked Crackers up in her arms and offered her cheek to her aunt.

"I can't kiss you, darling, whilst you are carrying that dog!" said Aunt Rose with her silvery little laugh. "He might lick me!"

"He wouldn't," said Susan. "He never licks anyone he doesn't like."

Jack gave her a nudge. Why *did* Susan always say things like that just when she shouldn't? Fortunately, his aunt didn't notice, because her sister-in-law came hurrying out with Jane.

"Rose dear! How nice to see you again! And how pretty you look!" cried Mrs Longfield, who hadn't an atom of envy in her nature. "Younger than ever! Isn't she, Cyril?"

"Yes," said Cyril proudly. He thought the world of his pretty, spoilt mother, and loved her little ways.

"Cyril's grown," said his mother. "People will soon be taking me for his sister, won't they!" She laughed her silvery laugh again.

"I hope Mummy never gets mistaken for *Jack's* sis . . ." began Susan in horror, looking at her mother. She got a nudge from Jane, who had kissed her aunt, and was now standing silently by, taking in all the frills and flounces,

73

the pretty, high-heeled shoes, and the necklace and earrings of pearls that her aunt wore.

Yes, Aunt Rose didn't look any the worse for her "shock". Indeed, Mrs Longfield thought, she looked even younger than before. Why, she looked almost as young as Melisande. It was very extraordinary. She glanced at Melisande. The girl had grown taller than her mother – and bigger! Her dress was almost bursting at the sides. For the first time her aunt realized that Melisande was no longer the slim, elegant girl who had come to Mistletoe Farm in the Easter holidays. She was a plump, well-grown young girl, her cheeks red with health.

They all went into the farmhouse, where Mrs Longfield had iced drinks ready, and some home-made biscuits. "Peter will be in to dinner," she said. "He's out in the hay fields. It's a busy time with us, you know, and his men have said they will work today, though it's Sunday."

"Poor Peter!" said his sister-in-law. "And poor David too! I suppose he'll be hard at work haymaking as well."

"Gosh! I'd like to be with him, then!" said Roderick.

"Oh Roderick darling! You could never stand work like that," said his mother fondly. "Why, don't you remember how ill you felt when you once tried to mow the lawn at Three Towers?"

Roderick went red. "I must have been an idiot then," he said. "I've helped every evening this week with the haymaking. Mother – and all day yesterday. I was hoping you'd come and help too, but I suppose you can't in that dress."

His mother heard him in amazement. Then her eyes fell on Melisande, who was trying to sit in a position that would ease the strain on her dress.

"Melisande, you've altered!" she said. "Yes, you have! Stand up and let me see you properly."

This was the last thing Melisande wanted to do. But she stood up obediently – and her dress split under one arm!

"Oh, that *dress*, Melisande!" cried her mother in an anguished voice. "That beautiful dress! You're fat, dear – yes, *fat*. You shouldn't have put on that dress."

"They're all too small now," said Melisande, red as a beetroot with everyone's eyes on her. Her aunt took pity on her.

"Go and put on a skirt and a cotton blouse," she said. "You look nice in those."

"Oh, I don't want her in school uniform today," said Aunt Rose. "Never mind, Melisande. I'll try and get you another dress when I go up to London. But, dear, you really are *fat* – quite coarse-looking. I did so hope you would take after me!"

She approved thoroughly of Cyril, who had on beige corduroy velvet trousers, a yellow shirt and a brown-and-yellow tie, flowing loose. "But I don't like the way you've had your hair cut, darling," she said. "All the waves have gone. And how's the poetry going?"

"All right, thank you," mumbled Cyril, furious at the grins he saw on Jane's face and Jack's. He wished his mother wouldn't ask these questions publicly.

His aunt saw his discomfort, and sent him out to get some more ice. He went thankfully, giving her a grateful look. Kind Aunt Linnie! He did hate to feel a fool in front of the others, and though Mother didn't mean to, she did embarrass him when she spoke to him as if he was five years old.

Susan, still holding Crackers, let out a colossal sigh. "Can I go?" she asked. "Crackers is awfully heavy, but I daren't put him down because of Aunt Rose's stockings. Though actually I can't see that she has any on."

Her aunt gave a little squeal of laughter and hit Susan playfully on the arm.

"Funny little girl! She's noticed my beautiful stockings!" cooed Aunt Rose, and put out a lovely ankle to be admired.

"Can I go, Mummy?" repeated Susan. "I've had two drinks, and I don't suppose you'll let me have any more. I *promised* Daddy I'd help him with the hay again this morning."

"Yes, you can go," said her mother.

"Can Roderick come too?" asked Susan. "He's an awfully good worker. Daddy says so."

"Oh, I can't spare my little Roderick!" said Aunt Rose, and put her arm round him, drawing him to her. "You don't want to go, do you, Roderick?"

Roderick hesitated. He did want to go. He wanted to go very badly. On the other hand, he wanted to be with his mother too.

"Well, dear?" said his mother a little sharply. "Answer Mother!"

"Mother, you come too," begged Roderick. "Aunt Linnie will lend you some proper shoes, won't you, Auntie? And you could take your hat off, and . . ."

"Roderick! Come into a *hay* field – full of horrible insects!" said his mother in horror. "And of *course* Aunt Linnie couldn't lend me shoes. Hers would be far too big."

Roderick felt that his mother was much more annoyed than she sounded. He sighed. He wouldn't be able to haymake this morning, that was certain. He would never, never be able to persuade Mother to come.

Susan went off with Crackers, giving Roderick a sympathetic look as she departed. Poor Roderick! That was what came of having a "butterfly" for a mother. Still, even butterflies went to hay fields, thought Susan. She was glad her own mother was so different Aunt Rose was pretty, she smelt lovely and had a sweet soft voice except when she was annoyed – but she didn't seem like a *mother* to Susan.

Jack soon excused himself and went off. His aunt looked after him. "Still the same old Jack," she murmured.

"What do you mean, the same old Jack?" asked Jane, suspicious of the tone of her aunt's voice.

"Nothing, dear! But he's so *dumb*, isn't he! So silent. Very like your dear father to look at. And you, dear Jane – how are you getting on at school? Are you up to Melisande's standard yet? Of course, Melisande had first-class governesses, and we let her travel a lot too . . ."

Melisande gave Jane a desperate look. Jane knew what it meant. It meant "For goodness sake don't say I'm in a class below you!" And Jane was loyal and said nothing, for which Melisande was profoundly grateful. Mother didn't understand things. She didn't belong to the world of Mistletoe Farm, where life was real and earnest, and there were a hundred and one things to be done and not enough people to do them. Melisande felt hot as the sun came through the window and fell on her shoulders, and she blew out a breath to cool herself.

Her dress split a little further. She interrupted her mother. "Mother, I'll have to go and get out of this dress. It's split some more. Anyway, I can hardly breathe."

"Well, go then," said her mother. "It's no good mending it, Melisande. Put on something else. What about that pretty red frock?"

"That's worse," said Melisande. "You'll simply *have* to get me a new dress or two, Mother. I hope there's enough money."

Her mother looked a little shocked. "We are not so poor as all that, Melisande;" she said with dignity.

"I'm going upstairs to put on shorts and a blouse," said Melisande. "I can't bear to put on my school ,skirt, Mother. It's bad enough to wear it on weekdays. You'd hate it."

"*Shorts!*" said her mother in disgust, and then re-membered that Jane had them on. "Well – all right. I keep forgetting you lead a simple country life here, poor child – no chance to wear your pretty frocks any more, I suppose. Oh, the parties you used to go to, Melisande. Do you remember? And you were always the prettiest child there. I remember Mrs Partington saying to me that you . . ."

"I'll hurry up and go now, Mother," said Melisande, knowing quite well that her mother hated to be inter-rupted, but despairing of her ever stopping her flow of talk.

"Dear, don't interrupt Mother," said her mother. "Oh, Melisande, I'm afraid your manners are not as good as they used to be. Well, go if you want to. I'll talk to Cyril."

Susan spent a happy morning with Crackers, Jane and Jack in the hay. They all got hot and dirty, and were very hungry indeed when they went in to their dinner. Their father went with them, groaning as he remembered he would have to make himself look really smart for the visitor.

Roderick had stayed all morning with his mother. He was shocked to find that he was very bored. It *was* boring to talk all the time. People hardly ever sat and talked and did nothing at Mistletoe Farm. They usually did their talking at mealtimes or when they were working.

He thought longingly of Susan and Crackers up in the hay field. What a good time they would be having! He wondered if he would be able to get his mother to go and see the ponies and the calves after dinner.

Melisande was now in clean grey shorts and a spotless white blouse. She looked very nice indeed, thought her Aunt Linnie, and very sensible. She wished Jane would try to keep her hands and hair like Melisande did – but she had almost given up trying to make Jane take any pride in herself.

She had to go and help Dorcas in the kitchen, and left the little family together. "Oh, Dorcas!" she said. "Rose is prettier than ever – she looks years younger than I do! How does she do it?"

"She does it by looking after herself so carefully and lovingly, Mam, that she hasn't time to look after anybody else, not even her own children," said Dorcas grimly. "There's more beauty in *your* face, seems to me, than there ever was in Mrs David's – and I'm not talking about skin and eyes and nose now, Mam. I'm talking about character. Your nature's writ plain in your face and makes it beautiful to all your family – yes, and to me too. But you'll look in vain for that kind of beauty in Mrs David's face!"

Mrs Longfield was touched. "You've got a soft spot for me, Dorcas," she said, beginning to beat up a batter pudding. "You always had!"

Dorcas had been nurse to Mrs Longfield and to her brother and sister when they were little. She had come back to her when she married, and now here she was still!

78

Mrs Longfield looked at her lovingly. Dorcas was plain, sharp-tongued and fat, but beauty came unexpectedly into her face too at moments: when she looked at Susan and teased her, when she fussed over a motherless lamb by the kitchen fire on a bitter cold night, or when she stood close beside her mistress, working hard with her at some urgent task.

The dinner was ready at last. All the family gathered round the big table. Dorcas put the dishes on the sideboard, and Mr Longfield got up to carve.

"Now then – everybody hungry?" he said, as he always did. And the answering cry came back at once.

"Ra-*ther*!"

CHAPTER ELEVEN

Poor Aunt Rose!

Aunt Rose's visit was not really a great success. Somehow her children saw her through new eyes, and she couldn't help sensing it. Roderick frankly wanted to get away and go to the hay field in the afternoon, once he found that his mother had no intention of going round the farm and visiting cows and horses.

Melisande found herself longing to get ouside in the sun and breeze. But her mother never sat in the sun, for fear of freckles. Cyril found that a pretty mother with a fund of light conversation was amusing for a little while, but now that he had got so used to being on the go all the time, he found it difficult to sit in the darkened room indoors, and converse lightly and amiably with someone who treated him like a small and delightful boy.

Very fortunately for everyone, Aunt Linnie had a real brainwave. "I think, Rose dear," she said, "that you really ought to have a rest this afternoon. You had a long journey this morning. Come up and lie on my bed."

Aunt Rose graciously consented. "I do feel rather tired," she admitted. "I have to take a little more care of myself than I used to, since the shock of the fire. Thank you, Linnie. I'll come up and lie down."

Soon she was lying down on her sister-in-law's bed, thinking that it was a very hard bed indeed. She looked at the furniture and thought it was very ugly.

"My poor Melisande, having to live in a place like this!" she thought. "Everything so plain and useful – nothing pretty. And no hot water anywhere, not even in the bathroom! My poor children! They look well enough on it all – Linnie is a very good cook – but I'm sure they can't be happy."

She closed her eyes and her long, curling eyelashes lay on her cheek. Melisande, peeping in quietly half an hour later, thought she looked like a beautiful china doll.

Everyone was relieved that Aunt Rose had gone to lie down. Crackers raced about unheeded. Roderick prepared to go up to the hay field with Susan. He was delighted. Cyril thought he would go too, as Jack said all hands were needed today in case the weather broke the next day.

"Melisande, you come as well," said Jane. "You've got shorts and a blouse on – just right for haymaking. You can't sit about all this lovely afternoon waiting for your mother to wake up!"

"No, I suppose it would be silly," Melisande said. "I'll peep in at Mother and see if she really is asleep, and if she is, I'll come. Dorcas can ring a bell for me to go back to her when she wakes. I'll ask her to."

Dorcas said she would. She and her mistress were busy doing the washing-up. They had told the two elder girls they need not help if they wanted to go and hay-make.

So all the six cousins went joyfully to the sunny hay field, and were soon tossing the hay and shouting and yelling at the tops of their voices.

"You go too, Mam," said Dorcas. "I can ring the bell when Mrs David wakes, and you can come back. Then you and she can have a cup of afternoon tea and a few cakes – the children and Mr Peter will have high tea as usual, I suppose."

"Well, Dorcas – I *would* like to go up to the hay field this lovely afternoon," said Mrs Longfield. "You ring the bell when Mrs David wakes, and put the kettle on straight away. I'll be a real society lady this afternoon and have four o'clock tea for once!"

She went off to join the rest of her family. Crackers came to meet her, barking a joyous welcome. Her husband smiled at her. He looked big and burly and brown, standing there mopping his forehead in the hot sun.

"Well, Linnie," he said with pleasure, "it's good to see you out here – you're so often down in the house. Now you sit behind this haycock and rest yourself."

"Oh, I don't want to," said his wife. "I've come to help! Rose is fast asleep, so she won't miss me."

Rose certainly was fast asleep. She slept soundly till a quarter to four, as still as a dormouse. Then she awoke with a jump as a cock suddenly took it into his head to crow loudly just under the window.

She looked at her watch, but it had stopped. What time was it? How quiet the house was! No sound of children's voices, no pattering of feet. Where was everyone?

"They're being quiet as mice so as not to disturb me!" she thought. "I'll get up now and go and find everyone. I really feel quite rested again now."

She put on her pretty frock, tied her hair and went downstairs. There was nobody in the dining-room and nobody in the sitting-room. Nobody in the little room off the stairs where Mr Longfield did his accounts either. *Where* was everyone?

She looked out into the little courtyard, peaceful in the afternoon sun. The fat goldfish jumped for flies, and a farm cat sat sunning itself on a warm paving stone, glad that Crackers was out of the way.

"Nobody there either," said Aunt Rose, puzzled. "What's happened? They can't all have gone for a walk and left me here by myself. And even if *Linnie's* children have gone to the hay field, mine wouldn't have – except Roderick, perhaps. Linnie wouldn't have gone, anyhow."

She thought she would go into the kitchen and see if anyone was there. She went quietly down the stone passage that led into the big old-fashioned kitchen, and at last found someone!

It was Dorcas – but Dorcas was lost to the world. She sat in her low armchair, her head back, her mouth dropping open. She was tired out, and had dropped peacefully off to sleep whilst she waited for Rose to awake.

On her lap was a fat tabby cat, who had jumped up there as soon as she had seen that Dorcas was asleep. He sat there, purring, kneading his paws in and out of her big white apron. He stared balefully at Aunt Rose as if to say, "Now don't you go and wake her. She's got such a nice big lap for me to lie on."

Aunt Rose felt annoyed. Nobody in the house at all to entertain her – and this fat old cook fast asleep with her mouth open. The kettle not even on for tea! She glanced at the big kitchen clock, and saw that it was past four o'clock.

"Four o'clock! And it's ages since we had lunch – or dinner, as they call it here," said Aunt Rose to herself. "They had it at twelve! And now it's four. Well, I suppose they'll all be in to tea soon. Had I better waken this fat old woman?"

She decided not to. She knew that Dorcas disliked her, and Aunt Rose didn't like being disliked. Dorcas always put on such a nasty, scornful sort of look whenever she came near her!

So Aunt Rose tiptoed out of the quiet kitchen, with its rows of scarlet geraniums in pots on the windowsill, and its well-scrubbed stone floor. She gave a parting look of dislike at Dorcas and the tabby.

She didn't see the worn old hands clasped together, or the tired, shapeless old feet in their bulging slippers, or the thin, grey hairs so neatly brushed back for Sunday afternoon. She just saw a fat, sharp-tongued old woman she couldn't bear, with a spiteful-looking tabby cat on her knee. Aunt Rose never looked very deep into anyone or anything!

Up in the hay field everyone was having an uproarious time. Some children from Roderick's class had come along to help, and there were mock fights and battles, accompanied by bloodcurdling screams and yells. The hay was being well and truly tossed, and was drying marvellously.

Nobody had a watch. Mrs Longfield listened for the bell that Dorcas was to ring when Aunt Rose awoke, or when it was four o'clock, but she heard nothing. She had exhausted herself for the moment and lay back panting against a haycock, looking young and happy.

Aunt Rose was sitting waiting for someone to come to her. She sat in the sitting-room, looking cross and feeling hurt and angry? What a visit! Why should everyone desert her like this? Was there to be no tea? She longed for a cup of nice hot tea with all her heart. Or for a drink of that iced lemonade. But that had all been taken up to the hay field.

Half-past four came. Five o'clock came! Dorcas awoke and looked at the clock in amazement. *Five* o'clock! Had she really been asleep so long? What must Mrs David be thinking? She got up in a hurry, emptying the cat off her lap as she rose.

"Maybe Mrs David is still sleeping herself," thought Dorcas, putting the kettle on. "I'll just creep up to the bedroom and listen to see if she's stirring."

So she crept up the stairs to the landing and stood outside the closed door of the bedroom, listening. But nobody was stirring inside.

"She's asleep still," thought Dorcas. "Well, she'd have come along and asked for tea, if she'd been awake!"

Down she went again, never guessing that an angry, haughty Mrs David sat upright in the sitting-room alone, waiting for someone to come and see to her.

The kettle boiled. Dorcas pushed it to one side of the stove, humming her little song. She began to cut small thin pieces of bread and butter.

In the sitting-room Aunt Rose could no longer bear being alone. She walked to the door and looked out, listening. The afternoon shadows were now lengthening, and the fields around and about were very lovely. Aunt Rose caught sounds of shouting and laughter on the breeze, and far away in a field she saw moving figures.

"I'll go and see what they're all doing," she thought, ready to do in her anger what she would never have done otherwise – walk in her high-heeled shoes through the farmyard, out of the gate and up the narrow, rutted path that led to the hay fields.

She was lying on her back . . .

84

It was hot in the sun. It was difficult to walk in high heels. But Aunt Rose persevered until at last she came to the open gate of the field in which the family was hay-making. What a tribe of children! What shrieks and shouts!

Goodness – was that – *could* that be – Melisande! It could be, and was. She was lying on her back, kicking away Susan and Roderick, almost helpless with laughter.

Cyril was chasing three children Aunt Rose didn't know. One turned, doubled back, tripped Cyril neatly and fell on him with shouts of laughter, trying to stuff hay down his torn shirt.

Another figure came flying by, chased by Jane and Jack. It was their mother! She was rescued by her burly husband, who swung her behind him, and proceeded to deal with Jane and Jack. His wife sank to the ground, untidy, hot, and weak with exercise and laughter.

She suddenly caught sight of the slight figure by the gate. She stared in dismay, then tried to tidy herself a little.

"Oh – Rose dear – have you really come all this way by yourself – in those shoes!" she said. "Dorcas was to ring the bell when you awoke, and I had planned a quiet little four o'clock tea together."

"It's almost half-past five," said Rose in a cold voice. "What a sight you look, Linnie! And I must say I don't approve of Melisande behaving in that way. And Cyril I've never known him so – so uncontrolled!"

She looked as if she was about to burst into tears. She felt thoroughly upset and dismayed. She had been absolutely forgotten whilst they had all been behaving like yokels! How *could* Melisande behave like that! Lying kicking and screaming in the field with Susan and Roderick flinging hay all over her!

"Melisande!" she called sharply. "Get up. Roderick, stop that! Cyril, whatever *are* you doing?"

Melisande jerked herself upright at once, and gazed at her mother in dismay. Cyril got up more leisurely, and brushed away the wisps of hay from his corduroy trousers.

Roderick took no notice, but fell on Susan and the two struggled together like puppies.

"Er – your mother says it is almost half-past five," said Mrs Longfield to Melisande and Cyril. "I'm afriad I didn't notice the time going so quickly. I had meant to have afternoon tea at four. We'd better all get back to high tea now."

Feeling very self-conscious and a little ashamed of being found haymaking like the youngsters, Mrs Longfield walked back to the farmhouse with a very silent, rather sulky Rose.

She tried to talk lightly, but it was impossible, and she was really very glad when at last they reached the house, and she could rush upstairs to tidy herself. She gazed in horror at her flushed, streaked face, and her hay-strewn hair. Whatever *must* Rose have thought!

"I'm really very sorry, Rose," she said when she got downstairs. "I can't think how it happened."

"I can," said Rose in a tight kind of voice. "I'm not wanted here – not even by my own children. I can see that. They're different. You've changed them."

"No, I haven't," said her sister-in-law, gently. "They've changed themselves. They were spoilt, Rose. Now they're not. They've adapted themselves well to their new surroundings. You ought to be proud of them, not ashamed."

"Well, I'm *ashamed*!" said Rose, and tears came into her eyes. "I don't believe they love me any more. And if they go on changing like this – I shan't love them any more either!"

"That is a very wicked thing to say, Rose," said Mrs Longfield sternly. "I have always thought you were a silly, selfish woman, but I did not think you would be wicked. To talk of not loving your own children is the wickedest thing any mother can say. I will not listen to such things."

She got up and left Rose, who was now very much ashamed of herself. She sat there alone till she was called into high tea by Melisande. She was silent and ate very little, but as there were nine children to tea – for the three visiting children had been told to stay too – there was very little chance for anyone to notice a silent person.

Only Cyril noticed, and was sorry. Poor Mother! They had changed and she hadn't. Cyril had not realized how much they had changed until he saw his mother again. He tried to be attentive and sweet to her, but got very little response.

The car came for her soon afterwards, and she made some polite farewells, kissed her three children, and drove away, even more a stranger than when she had arrived. Not even Roderick asked her to stay for the night!

"How sad!" thought Mrs Longfield as she went indoors to help to clear away. "How very sad that a mother should have three fine healthy children, and not plan with them to make a home, or talk to them about their father, or even please her youngest by going to see the horses and calves with him."

Cyril, Melisande and Roderick did not discuss their mother's visit at all. Each of them was very disappointed, but none of them liked to say so. They were loyal to her, and would not dream of saying a word against her.

But Susan was not going to let the matter pass without airing *her* opinion.

"I shouldn't think Aunt Rose will come again in a hurry," she said. "She thinks we're all awful – even Cyril and Melisande. Don't you think she does, Mummy?"

"Well, it was very shocking that we let her think we'd forgotten all about her this afternoon," said her mother. "It was a chapter of accidents, of course, but I'm afraid Aunt Rose doesn't realize that. She must think we all neglected her dreadfully."

"She could have come with us," said Susan.

"Oh, but she couldn't walk all that way in her high-heeled shoes this hot day," said her mother, quite forgetting that she had. But Susan hadn't forgotten.

"She *did* come, though," she persisted. "But she only came because she was *cross*. She wouldn't have come because we wanted her to. Mummy, you'd have come

87

because *we* wanted you to, and because you wanted to come yourself, too! You're a *proper* mother, and I'd rather have you than any other mother in the world!"

Her father twinkled at her. Susan always hit the nail on the head. You simply couldn't be cross with her!

CHAPTER TWELVE

Poetry and Ponies!

The end of the term came. The three girls broke up a day ahead of the boys, and were jubilant. Jane let Cyril ride to school the next day on Merrylegs, as she would not be wanting him

"I used to think I'd never, never let any of you three ride my pony," she said to Cyril. "But you do like Merrylegs, don't you?"

"I like every horse on the farm, even Boodi," said Cyril surprisingly. "You can't help liking all the animals really, can you, when you live so close to them. I mean — a farm's rather like one great big family, and even the tiniest chick belongs to it."

Jane stared at Cyril in delighted surprise. "Why, *Cyril*!" she said, "you're clever to think of that! I always knew it, of course — but somehow I never thought of it like that. I think what you've just said is miles better than any poetry you can ever say. I do really."

Cyril was quite overcome at this burst of praise from the usually scornful Jane. For once he was tongue-tied, and could only stare at Jane rather owlishly.

"You look like that sheep that stands at the gate and stares when we go by!" she said with a squeal of laugher. "You know, Cyril, if you put that thing you've just said into a bit of poetry, I'd listen to it."

"You never attempt to listen to *any* poetry," said

Cyril, "and I don't flatter myself you'd listen to any *I* made up, Jane."

"Well, I might, if you wrote a really sensible one with something in it like you said just now," persisted Jane. "But most poems aren't sensible. I don't think poets are sensible either. Farmers *are* sensible, now. For one thing, they most of them seem happy, even if they grumble."

"Give fools their gold, and knaves their power,
    Let fortune's bubbles rise and fall,
Who sows a field or trains a flower
    Or plans a tree is more than all!"

said Cyril, and grinned. "That suit you? Or isn't it sensible enough?"

"Well, actually I think that's rather good," said Jane, considering. "Do you know a poem about a horse? I wouldn't mind reading one if it had a horse in it."

"Yes, I know several about horses," said Cyril, amused at his cousin's sudden interest in poetry. "How's this?"

"She was iron-sinewed and satin-skinned,
    Ribbed like a drum and limbed like a deer,
Fierce as the fire and fleet as the wind,
    There was nothing she couldn't climb or clear!"

He stopped. Jane was listening greedily, understanding every word, picturing the beautiful horse racing like the wind.

"Go on," she said when Cyril stopped. "I like that. This is what I mean by *real* poetry! What comes next?"

"I don't know," confessed Cyril. "I've forgotten. I just remembered that bit because it seemed sort of spirited – like a horse is. You can read the whole of the poem if you like. It's called 'Britomarte.' I've got it in one of my books."

"Oh, thanks awfully," said Jane, little knowing that she had begun a course of poetry that was going to please her for the rest of her life! "I'll read it some time. Well, as I said, you can ride Merrylegs to school tomorrow if you like as I'm not needing him. Be careful if you meet one of those steam engine things, though. He's like Boodi; he hates them."

Roderick didn't like being the only one left to ride in on the bus. He went to find Susan. "Susan, Jane's letting Cyril ride Merrylegs tomorrow. Can I ride Boodi?"

"No. You know you can't," said Susan. "He doesn't behave with anyone but me."

"Well, but he knows me so well now," said Roderick "Look how he whinnies when I go to the stables. He only used to do that to you, and now he does it to me too."

"No. You can't have Boodi," said Susan shortly, and she turned and left him. She knew really that he could probably manage Boodi all right now, but she was jealous where her Iceland pony was concerned. He was hers, and she couldn't bear to lend him.

Roderick wandered off by himself, kicking a stone along. He wished ardently that he had his own pony. He thought how lucky Susan was, with both Boodi and Crackers. If he had a dog and a pony he would always be happy.

"Everybody who lives at Mistletoe Farm is lucky really," thought the little boy, stopping to look at the piglets running round their great fat sow-mother. "There's not only Crackers for them to have; there's all the farm cats, and the shepherd's dogs, and the farm horses and the cows and the sheep and the three pet lambs – though they're rather grown-up now. I hope Daddy does get a farm for us. I'd be so happy."

He began to plan his own farm. "I shall have a horse called Moonlight!" he thought. "A dark bay with a blaze like a streak of moonlight! And she'll go like the wind."

He told Susan about Moonlight when he next ran into her. She was feeding the hens, and he went to help to scatter the corn.

"Will you really have a horse called Moonlight?" said Susan. "That's a lovely name. Will you let anyone else ride him, or will you love him too much?"

Roderick thought about Moonlight. "Well – I wouldn't lend him to anyone but you," he said. "I'd lend him to you because I know you'd like him as much as I did."

"Oh *thank* you," said Susan warmly. Then she screwed up her nose and looked comically at her cousin. "Do you like Boodi as much as I like him? If you say yes, I'll lend him to you tomorrow after all."

And so it was that the three boy cousins all rode to school on the last day of term, Cyril on Merrylegs and Roderick on Boodi. Jack was on Darkie as usual.

Boodi played all his little tricks on Roderick! The boy loitered behind on the way home, enjoying the ride. Boodi put his ears back wickedly and began to side-step towards the hedge. Before Roderick had guessed what he meant to do, he was squeezing the boy's leg against the prickly hedge, dragging it along painfully!

"Boodi! Stop it!" yelled Roderick, and slid his leg out as soon as he could, resting it on the top of the saddle. "Bad Boodi! I'm ashamed of you. Get up, now!"

Boodi stood stock still and refused to move. He could be as obstinate as a mule. He stood there for five minutes, and a little crowd of children came and watched in interest.

"Woa there, woa!" suddenly cried Roderick, remembering that "Woa" meant "Gee-up, then," to contrary little Boodi. And Boodi suddenly tore ahead, and went into a glorious gallop – only to stop so very suddenly that Roderick flew right over his head and landed gracefully in a patch of nettles. He was very angry. He took Boodi's reins and shook them.

"What will Susan say, you bad pony? Now behave yourself! I'm badly stung."

He got home at last and related everything to Susan, who roared with laughter. "I'm sorry he behaved like that," she said. But secretly she was pleased. Boodi only behaved well with *her*, after all! She would let Roderick ride him again now that she knew Boodi misbehaved. It *was* nice to think that Boodi kept his best behaviour for his little mistress alone!

She took him two lumps of sugar as a reward for being loyal to her. "That's for misbehaving, Boodi!" she said in his ear. "But don't tell Roderick, will you!"

Everyone was glad that the summer holidays had come. Eight long weeks without any lessons to do! Melisande had to practise the piano, but neither Jane nor Susan learnt music, so they didn't even have to give up half an hour to the piano! Melisande was pleased to, however. Both she and Cyril were very fond of music, and it annoyed Cyril very much that he was not allowed to turn on the wireless whenever he pleased.

Roderick flew right over his head

He wished he could earn some money. "If I did, I'd buy myself a portable wireless," he thought. "Then I could take it somewhere by myself and tune in to the concerts I want to hear."

His aunt knew that Cyril liked to listen to special concerts sometimes, and although she thought it a good thing that Cyril had to consider the wishes of the others so much, she wished he could have what he wanted more often than he did. She was growing fond of Cyril, who, for all his posing, had a kind heart, and was always looking out for little things to do for her.

"I wish you could have the wireless on a little more in the evenings, Cyril," she told him once. "But this family only seems to use it for news, and for comic programmes! I'm fond of music myself, you know – but I couldn't force the others to listen to symphony concerts, they're so long."

"I wish I could earn some money," said Cyril. "I used to have more money than I could spend, Aunt Linnie – it seems incredible now, when I think of the pounds and pounds I used to have! Now, as you know, I only have a few shillings, and that soon goes on bus fares and things. If I could earn some money, I could save up for a little portable wireless. Then I could listen to what I wanted, without disturbing the others, because I could take it up into my room, for instance – or out into the fields."

"Yes, you could," agreed his aunt. "And I'd like to come with you and listen sometimes, Cyril! I used to be very fond of listening to concerts."

Cyril looked affectionately at his aunt, wondering whether she really meant this, or was saying it to him out of the kindness of her heart. He thought she really meant it. After all, she was fond of poetry too. He and she had evolved a little game together, finding a suitable poem to fit certain things they both admired.

Susan listened open-mouthed to this game, admiring them both, but Jack couldn't see anything in the idea at all. Susan had liked one poem very much, and had even written a bit of it out laboriously in her rather sprawling handwriting.

They had been out in the paved courtyard one day, she and

her mother, Jack and Cyril, feeding the goldfish. They turned to go in, and all of them stopped to look at the row of stately hollyhocks standing tall and dignified against the whitewashed wall of the old farmhouse.

"Aren't they nice?" said Susan, running to them and looking at the bees that went in and out of the pink, red or yellow blossoms. "And aren't they tall! Taller than I am – and taller than you, Mummy!"

Cyril and his aunt opened their mouths at exactly the same moment, and began to quote a verse. They stopped and laughed, looking at each other in amusement.

"Great minds think alike!" said Cyril. "It's an amusing little verse, isn't it, Aunt Linnie?"

"What is? You haven't said it," said Susan impatiently. "Say it, Mummy. Is it about hollyhocks?"

Her mother quoted it:

> "The stately Lady-Hollyhock
> Has graced my garden-bed for years,
> Sedately stiffened in a frock
> All frills and ruffles to her ears!"

Susan looked at the hollyhocks with pleasure. "Yes. They are all frills and ruffles to their ears," she said. "I think that's nice."

"Sounds a bit potty to me," said Jack. "But then I'm not going to be a poet, like Cyril. I'm going to be a farmer!"

"It's quite possibe to be both," said his mother, smiling at him.

"It's better to be a good farmer than a bad poet," said Jack, rather jealous of his mother's understanding with Cyril. He walked off rather sulkily. He wished they had Mistletoe Farm to themselves again. It was all very well for his mother to listen to Cyril and encourage him; she didn't have to put up with having him in the same room, scattering his beastly books about all over the place so that there wasn't an inch of room for a chap to call his own!

Cyril looked humorously at his aunt. She smiled back, and shook her head slightly at him.

94

"No, Cyril. You're not to make fun of Jack. He's not really the clod you think he is. He's a sound, trustable boy with the right ideas – even if those ideas don't include yours! He's good for you, you know – and you're good for him, though you do tread on each other's toes most of the time!"

"A bit more than you think, Aunt Linnie," said Cyril with his wide smile. "Our bedroom is so small that I can never seem to get out of the way of Jack's big feet! But seriously, Aunt – to come back to what we were talking about. Is there any way I can earn money? I can't ask Dad for any now he's so hard up – and I wouldn't ask Mother for worlds."

"Of course you wouldn't," said his aunt, thinking that it would do Cyril good to set to and earn something for himself. "Well, you could go plum picking soon. The farmers around are always glad of extra help then. But the pay is poor."

"It won't seem poor to me!" said Cyril. "I'd like to get my own wireless – and you shall share it whenever you want to!"

His aunt warmed to him. Cyril was certainly growing up! She liked his consideration for others, especially now that it was a little more than just good manners. She considered whether or not she should give him a wireless for his coming birthday.

Then she decided not to. No – that would be silly. Cyril had had too many things showered on him in his life, and so had Melisande and Roderick. It was good that he should want something badly, and have to get it by his own efforts. He would value it much more then, too.

"Well," she said, "you've got eight weeks in front of you, Cyril, to earn what money you like. You're strong and tall, though you're not burly like Jack; you can get plenty of jobs in and around the farms here, if you want to. But you cannot expect your *uncle* to pay for any work you do for him, you know."

"Of course not, Aunt Linnie!" said Cyril immediately, looking quite shocked. "As if I'd ever take payment from

95

somebody who's doing our family such a kindness as you are. You know I'd work full-time for Uncle Peter if he needed me."

"Well, you'll have to do a good bit, you and Jack, these holidays," said his aunt, giving a last glance at the frilly hollyhocks before she went indoors. "Harvest-time will soon be on us! I doubt if you'll feel like plum picking by the time your uncle has finished with you!"

> "He that will not live by toil
> Has no right on English soil!"

quoted Cyril with a grin. "Cap that if you can, Aunt Linnie!"

> "For men just work and women must weep,
> And there's little to earn and many to keep!"

flashed back his aunt at once. "I've six of you to cook for and keep, and if I don't go there won't be any pudding on the table today!"

CHAPTER THIRTEEN

The Holidays Begin.
Cyril Makes a Friend

Everyone was busy in the summer holidays. Mr Longfield was a man short on the farm, and Jack and Cyril had to turn to and do extra work. Cyril even had to walk the bull one day, much to his horror!

The bull had been brought to Mistletoe Farm for a week; then he was to go to another farm. He was a great big creature, with small, wicked eyes, and enormous horns. He lived in a reinforced corner of the stables, and the children had been forbidden to go and see him.

Roderick wouldn't have gone, anyhow. He was still scared of cows, and a bull was even worse. He kept out of the way well, and trembled when he heard the great creature bellowing.

Susan wanted to go and peep at him, but she knew better. She knew the difference between being brave and being rash. She would have liked to march up and peer in at the bull, to impress Roderick, but her common sense told her that this was silly. Besides, if her father found her disobeying him, goodness knows what would happen! Susan loved her father, but she had a very great respect for him and his commands.

Melisande had no interest in any of the animals at the farm unless they were beautiful or very young. She thought the sheep were too smelly and stupid for words, and the cows an ugly shape. The pigs smelt, the ducks were dirty, the hens foolish, according to Melisande. And now the bull was just the worst of all! She certainly wouldn't dream of going near him, and was very glad to hear he was only staying a week.

The bull's name was Rory, which Susan thought was a very good name for a bull. She thought it was spelt Roary, of course!

"He roars and he bellows," she said to Roderick. "I like hearing him."

"Well, I don't," said Roderick. "He sounds so bad-tempered. I'm always so afraid he'll come rushing out of the stable, and break his door down."

But Rory didn't do anything of the sort. He seemed quite peaceable until he grew restless and wanted exercise. Then he bellowed the place down, and the cow-man went to walk him. The bull had a big ring in his nose, and Jim put a stick through the ring, and led him by that.

"His nose is tender, you see," he explained to Roderick and Susan. "A pull at his nose-ring and he'll follow like a lamb! So long as I've got my stick through his ring, fixed there safely, I'm all right."

Then one day Jim hurt his arm and couldn't walk the bull. Jack had been sent to a neighbouring farm with some ducks. Nobody else could be spared to walk the bull, so Mr Longfield decided that Cyril must.

He dropped his bombshell at dinner-time. Cyril was really startled. Walk the bull! He couldn't. What a frightful job to give him to do! He didn't mind helping his uncle in the other jobs, but he did draw the line at walking the bull! He'd have to go all the way down the lane, round Long-Acre Hill and back again – and he'd probably meet some of the fellows from school.

Melisande spoke out at once. "Cyril can't walk the bull, Uncle! That's a man's job, you've always said so. It's not a fit job for Cyril to do, anyway!"

"Hold your tongue," said her uncle. "I won't have girls interfering with my orders. Cyril will walk the bull. If he's not enough of a man to do it, he can say so himself. If he helps his father on his farm, he'll be walking many a bull!"

He glared at Melisande, who felt the tears gathering in her eyes. She had never grown used to her uncle's rough tongue. He would not brook any interference with his ideas or with his orders, and Melisande was always running up against him by objecting to this and that.

"I'll walk the bull," said Cyril. "Shut up, Melisande."

"Can I go with him?" asked Susan eagerly.

"No. You can't," said her father. "Have some sense, Susan."

Nothing more was said, but that afternoon Cyril did walk the bull. Jim got the stick through the ring for him, and gave him one or two tips. "It's an easy enough job," he said. "Just keep command of the bull's nose, and you've got the bull under your thumb, Mr Cyril. Keep a firm hold, though."

And off went Cyril with the bull, decidedly nervous, hating every minute, but determined not to show it. Roderick watched him from a very safe distance. Susan watched from a little nearer. Melisande had retired to her room, angry with her uncle and afraid for Cyril.

The bull was very meek and mild. He ambled down the lane and round Long-Acre Hill and back again

"Hey! What's the day of the week?"

without so much as a snort. Cyril was quite disappointed! The bull's nose ws decidedly sensitive, and he followed every moment of the stick's guidance most obediently.

It was whilst he was walking the bull that Cyril made a new friend. Long-Acre Hill was a lonely place, with no houses or farms in sight. There were caves there, so Susan had said, but none of the children had gone to explore them with their cousins. As Cyril passed the place where the caves were supposed to be, a voice hailed him:

"Hey! What's the day of the week?"

Cyril stopped, astonished. A man came out of one of the caves. He was queerly dressed in some kind of long robe with a girdle. On his feet were sandals. His hair was rather long, and he wore a beard.

"Er – it's Friday," said Cyril.

"Thank you," said the stranger. "Living a life of contemplation as I do, I lose count of the time."

"Oh. Are you a sort of – er – hermit, then, sir?" asked Cyril.

"You can call me that if you like," said the bearded man. "I leave the world periodically to come and think and write by myself. We don't need the luxuries of civilization really, you know."

Cyril was rather impressed. The man looked most unusual. Perhaps he was a philosopher – or a poet. He had said he was a writer of some kind. He must be very serious over his work to come and live in a cave all by himself, like a hermit.

"Well – I must get on, because of this bull," said Cyril. "I'm sorry I can't stop."

"Come and see me again," said the hermit. "And I suppose you haven't a Greek dictionary, have you? I seem to have left mine behind."

"Yes. I've got one at home. I'll bring it tomorrow if I can," said Cyril. He longed to ask more questions, but he was afraid of keeping the bull waiting too long. He nodded to the stranger and went on again.

He went back the next day with the Greek dictionary. The hermit told him that his name was Benedict.

"Benedict what?" asked Cyril.

"Just Benedict," said the hermit. "I drop all other names when I retire like this."

He began to talk in a way that Cyril enjoyed very much. He seemed to have read a great deal. He told Cyril he was translating the *Iliad* of Homer in an entirely new way.

Cyril was even more impressed. He did his best to appear very knowledgeable himself. He and Benedict sat outside the man's cave in the August sunshine. Cyril was wearing his sandals again. He had given them up for a while, after a few remarks made by the boys in his form at school. But now, seeing his learned and impressive friend wearing them, he also took to his again, and wore them without socks, like Benedict.

He was very curious about the hermit's life. But

Benedict would tell him very little of his early life, or of what he did in "the world." "*This* is my life now," he would say, waving his hand round, embracing not only the cave behind him, but the hills, valleys and sky. "This is my world. I really have no other – though at times I have to return to attend to urgent business – to the publishing of my books, for instance."

He told Cyril that he had written many books. "On philosophy, on poetry and on music," he explained. "My interests are many. One day, when your mind is mature enough, Cyril, I will give you copies of my books. Till then they must be closed to you."

Cyril was flattered and fascinated. Once he was sent into the cave to fetch something, and looked round it with interest to see how Benedict lived. He certainly appeared to live very simply indeed.

His bed was a shelf of rock on which he had flung two or three rugs. He had very little crockery. There were a few books piled up together, among them Cyril's Greek dictionary, which he had not liked to ask for again yet. If Benedict needed it, he could have it!

Benedict could quote poetry by the hour. He appeared to like to hear himself reciting it too, and often when Cyril appeared silently round the rocky cliff in which the deserted caves were, he would find the hermit standing declaiming Milton or Shakespeare in a very imposing way.

Cyril felt that it was a wonderful change to have the hermit's company, after his cousins and uncle at the farm. "They honestly are clods," he said to himself. "Aunt Linnie isn't; but she's the only one who isn't, except Melisande who's an empty-head. Roderick's grown into a clod too. I need companionship that will cancel out the effect of living with so many turnips!"

He told no one about his new friend, but often he slipped away in the evenings, when he had done all the jobs his uncle had set him, and went to find Benedict. Roderick wondered where he went.

"He's always slipping off now," he told Susan. "Where does he go to? Do you think he goes and reads, or do you

101

think he says poetry out loud to himself, like that time we once heard him in the meadow?"

"I don't know. Let's track him one night and see," said Susan, always ready for mischief of any kind. He won't want us to know, so we must be very careful."

"Better not take Crackers then," said Roderick.

They hid behind the old barn and watched for Cyril that evening. He came out of the house, a book under his arm. Susan's sharp eyes noticed that his hair had not been brushed back, but had been allowed to lie in loose waves, such as his mother used to like. "He's gone all poetic and romantic again," Susan whispered to Roderick. "I bet he's going to spout poetry all by himself somewhere!"

Roderick giggled, but kept well out of sight. Cyril could be very hard-handed indeed if he caught his young brother doing anything he didn't like! The two children followed Cyril cautiously to Long-Acre Hill, unseen. As they came near the caves, they were surprised to hear voices.

"He's talking to someone!" whispered Susan. "Do you think it's Twigg the Poacher?"

"I hope so," whispered back Roderick. "I like Twigg and his dog, Mr Potts."

But it wasn't Twigg, of course; it was Benedict the hermit that Cyril was talking to. He and the hermit were sitting down in the evening sunshine. The conversation sounded very learned.

"Let's go up and surprise them," said Susan boldly, and, before Roderick could stop her, she had rounded the corner and walked in sight of Cyril and the hermit.

"Hello!" said Cyril astonished. "What on earth are you two doing here?" He looked at them suspiciously.

"Hello!" said Susan. "What a surprise to find you here, Cyril. What are you doing?"

"Who are these children?" asked Benedict.

"The boy's my young brother and the girl's a cousin," said Cyril. He looked annoyed. Now these two would go and tell his well-kept secret. He couldn't even have a special friend without his family knowing!

Benedict obviously didn't like young children. He

didn't like the way Susan stared at his big, rather dirty toes, sticking out of the end of his sandals. He didn't like the way Roderick looked at his beard as if he had never seen one like it before, or his long hair, that was now down to his neck.

"Why don't you get your hair cut?" asked Susan, also staring at his hair.

"Shut up and get out," said Cyril. "You're as bad as Jane. Don't you know it's bad manners to be personal?"

"I've never really found out yet what being personal means," said Susan. "I'm a person, aren't I, so how can I help being personal?"

"Don't be funny," said Cyril, glaring at her. "You can't be as stupid as all that."

Benedict, completely ignoring the two children, took up a book and began to read from it. It was a book on philosophy and Susan and Roderick didn't understand a word.

"Is he teaching you something?" enquired Susan when a pause came at last.

"Yes. A great many things," said Cyril. "For goodness sake, go. You've no right to intrude on Benedict's company."

"All right. We'll go," said Susan, now getting bored. "Goodbye. Come on, Roderick. Let's go back by the stream and float some sticks in it."

They went off, and Cyril heaved a sigh of relief. Benedict seemed quite undisturbed. He asked Cyril a few questions about the children, and then led on to Mistletoe Farm. Cyril thought the hermit was very flattering, the way he seemed to love to hear about the family, the farmhouse, and the stock. He seemed interested in everything, even in market days, and what happened there. Cyril had not hitherto taken much interest in the markets his uncle went to, but determined to go some time in order that he might relate all that happened to Benedict.

Cyril rather fancied himself as the hermit's link with the world. He did not know how long the man had been living his queer life. Benedict was always vague about time. He was vague about a good many things, and seemed to Cyril hardly to belong to this world at all.

At the back of the cave Cyril had seen a big suitcase, which went oddly with the hermit's simple abode and way of living. He stared at it, fascinated, wondering about the hermit's life before he had "retired" from the world. But Bendict would talk very little about himself.

"I am unimportant," he would say. "Let us talk about you, my boy, instead. One of these days you will make your mark upon the world I have left. But I think that you, like me, will one day wish to leave that world, and lead a life of contemplation such as mine."

Cyril wasn't so sure about that, but he was pleased to think that Benedict should have such a high opinion of him. Here was a well-read, learned, cultured man, who obviously enjoyed conversing with a mere boy. It was very soothing to Cyril's self-esteem, those holidays, to have the hermit's companionship, after a jumbled day of all kinds of tasks at Mistletoe Farm.

Susan and Roderick told the others about the hermit. "He's a kind of wild man, Mummy, I should think," she said. "His hair's down to his neck and he's got a beard, and he wears sandals and a girdle, and a kind of night-gown."

Jane laughed, and Jack roared. "So that's Cyril's new friend! Well, he's welcome to him!" said Jack. "I'm glad he's found someone as peculiar as himself!"

"Who is this hermit, Peter?" Aunt Linnie asked her husband that night.

"Hermit? What hermit?" said her husband, surprised. "Oh, you mean the odd fellow who sometimes turns up in the caves on Long-Acre Hill. He's cracked, I should think. Quite harmless, though, I imagine. Twigg says he meets him sometimes walking in the countryside at night, muttering some kind of stuff to himself. Why?"

"Oh, only because Cyril seems to have struck up a friendship with him," said his wife. "I wondered if he was the right kind of friend for him."

"It would be just like Cyril to get hold of somebody

cracked!" said Mr Longfield with a laugh. "Some long-haired fellow in sandals. Well, if he likes to make friends like that, let him! He'll forget him fast enough when he gets back to school."

CHAPTER FOURTEEN

The Doings of Twigg

Meantime, Susan and Roderick had made firm friends with Twigg. They had met him out one morning with Mr Potts, the golden spaniel. Crackers had gone bounding across the road to greet Mr Potts, and Twigg had waved cheerily to the children.

"Where are you going?" called Susan.

"To the woods, Missy," called back Twigg. "You come alonga me and I'll show you how to make whistles out of a bit of alder wood!"

"Come on, Roderick," said Susan, and the two at once followed Twigg to the woods, running to keep up with his rapid walk. His limp seemed to make no difference to the way he got along.

Crackers and Mr Potts gambolled along together, thrusting their noses down the rabbit-holes, and scraping up showers of earth as madly as they could.

"They're not really looking for rabbits, are they, Twigg?" said Susan. "They're just showing each other how well they can dig."

Twigg was a most entertaining companion. He made them each a whistle that blew shrilly. He cut them new briar shoots, stripped them and told them to nibble them and see how good they were. He showed them a little pond hidden deep in the wood, where, he said, a most enormous fish lay.

"Why don't you catch him, Twigg?" asked Roderick,

peering into the dark water, hoping to see a silvery fin moving there.

"Oh, I've tried lots of times, but he's too artful," said Twigg. "I come here late at night and try. That's a good time for fishing, you know. I come with a flare, and once I saw him plain as I see you. Ah, he led me a dance that night, he did. Nearly fell into the water after him – and then what happened? Why, I met Mr Potts – the policeman, I mean – as I was a-going home without any fish in my basket, and he tells me he thinks I've been out poaching!"

"What a shame!" said Susan. "Didn't you tell him you were only trying to catch the fish in this pool?"

"Ah, Mr Potts is so disbelieving-like," said Twigg. "Said he didn't believe in no fish and no pool, and he didn't believe in me, neither! He's a hard man, is Mr Potts."

"Twigg, have you met him since you told us about how you call your dog after him?" asked Roderick.

"Oh yes; once or twice," said Twigg, grinning as he remembered. "It's hard to meet Mr Potts now in the daytime. Seems as if he avoids me, like. Don't like me yelling, 'Mr Potts! Come here, you!' as soon as I see him."

"Oh, I *do* wish we could meet him when we're with you," said Susan earnestly. "Doin't you, Roderick?"

"Yes," said Roderick. "Let's stay with Twigg till he goes back to the village, and go back with him. We might just meet the policeman."

"Well," said Twigg, scratching his head. "I've got a few things to do in this here wood before I go back. Private-like things, see, that I don't like people watching because it makes me nervous all over. If you like to wait here and watch out for that old fish, I'll come back and get you in half an hour."

"What sort of things are you going to do?" asked Roderick with interest. He thought Twigg was one of the most interesting and delightful people he had ever met. He blew softly on his whistle as he waited for Twigg to answer. It made a lovely trilling noise.

Twigg didn't answer, and Roderick got a sharp nudge from Susan, which almost made him swallow his whistle. He looked at her indignantly.

"S'long!" said Twigg, and disappeared with Mr Potts at his heels.

"S'long," said Susan, imitating him exactly.

"Why did you punch me?" said Roderick. "I nearly swallowed my whistle."

"Because you're so *stupid*, Roderick," said Susan, impatiently. "The things he'll do are poaching things. Don't ask me what. Maybe he's after partridges or something."

"Oh," said Roderick. "Is he a bad man, then?"

"I suppose he is," said Susan, considering. "But he's awfully good too. He cured Daddy's grey cob once when he was almost dead. And one snowy night he went out with Hazel the shepherd to look for lost sheep, and he found them all and brought them back. But he was so cold, poor Twigg, that he shook and shivered for three whole weeks afterwards. He told me."

Roderick was impressed. He blew his whistle again, softly. Crackers looked up at him enquiringly, and then began to lap from the dark little pool.

"That's right, Crackers!" said Susan. "You lap it all up and we'll be able to see the fish!"

But Crackers wasn't as thirsty as all that. He went off to examine a rabbit-hole, and soon they heard him panting as he dug energetically for a rabbit that wasn't there.

Twigg came back after a time, with Mr Potts at his heels. "So you waited for me?" he said. "Come along. I'll take you by some honeysuckle and you can pick some for your mother. It's the finest anywhere around."

So it was. The sprays grew high up over a hawthorn tree, with long yellow trumpets full of sweetness. "You always know where the best of everything grows, don't you, Twigg?" said Susan, pulling down some fine sprays. "The best mushrooms, the best blackberries, the biggest nuts! I'd rather have you for my friend than the hermit up on Long-Acre Hill."

"What do you know about *him*?" asked Twigg sharply.

"Oh, Cyril's friendly with him," said Susan. "I think they say poetry to one another. We think they're both crackers."

The black spaniel looked up at the sound of his name, and Roderick laughed. "It's all right, Crackers," he said. "We're only talking about the hermit and Cyril."

"Mr Cyril shouldn't ought to be friendly with that chap," said Twigg. "Never did trust that fellow. Turning up suddenly in the caves, and then going off again when he's tired of it, and coming back when you don't expect him. Traipsing along the lanes at night and through the woods, frightening the life out of me! Mutter-mutter-mutter, he goes. I thought he was a ghostie in his white clothes!"

Susan and Roderick grinned quickly at one another. They could well imagine that Twigg wouldn't at all like the hermit wandering about at night, coming on him unexpectedly in the darkness. Twigg would not want anyone arriving suddenly near him, interrupting whatever he was doing in the woods. No wonder he disapproved of the hermit!

They were now out of the woods, walking down the lane to the village, Susan carrying great sprays of the sweet-smelling honeysuckle. She suddenly gave a squeal of delight, and pointed to the village.

"Twigg, look! There *is* the policeman, walking with his back to you. Oh Twigg! Do let's hear you call out for Mr Potts!"

Twigg grinned, and his wrinkled face wrinkled even more. He turned to his dog. "Sit," he said, and Mr Potts sat.

"We'll leave him, there," said Twigg. "He'll sit till I call him."

They went on rapidly, and came into the village street. The policeman was strolling slowly and with much dignity in the middle of the pavement.

Just as they got behind him, Twigg shouted loudly. "Mr Potts! Hey, where are you, Potts? Come here, you!"

Mr Potts the policeman jumped and turned round at his shouted name. He saw Twigg. He went scarlet, and looked at Twigg firecely.

"Now then!" he said, warningly. "Now then! None of that!"

"What?" asked Twigg, innocently. "Must get my dog, mustn't I? Hey, *Mr Potts*! You come here at once, you rascal, you!"

By this time all the people in the village street were standing and grinning. Susan and Roderick, afraid that they could not hold their laughter in any longer, went into the nearby shop, and rolled about there, almost knocking over the piles of biscuit tins that the grocer had stood in rows beside the counter.

The golden spaniel came running up at once and fawned round his master's legs, paying no attention at all to the angry policeman.

"So there you are, Mr Potts," said Twigg in a stern voice. "Where have you been? What you been a-doing of? You rascal, you scamp. Mr Potts. Ho, Potts is your name and potty is your nature!"

The real Mr Potts looked as if he was about to burst. Twigg patted his dog, nodded to the policeman in an amiable manner and went off down the street, bestowing winks and smiles on everyone he met, as if he were a well-applauded performer leaving the stage. As indeed he was!

The children came cautiously out of the grocer's shop when the policeman had gone. The grocer had given them a biscuit each, and they were nibbling them, with Crackers watching hopefully for crumbs.

"One of these days Twigg'll get the worst of it," said the old grocer. "He's a bad lot, he is, but he'd get a laugh out of a wet hen, he would! Him and his Mr Potts! I wouldn't trust Twigg with two pennyworth of peppermints, he's so slippery, but I'd rather have him for a companion any time than Mr Potts the policeman. *He* sends you to sleep in two minutes!"

Susan would have liked to stay and discuss the matter of

Mr Potts sending people to sleep, but Roderick pointed to the church clock. "Look! Five and twenty past five! We shall be late for tea – and Dorkie is giving us ham and eggs. She told me so this morning."

They tore back to Mistletoe Farm, and poured out all the happenings of their afternoon to everyone at table. Cyril frowned when he heard Twigg's opinion of his friend Benedict. He was so annoyed that he wouldn't join in the laughter over the Mr Potts incident at all.

Even Mr Longfield roared over that. "Twigg is a comic," he said. "He uses his fun to hide his bad ways; folks think he's such a comical fellow, they gloss over his sins. Well, he's been of great use to me, so I wish him well!"

"We do too, don't we, Roderick?" said Susan. "We think he's better fun than Benedict any day!"

CHAPTER FIFTEEN

Jack and Twigg

Somebody else was friendly with Twigg, as well as Roderick and Susan, and that was Jack. But he said very little about this to anyone, because he felt guilty. Twigg had shown him many little poacher's tricks, and Jack was afraid that his father would not approve.

Twigg's knowledge of wild animal and bird life was extraordinary. He knew every creature of the woods and fields, their ways and their haunts. Jack, too, was intensely interested in birds and animals, and he drank in eagerly every bit of information that Twigg gave him.

"Know them badgers I told you about?" Twigg said to him one day. "Well, they've moved!"

"Have they really?" said Jack. He had never seen one of these queer little bear-like creatures that turned up now and again in the countryside. "Why? What's made them move?"

"Well, I reckon a smelly old dog fox came and made his den somewhere near their sett," said Twigg with a laugh that wrinkled his face like a shrivelled apple. "And they couldn't bear his smell, so they upped and went! Badgers are particular creatures, they are – clean and tidy, and they won't put up with smelly neighbours."

"I wish I could see a badger," Jack said. "You've seen plenty, Twigg. They only come out at night, don't they? So unless I come out at night too, I won't see them!"

"Well, you come out at night, then," said Twigg. "If we don't see badgers, we'll see summat else. Wouldn't you like to see a few more of my tricks, Mr Jack? I wouldn't show them to everyone, but I don't mind putting you wise to a few."

This was a terrible temptation. No one was cleverer than Twigg at filling his pot with all kinds of forbidden animals and birds. Many a hare, many a partridge and pheasant, to say nothing of a fat trout, could have been found cooking deliciously over the poacher's fire. Sometimes Jack had been given a "bite" when he had popped in unexpectedly at Twigg's spick-and-span little cottage. Like the badger. Twigg was neat and tidy in his ways!

Jack hesitated. Twigg lighted his pipe and gave a few puffs. "Don't get me wrong, Mr Jack," he said. "I'm not *teaching* you nothing wrong, see? There's no harm in you watching, though – s'long as you don't give me away to P.C. Potts! And if you wants to see badgers and other night folk going about their business, you can't do better than come alonga me."

"I *must* come," said Jack, giving up with a sigh. It was no use. He'd have to go. It was such a chance, and Twigg was so knowledgeable, so interesting and so amusing. He might be up to no good most of the time, but the rest of the time he would spend on kindnesses and help for anybody.

"Now don't you say a word to nobody, then," said

111

Twigg earnestly. "Not to nobody at all, not even to Miss Jane, your twin."

"No, I won't," said Jack. "Though I wish Jane could come too. She'd love it."

"I wouldn't take her for all the gold in the world!" said Twigg. "Women! They can't hold their tongues for one minute. That sister of yours would talk the hind leg off a donkey if you let her!"

"Well, Jane is a bit of a chatterbox," said Jack. "But she's all right. She never splits on anyone."

Jack had begun going out with Twigg just before his cousins had come to live at Mistletoe Farm. He used to slip out of his window, and climb down the old quince tree that stood outside. Nobody ever heard him except Crackers, who wouldn't have dreamed of barking and giving him away. He joined Twigg at an arranged spot, and the two would go off into the woods or hills together, with Mr Potts, the golden spaniel, nosing at their heels.

Jack often wished he could take Crackers with him, but he was afraid Susan might wake up in the night and miss him. She might hunt for him and discover that his room was empty. So he reluctantly decided to go without Crackers.

Twigg was a most interesting companion. His ears were as sharp as a hare's, and his eyes, even on the darkest night, were as keen as an owl's. Many a time his hand went out and stopped Jack when the boy had neither seen nor heard anything at all.

"Fox," would whisper Twigg. "Vixen, I think. She've got cubs somewhere, and she's hunting food for them. Maybe I'll hear them growling together in the den if I listen!"

It was a wonderful experience for Jack, exploring the countryside at night, either under the moon, or with only the stars for light. He learnt to hear the almost soundless passing of an owl in flight. He caught the tiny gleam of some animal's green eyes looking warily from a dark bank. He heard the warning thump of an old buck

112

rabbit's hind legs on the hillside as they approached – the age-old warning that all rabbits heed when enemies come near.

"Everything's so different at night," thought Jack. "It's another world altogether."

He learnt other things besides these. Twigg taught him many tricks of his trade, delighting in the quick understanding of the boy. Jack might be slow of speech and clumsy in movement, but he was quick and deft enough in all the ways of the real countryman. He knew that Twigg should not use these tricks on land belonging to other people – he knew quite well it was against the law – but Jack was young and full of curiosity, and Twigg was a cunning and endlessly patient teacher.

"Look, Twigg, I know I oughtn't to learn all these things," Jack would say sometimes. "And, anyway, I don't like that snare you've shown me how to make. I don't know *what* my father would say!"

"He won't know nothing about it unless you go for to tell him," Twigg would say. "And you don't need to use the little tricks I've shown you, do you? You'll be a farmer one day, Mr Jack, and own land and all that's on it. You won't need to get your living and your food the way I do. Mebbe one day you'll be hounding old Twigg off your land and setting the law on him!"

"I should never do that," said Jack. "I shall never split on you, Twigg. We're friends. I can't think why you don't get a job on my father's farm and go straight. You know he'd give you a chance."

"Now, lookee here, Mr Jack," said Twigg, his keen eyes watching all the time for a movement in hedge or bush. "What's the use of knowing all the things I know if I don't use my learning? See? It would be a right down waste. Besides, there's a bit of excitement in this kind of life that there wouldn't be in a job on a farm."

That was the whole thing in a nutshell, of course. Twigg liked going against the law. It was exciting. He would rather bring home hares and trout by getting them in the wrong way than by earning money to buy them in the right way. Nobody would ever change him. He didn't even mind going to prison for the sake of his "beliefs" – though he did his level best not to give P.C. Potts the chance to crow over him in that way.

When Cyril came with Melisande and Roderick to live at Mistletoe Farm, and to share a room with Jack, the boy was dismayed. Now his night adventures with Twigg would be ended! He couldn't possibly slip out without Cyril knowing. So for some weeks Twigg went alone on his little excursions, with only his spaniel for companion.

The boy could only meet him in daylight, and there was not much excitement in that, though even then, Twigg had many interesting bits of information to impart.

"Do you know them bearded tits?" he said one day. "Them birds I once showed you in the marsh, among the reeds?"

"Oh, the reedlings," said Jack, remembering the pretty little birds with their long tails, the cocks with their strange little black, "beards". "Yes, of course I remember them. Why, have you seen them again, Twigg?"

"I was down in the marshes yesterday evening, when the rain was on," said Twigg. "And I hears 'Ching, ching! Ching-ching,!' And I says to meself, 'Ah, there's them reedlings again. Well, I looked about and I saw a pair – and didn't I just rub my eyes to see what they was doing, Mr Jack!"

"What?" said Jack, curiously.

"Well, they was sitting side by side in the rain on a reedstalk," said the old poacher, "and the cock bird had raised his little wing and he was holding it over his mate like an umbrella! What do you think of that for manners, eh?"

Jack hardly knew whether to believe this or not, because Twigg was not above a fairy tale or two. But it was plain that he was in earnest this time, and that the quaint sight had made quite an impression on him. Jack wished ardently that he too had seen it. He told Susan about it, and she listened in delight.

"I shall go down to the marshes and see it myself the

very next time it rains," she said. Her mother overheard this declaration and at once forbade it, knowing that Susan would come home quite unrecognizable for mud if she went plunging about in the marsh, looking for reedlings holding "umbrellas" over their mates!

"But I want to know if it's *true*," persisted Susan, who had an exasperating way of wanting to make sure of any fact told to her.

"Well, it *is* true," said her mother. "My own brother, your Uncle Will, actually saw it himself one day and told me."

So Susan had to be satisfied with that, and badgered Jack each day after that to find out if Twigg had told him anything more that was interesting. And Twigg, of course, always obliged, sometimes even bringing curious objects to show Jack or the others. A baby hedgehog, its spines still soft. A cuckoo's egg, taken from a meadow pipits nest. A mole, with its eyes so deep-hidden they could not be seen, and its forepaws just like spades, for digging hard in the ground! There was no end to the things that Twigg could produce.

One night, just before dark, Twigg came silently up to Jack as he ws finishing mending a gap in the hedge, through which a cow had wandered that day.

"Mr Jack! I'm going over to Marlins tonight," he said, in a low voice "To the river. If you like to come, there'll be otters about."

Jack looked longingly at Twigg in the dusk. He knew perfectly well that Twigg was going after trout, but he also knew that if Twigg said there would be otters about, well, there certainly would! And Jack had seldom seen an otter.

"I've got my cousin sleeping in my room," he said in a low voice like Twigg's. "He'd hear me go."

"Well, he won't know where you're going!" said Twigg "Come on, now. I ain't had you on my trips for weeks. You always said you wanted to see otters. You'll hear them too – whistling down the river!"

"I'll come," whispered Jack, seeing his father coming near. "Meet you same place."

Twigg melted away in the gathering shadows. Mr Longfield came up. "Who was that?"

"Only Twigg," said his father.

"Telling me about some otters," said Jack, feeling very guilty.

His father stood silent for a moment. "You be careful of Twigg," he said. "A sly rascal, he is, and he wouldn't mind putting you on the wrong road. Keep your wits about you, Jack. Don't be led away by his clever tongue and easy ways."

"No, Dad," said Jack, and made up his mind that he wouldn't go with Twigg that night after all.

But, lying awake in bed with the moon shining brightly through his window, he thought of the river and the whistling otters playing in the water. He heard Cyril's peaceful breathing, and his good resolutions melted away.

"I shall go!" he thought, and he sat up quietly. "Cyril won't hear. Dad will never know – and I shan't take any harm. It's such a chance to see the otters on a moonlight night like this. I'd be a mutt not to go!"

And he got out of bed and dressed. Down the quince tree he went and out into the night!

CHAPTER SIXTEEN

A Shock for Jack

What Twigg did that night Jack never really knew, because the otters kept him watching them all the time. They whistled, they gambolled, they swam at top speed, and they popped up and down in the moonlight, glistening like silver.

Twigg slid away as soon as he had ensconced Jack in an old hollow tree with a peep-hole through the rotten trunk. "Be back in an hour," he said. "S'long!"

He was back in just under an hour. The baggy pockets of his old leather-patched coat hung down, bulging. Jack did not enquire what he had in them. He knew better than that! He imagined that they were fat trout for Twigg's pot.

"There were seven otters," he told Twigg.

"Ay. There's a whole family about," said Twigg. "Or mebbe two families that play together. Wonderful swimmers they be, otters. I know where the holt of one family is. I'll show you next time we're across here. There's one entrance below water and one above. Clever creatures they are."

Jack slipped silently back with him, keeping in the shadows of the trees, because the moonlight was very bright. Halfway home Twigg stopped so suddenly that Jack bumped into him.

They stood without a sound under a big chestnut tree. Jack strained his ears, which were very sharp, but at first he could hear nothing. Then he heard a peculiar murmuring noise.

A figure came gradually nearer in the moonlight – a weird, rather frightening figure, dressed completely in flowing white. Jack's heart grew cold, and his hair pricked on his head, as if it ws trying to stand upright in fright.

Twigg pressed his hand on the boy's arm, warning him to keep absolutely still. The golden spaniel had frozen into a dark shadow at his feet. The murmuring grew a little louder, and the figure came nearer still, bright in the moonlight.

The strange apparition passed without seeing them, or at least without apparently noticing the man and boy in the shadows of the tree. There was no sound from Mr Potts the spaniel, and no movement from Twigg or Jack. The murmuring died away, and the white figure disappeared.

"Who was it?" breathed Jack at last. "That cracked fellow from Long-Acre Hill," said Twigg, contemptuously. "Wanders about like this at night, frightening folks into fits. Someone will push him into the river one of these nights!"

. . . a weird, rather frightening figure . . .

It was the hermit, of course, on one of his nightly wanderings. Jack was relieved that he was a real person! Mr Potts stretched himself and yawned. Twigg patted him, and he licked his master's fingers.

"He's a danger to decent folk like us," grumbled Twigg as they made their way home. "Never know when I'm going to run into him! Good thing he's always muttering as he goes – gives me good warning, anyway. I don't trust him. He'd give me away to the police any day he could."

Jack was very tired when he got into bed. Fortunately, Cyril, was still asleep. Jack gave a grunt and fell asleep too. He was late up in the morning, and could hardly get the sleep out of his eyes!

He got a shock at high tea that day. "I hear Twigg's been in trouble again," said his father, looking round the table. "He's a fool, that fellow. He's clever enough to get a fine job on any farm, and yet he must go and stage a robbery!"

Jack's heart began to beat fast. He stared at his father in horror, hoping that his face would not give him away. He wanted to ask all kinds of questions, but he could not say a word.

"What robbery?" said Jane.

"Well, Johns, over at Marlins Farm, went to market yesterday and sold a lot of his sheep," said Mr Longfield. "He didn't bank the money, but took it home. And in the night it went!"

"Gosh!" said Jane. "Do they think Twigg took it?"

"Well, Twigg was at the market and he watched the selling of the sheep," said her father. "And it's known he was away from his cottage last night, because someone went to get his help for a sick cow, and he wasn't there."

Jack's heart sank lower and lower. So that was what Twigg had been doing whilst he, Jack, had watched the otters playing in the river. It was hateful to think of Twigg sliding away through the shadows to rob Marlins whilst he had so unsuspectingly enjoyed the treat that the poacher had provided.

"Poaching is one thing, and bad at that – but stealing

money is worse," said his father. "Twigg will get no sympathy if he goes to prison *this* time!"

Jack was so worried and upset that day that no one could get a word out of him. Hazel the shepherd told him that Twigg's cottage had been searched, but no money had been found.

"That'll be buried deep in the middle of some field," said Hazel. "One of your father's fields, I don't doubt, Mr Jack."

Jack stared at the old shepherd dumbly. Hazel knew he was friendly with Twigg, and was sorry for Jack. "Don't you take on so," he said. "He'll get out of this all right, same as he's got out of a dozen scrapes. He says he was with a friend last night, who'll vouch for him, and swear he was nowhere near Marlins Farm."

This was an even greater shock for poor Jack. Would Twigg really say that he, Jack, had been out with him, and that they had never been near the robbed farm? Whatever would his father say to him? And how *could* he say that they had never been near the farm, when they had been on Marlins land most of the time?

The boy looked so miserable that his mother thought he was ill. She wanted to take his temperature, but he pushed her aside. "*No*, Mother! I'm not ill! I'm all right. Do leave me alone!" he said.

He hardly slept at all that night. He wondered if he should go to his father and tell him everything. He would get into a frightful row and perhaps even get a beating, but it would be better than this gnawing worry that never left him for a minute!

He determined that he would go to his father the next morning. But before he could do that, more news came in. Jim the cowman told it to Jack as he went out to help with the cows.

"Heard the latest about old Twigg?" said Jim. "He's got off all right! Swears he spent the night at Tommy Lane's over the hill, and that's why he was out of his cottage when he was sent for to Harris's sick cow. And what's more, Tommy swears the same."

Jack listened in amazement. How could this be? Twigg had most certainly been with him that night, and had been on Marlins land too – only about half a mile from the farmhouse itself! He supposed that Twigg had persuaded Tommy Lane to tell a lie for him.

"Funny thing is, he was seen coming out of Tommy's cottage early next morning too," said Jim. "Old Mrs Lucas saw him. Looks as if he might be telling the truth!"

Jack puzzled it out. Perhaps Twigg had not gone back home for some reason; perhaps he had gone to Tommy's and had actually slept there – which would account for Tommy's tale and for old Mrs Lucas seeing him in the morning. But had Tommy said what time Twigg had arrived? Probably that was where he had lied!

"Well, so it wasn't Twigg after all," said his father at dinner-time. "I have my doubts still – though I must say I've never known Twigg to go for money. Hares, rabbits, trout, birds – he'll poach all those – but I've never known him poach money!"

"Who could have stolen the money, then?" asked Susan.

"Anyone who was at the market and knew about Johns selling his sheep for such good prices," said his father. "Johns is a fool when he makes a good bargain. Goes shouting about it to everyone, slaps his pockets full of money, and boasts. Just the way to lose it! He should have banked it."

"You didn't bank *your* market money last week," said his wife, slyly.

"Well, Linnie, you know quite well the banks were closed, and I couldn't," said her husband. "And, anyway, no one knew I'd money on me, and I went and banked it first thing the next morning."

"Yes, dear, I know! I was just teasing you," said Mrs Longfield. "Poor Johns! It's a bad loss for him. All the same, I'm very glad it wasn't Twigg."

Jack's heart was very much lighter when he heard all this. Whether Twigg had been the thief or not, it was clear that he was not going to be had up for it. And he, Jack would not be dragged into the affair and get into trouble, after all. That was a great relief.

"All the same, I simply must have a word with Twigg," thought Jack. "I want it all cleared up. I shan't split on Twigg, but if he's taken the money by any chance, he'll have to return it somehow! This really is a horrible affair."

He got a shock when he met Twigg and spoke to him about the matter.

"Twigg, you know that night we saw the otters?" began Jack. "What actually did you do when you left me?"

Twigg looked at him, and a curious expression came over his wrinkled brown face. His black eyebrow-tufts shot up and made him look suddenly fierce.

"What you getting at, Mr Jack?" said Twigg in a dangerously mild voice.

"Well, you know what happened that night, don't you?" said Jack, beginning to flounder as Twigg's little eyes bored into him.

"Yes, I know what happened all right. You watched them otters and I got some trout for me and Tommy Lane," said Twigg, in a forthright way.

"Well," said Jack, beginning to feel distinctly nervous, "You see, Twigg . . ."

"I see that you got some very nasty suspicions of me, Mr Jack," said Twigg, looking at Jack as if he was a particularly unpleasant smell. "I'm surprised at you. Thought you was a friend of mine. I've satisfied the police, I'm satisfied meself, and there's no call for you to come along suspecting somebody what's as innocent as a new-born baby. I didn't say nothing about you being with me – wasn't going to give *you* away, o'course. Nobody knows nothing about that."

Jack badly wanted to believe in Twigg. He stared dumbly at the old poacher, getting more and more tongue-tied. Twig took pity on him.

"You're only a silly young lad," he said, and he no longer looked so fierce. His eyebrows descended to their usual place. "If I was going to rob and steal, would I take you with me? Have some sense, lad. I'd know you

122

wouldn't stand for me taking money, for all you shut your eyes to me snapping up a hare or a trout for my pot!"

"Oh, Twigg, I'm glad," said Jack, believing what the poacher said.

"I told old Tommy I'd be along with a fine dish of trout that night, and so I was," said Twigg. "And what's more, I slept along of him, as I often do – and that was lucky for me that night, I tell you straight!"

"Did Tommy say what time you arrived?" asked Jack.

"Tommy don't know the time!" said Twigg with a grin. "When the policeman asks me what time I come in to Tommy's, I looks at Tommy, and I says, ''Bout half-past eleven, weren't it, Tom?' and he says, 'Yes, that's right.' Tommy ain't never learned to tell the time, you know."

"I see," said Jack. "But . . ."

"And I'll tell you just one thing more," said Twigg, his eyebrows shooting up again like two black arrows, "Johns of Marlins says his dogs barked at two o'clock in the morning, and he says he reckons that's when the robbery was done. And where was you and me at two o'clock in the morning, Mr Jack? I guess you was in your bed again and fast asleep an hour or more. And I know I was with Tommy, a good feed of trout inside me, and meself in his old armchair, dreaming of nothing!"

"All right, Twigg. Sorry," said Jack. "Don't hold this against me, will you? I'm glad I've seen you."

"I tell you, you're just a silly young lad," said Twigg again, and he smiled in a friendly fashion that warmed Jack's heart. "I don't hold nothing against silly young lads. Never did!"

He went off, and Jack went home, feeling very much better. He was sure Twigg hadn't done the robbery now. Who had? Any one of the fellows who had been at the market and heard Johns boasting of his bargains! It was just chance that Twigg had been near Marlins Farm, and chance again that sent him off to poach trout, whilst Jack lay hidden in the old tree, watching the otters.

He debated with himself whether or not to go out with Twigg again. If he didn't, Twigg would most certainly think he hadn't believed him, and that would be the end of their curious but exciting companionship. Nobody else would take him about by night as Twigg did. He couldn't give him up.

And so on many other nights during that summer, Jack slid down the quince to meet Twigg and Mr Potts the spaniel. And if people wondered why Jack looked tired and seemed irritable next day, nobody ever guessed the reason why!

CHAPTER SEVENTEEN

A Visitor is Expected

Harvest-time came. The wonderful binder came into the fields of corn, and did the work of scores of men in a day. The children were fascinated to see the corn cut, made into sheaves, tied round with string and tossed out as the machine made its way down the field.

"Saves a lot of time, doesn't it?" Mr Longfield said to Melisande, who was watching, fascinated. "In the old days, when I was a boy, all hands had to come to help with the harvest, and we worked from early dawn to dark, cutting, binding, stooking."

"It's fine weather for reaping, isn't it, Uncle." said Melisande, who was burnt as brown as the others now. She had given up trying not to get sunburnt and freckled, though she had tried very hard at first to keep the sun from her face by wearing shady hats. "I wonder if Daddy is reaping too, on the farm he's working on."

"Shouldn't think so," said her uncle. "Scotland's harvest is much later than ours – and we're early this year. Look at those rabbits!"

Melisande looked, and felt sick. All the little creatures that had their homes in the tall, waving corn were now fleeing from it in panic. Melisande hated to see them so afraid and bewildered. She hated to see the farm men hit them with sticks and kill them for the pot.

"I think country ways are so often cruel," she said to her uncle. "There's such a lot that is lovely, but such a lot that is ugly."

"You have to take the rough with the smooth, my dear," said her uncle. "That's the way of the countryside, and the way of life too. You've had so much of the smooth that you've a horror of the rough. Still, you're toughening!"

He looked closely at his niece. Melisande was dressed in exactly the same kind of clothes as Jane – but what a difference in the two!

They both wore royal blue linen shorts and cotton shirts, open at the neck. Melisande's wavy hair was tied neatly back. She had no socks, but wore open sandals, like Jane. Her hands were burnt brown, but her nails were nicely shaped and well-kept. She looked pretty and neat and attractive.

Jane didn't! Jane's shorts were smeared with what looked like tar. She had dropped something yellow on them too. Her shirt was dirty, and a button was missing. One sleeve was torn. A buckle was off her sandal, and she had tied it up with string. Her straight, thick hair was all anyhow, and hung partly over her face. Her hands were black, and her nails bitten short.

"Why can't you look a bit more like Melisande?" said her father, suddenly. "You're dressed exactly the same – and look at you! Surely, Jane, you're getting to the age when you ought to take a bit more pride in yourself?"

Jane got the surprise of her life! She gazed at her father as if she couldn't believe her ears! She looked down at herself. What was the matter? "I look just the same as usual," she flared. "I was like this yesterday, and the day before, and you didn't seem to mind!"

"That's just it. You're *always* like that," said her father. "You never look tidy or even clean, it seems to me. I can't help noticing it when I see you beside Melisande."

"Oh, *Melisande*!" said Jane in a tone of the greatest scorn, and she turned rudely on her heel. " *I* can't spend hours a day doing my hair and my nails and titivating myself like *Melisande*. You can't make *me* into a butterfly!"

"Jane!" said her father sharply "Come back. Do you hear me?"

Jane came back unwillingly, her cheeks scarlet under their tan. She hated to be compared unfavourably with her cousin, especially by her father. Whatever could have come over him to pick on her suddenly like this?

"I won't have you speaking like that to me, Jane," said her father. "You're not too old to be sent to bed yet! Even if you can't look as trim as Melisande, you might at least sew on buttons and mend holes in your clothes! I'm surprised your mother hasn't spoken to you about these things."

Jane's mother had, of course. She was always begging Jane to put a button on, to stop biting her nails, to brush her hair and find a few more grips to keep it tidy. But Jane took very little notice. She had tried for a time to keep her nails nice, after Melisande's remark about not expecting her to make herself nice for her aunt, if she didn't bother to do so for her mother, but it soon wore off!

Poor Jane! She really never seemed to see how she looked. She honestly didn't think it mattered a bit having a sandal tied up with string, or a hole in her blouse. She couldn't see *why* people should bother about a bit of hair hanging over her face, or a smut on her cheek. As for hands, so long as they were strong and deft, what did it matter how they looked?

She was quite sincere in her contempt for Melisande and her ways. She had grudgingly begun to be a little tidier in her bedroom, but only because Melisande, in despair, had started to tidy up Jane's things and put them away in drawers and cupboards, so that she shouldn't have to walk over layers of clothes when she went into the bedroom they both shared.

"I never can find *anything* now!" Jane complained to

126

her mother. "Melisande picks up my things and puts them away, I never know where. Mummy, do tell her to stop it. She won't stop for me."

"Well, you can easily stop her yourself by picking up your own things and putting them away," said her mother. "I've never seen anyone so untidy as you, Jane. I really have given you up in despair. I shan't stop Melisande. I'm sorry for her, having to share your untidiness as well as your room!"

So Jane, rather sulkily, had begun to be a little tidier and stuff things away in her drawers. No wonder all her clothes always looked so creased and messy! She didn't dream of folding them properly when she put them away; she simply stuffed everything into a drawer anyhow.

And now her father had scolded her for not being like Melisande! Jane was angry and hurt about it. She rounded on Melisande when they were alone in the bedroom.

"If you had never come, Daddy would never have picked on me," she said, sulkily. "Nobody minded about me much before."

"Your mother did," said Melisande, brushing out her wavy, silky hair. "You told me so. Anyway, Jane, you've got very strange ideas of dressing, you know. In the winter I suppose you *live* in jodhpurs and riding jacket. I shouldn't be surprised if you go to bed in them when you sleep alone! In the summer you live in dirty, torn shorts and even dirtier blouses. I've never really seen you in anything spotless. And your hands! Ugh!"

"I can't *help* biting my nails," said Jane. "I never know when I'm doing it."

"Well, you'll be like one of my mother's friends one day," said Melisande. "She bit her nails so much when she was young that they stopped growing. And now she's grown-up and dresses beautifully, she's always trying to hide her hands with their disgusting nails! I wondered why she was so funny about her hands, and then Mother told me. Horrible!"

"Oh, be quiet!" said Jane, banging her brush down on the dressing table. "What with you and Mummy – and

127

now Daddy – I don't have a moment's peace. I've a good mind to have my hair cut as short as a boy's; then no one could keep nagging at me because it looks untidy."

Melisande laughed. "You try it! I wouldn't like to see your father's face if you try any tricks of that sort!"

Jane didn't try it. For one thing, she knew her mother would be grieved and her father angry – and also the boys would hoot with laughter, and she couldn't bear that!

One day Jack spoke to his mother at high tea. "Oh, I say, Mother – I nearly forgot – could I ask Richard Lawson over for the day? He's dying to see the farm and Daddy's prize heifers."

"Yes, dear, of course," said his mother. "Let me see, isn't Richard the boy who is a wonderful rider and jumper?"

"That's right, Mother," said Jack, pleased that his mother should have remembered. "He's a fine all-round athlete. Captain of the School Games too. Course, he's much above me, but he thinks I'm not bad at football, so we get on all right."

"Isn't that the one who's got that lovely horse you were telling us about one day?" asked Jane with interest. "What was his name? Lordly-One, or something peculiar."

"Yes. And it jolly well suits him, that name," said Jack. "He really is a magnificent horse – a real lordly one! You should see the way he holds up his head and paws the ground."

"Do you think he'd let me ride him?" asked Jane eagerly. "Is he coming on Lordly-One?"

"Oh yes. He'll ride over all right," said Jack. "When can I ask him, Mother?"

"Next Thursday," said his mother. "I'll give you an extra special dinner that day!"

Jane was as excited as Jack about the visit of Richard Lawson and his horse. She had heard so much of the boy and his fame at games and sports. She knew he went hunting too, and that his father kept a very fine stable. She made Jack tell her the names and histories of all the horses in Richard's stables that he could remember.

"You'd better ask Richard yourself," he said, with a grin. "You and he would get on well together! You're both mad on horses. You'll have to show him Merrylegs. He's a nice pony, and he'd like him."

Jane was pleased and excited. She looked forward to Thursday. When it came, she got up early and looked out of the window.

"A lovely day!" she announced to Melisande, who was still asleep. "I'm getting up. I shall give Merrylegs an extra grooming to make him look nice for Richard to see."

"Don't wake me up, you beast," said Melisande, turning over and hiding her face in the pillow, away from the light. "Groom all the horses in the stable if you like! I bet you won't groom yourself, though!"

Jane didn't, of course. She didn't bother at all about herself. She had a cold bath, then dragged on filthy jodhpurs, pulled a torn yellow blouse on, and looked for her riding boots. She wore ankle-length ones, and found them at last, very dirty indeed. She put them on.

She put a comb through her hair, didn't bother about her teeth, and clattered downstairs, waking up Susan and her mother. Her father was already out.

She spent an hour grooming Merrylegs till he looked beautiful. She scrubbed his hooves. She polished his tack, and even debated whether or not to clean out his stall.

She went in late to breakfast, and was about to sit down when Melisande objected.

"*Jane*! You've come straight from the stables and, honestly, you smell awful. You might at least wash!"

Everyone looked at Jane. "You're a perfect sight, Jane," said her mother. "Go and get clean at once."

Jane saw that her father was also about to voice his opinion, and she fled. "Blow Melisande! Nobody else would have noticed, I'm sure!" she grumbled to herself.

Except that she had wiped a smear off her face and washed her hands, and put a grip in her hair, there was not really much difference in Jane when she went back to the table. Fortunately for her, her father had now gone. Her mother was busy pouring out tea, and hardly glanced at her. Melisande gave her a quick, scornful look, but said no more.

Jane gobbled down her breakfast. She had suddenly thought that it would be a good idea to clean the window in Merrylegs' stall. Then, if Richard saw him for the first time in the stable, he would have a good clear light to admire him by.

So she slipped out when she had finished, leaving Melisande to tackle the washing-up alone, and to tidy up the bedroom.

"It's going to be very hot today, Melisande," said her aunt. "Wouldn't you like to put on one of those cool cotton frocks your mother sent for you? You haven't worn them yet, and they would be thin and cool for this weather. I want you to go shopping for me this morning, and you'll be just right for going into the village in a cotton frock."

"Yes. I'd like to," said Melisande, pleased. "If Uncle doesn't want me in the fields today, I'd like to put on a frock for once. I'm tired of wearing shorts!"

Melisande enjoyed walking into the village to do the shopping. The tradespeople liked the well-mannered, pretty girl with her soft voice, and served her well. She decided to take Crackers, if Susan would let him go.

When she had finished her household tasks, she ran upstairs and looked with distaste at the mess in her room. She bundled all Jane's things into the chest of drawers, and pulled her quilt straight. Then she went to wash.

She came back and brushed out her wavy hair. She no longer spent hours in training it into little curls and twists. She merely brushed it well, and let it go into silky waves, then she pinned it back with grips. It fell neatly over her ears, and shone like silk.

She cleaned her nails, and wished that her hands didn't feel quite so rough. Still, they weren't bad, and they were slim and well-shaped. Thank goodness she didn't bite her nails like Jane!

She slipped on her new cotton frock. It was very simple and inexpensive, blue, with a little white line running through it. Her mother certainly knew how to choose dresses, Melisande thought!

She put on a white belt, and went down to see what shopping her aunt wanted her to do. Aunt Linnie and Dorcas looked at her in approval.

"You look so cool and fresh!" said her Aunt Linnie. "That frock suits you, dear. You had got much too big for those other dresses. This one is just right."

Dorcas said nothing. She thought Melisande was conceited enough without being made more so. Nevertheless, she too thought the girl looked charming. Jane never looked like that – and yet Jane had a lovely thick mop of hair, a dear quaint little face, and fine straight-set eyes! Dorcas felt she would like to shake Jane for making so little of herself when she could make so much!

Melisande took the shopping basket and her aunt's list. It was a long one. "I hope I shall be able to carry everything, Aunt Linnie," she said. "It looks such a lot."

"Ask the grocer to send all the things I've marked with a cross, dear," said her aunt. "You should be able to manage the rest. I shall want them for dinner, so try and bring them. Don't hurry too much. It's so hot."

Melisande went down the path to the little gate. In the distance she saw Jane, looking hot and dirty and happy, carrying a pail of very dirty water. She waved to her. Jane waved back, and spilt some water down her jodhpurs.

"I've cleaned the stable windows!" yelled Jane. "Where are you going?"

"To the village, shopping," said Melisande. "I shan't be long! See you later, Jane – and do change out of those dirty things before Richard comes!"

CHAPTER EIGHTEEN

Richard and Lordly-One

Melisande went slowly down the lane, keeping as much in the shade as she could. Scarlet poppies nodded at the wayside, and bright blue chicory grew nearby. Melisande picked a buttonhole of chicory for her dress. It was exactly the same shade.

She went to the shops and gave her orders. Soon her basket was very full. The grocer said he couldn't send the things her aunt had marked – could she manage to take them?

"Oh dear. Well, I suppose I must," said Melisande, with a sigh. "The basket will be awfully heavy."

"I'll lend you another," said the grocer. "If you have one in each hand, the weight each side will balance, and it won't be too bad."

So Melisande was soon walking up the village street with a basket in each hand, rather dreading the long pull up the lane to Mistletoe Farm.

Someone came trotting through the street. Melisande turned and saw a well-set-up boy of about seventeen on a magnificent black horse whose coat shone like satin, and who had three white socks and a star.

The boy reined up when he saw Melisande. "Excuse me," he said, "but could you tell me the way to Mistletoe Farm?"

"Oh yes!" said Melisande, and she smiled. "I live there! I'm just going back home with the shopping!"

"Oh – are you one of the Longfields?" said the boy, thinking that this girl looked just about as nice as any girl he had ever seen. Not that he had much time for girls, but when he noticed them, he liked them to look pretty.

"I'm Melisande Longfield," said Melisande. "Are you Richard Lawson? You're expected!"

"Yes, I'm Richard," said the boy, holding in his horse, which had grown restive at a passing lorry.

"And is this Lordly-One?" asked Melisande, stroking him softly. "Oh, what a beauty! His name's exactly right, isn't it?"

"Do you think so?" said Richard, pleased. "I always think so, of course, but then he's mine! I say, how are you going to get back with those heavy baskets? Aren't you riding – or isn't there a bus?"

"I'm walking," said Melisande. "I wish it wasn't so hot! I shall be melted going up the hill to the farm."

Richard slid down from his horse. "Let's have an ice," he said. "I'm hot too. We could have an ice, and then, if it wouldn't offend you, you could, if you liked, get in front of me on Lordly-One, and he'll take us both up the hill, and the baskets too. He's as strong as a – as a . . ."

"Horse!" said Melisande, and though it wasn't very witty, they both laughed at once. "Yes, I'd love an ice. I've spent all Aunt Linnie's money, though, so I hope you've got enough to pay for mine!"

"Plenty," said Richard. He tied Lordly-One to a post, and they went into the dairy. It sold cream ices, and very good they were. Richard and Melisande had two each, whilst Lordly-One waited outside, whinnying with impatience.

"We oughtn't to keep a lordly horse like that waiting!" said Melisande. "And I'm sure Jack will be wondering why you're late. We must go. Do you really think your horse can take me too? I just hate the thought of climbing that hill with these baskets on such a hot day."

Lordly-One took them both easily. Richard helped Melisande up, and arranged the baskets very cleverly. He thought Melisande was not only a pretty girl, but a most amusing one. "She's so gentle, too, and has such a nice voice," he thought. "I don't know why, but I didn't imagine that Jack's sister would be a bit like this."

He had no idea that Melisande was Jack's *cousin*. When she had said she was Melisande Longfield, and lived at Mistletoe Farm, he had at once thought she was Jack Longfield's sister. He thought Jack was a lucky fellow to have a nice sister like this. They jogged on up the hill very slowly.

133

Lordly-One took them both easily

"I heard Jack say you're going riding with him this afternoon," said Melisande. "You'll enjoy riding over our hills."

"I hope you're coming too," said Richard at once. "You will, won't you? I'd like you to. I'm sure you ride well."

"I wish I could. But I expect I'll have jobs to do," said

Melisande. Anyway, she knew that Jane had planned to go with Jack and Richard on Merrylegs. There wouldn't be a horse for her, because nothing would persuade her to ride Boodi.

They arrived at Mistletoe Farm, and rode into the yard, Lordly-One's hooves clattering on the cobblestones. Jack and Jane and Susan rushed to meet Richard.

They were amazed to see Melisande riding in front of Richard. He helped her down, and grinned round at everyone.

"Sorry I'm late," he said. "I met your sister, Jack, and she had so much to carry I brought her along with me on Lordly-One."

"She's not my sister," said Jack. "She's my cousin. *This* is my sister," and he pushed Jane forward, whilst Susan hovered behind, her eyes on the magnificent Lordly-One.

Jane was a sight. There was no other word to describe her. She hadn't changed out of her dirty jodhpurs, not even to put on a cleaner pair. Her yellow shirt was now much dirtier. Her cheeks were streaked with dirt, and her hair was tumbled about anyhow.

After the cool, pretty Melisande in her blue cotton frock, she was quite a shock. Richard stared at Jane, and blinked. "Er – how do you do?" he said, and shook hands with her, taking hold of her dirty little paw rather gingerly.

"And this is Susan," said Jack. Susan grinned at him, and didn't offer to shake hands. "I like your horse," she said. "He looks high and mighty, like his name."

"You must see *our* horses," said Jane loudly. "Especially mine. He's called Merrylegs. I shall ride him this afternoon when we go for a ride together. Let's come and stable Lordly-One, and then we'll show you round."

Melisande had disappeared with the baskets. Richard was landed with Jane, because Jack went to stable Lordly-One, and Susan went with him. "What a lump of a girl!" he thought. And did she *have* to be quite so dirty? "She'll grow up into one of those awful horsy women who look as if they never get out of their riding breeches," he thought.

"Like my Aunt Judith - loud voice, big hands, always knocking things over! What a pity that girl Melisande isn't Jack's sister!"

Jane led the way proudly to Merrylegs, talking without a stop. She could always find plenty to say! She didn't give Richard a chance to say anything, and he rapidly grew bored. Jane was disappointed that he didn't rave over Merrylegs. He seemed interested in Boodi, though.

"Quaint fellow," he remarked. "Quite a character he looks. What is he? Oh, an Iceland pony. I've never ridden one of those. Who does he belong to? Melisande?"

"No! She'll never ride Boodi, because he misbehaves," said Jane. "He belongs to my little sister Susan. She's the only one who can manage him."

Melisande helped her aunt with the cooking all the morning, and did not appear, much to Richard's annoyance. He was getting very tired of Jane, who was determined that he should see every single animal on the farm and hear its history. Jack accompanied them, of course, but he never had much to say at any time, and with Jane talking the whole while, there was no need for him to say a word.

Susan went with them too. Richard liked the funny little girl, and he liked Roderick too, who suddenly appeared and trailed behind them, too shy to keep close.

"I like that kid sister of yours," said Richard. "The little one, I mean."

"Yes. She's a scream," agreed Jack. "Jane's not bad either."

"Melisande's the one to be proud of, though, isn't she?" said Richard, forgetting for the moment that she was not Jack's sister. "She's like Lordly-One – groomed down to the last hair!"

Jack was startled. He thought over what Richard had said. Yes, it was true. Melisande did have the groomed appearance of a well-cared-for horse – silky and shiny and clean and sweet-smelling. He looked at Jane, and saw her clearly for the first time. Richard saw him looking at her. He suddenly remembered that Melisande was a cousin, not a sister.

"Of course, Jane's nice too," he said, too hurriedly. "Only she's not the same type as Melisande, is she?"

Jack saw Jane with Richard's eyes – dirty, grubby, careless, with bitten nails and untidy hair. He was ashamed of her. He turned abruptly and led Richard to see the prize heifers.

The dinner was a very good one. "You've surpassed yourself, Mother!" said Jack, grinning at his mother, whose face was fiery red with cooking. "Richard, don't you think my mother's a good cook?"

"Rather!" said Richard, who had taken a great liking to the cheerful, twinkling mother of Jack, Jane and Susan. "I shan't be able to move this afternoon. I've eaten such a lot!"

"We thought we'd take a picnic tea over to Breezy Hill," said Jack. "Go on horseback, of course."

"Sounds a good spot for a hot day," said Richard. "Don't you think so, Melisande? What horse are you going to ride?"

"Well," said Melisande, and hesitated. "I'm not coming. I haven't a horse, you see. I'd *love* to come, but not on foot!"

"Oh, but you *must* come!" cried Richard, who had been looking forward to riding with Melisande, and was very anxious not to be landed with Jane all the afternoon.

Jane was looking very sulky. She didn't want Melisande to go. Already Richard had talked far more to her cousin at dinner-time than he had to her. Now here he was urging her to come riding, which meant Melisande would monopolize him the whole time. And Jane hadn't told him half she wanted to about the farm yet!

"I just can't come," said Melisande regretfully. "I know Susan would let me ride her horse Boodi, if I asked her, but I'm scared of Boodi's tricks!"

"And there's no other horse," said Jane triumphantly.

Her father had been listening to all this. He turned to Jack. "I shan't want Sultan this afternoon," he said. "If you like, you can ride him, Jack, and let Melisande have Darkie. Then she can go."

"Oh, *thank* you, Uncle Peter!" cried Melisande, delighted, and Richard beamed. Now at least he would have this nice, amusing girl part of the ride, instead of that lump of a Jane pouring out endless information into his ear the whole time!

Melisande went to change. Her jodhpurs were clean. Her yellow shirt was also clean and freshly pressed. Her riding boots shone. She looked dainty and well turned out as she mounted Darkie. Again Jack compared Jane with Melisande. What on earth did Jane want to look so awful for? Couldn't she at least make herself a bit decent when his friends came for the day? He felt angry with poor Jane.

The picnic was a great success for everyone except Jane. She couldn't make out why Richard didn't seem to want to listen to her, or even take any notice of her. Didn't she know much more about the farm and all the animals than that stupid Melisande? Even Jack seemed to snub her and look coldly at her. Jane fell silent, and was very miserable.

She liked Richard. He was tall and good-looking, and he had a merry laugh that showed extremely white teeth. She thought he must clean them at least six times a day to make them white like that, and she remembered rather guiltily that she hadn't cleaned hers for ages. She looked at Melisande's. Hers were white and gleaming too. She looked at Melisande's nice hands and at her gleaming hair.

She put her own hands into her jodhpur pockets, suddenly ashamed of the bitten nails. She scowled, and was angry when Jack gave her a punch and asked her what she was cross about.

Richard said goodbye regretfully that evening. "I've enjoyed my day," he said. "And thank you, Mr Longfield, for letting me go over the heifers. Wonderful beasts you've got. Well, Jack, come over to Treetop Hall some time, won't you – and bring Melisande – and – er – Jane too if you like."

He galloped off on Lordly-One, waving.

138

"A very nice boy," said Mrs Longfield.

"A good chap and a knowledgeable one," said her husband.

"He's fun," said Melisande.

"Thought you'd all like him," said Jack, pleased. "At least – I don't think Jane liked him. Did you, Jane? You went all mouldy halfway through the picnic!"

Jane scowled, and said nothing. The day had been a great disappointment to her. Jack felt cross. He was about to tell Jane a few things he had thought that day, but he stopped himself in time. No. It wouldn't be fair to say them in front of everyone. Jane would hate it, and probably throw something at him. So he waited his time, quite determined to point out a good many things to his twin as soon as the chance came.

It came two days later. A letter arrived from Richard for Mrs Longfield, thanking her for his nice day, and asking Jack, Jane and Melisande over to meet his mother.

"I'm afraid it won't be such a free and easy day as I had at Mistletoe Farm," he wrote. "In fact, I'm afraid it's a sort of party. But girls like parties, I know, so perhaps Jack could bring Melisande and Jane. We can arrange another day later to go riding together."

"What a very nice letter!" said Mrs Longfield. "He's a well-mannered boy, Jack. And how very nice for the girls to go to a party!"

Melisande was thrilled. Jane was silent. Jack sought her out that morning, when she was working in her mother's little garden, thinning out the lettuces. He sat down on a low wall beside her.

"Jane," he began.

"What?" said Jane.

"Look here, Jane," said Jack, and stopped, not quite sure how to go on.

"*What*?" said Jane. "Do say whatever it is you mean to say. I can't keep saying 'What?'"

Jack took the plunge. "Well, I may as well tell you, Jane, that I was jolly well ashamed of you the other day

139

when Richard came. I could quite well see what he thought of you – especially when he saw Melisande alongside."

"What did he think of me?" said Jane in a strangled voice, going on with her lettuces and keeping her head well down.

"He must have thought you were dirty and untidy, and had frightful nails, and your hair was all over the place and hadn't been brushed for weeks, and your shoes were filthy, and even your face had streaks of dirt down it," said Jack, beginning to warm up, and not realizing at all how upset he was making poor Jane. "Why do you do it? After all, you're a girl, aren't you? It's a girl's business to look decent, it seems to me. Like Melisande. I dare say she spends too much time titivating, as you girls call it, but it seems to me you don't spend any at all."

Jane said nothing. Her hands trembled as she pulled up the lettuce. Jack went on, thinking that Jane was sulking, and needed a little more trouncing.

"I could see that Richard was sorry Melisande wasn't my sister. He looked shocked when he found *you* were. Honestly, Jane, you looked a *clod*!"

This was really too much from her twin. A *clod*! That was what Melisande and Cyril called their cousins when they were fed up with them and their ways. And now Jack had said the same thing. Jane gave a gulp, and two tears dropped on to the lettuces. She didn't dare to look up. She never, never cried, and she couldn't bear Jack to see her tears. He would jeer like anything

Jack heard the gulp and was surprised. He bent down to look at Jane and saw the tears drop. He was struck with horror. Jane crying! She hadn't done that for years. He was suddenly sorry for what he had said.

"Jane," he said awkwardly, trying to pull her up. "I didn't mean all that. It's all right. I like you as you are. *Jane*!"

Jane pulled away from him and ran stumbling down the path. She shut herself in the barn in the dark. To think that *Jack* should say all that – and be ashamed of her. It was the very last straw. Something would have to be done. Blow! Blow! Blow! It was going to be beastly and hateful and miserable – but all the same, something would *have* to be done!

CHAPTER NINETEEN

Jane, the Party – and the Hermit

Jane did the most sensible thing she could have done. She went to her mother. Mrs Longfield was sitting out of doors on the little paved yard by the goldfish pond, darning the stockings that always filled her work-basket to overflowing. She was surprised to see Jane's solemn face.

"What's the matter, dear?" she said. Jane knelt down by the pond and began to dabble her hand in the water, looking fiercely at the bitten nails.

"Jack says he's ashamed to have me for a sister," she said after a minute.

"Well, that's a very unkind thing for Jack to say!" said her mother, startled.

And then it all came out – without any tears, because Jane was tough inside, and was not going to show any more weakness. Her mother listened in surprise, her busy needle going in and out without stopping.

"Well, there you are, Mummy," said Jane, who hadn't once looked at her mother all this time. "What am I to do?"

"Plenty, Jane dear!" said her mother. "But it won't be easy, will it?"

"I like hard things," said Jane obstinately. "If I choose to do them myself, I mean."

"Well, I'm glad you've chosen to, then," said her mother. "You have never done any of them for me. If

141

you can do them because you want to yourself, you should be able to make a success of it."

"I don't want Melisande to crow over me or make nasty remarks," said Jane.

"She won't," said Mrs Longfield, making a hasty resolve to warn Melisande.

"I'm going to be clean, and not bite my nails, and to remember to brush my hair, and look at my clothes before I put them on," said Jane. "But I feel I can't do any more than that yet."

"That will be a lot," said Mrs Longfield, trying not to smile. Jane was so very solemn and earnest. Her mother hoped she really meant all she said. If so, it would be a feather in Jack's cap to have been able to make Jane do what nobody else had succeeded in making her do!

Jack tried to make up to Jane for upsetting her, but she was very cool with him. Although she thought he was right and had made up her mind to do what he said, she couldn't forgive him for humiliating her so. And her cheeks burned whenever she thought of Richard and what he must have thought of her. She made up her mind that nothing would make her go to the party at Tree Tops Hall.

Melisande had a word of warning from her aunt. "Jane's turning over a new leaf," said Mrs Longfield. "Don't remark on it too much, Melisande, but help her if you can."

Susan also had a word of warning, and stared in surprise when her mother said Jane was going to try to make herself tidy and neat in future. "And don't you make any of your pointed remarks, Susan," ended her mother.

"I'll try and remember not to," said Susan earnestly. "But I'm afraid I shall forget. I suppose, Mummy, Jane was upset when Daddy was cross with her the other day. I dond't know if you've noticed it, but Roderick and I have really tried to be a bit cleaner since then."

Her mother hadn't noticed it, but she assured Susan that she was very pleased to hear it. Secretly, she thought that it was good for Roderick to get a bit dirty now and again – he had been *such* a proper little boy! But now, how all the six children were changing!

Jane was good at doing things once she had really made up her mind. She now scrubbed her fingers almost raw. She wouldn't put them near her mouth at all in case she bit her nails, but it was sometimes agony to her not to do this. It had been a habit nearly all her life!

She brushed her hair till her arm was tired, and was really surprised when it began to look as silky as Melisande's. She put so many grips into it to keep it tidy that her cousin protested.

"Really, Jane! Your hair is nothing but grips! Honestly, I think you must have about twenty in. Do take some out."

"It's got to be trained," said Jane, quite fiercely, as if she was talking about a badly behaved dog. "I'll gradually reduce the number. Don't bother me, Melisande."

Melisande didn't. She was very good about it indeed. It was an uncomfortable business altogether, because Jane was so determined and full of perseverance that everyone became really bored with the whole procedure. Still, she certainly began to look very much nicer, especially about the hair.

Instead of being straggly and messy and without a parting at all, it became thick and glossy and swung out on each side of her face, suiting her extremely well. Her father noticed it at once.

"Well, it's nice to be able to take pleasure in looking at you, Jane," he said. "Linnie, she's become quite good-looking, hasn't she?"

Jane pretended to scowl and look away, but secretly she was rather pleased. She had been so used to taking it for granted that Melisande was the pretty one and she was the ugly duckling that it was quite nice to be thought good-looking for a change!

The day for the party came near. Her mother began to wonder what Jane could wear. "I should think it's a kind of garden-party, as it's in the summer," she said. "You must wear your best frock, Jane."

"It's torn down the back," said Jane. "I can't wear it, Mummy! I don't want to go to the party, anyway. I thought I wouldn't go, as I'm not keen on parties."

"You'll certainly go," said her mother, and sent Jane to fetch her frock. She was horrified when she saw how torn it was.

"But *Jane*! How *could* you tear it all the way down like that! Even if I mend it beautifully, the tear will show!" she said.

"I fell over it on the floor," said Jane, beginning to look mutinous. "I caught my foot in it."

"But whatever was it doing on the *floor*?" said her mother. "Oh, Jane – your very best frock!"

"I don't leave my things on the floor any more," said Jane. "I really am remembering to put them away now. Don't scold me, Mummy, when I'm doing my best."

"Very well," said her mother with a sigh. "But I do wish you'd realize that a tear like this means a whole evening's mending for me – and *then* it won't look nice!"

"I don't want to go in a mended frock," said Jane obstinately. "I don't want to go at all."

"One more word, and you'll go out of the room and stay out," said her father suddenly. "You'll go to the party, and you'll go in whatever your mother says. Do you hear?"

Jane was scared at his tone. Daddy had seemed very cross with her lately. She said no more at all.

Melisande was sorry for her. She knew how she herself would have hated to go to the party in a mended frock. She went upstairs and began to rummage in her neat drawers. She soon found what she wanted. It was a dark blue frock in silk, with a full skirt, and a plain bodice. The dress had a little round white collar, and a white belt. Melisande looked t it, and wished it fitted her now. It had been one of her favourite dresses. She called Jane upstairs.

"Jane," she said, "*I'd* hate to go out in a mended frock. Look. Would this one fit you? It's almost new, because I've hardly worn it. Try it on."

Jane liked the plain little dark blue frock with its white collar and belt. She slipped it on. It was just a little too tight and a little too long.

But how it suited her! Melisande added a red silk bow to the neck, and silently showed Jane herself in the glass. Jane looked in amazement.

Why, she was quite pretty! Her thick hair shone smooth and silky, her face was clean and very brown, and her eyes shone very blue. What a difference it made when people looked after themselves even a little!

"Yes. I look quite nice," she said. "I wish the dress fitted me, Melisande. I can't ask Mummy to spend ages altering it, and I don't know how to myself."

"I'll show you," said Melisande, and she did. She unpicked various seams, and showed Jane how to sew them so that the dress gave her more room. She helped her to turn up the hem. Then it fitted her well.

"It's kind of you, Melisande," said Jane gratefully. "I do like it. I never did like dresses very much, but I really like this one. Do you think Jack will be ashamed of me in this?"

"No. He won't know you," said Melisande.

The funny thing was that not even Richard knew Jane when she arrived at the party with Melisande and Jack! He knew Melisande at once, and was delighted to see her, looking pretty and fresh in a frilly muslin frock. Then he turned to Jane and looked puzzled. He looked at Jack for help.

"Er – is this another cousin of yours?" he said as he held out his hand to Jane.

Jack went off into a roar of laughter. "No! It's Jane. My sister. Don't you remember her, Richard?"

"I didn't recognize her," said Richard. "You're different, Jane. Quite different! Let's go and visit Lordly-One, shall we? I'd like to show you his stable. Come along, Melisande. Jack, you go and talk to my mother for a bit."

Richard was really startled to think that this good-looking girl, with the lovely mop of hair and pretty

145

dress, should be the Jane he had thought of as a "dirty little grub". He kept looking at her in astonishment, and Jane couldn't help feeling proud of herself. Lordly-One welcomed them and condescended to take lumps of sugar in a very haughty manner from the palms of their hands.

"Pity you haven't jodhpurs on," Richard said to Jane. "I'd have let you take Lordly-One out. I bet you could ride him well. You know such a lot about horses."

It was really a very successful party, and Jack was very proud of both his sister and his cousin. He told them so when he took them home round Long-Acre Hill.

"I hope you won't slide back gain into being a dirty little grub," he said to Jane. "Gosh, Jane, even your nails are beginning to look like nails!"

"Except this one," said Jane, showing one bitten one. "I just seem to *have* to bite them sometimes, but I leave them all alone except this wretched finger. So at least I only have *one* awful nail!"

They were now near the caves on Long-Acre Hill, and Jack remembered that Benedict, Cyril's friend, lived there. They went cautiously round to the caves, but there didn't appear to be anyone around there. Jack went into the hermit's cave and had a look round.

"What colossal feet he must have!" he said to the two girls, holding up a pair of large sandals. "My feet are pretty big, but his are bigger still! Fancy wearing these things – all fancywork and holes!"

"It's quite a big cave," said Jane, looking round. "Is there another at the back – or is it just one cave? Some of these caves lead into one another, you know. Let's explore!"

She went to the back of the cave to see if it led into a further one – but an angry voice made her stop: "What are you kids doing here? How dare you come into my cave and mess about with my things? Come out at once!"

Jack and the girls went to the entrance. Benedict was there, looking very angry indeed.

"Sorry," said Jack. "We knew Cyril, my cousin, often came here to see you, so we thought we'd call and see if you were at home."

"It's a pity you haven't as good manners as your cousin," said Benedict coldly. "He would never dream of coming in unless he was asked. I may only live in a cave, but at least it is my own."

The three children walked off, not at all liking the look on the angry hermit. "I suppose it *was* rather awful of us to walk in like that," said Jane, at last. "But somehow caves don't seem very private – not like people's homes. But after all, that's his *home*, I suppose."

"I don't like him," said Jack. "I can't imagine why Cyril does. He really gives me the creeps. There's something *odd* about him. He doesn't seem to – to – ring true."

"Well, there *is* something odd about him," said Melisande. "That awful beard – and the long hair. And why wear a long white hermit's gown these days? Surely he could be a hermit and still wear ordinary clothes. Does he go and do his shopping in them?"

"Oh yes!" said Jack. "People stare at him like anything, but I bet he's idiot enough to like that. He even goes to market and buys butter and eggs. I've seen him, with a trail of giggling kids behind him, asking him why he doesn't get his hair cut!"

"How *can* Cyril be friendly with him?" said Jane in disgust. "Honestly, Melisande, Cyril is very odd sometimes."

"He's all right," said Melisande loyally, though she too thought Cyril had a very peculiar friend in the hermit.

Cyril was angry when he heard that his sister and cousins had intruded on his friend's privacy and had actually gone into his cave. "What *must* he have thought?" he kept saying. "What *must* he have thought?"

"I don't care *what* he thought. Or what you think either," retorted Jack, exasperated. "We didn't do any harm. He's crackers, I think. Bats in the belfry. Barmy!"

"Of course, no one could possibly expect you to appreciate a scholar when you see one, or even to realize that he *is* one," said Cyril sarcastically. "And you so seldom use your own mind that you have probably never even realized that there might be great thinkers."

"You can't tell me that your wonderful friend is a great thinker," said Jack bluntly. "If he was he'd think himself out of that awful cave pretty quick! Anyway, I bet he'll be out of it in two shakes of a duck's tail when the cold weather comes. He doesn't look as if he's made of very tough stuff. And oh, that hair! I suppose that's why you've taken to wearing *yours* long again these hols., Cyril – because *he* does! Well, I warn you, if you let it get any longer you'll hear about it from Dad."

Cyril went out and slammed the door. He went up into the room he shared with Jack and locked the door. He would read a little poetry and try and get calm again!

Someone banged at the door. It was Roderick. "Cyril! Are you there? Why have you locked the door? Aunt Linnie says will you come down and let her mend your coat, please?"

"Never any peace in this house!" muttered poor Cyril angrily. "What a place! What people! I've a jolly good mind to do what Benedict does – live in a cave away from everybody!"

CHAPTER TWENTY

The Time Goes On

The summer holidays ended. The last two weeks flew by at such a pace that they seemed like two days!

"Holidays always do that," complained Susan. "Mummy, why do horrid times crawl, and nice times fly? It's the wrong way round. I don't feel ready for school again yet. Do you, Roderick?"

"Not really," said Roderick, who had enjoyed the holidays at Mistletoe Farm more than he had ever enjoyed any time in his life before. His aunt looked at him. He was brown and sturdy and getting very independent. "It was

148

the best thing that could happen to him, to have to leave his mother for a while," thought his aunt. "He was such a silly little mother's boy, scared of everything."

There were great preparations for school. New school clothes had to be bought. Susan protested violently against wearing Jane's cut-down uniform, but had to have it all the same. "It's a question of money, Susan," said her mother. "Autumn is an awkward time for Daddy. He's buying lots of new stock, and so his money is in the cattle and sheep and crops, instead of in the bank."

"Go and ask Buttercup the cow if she'll let you have a few pounds to buy a new uniform, Sue," suggested Roderick with a grin. Susan sighed, and gave in. There was always this battle about clothes. Perhaps one day she would be as big as Jane, and then she could have new clothes too.

Melisande was quite pleased to be going back to school. She felt that it would be very nice to have a change from so much housework, especially since Dorcas had not been well, so that Jane and Melisande had had to do extra household jobs.

Jane loved school, and the chatter and noise and games and general excitement. She was really pleased to be going back.

"I don't expect I shall have so many remarks in your report about untidiness and carelessness this term, Jane," said her mother slyly. "You're certainly managing to keep your word, aren't you?"

"What about? Oh, you mean about my hands and nails and clothes?" said Jane. "Well, you know when I say I'll do a thing, I always do do it, Mummy. But, oh dear, I still haven't been able to get this one nail right. I still seem to keep it for biting!"

"Well, one bitten one is better than ten!" said her mother. "Jane, I suppose you wouldn't like to take it in turn with Melisande to ride Merrylegs in to school each morning, would you? She's really been very good in the house these last two weeks."

"Oh, *no*, Mummy!" said Jane, looking horrified. "I couldn't *possibly* do that. Merrylegs would hate it."

"I'm not thinking about Merrylegs," said her mother. "He will do whatever you tell him. Well, I didn't really think it was possible for you to be as unselfish as that, Jane!"

"No. I don't think I could be," said Jane. "I wish Melisande and the others would go away! I want our home to ourselves again. I don't want them here for Christmas, Mummy. Do you?"

"Well, it *will* be nice to have the house to ourselves," said her mother. "But I've grown very fond of your three cousins, Jane – especially little Roderick. Susan would miss him dreadfully. She was rather one on her own, you know, because you and Jack, being twins, always went about together."

Cyril was bored at having to go back to school. After his time with Benedict, and having listened with awe and respect to the many theories and ideas that the hermit expounded to him, Cyril felt that school was elementary and a waste of his time. He hadn't got back his Greek dictionary yet, and he hardly liked to ask for it. So he bought another out of his meagre store of money, though he could ill afford to.

He had spent most of his money on a little portable wireless. He had gone plum picking, as his aunt had advised him, in the plum season, and had earned about twelve pounds. It had been very hard work, because it had not been a well-paid job, and Cyril had had to put in very long hours to get enough money for the wireless.

But the wireless was worth it! It was wonderful to have one of his own. He took it away into quiet corners of the farm whenever there was any lovely music he wanted to hear, and the ducks and hens grew quite familiar with Beethoven and Mozart. The cows chewed the cud and looked languidly at the tiny machine that sang strange sounds to them. Cyril did not dare to leave it anywhere, if he was called away, because the cows were so inquisitive – and as for Boodi, if he was anywhere about he would be quite likely to lick it till it dripped!

It was Cyril's most precious possession; not because it was the most expensive thing he had ever had, for it certainly was not! It was precious because he had had to work for it himself, he had wanted it very much, and he had gone to buy it with his own money.

He had been very disappointed because Benedict hadn't seemed as pleased about it as he had hoped he would. Benedict liked to talk, and the wireless prevented that. He talked one day whilst Beethoven's Fifth Symphony was on, and Cyril was so shocked about this, that he dared to expostulate.

Benedict had seemed surprised. "My boy," he said in lofty tones, "the music I love best is the song of the birds, the hum of the bees and the sound of the little waterfall nearby. Nature's music is finer than any other."

"But you said you liked music so much," said Cyril, unable to hide his disappointment. "This is such a lovely thing they're playing, Benedict."

The hermit saw that the boy was surprised and hurt, and he listened in silence to the rest of the programme. But it was spoilt for Cyril, and he took the little wireless away and did not bring it back. Instead, he put it into his room at Mistletoe Farm, and only brought it out for himself after that – until one day, when Aunt Linnie stole round the corner of the barn and seated herself beside him in silence, to listen to a ballade of Chopin's.

"Lovely!" she said when it was finished. "I wish I could stay longer, but I must feed the hens. Let me know when anything special is on, Cyril, and, if I shan't intrude, I'll come and listen too."

Except for his disappointment over the wireless, Cyril thought more of his friend than ever. He was sorry to think that he would see so little of him when school began. Jack felt the same about Twigg. He knew he would not be able to go for many more night trips with the poacher, because they would make him too sleepy in school the next day.

"But, Twigg, if there's anything special to see, I simply *must* come," he told him. "You know – like the badgers, for instance. I've never seen them yet."

151

"Well, you'll have to come before they set about hibernating or the winter, then," said Twigg. "Once they go below, they'll sleep the sleep of the dead. I'll keep my eye open, Mr Jack, and let you know if there's badgers to be seen."

The mystery of the stolen money had never been solved. Not only that, but several other robberies were unsolved too! More market money had been stolen, and farmers were beginning to be very careful about banking their money now. It was whispered that Twigg and his friends were responsible, though Twigg stoutly denied it. P.C. Potts, anxious for promotion, prowled about continually at night, hoping to come across something suspicious.

He never once saw Twigg, though that sharp-eyed little fellow often saw him! Sometimes the policeman came almost close enough to touch Twigg and the golden spaniel, who were both as still and silent as a tree-shadow! Often the screech of a barn-owl that caused Mr Potts to jump out of his skin was made by Twigg signalling to Tommy Lane that the "bobby was about agen!"

At times Mr Potts got a shock when he saw the hermit on *his* nightly wanderings too. But, as he always gave warning of his presence by his curious habit of muttering or murmuring, the policeman at last got used to him. He was quite sure that the hermit was mad, though he talked in a remarkably sane manner at times.

"You ever see anything of that feller Twigg?" Mr Potts asked the hermit one night when he had gone to the poacher's cottage and discovered he was out.

"Twigg? Now who is he?" asked the hermit. "Ah yes, Sergeant. That little rat-like fellow in gaiters, you mean?"

P.C. Potts was pleased at being called "Sergeant." He swelled up visibly. He was also pleased to hear Twigg called rat-like. He began to think the hermit was a lot more sensible than people made out. They had quite a nice conversation about poachers and wrong-doing, and Twigg and Tommy Lane and one or two others.

"Well, sir, it's a strange habit of yours, this, wandering

about in the dead of night in that there gown of yours," said P.C. Potts, preparing to go, "but it's your own business, I suppose. And if so be as you'd just keep an eye out for anything suspicious-like at night, I'd be glad to hear from you. It's all right you and me being out in the dark, sir, but if folks like Twigg and Tommy Lane get about at night, there's something in the wind."

"I am on the side of law and order," said the hermit. "I will help you if I can. Good night to you, Sergeant." And he went off through the woods, muttering something that sounded most impressive to P.C. Potts.

A barn owl screeched very near to him, and he jumped. It semed a funny thing to him that the woods were so full of barn owls now. Must be a good year for them, he thought.

Twigg too was out that night. He had a good many things to see to, and he and Tommy Lane were working round a mile or so, intending to meet later. It was that night that Twigg saw the two badgers.

The moon came out suddenly, and there, on the bank not far off, were the little bear-like creatures, standing absolutely still.

Twigg put his hand on Mr Potts' collar, and the dog froze. The wind was blowing from the badgers to Twigg, which explained why the two creatures had not smelt or heard him. Mr Potts' nostrils opened wide as he sniffed badger, but he made no sound. Twigg watched closley.

Another badger joined the two. It was a young one. A small sound made all three turn towards the dog and the man. Twigg could clearly see the black-and-white markings on their faces, which so closely simulated the streaks of white moonlight and black shadows. Twigg's eyes were sharp, but even as he looked at the badgers they seemed to disappear, so clever was the camouflage of their markings. He blinked. A badger moved slightly and came into focus again.

Then they fled silently away through the night as Tommy Lane came towards them to look for Twigg. Mr Potts stretched himself and yawned. Twigg went to look at the bank where the badgers had been, and discovered a deep hole at the back.

Another badger joined the two

"That's their hole," he decided. "I reckon if Mr Jack comes along next time there's a moon, and watches out for them badgers, they'll oblige him!"

He told Jack next time he saw him. "Saw them badgers again," he told the interested boy. "Three of them on a bank. Their sett's there, or I'll eat my hat. If you come along the next moonlight night when I'm out, you can see them. I'll send word when I'll be out."

"Thanks, Twigg," said Jack eagerly. He did not see his father talking to Jim the cowman as Twigg went, and he was surprised to hear him call him.

"Jack! Come here! I want you a minute."

154

Jack went over to Jim and his father. They both looked grave.

"Look here, Jack," said his father. "I'm going to tell Twigg he's not to come on my land any more. Jim here says it's pretty certain that Twigg and Tommy Lane are working the robberies between them that have been going on this summer. He's an artful old rascal, and Potts is after him all the time. Sooner or later he'll find himself in prison again. I don't want you to have anything to do with him."

Jack stared at his father in dismay. "But, Dad!" he said "Twigg's a good friend of mine. He's been awfully decent to me, and taught me no end of interesting things about birds and animals. Whatever will he say if I don't have anything to do with him?"

"He won't be surprised!" said his father. "He knows he's suspected now. He won't get out of things by saying he was up at Tommy Lane's next time anything happens!"

"He's a bad lot," said Jim. "Always was since a boy. I went to school with he. Slippery as an eel, was Sam Twigg."

"Well, I like him," said Jack, obstinately.

"You hear me, don't you?" said his father sharply. "Nothing more to do with him! No going out on excursions with him! And I expect you to warn him off our land if you see him on it."

Jack turned away, dismayed. Poor old Twigg! To be turned off his father's land – and by Jack as well. Jack felt that he could never do that. He hoped Twigg wouldn't turn up again, now that his father was going to warn him off. Then Jack wouldn't need to show him that he mustn't be friends with him any more.

"I shan't see the badgers now," thought Jack as he went off to help to milk the cows. "Blow! I don't believe Twigg's a bad lot. I don't care what *any*one says. I just – don't – believe it!"

CHAPTER TWENTY-ONE

An Alarming Idea

Everyone settled down well at school, even Cyril, who found to his surprise that he had become quite good at games!

He had grown strong and muscular with all the work he had done on the farm, and discovered that he was unexpectedly good on the football field. The others found that they were up against someone tough now when they tackled Cyril, someone sturdy and hard as nails. He began to delight in his strength, and no longer sneered at Jack when he grew enthusiastic over the school matches. In fact, he and Jack had animated discussions about teams and method of play, much to the quiet amusement of Mrs Longfield.

Melisande was enjoying herself too, although she was still a form below Jane. Her class were doing a play that term, and Melisande knew she was good at acting. She hoped against hope that she would be chosen as the Princess of Granada in the play, and pictured herself in crown and flowing robes, holding the centre of the stage.

But her hopes were not fulfilled, partly because the teacher had come up against Melisande's vanity the term before, and was determined not to let the girl show off too much. Instead, she gave Melisande a small character part, in which she had to make herself up as a comical old woman.

Melisande was disappointed and angry at first, but soon saw possibilities in the part, and put it across well. She was also excellent at the dresses and scenery, having a natural flair for decoration and colour. She enjoyed herself thoroughly, and looked so happy and excited when she was telling the others about her play that her aunt was quite astonished.

"Why, Melisande," she said, "you sound as if you like

school after all! You couldn't bear the idea of going last term."

"Wouldn't you prefer a private governess again?" asked Jane, grinning.

"Heavens, no!" said Melisande at once. "To have lessons all by myself – never share a thing – never get kicked under the desk – never get ticked off for whispering – not have all the fun of this play! I couldn't bear it. I only wish I'd gone to school all my life now. To think I'll have only two more years of it! How wasted my life has been!"

She put on such a comical expression that everyone laughed. Susan put out her hand and touched Melisande lightly.

"You're different," she said. "I don't want you to go away after all, Melisande. I like you here."

Melisande was touched. She didn't say anything, and the moment passed. But Melisande didn't forget. Because of Susan's words, she suddenly seemed to belong to Mistletoe Farm, and Three Towers seemed to be gone for ever. It was odd, Melisande thought, but she liked the warm feeling it gave her.

Jane, too, was getting on much better at school, because she was having fewer order marks for untidiness and carelessness. Everyone had been amazed to see her at first, looking so unlike herself.

"Gosh! You look quite passable!" Patricia, the head girl of the form, had said to her, and this was praise indeed. "It looks as if we shan't suffer too much from your long list of order marks this term."

"Don't talk too soon," Pam had said. "This may be a flash in the pan! Tomorrow Jane will have a button off her shoe, she'll have lost her hair-grips, and her hands will be all over ink!"

Jane grinned. She never minded being teased by the girls. She loked proudly down at her hands when she held them under the desk in class. Only one nail bitten now! The others were all long and, to her surprise, as shapely as Melisande's. Well, it would be a good thing for her class if she didn't get as many order marks as she usually did! However popular she was, it wasn't fair to the class to load them with bad marks and expect them not to mind.

The term sped on into October. The weather was fine and warm. Work on the farm went on well. Mr Longfield had had his corn threshed already, and was very proud of the good yield.

"We've actually got money in hand!" he told his wife. "And when I've sold the young heifers, I shall be quite a rich man!"

"I hope your brother David will do as well," said his wife. "We haven't had a letter lately. As for Rose, except for her weekly letter to her children, we never hear a word. It's extraordinary that she doesn't even *ask* to come and see them."

"Her day here was too much for her!" said Mr Longfield, smiling as he remembered it. "Well, there's one thing; she's at least somewhere near David now, and will be seeing him sometimes. She won't like living in Scotland though, so far away from all her friends, if he takes a farm there."

"I shall be quite sorry to lose the children," said Mrs Longfield, taking up a stocking of Cyril's to darn. "They really have improved since they came, Peter."

"So have ours," said her husband. "They've all changed, you know."

"Except Susan," said Mrs Longfield. "I don't really think she's changed a bit. She's so very much herself, isn't she?"

"I don't know that I want Sue to change," said Mr Longfield. "She says awkward things at times, but she's so honest and straight forward that we oughtn't to mind! Will you really be sorry when the other three children have gone, Linnie? It's been such a lot of extra work for you and Dorcas."

"I shall miss them," said his wife. "I wish they were not going so far away, because they will miss us, too, Peter!"

Susan came in with Crackers at her heels. "Twigg's outside," she said. "He's got a message for Jack. Where *is* Jack?"

"I've told Twigg he's to keep off my land!" began Mr Longfield, rising up in rage. "If I catch him here, I'll . . ."

"He's gone," said Susan, looking out of the window. "There he goes, look! I wish you wouldn't chase him away, Daddy. I like him."

Mr Longfield sat down again when he had watched Twigg out of sight. He took up his paper and forgot all about Twigg. Susan wandered out with Crackers to find Roderick.

Jack was some way away, beside the old barn. Susan went over to him. "Twigg was here, looking for you," she said.

"I know," said Jack.

"Did he give you his message?" asked Susan.

Jack nodded. He turned away, but Susan followed him.

"What was the message?" she asked, filled with curiosity.

"Nothing much," said Jack. "Stop asking questions, Susan. You hardly ever open your mouth without asking a question."

"Don't I really?" said Susan with interest. "Are you sure? Oh, that's another question, isn't it? And so is that!"

Jack made an impatient noise and left her. He had had Twigg's message all right. Twigg had told him about the badgers, and said that soon there would be a cold spell and the little bear-like animals would hibernate for the winter. He was going out on Thursday night; if Jack liked to come with him, he'd have a chance of seeing the badgers in the moonlight.

Jack had listened in silence, looking uneasily around in case his father should see him talking to Twigg. He knew he should have told Twigg to go, but he couldn't. After all, the old fellow had come with a kindly message.

"Will you come tonight, then, Mr Jack?" Twigg had asked, surprised at the boy's silence.

"I don't think so," Jack had answered. "My father's making things awkward for me to come with you, Twigg. I'm sorry about it, but it's not my fault."

"That's all right, lad," said Twigg. "I seem to a' got a lot of enemies lately. Well, if you don't come, you don't. It's your last chance of seeing them badgers, that's all. Meet me same place, same time, if you want to."

He went off, and Jack stared after him. He knew that everyone was saying old Twigg and Tommy Lane were robbing here and there, and sooner or later it seemed likely that both the old poachers would be taken off by P.C. Potts. That would be the end of all the little trips and excursions for always.

He met the postman as he turned to go to the house, and took the letter from him. There was one for his father and two for his mother. He took them in.

It was getting dark. Jack went to wash, and then joined his family in the big sitting-room. His mother had just lighted the oil lamp, and its yellow glow was spreading over the room.

"Thank you, Linnie," said his father, and opened his letter to read. Jack took his homework and sat down to do it. Cyril was finishing his. Jane and Melisande were arguing about something at school, and Susan and Roderick were playing one of their everlasting games of draughts, with Crackers watching as intently as if he knew how to play himself. Susan always said that if he could use his paws properly and move the pieces, he really would be able to play, but only Roderick believed this tall tale!

There was an exclamation from Mr Longfield. Everyone looked up. Jane and Melisande stopped arguing.

"What is it, dear?" asked Mrs Longfield, putting down her mending.

"Listen to this," said her husband. "You know Holly Farm?"

"Yes, of course," said his wife. "Dear little place, about four miles from here. Rather like ours, but much smaller. What about it?"

"It's on the market," said Mr Longfield. "First time for years! Roker owns it, you know. And this is a letter from him. He wants to know if I want it."

"Want it? Why ever should you want Holly Farm?" said his wife, astonished. "You've got your own good farm, Peter."

160

"Yes. But think of Holly Farmhouse!" said her husband. "You've seen it, dear – a trim little place, with electric lights, water laid on, good drainage system – very modern and labour saving!"

His wife thought about it, and so did all the children. Susan cried out in alarm. "Daddy! You wouldn't leave Mistletoe Farm, would you? You don't mean *that*, do you?"

"Well, that's just what I did mean," said her father. "Think what hard work it is here for your mother and Dorcas: all the oil lamps to clean and fill, that great kitchen floor to scrub, no water from taps except the cold one in the bathroom and one downstairs, no gas to cook with! I've heard your mother groan hundreds of times about those things."

Jane, Jack and Susan looked at their mother with faces full of fear at the thought of leaving their home. "Mummy," said Jane in a trembling voice, "you won't say yes, will you? We do so love Mistletoe Farm. We know – we know every single corner of the farm."

Then Jack turned reproachfully to his father. "Dad! How can you think of it? You've often told me how your father lived here, and your grandfather was born here, and how *his* father built the L-wing of the house. Dad, how *can* you want to leave? I did think it would be my home for always."

"I don't want to leave Mistletoe Farm," said his father. "But your mother has to carry a heavy load here because it's so old-fashioned. Maybe in a few years' time we'll get the electricity and things will be fine, but here's this trim little Holly Farm going, and we've got the first chance of taking it!"

"Well, it's up to Mother then," said Jack soberly. "It's quite true what you say, Dad. It's hard work here for Mother, and since Dorcas hasn't been very well it's been harder still."

All eyes were now turned on Mrs Longfield. She had put down her mending and was looking round at her family. Even Melisande, Cyril and Roderick hung on her words.

"I can't decide all at once," she said. "Have we got to say yes or no immediately, Peter? And even if I said yes, we couldn't go at once, because Holly Farmhouse is smaller than Mistletoe Farmhouse, and there wouldn't be room for Melisande, Cyril and Roderick. We can't turn the poor children out when they have no home of their own!"

This was a most alarming thought, and the three cousins looked at each other in consternation. Their aunt smiled at them. "Don't look so upset! I wouldn't do that to you. You know that. But, oh dear, Peter – Holly Farm is so small and so modern, and so easy to run. What a temptation it is, to be sure!"

"To think of leaving the pond and the goldfish, and the fruit trees and the old quinces, and the tumbledown barn and the dairy," said Susan in such a mournful voice that her mother laughed.

"It wouldn't be as bad as what happened to *us*," said Melisande. "*Our* house was all burnt down, and we *had* to leave it behind, in ruins."

"Yes, but you were lucky. You came *here*," said Susan. "This is miles and miles better than Three Towers!"

"Well, Linnie," said her husband, folding up the letter, "we've got a week to think it over. Don't hurry yourself. You shall choose. I don't want you to think of anyone but yourself, of any wishes but your own. You've worked and cared for us all these years, and now, if you feel you would like an easier place to run, then you shall have it! You'll deserve it, Linnie!"

CHAPTER TWENTY-TWO

A Night with Twigg

Jack couldn't get to sleep that night for thinking about Holly Farm. He couldn't bear the thought that he might have to leave Mistletoe Farm. He loved it very much, and had always thought that it would be his.

"It's in my very bones," thought the boy, turning restlessly over and over. "Why, there's still the mistletoe growing on the old oak trees in Top Field that gave the farm its name a hundred and fifty years ago. Dad would never be happy at Holly Farm. Nor would I. Yet Mother does deserve something easier."

Cyril sat up and spoke to him. "For goodness sake, Jack! You'll keep me awake all night long. What's the matter?"

"I'm worrying about the farm," said Jack, and gave his pillow a vicious thump.

"Well, don't. Your mother's going to settle the matter, and I could quite well tell you what she's going to say, though she doesn't know herself yet," said Cyril surprisingly.

"Women think such a lot of things like electric light and gas cookers," groaned Jack. "Oh, blow! I shall never get to sleep!"

"Well, get up and go for a night walk, like Benedict does when he can't sleep," said Cyril. "For goodness sake, let *me* get to sleep."

"Right. I'll get up," said Jack, suddenly remembering Twigg's message. He'd slide down the quince and go and meet Twigg! He'd see the badgers, tire himself out and come back and sleep like a top!

He knew his father had forbidden him to have anything to do with Twigg, but just then Jack did not feel inclined to respect his wishes at all. He felt angry with his father for even suggesting that they might go to Holly Farm. He dressed and got out of the window.

163

"I'm going down the quince," he informed Cyril, who was still awake.

"You needn't tell me that. I've watched you before!" said Cyril, much to Jack's surprise. "It's all right. I've never split on you, idiot. I guessed you were out with Twigg, though why you want to make friends with that disreputable old poacher I really don't know."

"He's a jolly sight better than your fraud of a hermit!" retorted Jack. "Silly old poser, he is!"

He disappeared into the night. Cyril settled down to sleep with a contented grunt. No one heard Jack sliding down the quince except Crackers, who raised his head, sniffed, smelt a whiff of Jack, and put his head down again, satisfied.

Jack made his way to where he was to meet Twigg. He was there, alone. "Sssst!" he said. "This way!"

He led Jack through the wood, out again and into another little wood, where, in the spring, the primroses blossomed by the thousand. "Now go quiet!" he whispered, his hand on Jack's arm. Mr Potts, who was at Twigg's heels, sniffed delicately and gave a tiny whine.

"He's smelt them," whispered Twigg. "We're all right with the wind: it's blowing to us not from us. The badgers can't wind us. Stay quiet now."

But the badgers didn't appear, though Mr Potts could quite plainly smell them.

"They'll be in their sett," whispered Twigg. "We'll sit down here and wait."

A bat skimmed against Jack's head, and he jumped. Night moths appeared in the moonlight. A rabbit leapt so close to Mr Potts' nose that he started in surprise, but with very great self-restraint did not pounce after the rabbit.

Jack began to whisper to Twigg, telling him about Holly Farm. It was a comfort to pour it all out to someone. Twigg listened in silence.

"That's a toy farm, is Holly Farm," he said when Jack had finished. "Mistletoe Farm now, that's a real proper, set-up farm. Your grandad and his grandad, too, farmed it. It's got Longfield's blood and bones in it, so it has, just as it's in your blood and bones. Don't you leave it, Mr Jack."

Jack sat silent for a long time. He and Twigg thought about many many things. Then there came a tiny movement from Mr Potts, and Twigg's sharp eyes looked towards the badger bank. He gave Jack a nudge.

"Sssst!" he said, very softly. And Jack saw the three badgers, their black-and-white streaked faces moving here and there in the moonlight, difficult to see at times, but there all right!

Mr Potts might not have been there, he was so still. He really was a marvellous dog, Jack thought. He was certain that Crackers would never keep so still. The badgers moved about, sniffing. Then they seemed to have a little conference together, and one of them went off.

The other two began scraping in the ditch nearby. "Mebbe they're getting moss and leaves to prepare their winter den," whispered Twigg, right in Jack's ear. "It's getting near the time they go underground for the winter."

The third badger came back after a time and there seemed to be another conference, accompanied by a few low gruntings. Then the biggest badger, raising his black-streaked face in the moonlight, sniffed the air suspiciously – and immediately all three badgers slid through the bushes and were gone!

"They winded us at last," said Twigg regretfully. "Well, we got a good view of them. Funny critters they be; keeps themselves to themselves. And clean! You should see the way they take their bedding out to air when they wake up from their winter sleep!"

Jack gave a little laugh, though he did not feel like laughing. The little interlude with the badgers had taken his thoughts away from his own worry about losing Mistletoe Farm, but now it came back and gnawed at his tired mind.

"You're proper down in the mouth tonight, Mr Jack," said Twigg, sympathetically. "You go back home and have a right good sleep. Best thing to face worries on, a good night's sleep!"

"I shan't sleep," said Jack, gloomily. "I know I shan't. What are *you* going to do, Twigg?"

"Well, I was going home," said Twigg. "But what about a good sharp walk, Mr Jack? That'll tire you out, and I'm always one for the night-time. Nice and quiet, and not too many people about. Come on. It's a fine night, and you can say what you like to old Twigg. He don't split on anyone!"

"Good old Twigg!" thought Jack. He fell into step beside him, with Mr Potts nosing at their heels as usual. Jack no longer felt like talking, so Twigg talked. He told Jack that his father and grandfather and great-grandfather Twigg had lived in the district, too, and how they had worked for the Longfields and known them all.

"And I used to hear my grandad say that he and your great-grandfather used to cut the mistletoe from the oak trees to take to the farmhouse each Christmas," said Twigg. "Ah, I'd be sorry too, to see the Longfields leave Mistletoe Farm. Pity your father can't run the two farms, lad."

"That wouldn't be much good, Twigg, if we went to live at Holly Farm," said Jack. "I don't want to *leave* Mistletoe Farm, even if it still belonged to us. Oh, why did Mr Roker write and tell Dad he could have first chance of buying Holly Farm?"

"Mr Roker's a rich man now, I reckon," said Twigg, considering. "Done well the last six years, he have. And his things always fetch the highest price at the market. I were there today, and his colts went for the highest price I ever did know colts to fetch. Course, their sire was a champion all right, and . . ."

So Twigg went on, talking away, doing his best to talk Jack out of his black mood. For two hours they walked over the moonlit countryside, Twigg's eyes always on the watch for any sound or movement, and Mr Potts hoping for a halt, so that he might put his nose down a rabbit-hole.

Jack was tired out at last. He said good night to Twigg gratefully. "You're a good friend, Twigg," he said. "I'm

166

sorry Dad won't let you on his land now. He doesn't know you as well as I do!"

"Mebbe he knows me better!" said the old poacher with a grin that showed his teeth in the moonlight. "S'long, Mr Jack! My! There's three o'clock striking!"

The strokes of the church clock came clearly through the still air. Three o'clock! Jack yawned widely, and turned to go home. Over the farm, through the yard and up the quince. Cyril didn't stir. He was fast asleep and dreaming.

Jack tossed a few times, and then fell asleep suddenly. He awoke when he heard Cyril getting up. "Blow! Is it time to get up?" he said, sleepily.

"Yes. It jolly well is," said Cyril. "I'm late too. Come on, we'll never get our jobs done before we go off to school. All right, Crackers. We're coming! Thanks for waking me!"

Crackers always came to wake the boys if he thought they were late in stirring. He would put his paws up on Jack's bed or Cyril's, and solemnly lick their noses till they opened their eyes.

The boys raced through their jobs, gobbled down their breakfast and set off for school. Jack had to get Darkie, and Cyril ran for the bus. There wasn't a moment to spare. The others were not so late, and had a more leisurely time.

Jack had an errand to do for his father in the town after school that afternoon, and he was late in getting home. Susan was waiting for him with Roderick, their faces full of gloom. "There he is!" cried Susan, and rushed to meet Darkie and Jack.

"What is it?" asked Jack. "Anything wrong with old Crackers? You look very solemn. Oh, no. Here's Crackers. Hello, old fellow!"

"Jack! Something awful's happened!" said Susan.

"What?" asked Jack, lifting off Darkie's saddle.

"Twigg's in prison," said Susan, and she began to cry.

Jack stared at her in alarm and dismay. "What do you mean? What's he in prison for? Stop crying and tell me."

167

Roderick told him. "Last night Mr Roker's money was taken – the money he got at the market for his colts."

Jack stood as if he was turned to stone. He was thinking rapidly. "What time? Do they know when?"

"Yes. Mr Roker heard his dogs barking at half-past one, he says. And when he went down, he found his safe opened, and his money gone. They think the thief climbed up a gutter-pipe and got in at an upstairs window," said Roderick.

"Half-past one!" said Jack, with relief. Then it *couldn't* have been Twigg! Thank goodness for that! *He* was with Twigg at half-past one, walking through the countryside, listening to the old poacher talking.

Another thought struck him. "But why was Twigg arrested? he asked. "It wasn't Twigg who stole the money. I know that. What right had P.C. Potts to take him to prison?"

"Somebody saw Twigg near Holly Farm at just past one o'clock," said Susan, wiping her eyes on her sleeve.

"*Who* saw him?" asked Jack, disbelievingly.

"I don't know," said Susan. "Anyway, Twigg was out of his cottage again last night, they say. And, what's more, there was someone *with* Twigg, and they say it was Tommy Lane."

Jack was astounded. Neither he nor Twigg had been anywhere within miles of Holly Farm! How could anyone possibly say that Twigg had been there at one o'clock – with somebody who was thought to be Tommy Lane?

He was half inclined to burst out then and there to the two upset children, and tell them that *he* had been with Twigg all the time, and that they hadn't been near Holly Farm. But he didn't. A little core of fear crept into his mind. Twigg had actually been arrested. Suppose – just suppose – he, Jack, got into trouble too, for being with Twigg at a time when the old poacher was supposed to be robbing Holly Farm? Suppose nobody believed him? Suppose they even thought he might have been engaged in the robbery too!

Feeling rather sick, Jack rubbed Darkie down and then

went in to high tea. He didn't feel as if he could eat anything at all, but he forced himself to, in case his mother drew attention to him. What bad luck that once again he should have been out with Twigg on the night of a robbery!

His father looked up from his paper, and noticed Jack sitting silently eating. He knew that Jack liked Twigg, and that the boy would be upset at the news of his arrest, "Pity about Twigg," he said. "I knew he'd get caught sooner or later. He should have stuck to poaching! Now you see how wise I was, Jack, to forbid you absolutely to have anything more to do with Twigg! Suppose you'd been out with him last night! You would be involved in this horrible affair too."

Jack almost choked. He couldn't swallow his mouthful of ham at all. He wanted to shout out that he *had* been with Twigg, and that the old poacher hadn't been *near* Holly Farm, and wasn't a thief. But he was afraid to; and, besides, he wanted to think everything out for himself. He wished he knew if Twigg had said that he, Jack, was with him last night. That would let Twigg out at once – if he was believed.

"Do you know who saw Twigg near Holly Farm last night, Daddy?" asked Jane.

"Oh, yes. It was that friend of Cyril's – what's his name – fellow I can't stand the sight of – Ben something," said her father.

"Benedict," said Jane.

"Yes. Apparently he was on one of his usual nightly prowls, and spotted Twigg and somebody else, hiding near the barn round by Holly Farm," said Mr Longfield.

"Has Tommy Lane been taken off by P.C. Potts, too?" asked Jane.

"No. This fellow Benedict apparently only recognized Twigg for certain," said her father. "But if it *was* Tommy, he'll soon be in prison with Twigg."

Jack felt a surge of anger towards Benedict. What lies! How dare he say things like that? He probably saw two figures hiding, and thought he recognized one of them as

169

Twigg, and because of that, poor old Twigg, who was perfectly innocent, was in prison. The thing was: supposing Jack came out now with his proof that Twigg was innocent and said why, would his word be taken against Benedict's? And if Benedict was believed, would Jack be hauled off to prison, too, for admitting that he was with Twigg, and therefore might have been involved in the robbery?

He left his tea and got up abruptly. He went out into the dusk of the evening. A dark figure detached itself from a thick bush and came towards him.

"Ssss!" said the figure and Jack jumped, thinking for a moment it must be Twigg who had somehow escaped from prison. But it wasn't. It was Tommy Lane, Twigg's old and most disreputable friend.

"It's me, Tommy Lane," said the figure. "I've seen Twigg today. He's sent me with a message. You're to keep your mouth shut about last night. He ain't said nothink about you being with him, and you're not to either."

"Yes, but, Tommy – I can clear him," said Jack. "If only people would believe me!"

"You might get into trouble, Twigg says," said Tommy. "And you're but a young lad yet. You don't want to get a bad name, do you? You got your Ma and Pa to think of."

"But – Twigg's in prison, and he'll stay there unless I can make people believe he wasn't anywhere near Holly Farm last night," stammered Jack.

"Yes. He'll stay there all right," said Tommy. "But he says, not to worry. He'll make out all right. But he says you and me's got to look into this. We've got to find the right thief! If that fellow what's-his-name saw somebody round Holly Farm last night, that's the one we're after!"

"Yes. I'd be very glad to snoop round and see if I can find out anything," said Jack, thinking with relief that it would be something to do. "When can we go and have a look round, Tommy?"

"It's Saturday tomorrow," said Tommy. "You and me'll go along then. Now don't you say nothing to anyone! Good night!"

CHAPTER TWENTY-THREE

A Little Detective Work

Cyril said very little to Jack that evening. He knew that Jack had been out with Twigg, and he saw how worried his cousin was over the whole affair. He wondered if Jack would say anything to his father about his being out with Twigg, and was rather surprised that he didn't.

When they were in bed that night Jack spoke to Cyril. "That beastly friend of yours was lying when he said Twigg was anywhere near Holly Farm last night. He wasn't. I was with him till three o'clock. We heard the church clock strike, and we were neither of us anywhere near Holly Farm at any time."

"Why don't you tell your father that, then?" asked Cyril, reasonably enough.

"Because I'm jolly well going to find out who's at the bottom of all this." said Jack. "And let me tell you this: I don't think much of that Benedict for swearing he saw Twigg when he didn't. Whoever he saw, it wasn't Twigg. He's a real rotter, that friend of yours – swearing a man into prison without being dead certain."

"He *is* dead certain," said Cyril. "He's met Twigg plenty of times. He told me today he knows it was Twigg. And somebody else he couldn't see."

"But how *could* it be Twigg if I was with him, miles away, at the time?" said Jack, beginning to talk loudly in his anger.

"Sh! You'll have your father up here," said Cyril sharply. "I do hope, Jack, you weren't the person who was with Twigg near Holy Farm! If you and Twigg weren't anywhere near, I can't think why you don't tell what you know, and get Twigg out of prison."

"Because it would be my word against Benedict's, and a grown-up's word would be taken against mine any day!" said Jack, still loudly. "And I've told you: I'm going to go into all this and see what I can find out. And it'll make your fine friend feel pretty foolish when he has to eat his words and admit it wasn't Twigg he saw!"

"Benedict wouldn't lie," said Cyril. "He despises that kind of thing. You haven't the least idea what a cultured and – and – unworldly sort of fellow he is, Jack. I wish you wouldn't talk like that. I'm pretty certain it *was* Twigg he saw last night. I believe you're just trying to shield the old poacher when you say you were with him all the time and didn't go near Holly Farm."

Jack felt such a surge of anger that he wanted to hit Cyril. He clenched his fists and lay still, trying to overcome his rage. It was no good starting a fight in the bedroom. It would only bring everyone up, and then things would have to come out.

Cyril sensed Jack's fury. He was honestly sorry for Jack in his worry, though he only half-believed his story, and felt certain in his mind that Jack was shielding Twigg.

"I'll come with you tomorrow, and we'll see if we can discover anything that will help," he said at last.

Jack's anger went, and he relaxed. "All right," he said. "Thanks. Tommy Lane is coming along too. We'll take Crackers as well. He might be a help in sniffing about."

So, the next morning, Jack set out on Darkie, and Cyril on Merrylegs, lent to him by Jane. Crackers ran beside them. Tommy Lane was to meet them at the group of holly trees outside Holly Farm, at the corner of the lane there.

He was there, looking more bent and shrivelled up than ever, and smelling very strongly of fish. Obviously he had had fish in those baggy pockets of his not very long since! He touched his cap.

"Morning, misters. You going along to ask permission to look around a bit first? Don't want no trouble from the farm dogs, do us? Nor from Mr Roker neither."

Mr Roker came up himself at that moment with his two fine dogs, a dapper little farmer in highly polished leather gaiters and tweed suit. "Morning!" he said. "Come to have a look round Holly Farm, Jack, my lad? Haven't

He was there . . .

heard from your father about it yet. I hope he'll get it.
Fine little farm, you know – and a farmhouse that's the
envy of all the women round!"

"My mother's going to do the deciding, yes or no, sir,"
said Jack. "May I look round? Thank you. And – er – I'm
sorry to hear you had a robbery the other night. Where do
you think the thief got in?"

"See that window there?" said the farmer, pointing with
his stock-whip to a small window on the first floor. "That's
the only window that was left open that night, so we
reckon the thief must have got in there. All the doors were

locked as usual. I don't doubt it was Twigg – though he must be pretty nippy to swarm up that old gutter-pipe!"

Tommy Lane had melted away at the farmer's approach, but as soon as he had gone striding up the lane, he appeared again. "He's taken his dogs with him," he said in satisfaction. "Come on, lads."

The boys tied up their ponies and went into the farmyard. It was spick and span, and every shed and barn was well-roofed, well-kept and neat. The farmhouse had been recently whitewashed, and looked very attractive.

"It's like a model toy farm," said Jack to Cyril. "It's not real!"

"I must say I like it," said Cyril. "I don't like having to wade through all the muck at Mistletoe Farm. I don't see why farms can't all be kept like this. And that farmhouse would be jolly easy to run – not like the old house you have, all rambling and wanting painting and mending, too big for anything!"

"You haven't lived there all your life as I have," said Jack, feeling fierce. "It isn't in your bones as it is in mine. You're a townsman. You simply don't understand."

"Right. I don't," said Cyril. "Come on, Crackers. Do a little snooping for us!"

They went all round the farmhouse. Tommy Lane traipsing behind, his washed-out little eyes missing nothing.

They came to the flower bed below the first floor window. Jack and Tommy looked at the ground carefully there. There was no sign of the earth being disturbed at all.

"Doesn't look as if the thief even *trod* on the soil," said Jack, surprised. "But he must have done to get to that gutter-pipe."

"Well, he didn't," said Tommy. He pointed to the bed. "Get to it, Crackers," he commanded. "Anything there?"

Crackers sniffed all round obligingly, but found nothing interesting at all. He wagged his tail and looked up inquiringly at the others, as if to say, "Well, what next?"

"It's queer," said Cyril. "It really doesn't look as if this is the way the thief got in."

"Well, it's not the way Sam Twigg would use, I do know

that," said Tommy Lane. "He's that rheumaticky in his shoulders, he couldn't shin up a pipe, you take my word for it."

"Then he must have got in somewhere else," said Cyril, and Jack scowled. He knew perfectly well that Twigg hadn't got in anywhere!

They went slowly round the trim little farmhouse. They came to the dairy. The door was open, and Mrs Roker was there, making butter.

"Well, boys," she said, "come to see if you like Holly Farm enough to take it?"

Jack smiled politely. "Mother's doing the deciding," he said. "At the moment Cyril and I are just trying to make out where the thief got in the other night."

"I wish you could get back the money!" said Mrs Roker. "I hear that Twigg's cottage and garden have been searched, but nothing has been found!"

Tommy Lane had again made himself scarce. He had hidden behind a bush that jutted out alongside the dairy wall. It was very thick, but rather prickly, because it was holly.

Mrs Roker chatted away to the boys. "I say the thief must have gone into my dairy," she said. "And helped himself to some of my cream! What's more, a bowl of it was knocked over. Mr Roker says it was Sally the cat, but she couldn't get in, because I'd shut the door leading into the house, as I always do."

A bell rang somewhere. "That's the telephone," said Mrs Roker. "Excuse me a minute!"

She went off to answer the telephone. From out-of-doors a familiar noise came to the boys' ears: "Ssssst!"

It was Tommy. His wizened face peered out from behind the big holly bush. He beckoned. The two boys went to him. He pointed silently down to the earth in which the holly tree grew.

Someone had been standing there – someone with large-sized feet! "Them's not my prints," said Tommy, looking excited. "See. These are mine. I got feet as small as Twigg's. I reckon someone was hiding here the night afore last. Yes, and it was him what got into the dairy and upset the cream, too!"

Crackers was also very interested in the large footprints. He snuffed at them and then tried to paw them over, but the boys stopped him quickly. They might be a very valuable clue. Jack pointed to one very clearly marked print.

"Look at that! It's a curious kind of print – not shaped like mine or Tommy's at all – very broad and flat. It's – it's like a *sandal* footprint!"

It was. Silently Jack bent down, measured it from end to end, and wrote down the length. Then he made a rough drawing of it and put it away in his notebook.

"Looks as if the thief waited here till the coast was clear, and got into the dairy," he said to Tommy. "He couldn't get into the dairy windows; they're too small. He must have gone in through the door."

Mrs Roker still hadn't come back. The boys, Tommy and Crackers went into the spotless dairy. They looked round for some place there in which a man could hide. There was a cupboard at the far end. Jack went over to it.

He opened it and peered inside. It was full of old junk – a broken churn, an old chair, some pails and a pile of what looked like old curtains.

"He could have hidden in here," said Jack. "Under those curtains!"

He went into the cupboard and looked around. He remembered that he had a small torch in his pocket, and he switched it on.

It did look as if someone had disturbed the old curtains, for some of them were disarranged out of their pile. Jack's torch travelled round the cupboard. He was about to switch it off when he saw something that was caught on a broken piece of the churn. He pulled it off, and took it into the dairy.

It was a bit of white stuff – probably a piece of torn curtain. Crackers suddenly sniffed at it and gave a little whine. He recognized the smell it had.

Jack looked down at it. Where had he seen stuff like

this before? Yes, of course: it was the same material as the hermit wore! It was! It was!

His face grew red at the thoughts that came pouring into his mind. That big sandal-print behind the holly bush, this bit of torn cloth, Benedict's lie about Twigg, his nightly prowls, his attendance at the markets and his knowledge of the sales that went on there – could there *possibly* be anything in all this? He turned to tell his thoughts to Cyril, and then stopped.

Cyril would deny everything strenuously. His quick wits would find ways out. He would do his best to muddle Jack, and he might warn Benedict. Better not to say anything.

The boy turned to look round the dairy again. He saw that bowls of cream were arranged on a low table near the cupboard, and others round the walls on shelves. He wondered which had been upset the other night. Mrs Roker came back at that moment, and he asked her.

"One on that table near the cupboard over there," she said, pointing. "Just as if someone had knocked into it, given it a good shake, and upset the cream. Splashed all over the floor it was!"

"Did you lock the dairy door the other night, Mrs Roker?" asked Jack.

"Oh, yes. I always lock it myself," said Mrs Roker.

"Was it still locked when you came to the dairy next day?" went on Jack.

"Yes. But the key had fallen out of the lock on to the stone floor," said Mrs Roker. "Why all these questions, Jack? No thief could walk through a locked door!"

"I know," said Jack, and he began to reconstruct everything slowly in his mind. The thief had hidden behind the holly bush till he could slip into the open dairy door unseen. He had gone to the cupboard to hide. In the night he had crept out, forgotten the table carrying the bowls of cream and bumped into one of them. He had then gone through the house to get the money out of the locked safe – must have had a skeleton key or something – and then escaped through the dairy door by the simple process of

177

unlocking it, taking the key out, going out of the door, locking it from the outside, and then pushing the key under the door to look as if it had dropped from the lock the other side!

There was a wide space between the bottom of the door and the floor, quite big enough to push the key through. Very clever! Jack was quite sure that was how the robbery had been committed. No wonder there were no marks on the earth under the landing window. The thief hadn't used that window at all, or the gutter-pipe either!

There didn't seem much more to be found at Holly Farm. The boys said goodbye to Mrs Roker and went. They were joined by Tommy Lane outside in the yard. He had disappeared again when Mrs Roker had come back.

"Where are we going?" asked Cyril as they made their way to their horses. "Back home?"

"No, " said Jack. "I'm not. You go home, though. I've got somewhere else to go."

"Where?" asked Cyril in a strained voice. He looked pale.

"Never mind," said Jack, and mounted Darkie.

"Jack, I know where you're going," said Cyril. "You're going to Benedict, aren't you? I know what you're thinking, but you're wrong! It's unthinkable that he should have anything to do with it. That bit of cloth might be from anything – and other people wear sandals too!"

"Yes. That's why I'm going up to the cave," said Jack. "If the piece of stuff doesn't match Benedict's robe and his sandals don't fit the drawing I've got of the print, then it's all right. But don't forget that he told a deliberate lie about Twigg, Cyril. Don't forget that! There's a much, much stronger case against Benedict than there ever was against poor old Twigg!"

Tommy Lane was listening to all this in amazement. He called out sharply as Jack swung Darkie round, ready to go off. "Hey! I'm coming too! Let me up behind you. My weight won't hurt Darkie. This is my business as much as yours. I'm coming too!"

CHAPTER TWENTY-FOUR

The Real Thief at Last

Jack let the old fellow clamber up behind. The more the better perhaps! Benedict might turn nasty, and Cyril might be no help at all. He glanced at his cousin, and was surprised to see his face so pale and pinched.

They rode off to Long-Acre Hill. They dismounted at a clump of trees near the cave where Benedict lived, and tied up the horses. Then the three of them went on foot to the cave.

"Call him," said Jack to Cyril.

Cyril called, in rather a shaky voice. Nobody came out. He called again. Still nobody came.

The boys and Tommy Lane walked to the cave entrance and looked in. The cave stretched back, dark and not very inviting. It might be all right in the summer months, but it was certainly not very pleasant now that the weather was getting colder!

Jack switched on his little torch and looked round the place. It was curiously tidy and bare. The rugs had gone from the shelf that served the hermit as a bed. A few books were piled up untidily, and some pieces of crockery still stood on the shelf. Rolled up in a corner was the hermit's white gown.

"He's gone," said Jack.

"He can't have," said Cyril. "He would have told me he was going. He would never have gone without saying goodbye and giving me his address!"

"Maybe he didn't want to leave an address," said Tommy Lane drily.

Jack went over to the gown and unrolled it. It was dirty. The boy shook it out. Just below the waist there was a hole – a rough, torn place. Jack silently fitted in the little bit of white material he had taken from the broken churn in the dairy cupboard. It was quite plain that it had come from that very robe, and that very place.

179

Cyril was now quite white, and looked shaken and scared. Jack felt sorry for his cousin. He tossed the gown away, and looked round to see if the hermit's sandals were anywhere about.

He found them at the back of the cave and turned one upside down. He took out his sketch and compared the measurements. The sandal fitted them exactly.

"It's no good, Cyril," he said. "It was Benedict. You might as well face it."

Cyril turned away, feeling sick. A cry came from Tommy Lane, who was doing a little exploring of his own. "Hey! There's a place back here – kind of little cave."

They went to him. He had crawled into a tiny place, not really a cave, but more like a big hole, and was feeling all round.

He gave another shout. "There's a hole leads out of it – and there's rubbish stuffed here. Wait till I throw it out."

He dragged it out at last. It was strange rubbish! There wer two battered cash-boxes, and three battered deed-boxes. Evidently money and notes had been in these, locked up, and had been got out by bursting open the metal boxes. Tommy pulled out a couple of leather wallets too, and one or two canvas bags such as are used by banks when they put a large amount of silver together to be used as wages.

Jack whistled. "My word! This settles it all right. We'd better go to the police – or, better still, bring my father here!"

Cyril said nothing at all. He was very shaken, and his mind was full of horror. To think that a man he had liked so much, and trusted, and believed in, should turn out to be a thief, a common burglar. One who had had no hesitation in getting poor Twigg put into prison for something he himself had done!

"I'll walk home," Cyril said in a trembling voice. "Tommy can ride on Merrylegs."

Jack nodded to Tommy, who mounted Merrylegs at once. They went off round the hill.

"He's hard hit, isn't he?" said Tommy. "Friends,

weren't they? Now, if your Pa had ordered *that* fellow off his land 'twould have made more sense than sending off Sam Twigg. Folks is queer."

Mr Longfield could hardly believe Jack's tale when he told him. Tommy Lane went too, and sat by Jack, nodding and saying "Ah!" to back Jack up whenever he could.

"This is a most extraordinary tale," said Mr Longfield when he at last grasped it all. "Why on earth didn't you tell me you were out with Twigg on Thursday night and could vouch for him? Surely the fact that you had deliberately disobeyed me didn't scare you enough to prevent you from owning up at once? And Twigg never said a word about you either! Now why was that?"

Tommy spoke up. "He said Mr Jack here was only a young lad, and he didn't want him to get a bad name on account of being with him that night, Mr Longfield, sir. Sam Twigg's right fond of your boy. He wouldn't do him no harm for worlds. He'd a long sight rather go to prison."

Mr Longfield sat silent, thinking of how he had forbidden Twigg to set foot on his land. He'd have to make it up to him! Twigg was a puzzle. He was a bad character – and he was a good character too. What were you to do with a man like that?

"We'll have to get going," he said, standing up. "First, Twigg must be set free. Then the police must get after this Benedict. They'll have to get in touch with Scotland Yard and find out the man's history. I've no doubt he's got quite an interesting one, as far as the police are concerned."

"Cyril's a bit cut-up, Dad," said Jack. "They were very friendly, you know."

"More fool Cyril," said his father shortly. "He was warned. It'll be a lesson to him. Pity you boys have to choose the wrong friends."

Jack didn't dare to argue that Twigg was all right as a friend – and a very loyal one, too. Perhaps his father *was* right. A poacher was a poacher, and against the law.

"A man is known by the company he keeps," said Mr Longfield. "That's an old proverb, but it's a good one for a young lad to remember."

181

Things began to happen quickly after that. The Inspector was called in from the next town. P.C. Potts was instructed to free Twigg at once. All kinds of interviews went on – with Mr and Mrs Roker, with Twigg, with Tommy Lane, and with the two boys, Cyril and Jack.

The Inspector was soon in touch with Scotland Yard and it was not long before he had a nice little history of Benedict, the hermit, telephoned down to him at Mistletoe Farm. He related it to Mr Longfield, who later on gave a short version of it to Jack and Cyril.

"He was a clever rogue. At one time he had been an actor, and was a clever impersonator. He was very well educated, and quite a good musician, and was once in a dance band as first violin. He liked to pose as a cultured scholar, and had committed many frauds. He had been in prison twice. This hermit act of his was a good ruse to put the police off his track, and to hide away from people, but he needed money for the time when he returned to his ordinary life, and so robbed the farmers to get it."

This, in brief, was Benedict's story. The two boys listened in silence, shocked and horrified. Cyril squirmed when he thought of how completely he had been taken in. How Benedict must have laughed at him in secret! Cyril remembered, too, the many questions that the hermit had asked him about the various farmers and their ways. His interest, of course, was based on the necessity for getting to know any fact he could which might help him to learn of any farmer with money, and the whereabouts of his farm. His nightly prowls had taught him the various roads and ways. It had been a clever stroke on his part to implicate Twigg in the last robbery. Twigg had been put into prison and Benedict had been able to get away in safety.

"By the way, his name isn't Benedict, of course," said Mr Longfield. "It's Raymond Jones; and in my opinion that suits him better than Benedict!"

"Will he be caught?" asked Jack.

"No doubt about it," said his father. "He seems unable

to stop posing as a fine scholar, and he'll give himself away sooner or later. Most rogues have their weak spot, you know. That's his."

He left the two boys and went out to get his cob Sultan, to ride over to Holly Farm and tell Mr Roker the latest news. The boys looked at one another. Jane and Melisande came into the room, looking scared, followed by Susan, Roderick and Crackers.

"Oh, Cyril!" said Melisande, and promptly began to cry.

"What have *you* got to howl about?" said Cyril. "I'm the mutt, the idiot, the prize ass! I'm the one you are all ashamed of! What do you suppose I feel like now? Didn't I ape Benedict – no, give him his right name, Raymond Jones – and pride myself on being very like him in my tastes and my ways? Pah! I can't bear to think of it. I've got a nasty taste in my mouth the whole time. If that's what education and scholarship and culture make you, I'll be a farmer!"

"But it's not what they make you!" said his aunt as she came into the room and heard what he said. "It was Benedict's own character that made him a rogue, not his education and culture – because apparently he *was* quite cultured. Stop crying, Melisande, I thought you'd given up weeping when things went wrong!"

Melisande sniffed, and dried her eyes. "I feel so sorry for Cyril," she said.

"Well, don't," said Cyril with a scowl. "It's the last thing I want. I've been a donkey, and I've kicked myself for it, and I jolly well won't be taken in again by anyone. I don't feel sorry for myself; I deserved all I got – so for goodness sake don't weep all over me and sympathize, Melisande."

His aunt was secretly surprised at this sensible speech from Cyril, and very pleased. She was debating how to end this rather emotional discussion when there came the sound of hooves outside in the yard. They all looked out of the window.

"It's Richard – and Lordly-One!" squealed Susan. She

ran out with Roderick and Crackers. Jane glanced hastily at herself in the glass. Was she tidy and clean? Melisande sniffed and fled upstairs, anxious that Richard should not see that she had been crying. Jack and Cyril went out to Richard.

"Hello!" said Richard, looking very sturdy and straight on Lordly-One's back. "I heard about all the fuss here – police and everything. It sounded too exciting for words. I've come over to hear about it."

Mrs Longfield smiled. This was just the best thing that could have happened. They would all be so excited at telling Richard the extraordinary story that everything would begin to seem ordinary again afterwards, and Cyril would be himself once more, and Jack shake off his worried look.

Soon Jane was riding Lordly-One in glee, enjoying being on such a big horse. P.C. Potts, the policeman, could hardly make himself heard as he picked his way towards the farmhouse with a message.

"Here's Mr Potts!" cried Roderick, and Susan at once looked for Mr Potts, Twigg's golden spaniel, and was bitterly disappointed to find it was only the policeman. He muttered something and disappeared to talk to Mrs Longfield.

"Oh, I *wish* Twigg would come now. I do wish Twigg would come," sighed Susan. "With Mr Potts at his heels. Don't you, Roderick?"

And, by what Susan and Roderick thought was a very lucky chance indeed, Twigg did indeed arrive just as P.C. Potts was leaving!

Mrs Longfield was just seeing the policeman off, when she was amazed to hear a shriek from Susan.

"Mr Potts! Come here, you! Hey, Mr Potts, you rogue, you! Don't you know enough to come when you're called, Mr Potts?"

"*Susan!*" cried her mother, shocked, and P.C. Potts scowled. He saw Twigg and Twigg saw him. Twigg resented having been arrested by Mr Potts when he was innocent, and he was feeling rather cock-a-hoop about the whole matter now.

"Potty!" he called. "Here, Potty! Come to heel now! Come to heel!"

P.C. Potts decided to go another way home. Very red and angry, he departed down the kitchen path and slammed the gate behind him. Richard went off on Lordly-One, doubling up with laughter at the memory of P.C. Pott's face.

"Susan! How *could* you call out like that when Mr Potts was here?" said her mother. "I'm ashamed of you. Twigg, would you like a cup of tea? I'm sorry about your mistaken arrest. Still, it's all put right now. Go and ask Dorcas for some tea, and tell her I said so."

"Thank you kindly, mum," said Twigg, and departed to the kitchen door.

Jack went with him. "Thanks, Twigg, for not saying anything about me," he said. "It's a good thing it's all cleared up, isn't it? Dad says I can go out with you if I like. I'm jolly pleased about that."

"Your dad's a fine man," said Twigg. "Me and Tommy thinks the world of him. Good day, Miss Dorcas. Cuppa tea for me, please – and the Missus says so!"

CHAPTER TWENTY-FIVE

If Wishes Came True . . .

After the excitement about Twigg and the hermit had died down, the matter of buying Holly Farm loomed up again. Mrs Longfield had still said nothing about her decision. Worse still, she had actually gone over to Holly Farm to see it!

"She wouldn't have done that if she wasn't really and truly thinking of leaving Mistletoe Farm and buying it," groaned Jane.

"I keep on talking about the lovely things there are here," said Susan. "Hoping it will soften Mummy's heart."

"Yes, we all know that!" said Jane. "The snowdrops that

185

come up in February outside the kitchen window, the primroses out in the wood in spring, the old barn where the cats have their kittens! Bit silly, I think, because there'd be snowdrops and primroses and cats having kittens over at Holly Farm too! I wish you'd stop it. It makes *me* feel awful, not Mummy!"

"Boodi would simply *hate* to live in another stable," said Susan. "He'd be miserable."

"Well, leave Boodi behind, then," said Melisande heartlessly.

There was an unexpected visitor the next day, when the children got back from school. Their Uncle David! He welcomed them all, and stared in amazement at Melisande, Cyril and Roderick.

"I wouldn't know them!" he kept saying. "I honestly wouldn't know them! Cyril's as sturdy as Jack now. And Melisande's fat!"

"I'm not," said Melisande, who didn't like this adjective at all. She was delighted to see her father, and thought how well he too was looking.

"No. Melisande isn't fat. She's just right," said Aunt Linnie, coming to the rescue as usual. "What do you think of Roderick, David?"

"He's fine!" said his father, and Roderick glowed. "Stands on his own feet now, I can see!"

At high tea, when all the news had been given from everyone, the talk turned to Holly Farm. The three grown-ups discussed it thoroughly. To the children's dismay, both their father and mother seemed to think it a wonderful little place.

"We'll take you over to see it tomorrow, David," said Mrs Longfield. "That's where the last robbery was, too, you know – that the children have been telling you about."

After high tea had been cleared away, the children sat about the room, talking, doing homework or mending. Uncle David talked about his work. He obviously enjoyed it very much. He spoke of Aunt Rose too, and how she had done her best to get as near him as possible, and was

186

longing to have a home of her own again, with him and the children.

"If you get a farm up in Scotland, will Aunt Rose like that?" said Susan. "I don't think she likes farm life."

"It's that or nothing," said her uncle, looking serious. "Farming is my job from now on."

Later that evening the three grown-ups went into Mr Longfield's little study to discuss a few matters in private. The children heard the door closing, and looked at one another.

"What's Uncle David come down for?" said Susan. "Has he come to take you three back with him, Cyril?"

"I don't know. Something's in the wind," said Cyril uneasily.

"Well, you may get your wish sooner than you think, Jane," said Melisande.

"What wish?" said Jane.

"That we should all be gone and leave you your house to yourself," said her cousin. "And you would at last have your own bedroom again."

"And Susan would have Crackers to herself instead of having to share him with me," said Roderick.

"And Jack would be rid of Cyril," said Melisande. "I do believe we'll be gone soon. I can feel it!"

There was a silence. Jack, Jane and Susan were all thinking hard.

"I don't want you to go away where we'll hardly ever see you again, Melisande," said Jane suddenly. "I've got sort of used to you. I know we bicker and squabble, but I honestly should miss you awfully now."

"*Would* you?" said Melisande, pleased. "That's nice of you, Jane. I feel the same."

"And I should feel lost without Jack!" said Cyril surprisingly. "He's a rock, is old Jack! Shouldn't like to feel we weren't going to see each other every day as usual."

"It's your turn now, young 'uns!" said Jack, looking shy at Cyril's sudden speech.

Roderick and Susan looked at each other. "*I* shall ask Mummy if we can keep Roderick," she said in a very determined voice. "You don't want to go, do you, Roddy? You like Mistletoe Farm, don't you?"

Roderick was surprised at being suddenly called Roddy – and very pleased. "Yes. I love Mistletoe Farm," he said. "I don't want to go. Perhaps I could be here for the term-time and go home for holidays."

"I'll see what I can do about it," promised Susan. "Crackers would hate you to go. Wouldn't you, Crackers? I don't want anybody to go, really. I like us as we are now, though I hated you all so very much at first!"

Everyone laughed. Susan was always so devastatingly honest. A voice floated down from Mr Longfield's study to the sitting-room.

"Susan! Roderick! It's time you went to bed."

"Blow!" said Susan, getting up. "I thought they'd forgotten us. Come on, Crackers. Bed for you too! I'm going to weigh you on the bathroom scales tonight. I think you're getting a tummy!"

Two days later Jack went to Holly Farm with a message for Mrs Roker from his mother. As he was leaving, Mr Roker called to him.

"Well, young Jack! How's the detective business going? Pretty smart work you did here last week! Did you hear that fellow's been caught, and I've got all my money coming back to me?"

"No! I *am* glad!" said Jack. "Where was he caught?"

"He had his beard and long hair cut, and was caught then," said Mr Roker. "The police notified all the barbers in London that a man might be coming along wanting a beard and long hair cut, and the barber he went to got on to the police at once! Bad lot, that hermit was."

"Yes," said Jack. "Well, good evening, sir."

"Good evening to you, lad," called back Mr Roker. "Glad your father's decided to buy Holly Farm!"

Jack was riding off on Darkie when this last sentence hit him like an arrow. He reined up Darkie and looked round. But Mr Roker had gone into the farmhouse, and the door was shut. Troubled and unhappy, Jack rode back to Mistletoe Farm.

So it had happened! His mother had made her decision, and his father had actually told Mr Roker he would buy Holly Farm. They would have to leave; and no doubt that was really why Uncle David had come down from Scotland, to arrange to take Cyril and the others back with him. There would certainly be no room for them at Holly Farm!

He rode back to Mistletoe Farm completely miserable. How could his father consent to letting his own farm go – the farm that had been in his family for so many generations? His grandfather had planted that big oak. His great-grandfather had planted that big copse of trees on the hill yonder to shelter the field there from the cold north winds, so that his crops would grow well. It was Longfields' land, and it always ought to be!

He found the others in the sitting-room when he got back, and broke the news to them.

"Dad's bought Holly Farm," he said flatly. "Mr Roker told me."

There was a horrified silence. Jane was so shocked that she felt tears coming to her eyes, and hastily blinked them away. Susan wailed aloud. The others looked really dismayed.

"I don't think we're supposed to know yet," said Jack. "So we'd better not say anything. The week is up tomorrow, and I expect Mother meant to tell us then – break it gently to us, I suppose!"

He spoke bitterly. Jane slipped her arm through his. At moments like these the twins were very close together. Jack squeezed Jane's arm gratefully.

"So that's why Daddy came down from Scotland," said Melisande. "To take us back. How awful!"

Mrs Longfield was helping Dorcas to make the first batch of Christmas puddings and mincemeat that night, so, much to the children's relief, she did not appear in the sitting-room for more than a few minutes. She liked to get her puddings done very early, and then give them what she and Dorcas called a "good boil-up" every now and again, till they were as black as could be!

189

She popped her head round the sitting-room door. "Children! The pudding is ready to stir. You must each come along to the kitchen and stir, and wish your wish as usual."

She disappeared. The six children looked round at one another, exactly the same idea in their minds. "We're all to wish the same wish!" said Jane, fiercely. "We mustn't say what it is, but you jolly well all know it! See?"

"Yes!" said everyone, and they trooped down the stone passage to the big kitchen. Mrs Longfield and Dorcas were there, very red in the face with their exertions. Mixing a Christmas pudding was a difficult job!

Each of the six cousins stirred and wished in silence. Jane wished last of all. "I wish to stay at Mistletoe Farm," she wished fervently. "I wish that it shan't be sold!"

"Crackers wants to wish too," said Susan, and she lifted him up, put the spoon in his paw, held both paw and spoon herself, and stirred. Crackers looked faintly surprised, and sniffed longingly at the mixture under his nose.

"Wish, Crackers! Wish" cried Susan. He looked up at her solemnly. "He wished," she said. "And it was the same wish that we all wished!"

Next day, at high tea, Mrs Longfield interrupted the conversation. "Daddy and I and Uncle David want to talk to you all," she said. "Jane and Melisande, clear away. Dorcas will wash up. It's about Holly Farm."

There was a silence. Susan clutched Crackers and whispered in his ear. "You did wish, didn't you, Crackers? You'll go too if you didn't!"

Jane and Melisande whipped the things off the table and took them out to Dorcas. Soon the whole family was sitting together. Mr Longfield was discussing market prices with his brother. His wife tapped him on the arm.

"Come along, Peter. The children are waiting for the news."

"Oh, yes. We said we'd tell them today, when everything was signed and sealed, didn't we, Linnie?" said her husband. He turned to the waiting children and smiled. "Well," he said. "I've bought Holly Farm today."

190

There were groans and moans, and a cry from Susan. "But we wished. We wished!"

"Whatever's the matter?" said Mr Longfield, surprised. But Mrs Longfield knew.

"Children," she said, "it's all right. We have bought Holly Farm, it's true, but it's for your Uncle David, not for us! We're staying here! I couldn't leave after all. I just couldn't. Your father loves it too much, and you've grown up here, and I love it too, in spite of its hard work."

She could hardly finish because her three children were on top of her. "Mummy! We never guessed! Mummy, it's too good to be true! Oh, thank you for saying we can stay!"

Mr Longfield and his brother laughed. They looked at Cyril, Melisande and Roderick. Their eyes were shining too.

"Daddy!" said Melisande. "We shall be quite near Mistletoe Farm, then. And I can go on going to the same school, and so can the others."

"I shan't," said Cyril. "I'm leaving, Dad! I'm going to help you on the farm. You'll want some good, strong hands."

"Shall we have ponies of our own?" said Roderick hopefully. "Oh, Dad, this is fine. I do like being on a farm – and now we'll have our own."

"Thanks to your uncle's goodness and belief in me," said his father. "He's putting up the money, and I'm going to do the work. Mother will come and join us as soon as we can get in. She'll like that trim little Holly Farm, I think, once she's in it."

There was a perfect babel of voices after that. "We thought you had sold Mistletoe Farm! We thought you had bought Holly Farm for us!"

"Now I shan't have to take you all round the farm Roddy, so that you can say goodbye to everything. And Crackers won't have to say goodbye to you, either!"

"When are the Rokers going? Oh – just before Christmas. Then you'll be able to have your first Christmas there all together. How lovely!"

"But you'll have to come over and share Christmas dinner with us. And you must get a dog like Crackers – or Mr Potts."

"Well!" said Mr Longfield, his big voice booming over everyone else's. "This is very nice, to hear you all so pleased. It's not so very long ago since the six cousins would have been very glad to have seen the back of each other! Now you sound like long-lost brothers!"

"I was so afraid you'd sold Mistletoe Farm, Dad, when you bought Holly Farm," said Jack, looking radiant. "I felt sure we'd have to go."

"*I* didn't," said Susan. "Did I, Roddy? I *knew* we shouldn't have to go. I ab-sol-utely knew."

"How?" said Jane. "You couldn't have known. None of us did. Don't be silly, Susan!"

"What about our Christmas pudding wishes?" demanded Susan. "I knew they'd come true. And they did. Oh, I feel so happy I'd like to hug simply everybody, even Melisande."

"Well, don't," said Melisande. "Hug Crackers instead. Aunt Linnie, thank you for having us here so long, and if only we can make Holly Farm as lovely a home as Mistletoe Farm, I'll be proud!"

"Good old Mistletoe Farm!" said Cyril, and the cousins echoed his words in their hearts.

Good old Mistletoe Farm!

THE END

Six Cousins Again

First published in a single volume in hardback in 1950 by
Evans Brothers Ltd, London
First published in paperback in 1967 in Armada

CHAPTER 1

The Six Cousins Talk

"LET'S all go over to see Holly Farm!" said Jane, on a fine December morning. "The Rokers have gone now. They went yesterday so it's empty."

"Yes, let's!" said Roderick and Susan, delighted. Melisande nodded too. She felt excited at the thought of seeing their new home.

Jack and Cyril came by the window, and the others yelled to them. "We're going over to see Holly Farm – the Rokers have gone. Are you coming too?"

The two boys opened the window wide enough to jump in. "What's all the shouting about?" asked Jack.

"Haven't you finished your Saturday jobs yet," said Jane. "We've decided to go and look at Holly Farm."

The six cousins began to talk at the tops of their voices. Jane and Jack were twins, getting on for sixteen. Susan was their little sister. She was twelve.

Melisande, Cyril and Roderick were their cousins. Cyril was sixteen, Melisande was fifteen, and Roderick was the youngest of the six cousins, even younger than Susan. They sat there, talking nineteen to the dozen, with Crackers, the black spaniel listening as if he understood every single word.

'We've been staying with you so long now that Mistletoe Farm seems like home," said Melisande, looking round the cosy, rather untidy sitting room. "I shall miss it."

"Yes – it's almost eight months since we came," said Cyril, counting up. "Our house was burnt down then, and we came to you."

They all sat silent for a few minutes, remembering that

far-off April evening, when the telephone bell had shrilled out, and the news had flashed through. Susan especially remembered everything clearly. She never forgot anything!

"Jane went to the phone first," she said, "then Mummy went, and we heard her saying she was horrified, and terribly sorry for you. We couldn't think what had happened."

"It seems a long time ago now," said Melisande. "I don't mind telling you we all three hated the idea of coming to stay with you – Mistletoe Farm seemed dreadful to us after lovely Three Towers."

"Well, we didn't want you either," said Jane. "None of us did – except perhaps Mummy, but she's always so sorry for people when things happen to them. I remember how I hated having to clear out a chest of drawers for you to put your clothes in, Melisande. I couldn't bear the idea of sharing a room with you. Well, I still don't like it, actually, but I've sort of got used to it."

"And Roderick hated that little room up near the cistern," said Susan. "You were afraid of the gurgles it made – do you remember, Roderick?"

"Gosh, yes – I must have been an idiot," said Roderick. "I never even notice the noises the cistern makes now."

"You'll probably miss them when you get to Holly Farm," said Jane, with a laugh. "I'm sure everything is absolutely up-to-date and well-behaved at Holly Farm – even the cistern! It seems funny to think you'll be moving in so soon."

"Yes – it'll feel strange to be only three of us instead of six," said Jack.

"Strange for us too," said Cyril. "But after all, we're not very far away. And if Dad can get us each a horse, we'll be riding over pretty often."

"It's almost four miles by the road, but it's only two-

and a half by the fields," said Susan. "That's what Twigg the poacher told me, anyway. He says he'll show me all the short cuts when you move."

For eight months the six cousins had had to live at very close quarters indeed with one another.

Mistletoe Farm was certainly not meant for six children – it was hardly big enough for three! It had meant sharing rooms, living on top of one another, and being altogether very uncomfortable.

Added to that, the three Mistletoe Farm cousins were real country children, and the other three whose house had been burnt down, were real town children, who turned up their noses at life in the country. So there had been quarrels and bickering and bad temper – but then somehow or other the corners had got knocked off, and now the six cousins were genuinely sorry to part.

"It's jolly decent of your father to buy Holly Farm for *my* father, and set him up there," said Cyril to Jack. "I guess Dad will be happy, running a farm himself. It's what he always wanted to do, but he just had to live in a town because Mother hated the country."

"She'll still hate it, I expect," said Susan. "But it's her turn to do something she doesn't like. Your father had years of living somewhere *he* hated."

Jane gave her a nudge. Susan was always so tactless. Melisande frowned.

"Don't talk like that about my mother," she said to Susan. "I wouldn't dream of saying things like that about *your* mother!"

"No, because she's not like . . .," began Susan, and got another, sharper nudge from Jane. Now it was Susan's turn to scowl. She never could understand why she couldn't always say exactly what she was thinking. And she was thinking that her beautiful, well-groomed Aunt Rose would most certainly hate to live on a farm and run a farmhouse! In fact Susan simply couldn't imagine her doing it.

Aunt Rose, the mother of Cyril, Melisande and Roderick, was so different from Susan's own hardworking, cheerful, sensible mother. Certainly Aunt rose always dressed much better than Susan's own mother, who was nearly always in overalls as she raced about the house doing the hundred and one jobs that were for ever waiting for her – and certainly Aunt Rose smelt nice and had pretty hair and walked almost as if she was floating on air.

But on the other hand Susan's mother, according to Susan, was the best in the world – she was a *mother*, and in Susan's opinion Aunt Rose wasn't a real mother at all. Hadn't she let all her three children live at Mistletoe Farm for eight months and only come to see them once? Susan opened her mouth to remind Melisande of this, and then shut it again. Jane would nudge her for the third time if she said anything more about mothers!

They all began to talk about Holly Farm. It had just come onto the market at the right time. At first the children of Mistletoe Farm had been afraid that their father was going to buy it for their own mother, because Mistletoe Farm was old-fashioned, and very hard to work. But their mother had said no she couldn't leave dear old Mistletoe Farm – and so Holly Farm had been bought for the cousins. Their father, brother to Susan's father, was to run it, and his wife, Aunt Rose, was to come down from Scotland, where she had been staying; and so once more the family, split by the burning down of their old house, were to be together again.

"Holly Farm's got electric light and gas," said Roderick. "That'll please Melisande – no more cleaning oil lamps and filling them!"

"And it's got a proper water supply," said Jane. "And

"They cantered off in the crisp, frosty morning. Jack looked back at Mistletoe Farm as he went."

Dad says the cows' milking shed is all tiled! Fancy cows having a place that's tiled. Do you suppose they like it?"

"I don't care if they like it or not," said Melisande "*I* shall like it. At least it will be easy to swill down and clean, and won't smell as horrible at the cowsheds here."

201

"They *don't* smell horrible!" said Susan, indignantly "Cows smell lovely."

"The stables are fine too," said Cyril. "Of course, they're new. The ones here must be very old. I shall like the new ones – but there's a kind of *feel* about the old ones here that I love."

"Yes," agreed Susan, "as if they're still remembering all the nice old horses that ever stood there. I know what you mean."

"Well, if we're going to have a squint at Holly Farm, we'd better go," said Cyril, getting up. "Come on – we'll ask your mother for the keys, and go over. You three ride on your horses, and we three will catch the bus that goes in ten minutes."

Cyril got the keys, and he, Melisande and Roderick went to catch the bus that went to the bottom of the lane in which Holly Farm stood. The other three cousins went to get their horses.

They cantered off in the crisp, frosty morning. Jack looked back at Mistletoe Farm as he went.

"I'm glad *we're* not going to Holly Farm!" he thought. "I'm glad Mistletoe Farm is ours. But Holly Farm will suit the others down to the ground. They'll love it!"

CHAPTER 2

Holly Farm

The three children on horseback got to Holly Farm before their cousins did. The bus had to go a roundabout way on the roads, but the three riders took short cuts over the fields. They arrived at the trim little farmhouse with pleasure.

"Let's tie our horses here," said Jack. "The stables may be locked. They'll stand at this gate all right. Susan, tie Boodi as far away from Merrylegs and Darkie as you can – I don't want him nibbling their tails!"

"All right," said Susan, obligingly. Boodi was her own pony, a real character. He had come from Iceland, and was like a little barrel, sturdy and strong. But he had several bad little tricks of his own, and one was nibbling the tail of any horse in front of him.

Susan tied him up a good distance from Darkie and Merrylegs. "All the same, I do think it's silly of the others to keep standing with their tails touching his nose," she said, giving Boodi a loving pat. "If *I* was a horse and knew Boodi, I'd always face him. I wouldn't give him a chance of nibbling my tail."

The three of them waited for their cousins to arrive, and soon they heard them coming up the lane. "Buck up" shouted Jack. "Come and have a good look at your new home."

Jane stood and looked at the pretty little farmhouse, where her three cousins were so soon going to live. It was whitewashed, and shone in the pale December sun. It was not so old and rambling as Mistletoe Farm, nor did it look so untidy, because the creeper on the house was neatly

203

trimmed, and flowerbeds nearby were neatly dug. The crazy paving paths were neat too, and not a weed grew in the cracks. No moss grew on the roofs, as it did at Mistletoe Farm, and not a scrap of ivy had been allowed to grow anywhere.

Holly trees and bushes stood all about. They had given the little farm its name. Trim holly hedges enclosed a square farm garden. Jane pointed to it.

"You'll be working there next year, Melisande, growing lettuces and radishes and parsley and mint, just like we do. And flowers for the house. It's not quite as big a garden as ours, so you ought to be able to manage by yourself, if your mother helps you."

For the first time Melisande's heart sank. She had helped in the garden at Mistletoe Farm – she had thinned out a few lettuces, and weeded a few beds. But now she suddenly realised that quite probably she would be the only one here at Holly Farm who would have either time or inclination to do the garden. A farm garden was always supposed to be women's work – no farmer dreamed of sparing one of his precious men to help with that. The farmer's wife and daughters did it.

And Melisande's heart sank because she felt sure that her mother wouldn't know a thing about the garden – and she, Melisande, would have to do it all by herself! Things wouldn't be quite such fun at Holly Farm as they were at Mistletoe Farm – there wouldn't be so many people to do them with, for one thing. And for another, who, except her father, would know *how* to do anything? Certainly her mother wouldn't know when to plant seeds, or how to thin lettuces.

"And what's more I don't believe she'll want to know," thought Melisande. Then she cheered up. "But after all, when Mother's really here, running this dear little place, she'll surely love to learn everything. I've quite enjoyed

204

all the things we did at Mistletoe Farm – though it's true that at first I hated everything. Oh dear – I do hope Mother won't hate things."

Cyril was looking with pleasure at the farmhouse, and the farm beyond. How well-kept – how neat and trim! Not a tile was missing from the barns, not a fence was broken anywhere. The hedges were well trimmed, the ditches were clean. It certainly was a model little place.

"I could almost run this myself!" said Jack, suddenly to his cousin. "It's in such shipshape order! Nothing to be mended, nothing to be altered – you've only just got to run it as it is. Your father's lucky, Cyril."

"Yes. And Mother will be lucky too," said Cyril, going up the neat path to the gleaming front door. "This will be play to run properly – not like Mistletoe Farm with its bad lighting and no hot water, and leaky roof. Let's go in and look."

Cyril pictured his pretty, smiling mother in Holly Farm. Surely it would suit her? He remembered his old home, Three Towers – his mother must have run that beautifully for there were always punctual meals, excellently cooked, the house was always shining and spotless, with lovely soft cushions everywhere, and well-swept carpets. He thought of the carpets at Mistletoe Farm.

"Worn and old, with holes you catch your feet in," he thought. "And dirty old cushions, because Crackers is allowed to jump on them, and the cats sleep there. And the curtains so faded. I've enjoyed my stay at Mistletoe Farm – but it *will* be lovely to have a *beautiful* home again, and well-polished silver on the table and things like that."

They were now inside the farmhouse. It wasn't really like a farmhouse at all – it was more like a town band-box of a house. The rooms were trim and small, most of them square. There were built-in cupboards in every bedroom so that no wardrobes would be needed – and to

205

Melisande's enormous joy, there were fitted basins there too!

She ran to turn on a tap. Water spouted out at once. "Look!" she said. "It's just like we had at Three Towers, Roderick – basins in our bedrooms. Look, Jane – won't you envy me, being able to wash in my own bedroom, and not even having to pour the dirty water away! No wardrobes, no washstands – my, this place will be easy to run."

It was completely modern. A gas stove stood in one corner for cooking. A boiler stood on the big hearth, excellent for heating water all over the house. Jane looked at it silently.

"I suppose all this *does* save a lot of work," she said, reluctantly. "But I do like our big old range at home, where Dorcas does the cooking – I love all her pots and pans and kettles on top, and the great big oven. It's nice to sit by too."

"You're old-fashioned," said Melisande, looking into the larder. "Look here – tiled all round too, just like the kitchen – and there's even a 'fridge! We can have ice cream whenever we want it!"

"Good," said Roderick. This was the first word he had spoken so far. He hadn't like the inside of Holly Farmhouse at all. It didn't feel right to him, after the friendly cosiness of the rooms at Mistletoe Farm. Everything here was so *proper*, he thought. He was sure he wouldn't like it as much as dear old Mistletoe Farm. Still – he would have his mother again. He had missed her very much, more than either Cyril or Melisande had. It would be lovely to have her back again.

He pictured her sitting at the head of the table at high tea each evening, just as his Aunt Linnie did at Mistletoe Farm. Aunt Linnie had a very nice face, he thought loyally, but his mother was so pretty, and her hair was never untidy like his aunt's. Yes, decidedly it would be lovely to have her here at Holly Farm, looking after him, and fussing him as she used to do.

The children examined the house and the farm thoroughly from top to bottom. The house was just big enough to take them all, if Daddy didn't have a dressing-room, but kept all his things in Mother's room, or out in the cupboard on the landing.

"Mother won't like that much," thought Melisande. "But I expect she'll soon get used to it. Roddy's got a dear little room – he'll like that. But he'll certainly miss his cistern!"

The barns were in excellent order, and so were all the sheds. What machinery the recent owner had left for Cyril's father to buy was gleaming like new in its own shed. There was a tractor there, and Roddy's eyes gleamed when he saw it.

"I hope Dad will let me drive that," he said to Cyril. "Is he going to have a car?"

"Of course," said Cyril. "He'll have to, to get to market and back, and fetch and carry things from the station."

There was no livestock on the farm at all. Mr Roker, the last owner, had taken it all with him to a bigger farm. Cyril's father was going to restock Holly Farm with the help of his brother at Mistletoe Farm. That would be exciting, Roddy thought.

"When do we move in?" asked Roddy. "I want to be here in good time for Christmas. I want to have my Christmas dinner here for the first time this year. When is Mother coming?"

"She's coming soon, with Daddy, to get the house ready for us, and to have everything shipshape for Christmas," said Melisande. "I wish it wasn't still term-time – it would be fun to help to get everything straight. Perhaps we could come over on Saturday and Sunday and do a few jobs ourselves."

They had spent about two hours wandering over the house and farm. Reluctantly they decided it was time to go home. "Though 'Home' will soon mean here, and not Mistletoe Farm!" thought Melisande. "It *will* be nice to have a home again – just our own family, and not anyone else – though I do like Jack, Jane and Susan. Still, we shall often see them."

She and Cyril and Roderick went off to catch the bus. The others untied their horses and cantered over the field-paths home.

"What do you think of Holly Farm?" asked Susan, after a while.

"It's nice – but it's a toy farm, not a real one!" said Jack. "Give me Mistletoe Farm every time!"

And on the bus Cyril was asking Melisande the same question. "What do you think of Holly Farm?"

"Oh, it's *lovely*!" she was answering. "It's not old and dark and overgrown like Mistletoe Farm. Give me Holly Farm every time!"

CHAPTER 3

Moving In

The next excitement was moving in, of course. Everyone at Mistletoe Farm was thrilled with this, not only Cyril, Melisande and Roderick. Even Dorcas got "all worked up," as she called it, and went over to see it she could do any scrubbing.

Mrs Longfield went with Jane to hang the new curtains that had arrived in good time. They looked very nice indeed. "Aunt Rose certainly has good taste," said Jane, as she looked at the new hangings, half wishing that she had such pretty curtains at her bedroom window too. She didn't even know what colours hers were supposed to be, they were so old!

"Mummy, wouldn't *you* like some new curtains sometime?" she asked suddenly, watching her mother look admiringly at the blue ones she had just hung in Aunt Rose's bedroom.

"Yes. I'd love some," said her mother. "But things like that have to wait, if you run a farm there always seems to be something much more important to buy – machinery, or new hens, or feeding-stuff. I've kept meaning to make *you* some new ones, Jane – yours are the ones I had in my bedroom at my own home when *I* was a girl! It's a shame that I can't give you a pretty, dainty bedroom like Melisande is going to have. Especially now that you have got so much tidier in your ways!"

Jane grinned. She had had to share her small bedroom with Melisande for eight months and Melisande had grumbled bitterly at the way Jane scattered her things everywhere. She had even threatened once to throw Jane's "smelly old jodphurs" out of the window if she left them lying about the bedroom any more.

"Yes. I *am* better now," said Jane. "But I don't know if I'll be able to keep up my good ways when my bedroom is my own again, without Melisande there to grumble if I'm too untidy."

"Oh, don't say that, Jane," said her mother with a groan, unpacking some brown-red curtains for Cyril's bedroom. "It's been such a pleasure not to have to grumble at you so much. Dear me – how we shall all miss your three cousins now."

"Yes. But it will be lovely to have you all to ourselves again," said Jane. "I don't like sharing you with so many people."

"Don't I take enough notice of you, when I've six children instead of three?" said her mother, with a chuckle. "All right, you wait – I'll begin to notice all kinds of things when I've more time – your dirty shoes – buttons off. . . ."

Jane laughed. She climbed up on the window sill to slide the curtain rings on to the rod there. Out in the yard Roderick and Susan and Crackers were unpacking a big crate, performing peculiar feats with a chisel and a screwdriver. Mrs Longfield, looking down too, thought it all looked very dangerous indeed.

"I suppose they think they're helping," she said. "But all that will happen is that the chisel will slip and cut somebody's hand – or jab Crackers' nose. He sticks it into everything!"

They had planned to lay the linoleum and the carpets, and hang the curtains before the new furniture came in. It wouldn't take long then for everything to be straight, and Aunt Rose hoped to have the children in their new home at five o'clock on the afternoon of moving-in day.

"Who's going to help Aunt Rose?" asked Jack, wandering in to see how his mother and Jane were getting on. "Is she going to have somebody like Dorcas?"

"She's bringing someone," said his mother, shaking out another curtain. "And Dorcas has got her niece to come in every day and help. So Aunt Rose should be very comfortable indeed – she'll lead the life of a lady – quite different from mine! She'll be able to keep her hands nice, for one thing, and she'll be able to look pretty when Uncle David comes in from his work – which I never do when Daddy comes in! I'm always too busy!"

"Oh Mummy – why, I think you *always* look nice!" said Jane, surprised. "I'm sure Daddy does too – even if he doesn't say it. Anyway I'd rather have you than Aunt Rose any day."

210

"Sh!" said her mother, as Melisande came into the room, looking flushed and pretty with excitement at helping to get her new home ready. "Hello, Melisande – finished putting up Roderick's curtains yet?"

"Yes. And I've helped Cyril to put down the carpet in my room and in his," said Melisande. "Isn't it fun, Aunt Linnie? I'm just longing to move in."

"We'll feel strange without you all," said her aunt. "But it will be nice for you to have your mother and father again and be one united family. That's what families are meant for – to live together in friendship and love."

"Like yours, Aunt Linnie," said Melisande unexpectedly. "I wish we were going to live a *bit* nearer to you – not two or three miles away. I've a sort of feeling we'll want to keep popping in and out to ask how we do this and how we do that! It's a good thing Mother has someone she's bringing here to help – and Dorcas has got her niece to come. She couldn't manage like you do."

"Well, my dear, if you're in difficulties, you know quite a bit about household and farm affairs now, you and Cyril and Roderick," said her aunt. "You can surely help in all kinds of ways. You can't live on a farm like Mistletoe Farm for eight months without knowing a good deal of its running!"

By the time they left that day, Holly Farmhouse looked quite homely! The carpets down on the floor and the curtains hanging at the windows gave the house a friendly look. Melisande looked back at it, and felt very glad they were all going to live there.

"Daddy will love it," she thought. "He'll be really happy in the country. So shall I, though I never thought I would. How lovely to have Christmas Day in our own house!"

Moving in day came at last. It was on a Friday, so Cyril, Melisande and Roderick were all at school. They begged to help, but their father said no. "You'll be better out of the way!" he said. "Your mother's seen the house and she's got the plan of it. She has arranged exactly where all the new furniture is to go. We'll manage fine."

In great excitement the three children took a different bus from their usual one that Friday afternoon, rode in the opposite direction, and got out at the end of their lane. Up the lane they raced in the darkening evening. The sky was very clear, and the evening star hung low and bright. They crunched their way over frosted puddles, and looked out for the first glimpse of their new home.

"There it is!" said Roderick, suddenly, as he saw a light shining out from a window, and then from another. "Oh – it does look nice and welcoming! Mother will be there."

They raced in at the gateway and up to the front door. It had been left ajar for them. They tore into the little hall, feeling the warmth at once – for Holly Farm actually had central heating, and the whole house was warm from top to bottom. What a change from the chilly rooms at Mistletoe Farm!

"Mother! Where are you?" shouted Roderick, impatiently, and flung open the sitting room door. And there was his mother, sitting by a bright log fire, waiting, looking as young and pretty as ever.

The three children flung themselves on her, and both Melisande and Roderick thought the same thing at the same moment. "Why! We're bigger than Mother is now!"

Their mother gasped at the onslaught of the three hefty children, and pushed them back, laughing. "One at a time, dears! Melisande, how you've grown – and you really *are* fat! Cyril – you don't look the same!"

"Well – I've grown too," said Cyril, marvelling at the slightness of his mother.

"No – it's the way you've had your hair cut," said his mother. "It's so *terribly* short! We'll let it grow long now, just as it used to be. And how is mother's boy, my darling little Roderick?"

Roderick was so delighted to have his mother again that he didn't even mind being called "mother's boy" He tried to sit on the arm of her chair, and hugged her.

"Oh dear – how you rumple me!" said his mother. "What enormous children I've got now. Well, how do you like your new home, dears?"

"It's *lovely*," said Melisande, at once, looking round at the sitting-room, and marvelling how different it was from the rumpled, untidy room she knew so well at Mistletoe Farm. "Oh Mother – it's so nice to have pretty cushions about again – and flowers everywhere – and the fire irons shining – and everything so tidy!"

"And a fine wireless!" said Cyril, joyfully. "I was hardly ever allowed to put the wireless on at Misteltoe Farm, because Uncle wanted to read the paper, or something. Even though he knew that Aunt Linnie might like to hear a concert!"

"He's such a boor, your dear uncle," said his mother's soft voice. "Well, you can turn on the wireless whenever you like now. This is your own home and you can do what you please. No cross uncle to say you mustn't do this and you mustn't do that – and no busy Aunt Linnie rushing round with a red face, sending everyone to do jobs!"

Roderick drew back a little. He was very fond of his Aunt Linnie. "She's awfully nice, all the same," he said, loyally.

"Oh, of *course*," said his mother, and pulled him towards her again. "But surely I'm the kind of mother you want, aren't I? Just look at me and see!"

They all looked at her. She laughed up at them, as pretty as a picture, her hair shining. The little pearly earrings in her ears caught a spark of fire-light as they swung.

"You look so *young*!" said Cyril. "And you smell so

213

nice – and you've got a pretty new dress on. Yes – you're the kind of mother we want!"

"But Aunt Linnie's nice all the time," said Roderick in a small voice. "You're much *prettier*, Mother – but Aunt Linnie *is* nice!"

CHAPTER 4

Teatime At Holly Farm

"Well, let's have tea," said Mrs Longfield, pushing Melisande away and getting up. "Ring the bell, dear. Everything's ready. We got straight so quickly, because you were clever enough to put up the curtains and put down the carpets for me. Daddy will be in soon, I hope. He's just gone round the farm – not that there's much to see yet."

The door opened and a maid came in. She looked very smart indeed in a black frock and frilly white apron. She carried a silver teapot and hot water jug on a silver tray. The children stared at her.

"These are the children, Ellen," said Mrs Longfield. Ellen gave them a stiff smile and a nod.

"Yes, Madam," she said. "Er – somebody's left the front door wide open. Shall I shut it?"

"I will!" said Cyril, and rushed out. They had all been so excited at coming "home" for the first time that nobody had remembered to shut the front door behind them!

"I don't like her much," said Roderick, when the door had shut behind Ellen, and her footsteps could be heard tap-tapping down the hall.

"Now you musn't be awkward, dear," said his mother,

214

sitting down at the table, and lifting up the teapot. "We're lucky to have persuaded Ellen to come down to the country – she wouldn't have come if we hadn't had such a modern farmhouse."

Melisande looked with pleasure at the pretty teacloth, the plates with lace mats on them, and the silver teapot. It was a long time since she had seen such a dainty meal. She compared it with Mistletoe Farm – the big cloth that entirely covered the table and so soon got spotted – the great brown teapot – the plates covered with food, but with never a lace mat to grace them.

"It's lovely to have things nice again," she said. "I didn't know how much I'd missed all this kind of thing till I looked at this tea table. It's just like it used to be at Three Towers, before we lost everything in the fire."

"Yes – I was afraid you wouldn't like pigging it at Mistletoe Farm," said her mother, sympathetically.

"Well, dear, if it rests with me, we shall never "pig it" – we shall live as we used to live, even if we are in a much smaller place, and haven't so many lovely things."

Roderick was also surveying the table – but with very little pleasure. Silver teapots and lace mats meant nothing to him – what *he* noticed was the lack of food! Where was the dish of ham, the big fat scones, the great fruit cake, the round cream cheese, the big pats of butter that had always accompanied high tea at Mistletoe Farm? He was hungry, and didn't much like the look of the plate of thin-cut bread and butter, and the biscuits and little buns on this tea table. Why, he could eat the whole lot and still be hungry!

"Is this all we're going to have?" he began – and then someone tapped at the window, and a voice outside cried: "What a glorious sight! All my family together again!"

"Daddy!" yelled Roderick, and pushed back his chair so suddenly that it overbalanced and fell with a crash to the floor. He tore out into the hall, followed by Melisande and Cyril. Soon their father was being hugged and squeezed, and everyone was laughing happily.

"It was a wonderful sight to see you all sitting round the table like that," said Mr Longfield, taking off his heavy coat and hanging it in the hall cupboard. "I must just go and kiss your mother before I wash. She looked like Melisande's sister, sitting there at the table. Rose, here I am! Welcome me to our new home!"

His wife smiled at him, pleased that he said she looked like Melisande's sister. But she noticed that his boots were dirty and his hands too, and she gave him a little push after his kiss.

"Go and wash, you dirty boy! And just you be careful never to come in smelling like your brother at Mistletoe Farm! Hurry up, and we'll all have tea."

Mr Longfield was soon back, and took his place, beaming. This was the first time for eight months that he had had his whole family together under one roof in a home of their own. He was delighted. He loved them all so much – and now he was going to lead the life he liked. He was going to be a farmer, and live in the country!

He looked admiringly at his wife. He was lucky to have someone so dainty and pretty – not like his brother's wife, Linnie, who seemed to go about all day long in overalls, and always looked hot and hurried. She had turned into a typical farmer's wife and he was glad that Rose showed no signs of it. He wanted someone decorative, someone whom everyone else would admire.

Roderick sat close to his father, glad to have him back again. He had taken a thin piece of bread and butter on to his plate, and doubled it up, – and then put it into his mouth whole! It really only made one mouthful and was gone in a minute.

"Roderick! You really can't eat like that now you're at

216

home with me," said his mother, horrified. "Oh dear – the children will have to learn their manners all over again, I'm afraid David. Their stay at Mistletoe Farm may have done their health a lot of good – thought I do think Melisande is much too fat – but how it has ruined their manners."

"Mother! How has it ruined mine?" said Melisande, hurt. "You want to see Jane's, if you really would like to know what bad manners are!"

"Jane has no manners at all," said her mother. "Neither has Jack. As for Susan – and that perfectly awful dog, Crackers . . ."

"Crackers isn't an awful dog," said Roderick swallowing a piece of bread-and-butter so quickly that he almost choked. "I'm going to miss him very much. Don't say anything against Crackers. And I say – is this all there is to eat?"

"Roderick dear – you're over-excited or something, I think," said his mother, in a gentle voice. "What else should there be to eat at teatime?"

"Well – ham – or eggs – and a jolly big fruit cake – and some of that lovely cream cheese," said Roderick, re-membering all the things he had had at high tea at Mis-tletoe Farm. "And perhaps sausage rolls – and pickles . . ."

"Pickles! Sausage rolls! At teatime!" said his mother. "Surely you didn't have those things at Mistletoe Farm!"

"Yes, we did. Every single day," said Roderick. "Didn't we, Melisande?"

"Yes. You see, they had high tea there, Mother," ex-plained Melisande. "I suppose *we'll* have afternoon tea and then dinner later – or supper?"

"Of course," said her mother. "You'll soon get used to it. We'll simply have to get you back to proper ways again."

217

Roderick looked very gloomy. "I don't know how I'm going to last out till supper," he said. "I'm always so hungry when I get back from school. Wouldn't Daddy rather have high tea too? Won't he be hungry when he comes in?"

"I suppose it wouldn't be possible to have a more substantial sort of tea than this?" said Mr Longfield to his wife. "Farming's hungry work. I got used to a big meal about six o'clock or so, when I was farming up in Scotland."

"I do hope you don't expect me to do without all the nice ways I've been accustomed to," said his wife, looking suddenly tearful. "After all – I've come to live in the country, when I much prefer the town. That's a big thing for me to do. And if you want me to give up all the little ways I've been used to. . . ."

"No, dear, no," said her husband, hastily. "I wouldn't dream of it. We certainly won't have anything you don't want. You've had a hard time this year, what with that dreadful fire, and losing all your nice things, and having no proper home for months. You deserve to have your own way now."

"Besides," said Rose, looking more cheerful, "we have Melisande to think of. She really ought to have things done nicely. It would be a shame not to bring her up properly."

Having her own way, Mrs Longfield was prepared to be charming again, and things went smoothly. She could be very witty and amusing when she liked, and had a pretty, silvery laugh. She exerted herself to conquer everyone at the table, and succeeded. By the end of the meal they were all thinking that surely it was the best thing that ever happened, their coming to Holly Farm and being all together again.

Roderick still felt hungry, however, when he got up

218

from the table. He didn't like to say any more to his
mother, so he went quietly out of the room and down to
the kitchen. Perhaps Ellen would give him a bit of bread
and cheese.

Ellen was sitting in a chair by the fire – reading. Out in
the scullery someone was doing something, but Roderick
couldn't see who it was. Ellen looked up as he came in.

"What is it?" she said, coldly.

"Have you got a bit of bread and cheese I could have?"
asked Roderick, staring round the neat, small kitchen,
comparing it most unfavourably with Dorca's big warm
kitchen at Mistletoe Farm with its geraniums on the
windowsill and its fat clock ticking away.

"What next?" said Ellen. "A bit of bread and cheese
and you've just finished tea! Did your mother send you
out for it?"

"No. I came because I didn't have enough to eat," said
Roderick.

"Well, I'm sorry. But I don't encourage children in my
kitchen, and unless your mother says you can have bread
and cheese, I can't give you any," said Ellen. She returned
to her reading, and Roderick, rather scared, tiptoed out of
the kitchen.

He suddenly felt homesick for Mistletoe Farm, and his
cousins and Aunt Linnie and fat, comfortable old Dorcas
in the kitchen – and above all for Crackers! He didn't want
to go back to the others. He went to the garden door,
opened it and slipped into the dark garden. Roderick
wasn't at all sure that he liked Holly Farm after all!

219

CHAPTER 5

Mostly About Roderick

There was a light in the window of the scullery. Roderick remembered that he had heard someone out there. Who was it? A friend of Ellen's?

He went to the window to see. At the same moment the backdoor opened and somebody came out with a pail in her hand. Roderick knew her at once!

It was Sally, a niece of Dorcas's, who had sometimes come to see her aunt at Mistletoe Farm. She was a plump, round girl of about seventeen, with cheeks like an apple and a mop of dark hair.

"Sally!" said Roderick, in a loud, delighted whisper.

She jumped. "Oooh, who's that? Why, it's you, Master Roderick! What are you doing out here in the cold?"

"Nothing," said Roderick, truthfully. "Except I was wishing that Ellen was Dorcas."

Sally gave a little snort. "They'm different as chalk from cheese," she said. "Miss High-and-Mighty would fall foul of Dorcas in two minutes. Did I hear you say you wanted a bite of bread and cheese? You wait and I'll get you some."

She disappeared and came out with a generous hunk of bread and cheese. She pushed it into Roderick's hand. "There you are. Dorcas would have done the same – she knows what hungry boys are like. If you want any snacks, you just come to me, not to Miss Sour-Puss in there!"

Roderick gave a small chuckle. Miss High-and-Mighty! Miss Sour-Puss! What lovely names for the haughty, sour-faced Ellen. He whispered his thanks to Sally and went off to eat his bread and cheese in a nearby shed. He began to think of Crackers the spaniel again, and wondered how many dogs his father would keep.

"Farmers always have to have dogs," he thought. "I hope Daddy gets his quickly. Then I could have one of them for my own."

He went back indoors again, feeling much better after his talk with Sally and his bread and cheese. He determined to ask his father about dogs as soon as he got a chance.

Ellen had cleared away the tea. The sitting room looked cosy and friendly, with the curtains drawn, and a big log fire sending up flames and sparks. It crackled loudly. His mother was sitting making a new cushion cover by the fire, and Cyril was fiddling with the radio in the corner. Melisande was trying to make up her mind to leave the cosy room and look at her bedroom upstairs. She hadn't yet seen it all nicely furnished.

Mr Longfield was reading the paper contentedly in an armchair. From time to time he glanced at his wife and smiled. He felt very happy. A home again – and all his family round him – and a farm outside waiting for him to tend it and care for it as best he could. He would cover his fields with crops, set cows in his pastures, have sheep on the hills, and hens in the yard. There was a fine pigsty too – with a tiled floor almost good enough for him to eat off! He was lucky to get such an up-to-date little farm.

"Have you been up to see your bedroom?" Mrs Longfield asked Roderick. "Do you like it?"

"I haven't been yet," said Roderick.

"Where have you been all this time then?" asked his mother. Roderick remembered that question of hers of old. She always liked to know where everyone had been and what everyone had done. He answered vaguely.

221

"Oh – I've just been wandering about." He didn't like to say he had been to ask for bread and cheese in the kitchen, and he certainly wasn't going to give Sally away.

"I'm going to see my room," said Melisande getting up at last. "Come with me and see yours, Roderick. You coming too, Cyril?"

"Yes," said Cyril. "I must say it's marvellous to be so comfortable on moving-in day. Everything arrived and unpacked and set in place."

"Except the pictures," said his mother. "Daddy is going to put those up tonight. I'll come up with you and see if you like your rooms."

They all went up together, and came out on a small, but fairly wide landing. Three doors opened off it, and round a corner was another door, leading to the bathroom.

"Here's my room," said their mother and opened the door, showing almost exactly the same kind of bedroom that the three of them remembered at Three Towers, though this one was much smaller. Everything was new and pretty, and the bedspread matched the curtains just as all the bedspreads had done at their old home.

"It looks just like you, Mother, this bedroom," said Melisande, revelling in the daintiness. "Quite different from Aunt Linnie's, isn't it?"

"Ugh! Aunt Linnie's room is dreadful!" said her mother, with a shudder. "So bare – and the bed so big and hard – nothing pretty in it all. The only drawback here is that Daddy hasn't a dressing room. He'll have to share my room for his clothes, and I don't like that at all. Now let's come and look at your room, Melisande."

All the other rooms were pretty and neat and altogether charming. Mrs Longfield certainly knew how to choose curtains, carpets, furnishings and furniture! Melisande was delighted with her room, which looked

222

out on to the orchard – though by now, of course, it was too dark to see anything outside.

The boys liked their rooms too, though privately Cyril thought his was a bit girlish. He had been so used to sharing Jack's bedroom, with its bare boards, old curtains and old, battered furniture that somehow this new room of his seemed more suitable for a girl than for him. A soft carpet covered the floor, a silk bedspread covered the bed, and coloured towels to match hung by the basin. The lamp by his bedside was very pretty-pretty too – he could picture Jack grinning at it when he saw it.

"It's a lovely house, though it's so small," said Melisande. "Where does Roderick sleep?"

"There's a little stairway beyond the bathroom," said her mother, leading the way. "Ellen sleeps in a bedroom up there, and next to it, under the eaves, is a funny little room that used to be a boxroom. It will do beautifully for Roderick."

"Oh – I do hope it's next to the cistern!" said Roderick, to his mother's astonishment. "If it made a noise like that one at Mistletoe Farm, it would be nice and friendly. I should like that. It would remind me of my little room at Mistletoe Farm."

"I should have thought you wanted to forget that horrible little room, not remember it," said his mother, opening the small door at the top of the little stairway. Roderick gazed inside. He liked it enormously. It was a funny shape – all awkward corners and slanting ceilings. The window was set very low – why, the sill only reached his knees when he stood by it!

A low, built-in shelf ran along one side of the room. His mother had put some books there and a few toys saved from the fire. Roderick recognized them in delight.

"It's a *smashing* room!" he said. "The best one in the house." He looked out of the window, and just made out a

223

tree that reached the windowsill "It's got a tree outside," he said. "Does my window look down in the yard? Oh, good – I shall be able to hear the cock crowing in the morning and the hens clucking and the pigs grunting – when we have them."

The others left him up in his funny little room, pleased that he liked it. Neither Melisande nor Cyril would have liked it at all! "We'd always be bumping our heads on those awkward corners and slanting ceilings," said Melisande. "And thank goodness he's tucked right away from us so that we can't hear his singing and whistling. He's awfully noisy sometimes."

Roderick felt happy in his little room. He thought how much Susan would like it. And Crackers too! Crackers would sniff into every corner, and learn the whole room with his nose. Then he would sit down on the mat and look round as if to say "Yes, it's a nice room. And if I lived here I wouldn't mind coming and sleeping with you on this little bed at night. Just in case you felt lonely."

It didn't do to think of Crackers. Roderick hadn't realised how fond he was of the little black spaniel with the melting brown eyes. If only, only he could have a dog of his own. What would he call it? Roderick went into a long dream in which names for dogs floated about, trying to find one for the particular dog he might have. But he couldn't think of one nice enough for his dog.

He went downstairs at last and spoke to his father, "Daddy – farmers have to have dogs, don't they? Like Uncle has over at Mistletoe Farm. Are you going to have any?"

"Yes. The two I had up in Scotland are being sent down here," said his father, laying down his newspaper. "They're fine dogs – both mongrels though. I couldn't afford to buy pedigree dogs when I was working up there. You'll like them."

224

"What are they called?" asked Roderick, pleased.

"Punch and Pouncer," said Mr Longfield.

"They'll live in the house, won't they?" said Roderick, hopefully. But before his father could answer his mother spoke.

"No, of course not. Whoever heard of farm dogs being allowed in the house! They'll live out in the kennels."

"Daddy, can I have a dog of my own?" asked Roderick, feeling perfectly certain that neither Punch nor Pouncer would ever put a foot inside Holly Farmhouse.

"Well – I don't see why you shouldn't," began his father, pleased that Roderick, who had once been so afraid of dogs that he yelled if one went near, now wanted one of his own. But his wife interrupted at once.

"No, Roderick. You can't have a dog. Nasty noisy, messy creatures, covered in fleas!"

"Crackers never had a single flea!" began Roderick, indignantly. "I *wish* you liked dogs, Mother."

"I might get a cat, perhaps," said his mother.

"Pooh – a *cat*!" said Roderick, with the utmost scorn. "Who wants a cat? I bet there are dozens out in the stables anyway. There always are at a farm. Why can't I have a dog? I'd train it myself and I'd never let it worry you at all, Mother."

"Please don't bother me about a dog any more," said his mother. She saw Roderick's mutinous face and put out her hand to him. "What a dreadful face for mother's boy to put on the very first evening at home! Come here, darling."

But Roderick didn't come. He sat where he was, looking at the floor, sulking. He didn't want to be Mother's silly darling boy. He just wanted a dog.

CHAPTER 6

First Night At Holly Farm

It was fun to go to bed that night in the cosy bedrooms. It was lovely to have a hot bath and not have to carry up heavy pails of hot water, as they had had to do at Mistletoe Farm whenever anyone had had a hot bath. It was grand to switch on the reading lamp by the bed, instead of having to try and read by a guttering candle.

Melisande and Cyril took a long time undressing and messing about in their rooms that night. Both of them enjoyed the little luxuries of a soft carpet instead of bare boards with shabby thin rugs on them. Both of them liked to turn on the water in their basins instead of having to go and bang on the one bathroom door at Mistletoe Farm and yell to someone inside to buck up, they wanted to wash too!

The beds were soft and warm. The reading-lamps gave a bright, clear light, making reading in bed a pleasure. Melisande welcomed her mother warmly when she came in to say good night to her.

"Oh Mother – it's so lovely here, after Mistletoe Farm!" she said. "We *did* pig it there, you know! Now that I'm back in a decent place like this, I realize all I had to put up with – though the last few months I was there, I didn't seem to notice it. But this is something *like* a home!"

Her mother was pleased. She kissed Melisande good night and went in to Cyril.

"You must be very pleased to have left the hard life at Mistletoe Farm," she said. "I did feel so sorry for all you children having to stay there for so long."

226

Cyril was more loyal than Melisande. He remembered how hard his Aunt Linnie had had to work to look after six children instead of three for the eight months they had had to stay with her.

"I think perhaps it was good for us, Mother," he said. "It made me tough, you know – and I think I was a bit milk-and-watery before."

"Oh no, dear, you weren't," said his mother. "You were a well-mannered, well-brought-up boy – and there was no need for you to be tough! I want you to go back to your old nice ways now – and to begin with, dear, *don't* have your hair cut so short. It doesn't suit you."

"I'm not very keen on the kind of fellows who wear their hair long now," said Cyril, shortly. "And as for being tough – I'll need to be now if I'm going to help Dad on the farm."

"Oh, I couldn't allow that!" said his mother, shocked. "This is the first I've heard of such an idea! Why, you're only sixteen. You must go to school, of course – and perhaps to the university later – but you'll have to win a scholarship now, I'm afraid."

"I'm not clever enough," said Cyril, who had no illusions about his brains now. "I know I'm fond of poetry and music and reading and all that – but that won't win scholarships, just being fond of things! I've had to work harder since I went to Jack's school than I've ever had to work before, and I can see I've not got such good brains as any of the boys who win scholarships. So put that out of your head, Mother. I'm going to help Dad on the farm after this term."

His mother didn't argue with him. She felt quite sure that she could talk his father out of this idea, and persuade him to send Cyril back to school. She couldn't bear the idea of poor Cyril going on the farm so young – such hard work for him, too!

She said good night and went away. She wondered if Roderick was asleep. He had said rather a curt good night two hours before, and gone up to bed after making an enormous supper. She felt a little hurt. After all, Roderick was her youngest, her boy that she hadn't seen for so long. He had seemed to be the only one of the three who at all regretted leaving Mistletoe Farm.

She opened Roderick's door and went into the room without switching on the light. "Who's that?" said Roderick's voice at once.

"It's only Mother, darling," said Mrs Longfield, and went and sat on his bed. She stroked one of his hands, and wished he would put his arms round her as he used to before he went to Mistletoe Farm. He took his hand away.

"What's the matter, Roderick?" she said. "Aren't you glad to have Mother again?"

"Yes, of course," said Roderick. Then he burst out. "But if you were glad to have *me*, you'd give me a dog! What's the good of loving a person if you just won't give then what they want most in the world!"

His mother was startled. Roderick had never, never spoken like this to her before. Why, he sounded as if he didn't love her a bit! That's what came of letting him go to that awful Mistletoe Farm – he'd lost all his nice ways and nice talk. She debated what to say.

If she said firmly, no, he couldn't have a dog, he might sulk for days and spoil everything. If she put him off a little, she would soon win him round – after all, she had always been able to wind Roderick round her little finger. So she spoke gently to him.

"We'll see, Roderick. We'll just have to see."

"That means you won't give me one," said Roderick, at once. "Oh, I wish I was back at Mistletoe Farm with Susan and Aunt Linnie and Crackers. I shall go back there if I can't have a dog."

228

"Roderick lay and pictured Crackers' funny, mournful face."

"You're being silly," said his mother, shocked "You're just over-tired with all the excitement of the new house. Go to sleep now – and as I said, we'll see if you can have a dog. I'm not making any promises to a rude little boy."

She kissed him good night and went down the little flight of stairs, angry and disturbed. All this dog business! It would be bad enough to have two farm dogs rushing at her whenever she appeared outside, without having a tiresome dog in the house too.

Roderick lay awake, scowling. He knew he had been rude and unkind, but he was homesick for Mistletoe Farm. He wanted his Aunt Linnie. She didn't paw him about and pretend to be fond of him as his mother did – she really did like him and looked after him – she would have given him a dog, he knew she would!

And Susan would have said he must have one too. So

would Crackers, if he could talk. He *could* almost talk. Roderick lay and pictured Crackers' funny, mournful face, long black silky ears and loving, brown eyes. Now, if only he could have a dog like Crackers, he would be able to put up with anything at Holly Farm.

The cistern in the tiny box-like place next to his room gave a little gurgle. Roderick felt pleased. It sounded like Mistletoe Farm to hear that gurgle. He fell asleep listening for another gurgle, imagining that he was back in his room at Mistletoe Farm, with Crackers about to come into his room and jump on his feet.

Downstairs all was happy and peaceful. His mother and father sat beside the fire, happy to be together again. His father glanced at his pretty, young-looking wife with pleasure, thinking how fine it would be to have her here in the farm house looking after him and the children again. She would look nice even in the dairy, making the butter and setting out the bowls of cream. She would look nice feeding the hens. They would plan out the work together, and she would surprise him by doing it as if she had been country-born!

Mrs Longfield was pleased to have a home of her own again too. Of course, it was quite different from the lovely one she had had. Now she was a farmer's wife – but she would show everyone that it was possible to be a farmer's wife, and yet look pretty and dainty, and go to theatres and sit on committees just as she always used to do.

It didn't enter her head that her husband was expecting her to do any work on the farm. She had no thought of feeding hens, or grading eggs, and certainly not of washing them. As for making butter, well, she didn't even know how to, so that thought never occurred to her.

She sat there, peacefully sewing at the cushion, pleased with her good-looking husband, her "tough" Cyril, her pretty (though too-plump) daughter, and her youngest –

yes – pleased with him too even though he was so funny and obstinate. She would soon win him over.

Out in the kitchen Ellen sat reading by herself. She put down her book as the clock struck ten and got her hot water bottle. She yawned – a polite little yawn covered by her hand – not a vast, groaning yawn like Dorcas often gave, tired out at the end of the day.

She thought of Sally, who had gone home for the night, and was due to come back at seven the next morning. She didn't know whether she was going to get on with Sally or not. Sally was nothing but a rough, country girl without a thought in her head. Only seventeen too. Well, she would have to learn a few manners if she was going to share Ellen's kitchen.

As for those children, thought Ellen, she would keep them in their place from the very beginning. Master Cyril seemed all right – quiet and nicely spoken. Miss Melisande might want too much waiting on. As for that Master Roderick, demanding bread and cheese immediately after a meal, well, she would soon stop that kind of thing!

She thought of her mistress. Mrs Longfield was gentle and sweet – there wouldn't be much trouble with *her*. Ellen liked her all right. Thank goodness there were no dogs rampaging about the house. She wouldn't stay a week if there were – messing up everywhere and barking and wanting food at all times!

Ellen slipped quietly up to bed. Now only Mr and Mrs Longfield were left downstairs. Rose looked at her husband. "Are you going to be up early, dear?" she asked. "That's the worst of being a farmer. You have to be up so early, and go to bed so early too. There never seems any evening at all, in a farmer's life!"

"Rose, dear, if you want nice, long evenings you can have them," said her husband. "*You* won't need to get up early. You can have your breakfast in bed. And even though I'll have to get up about six, I shall try not to wake you – and I'll stay up as late with you at night as you wish. I won't become a country clod, I promise you!"

Rose smiled. She hadn't very much liked saying that she would live in the country. In fact she had fought against it for a long time. But if she could get her own way in everything, it wouldn't be so bad. It would be easy to make everyone do as she wanted them to do – she had always found it easy!

But it wasn't going to be as easy as she expected. There were plenty of shocks coming to the little family at Holly Farm – shocks that not one of them suspected on that cosy, happy night when they were all together under the same roof once more.

CHAPTER 7

Saturday

The six cousins did not see one another over the weekend. Jack, Jane and Susan had been told by their mother not to visit Holly Farm on Saturday and Sunday, but to let their three cousins settle down in their new home. They wondered and wondered how they were getting on.

"Melisande will be so pleased to have that nice bedroom for her own, instead of sharing with me as she's had to do for so long!" said Jane. "But *I'm* pleased to have my room to myself again, I really am. It's nice to have got rid of all Melisande's bottles and jars and boxes off my dressing-table. *I* shall never want to use face cream at night like she does."

"Well, I rather hope you will, when you're old enough," said her mother. "You don't want to look like one of those weather-beaten, dried-up women, do you, that we sometimes see at the market? Why *shouldn't* you look nice? Daddy and I much prefer looking at you when you're clean, and your hair is shiny, and your nails are nice."

"So do I," said Jack, unexpectedly. "You did use to look simply awful, Jane. And you smelt too."

"She only smelt of horses," said Susan. "Who minds that?"

"Quite a lot of people," said her mother. "Anyway, even *you* sometimes say that your precious Crackers smells dreadful, when he's got wet out in the rain. So he does."

"Well, even if he does, I don't really mind," said Susan, hugging him. "Mummy, I bet Roddy's missing Crackers, don't you? Do you suppose Aunt Rose will let him have a dog? I'm sure she won't."

"I hope she *will*," said her mother. "I believe Cyril and Melisande would like one too – but Roddy really *needs* a dog – something he can love and call his own. He's a funny boy."

"I quite miss him," said Susan. "And I'm sure Crackers does. Crackers went up to the room by the cistern this morning, where Roddy slept, and sniffed all round like anything. He's awfully puzzled – he can't think why Roddy and the others have disappeared all together so very suddenly."

"Well, he'll soon see them again, I've no doubt," said her mother. "Now, are you going to clean out the hen-house for me today, or are you not, Susan? You said you would, so I imagine you are – but if you don't hurry up you'll have to rush over it, and I know you like to take hours and hours."

233

"Yes, I do," said Susan. "It's a nice job, cleaning out the henhouse. And I like putting down the peat on the floor afterwards – it looks so clean and brown. And I like putting new straw into the nesting boxes. The hens like me fussing round too – they all like to come into the henhouse to talk to me. And I talk back – like this. . . ."

And Susan gave such a very good imitation of clucking that an enquiring hen put its head in at the open garden door to listen.

"There you are!" said Susan, triumphantly. "See that hen? It came into see what I was saying in hen language."

"Go on with you!" said her mother, shooing Susan and the hen out together. "You cluck all day long, either in your own language or someone else's! Go and talk to the hens and the ducks – I've got work to do."

Susan wandered off happily, with Crackers at her heels, his long black ears brushing the ground whenever he put his head down to sniff at any exciting smell. Susan loved school – but she loved Saturdays too. There were so many nice jobs to do on Saturdays. She would clean out the henhouse – she would go round the farmyard and look under all the nearby hedges to see if any hen had laid away. She would count up all the eggs that had been entered in the eggbook that week. She would grade all yesterday's and today's into different sizes and wash them all. She would. . . .

And Jane was happy too, about quite a lot of things. She had got her bedroom to herself again. She had done quite well at school that week. She hadn't got a single order-mark against her form. She had all the weekend to mess about in. What should she do?

"I'll groom Merrylegs," she thought. "I'll groom him down to the last hair of his tail. Then I'll clean out his stable. Well, I might perhaps clean out all the stables, it's such a nice cold day. And I might go and have a try at mending that bit of broken fence I saw the other day. I know where there's a bit of wood exactly the right size!"

Merrylegs, her pony, put his lovely head over the stable door as she came nearer. He whinnied softly. He adored Jane and she adored him.

"Hello!" she said, stroking his velvety nose. "You're the nicest animal in the world. And I'm going to make you look beautiful. No school today Merrylegs. It's Saturday."

Merrylegs knew that already, of course. All the three horses that the children rode knew when Saturday came. Jane opened the stable door and Merrylegs trotted out.

He was a bright chestnut pony from the New Forest. He had four white socks and a white star on his forehead, and was very loving and sweet-tempered. He swished his long tail, and nuzzled against Jane's shoulder.

Jane hissed as she groomed him. He liked that. Sometimes she whistled and he liked that too. Boodi, Susan's pony, put his wicked little head over his stable door and watched.

"I'm not grooming *you*, Boodi!" said Jane, severely. "You got loose yesterday at the stables where you waited for us to come out of school, and put your head in at a window and ate all the leaves off a plant standing on a table there. You're a bad horse, always into mischief!"

Boodi blew at her. He only really liked one person and that was Susan, though he had got used to Roderick too now. Jane would never ride him. He would gallop at top speed and then stop dead, just for fun, to see if he could throw his rider over his head. But he never did that to Susan.

Jack was happy too. He was glad to have his home and his mother to himself again, without his three cousins always demanding room and attention. He had gone up to his bedroom after breakfast and had rearranged the room completely, much to his mother's surprise.

235

"Merrylegs swished his long tail and nuzzled against Jane's shoulder."

"Well, Mother – I've felt it was Cyril's room more than mine, the last few months," said Jack. "All his books everywhere, and his bits and pieces. Now it's going to be mine and I've arranged it the way I like it."

236

Now he was out with his father, riding round the farm. His father rode his grey cob, Sultan, and Jack was on his own horse, Darkie, a Dartmoor pony with a black mane and tail. Jack liked these rides over the big farm with his father.

They looked at all the fields, lying brown and bare in the December sun, the frost getting at the earth and making it fine and powdery when the clods crumbled. They examined hedges to see that there were no gaps that the cows could squeeze through and get out on to the road. They looked solemnly at the herd of cows, and the cows looked back just as solemnly, chewing hard.

"They always look as if they were chewing gum, like the Americans do, don't they, Dad?" said Jack, and was rewarded by a guffaw of laughter from his father. They rode over to the hill where the sheep were. They looked well and healthy and their coats stood out round them, thick and curly.

"It's been a good year, Jack," said his father as they turned to ride back, after having a word with Hazel the shepherd about three sheep that were expecting very early lambs. "A very good year. That's how it was I was able to buy Holly Farm for your uncle."

"Suppose he has a bad year next year?" said Jack. "Will you lose money, Dad?"

"Yes. But he's a good worker, your uncle, and he understands farming, though living a town-life for years has set him back a bit," said his father. "It's your Aunt Rose that's going to be the making or marring of that trim little farm. She must help him. If she doesn't, he won't get far."

"Will Cryil help him too, Dad?" asked Jack. "Is he really going to leave school, as he said, and help on the farm. Why can't I leave too, and help *you*?"

"Because there's no need for you to," said his father

237

"I've got good men – and I want you to learn to use your brains, so that when you do come on the farm, you'll never be at a loss. And I want you to go to a farming college when you leave, and learn all the up-to-date methods. You'll be more help to me trained than untrained!"

"Will *Cyril* leave school this term, though?" persisted Jack.

His father hesitated. "Well – there'll be no real need for him to," he said. "Your uncle's got a few good men, and when he gets his cows and sheep and pigs and the rest, and gets on to his planting, he should be all right with the labour he's got. But Cyril wants some sense knocking into him – he's too la-di-da for my taste. It would really do him good to knock about the farm for a bit."

"He'd have to wear good leather boots and gaiters then, and not sandals!" said Jack, with a grin, remembering how Cyril had worn sandals, and artistic shirts and flowing ties that year. "Still, Dad, Cyril's come on a lot since he lived with us. He's jolly good at football now too."

His father reined in Sultan to shout to one of his men who was spreading mangels over a field for the stock. Jack listened with half an ear, taking in the quiet fields and the distant hills and the view of the rambling old farmhouse not far away.

He glanced at the bare oak trees on which enormous clumps of mistletoe grew – the mistletoe that gave the farm its name. How many years was it since that mistletoe first grew there, planted perhaps by some thrush who scraped his sticky beak on a bough and left a mistletoe seed behind? How many years had his father, and his grandfather and his great-grandfather too, gone each Christmas to the oak trees, and got down mistletoe for the old farmhouse?

"I'd hate to have gone to Holly Farm," thought Jack,

for the hundredth time. "This farm is in my blood and I'll never leave it!"

"What are you dreaming of, Jack?" said his father, surprised at the serious, far-away look on Jack's usually stolid face. "Something nice, I hope?"

"Yes. Very nice," said Jack, but he was too shy to say what it was. Off they cantered together in the bright December sun, the horses' breath steaming in the crisp and frosty air.

CHAPTER 8

Roddy Goes By Himself

The next day, Sunday, the children's mother rang up Aunt Rose at Holly Farm. "How are you all getting on?" she asked, kindly. "I do hope you've settled in nicely."

"Oh *yes*," said Aunt Rose. "It's all quite perfect. The children are *so* happy."

"That's splendid," said Mrs Longfield. "We do miss them. I wondered if you'd like to come over to tea today."

Aunt Rose hesitated. A vision of high tea at Mistletoe Farm came into her mind – table loaded with far too much food, she thought – her own children gobbling and guzzling with their cousins – just as they had nicely settled in and she was trying to get back to better ways! No – it would be too upsetting!

"Well, dear, thank you for asking us, but I think it would be nice for us to be just ourselves here our first weekend," said Rose, in a cooing sort of voice. "I don't

239

really think any of the children would want to leave. They'll all see each other at school tomorrow."

Roderick was in the hall, and he heard all this. He leapt towards his mother. "Oh, let's go!" he cried eagerly. "It would be fun. Susan would love us to go, I know she would."

"Be quiet," said his mother, sharply. She was afraid that his Aunt Linnie would hear what he said. She turned to the telephone again and began to tell her sister-in-law all about the house. Roderick wandered away, disappointed.

Why *shouldn't* they go over to Mistletoe Farm to tea? There was nothing to do on Holly Farm yet – no hens to feed, no stock to look after, no milking to do – nothing interesting at all. A farm wasn't a farm till you had lots of animals about. Why, there weren't even any dogs!

"We could just as well have gone," said Roderick to himself, and he went out into the tidy yard and kicked a stone round and round it. He thought it would be very nice to have high-tea again too – there was always an extra special one on Sundays at Mistletoe Farm, because old Dorcas baked on Saturday afternoons, and her cakes and scones were at their very best on Sundays.

He considered things carefully. Would it matter if *he* went? He badly wanted to see Crackers. He went to find Melisande and Cyril, who were reading in the sitting-room. It all looked very tidy and proper, and the room was hot.

"Phew!" said Roddy, and opened a window. "It's stifling in here! Why don't you two come out? It's a lovely day."

"For goodness sake! Shut that window, you idiot," said Melisande, crossly.

Roderick shut it and sat down with a heavy sigh. Cyril looked up.

"What's the matter with *you*? I suppose you're mourning for Crackers!"

"Well, I do miss him," said Roderick. "Don't you? Didn't you like him awfully?"

"He smelt," said Melisande.

"So do you," said Roderick, rudely. "You've got scent on again. *Smell*isande!"

Melisande stared at her small brother in angry surprise. Cyril reached out and slapped him. "Get out," he said, curtly. "Go on – get out of here till you're in a better temper."

Roderick didn't move. He went very red and pursed up his lips. He knew he had been rude to Melisande and he felt rather surprised at himself. But he wasn't going to apologise after that blow.

"I told you to get out," said Cyril again. "If you've got anything sensible to say, say it, and clear off."

"I came to say that Aunt Linnie had telephoned to ask us all over to tea," said Roderick. "Do you want to go? Mother's refused for all of us."

"Well, that's that, then," said Cyril. "Anyway, I don't want to go. There's something I want to hear on the radio. I bet Melisande doesn't want to turn out on a cold evening, either!"

"No, I don't," said Melisande. "Do go away and don't bother us any more, you little pest."

"Would it matter if *I* went over to tea?" persisted Roderick.

"Poor boy – homesick for his precious Aunt Linnie and Susan and Crackers!" said Cyril with a laugh. "Go and ask, Mother. I bet she won't let you go. Who's going to get out the car for *you*, anyway, and run you over? And there's no bus on Sunday afternoon."

"I could walk there," said Roderick, gloomily.

"You don't know the way. Stop kicking at the carpet and do something," said Melisande.

Roderick wandered out, scowling. He wondered what Susan was doing. He wondered if Crackers had done anything funny or clever that weekend. You never knew what a dog like that would be up to. He wondered if Dorcas had baked any of the ginger cake he loved.

"I shan't ask Mother if I can go," he thought. "She'd say no and then she'd be cross if I disobeyed. I'll go without saying anything. I'll say *I* wanted to accept the invitation, even if the others didn't."

So that afternoon, about three o'clock, Roderick set off over the fields by himself. He hoped he would be able to find the way all right. He had to go across those fields by the stream, then up the hill and over it, and then make his way towards the wood. After that – well, he guessed he'd find out all right which way to go. So, with his thick coat on, and a scarf, and his rubber boots, he set off secretly. Nobody saw him go.

Teatime came and his father, mother, Cyril and Melisande sat round the tea-table. "Where's Roderick?" asked his mother. Nobody knew.

"He'll come along soon," said Mr Longfield. "He hasn't much idea of time. He's probably gone for a walk. I wish he'd told me, because I'd have gone with him."

Roderick didn't turn up at all – because he was miles away, stumbling over the fields, completely lost. He didn't know the countryside nearly as well as Susan did. She wouldn't have been lost. She seemed to have a nose like a dog, where direction was concerned. But poor Roderick had taken as many wrong turnings as it was possible for him to take, and now he hadn't the remotest idea where he was at all.

To make things worse, there didn't seem to be any house in sight, and he met nobody at all. And now it was almost dark! He began to get frightened.

He was also extremely hungry. He simply couldn't *bear*

242

to think of the laden table there would undoubtedly be at Mistletoe Farm. He stumbled on over marshy ground, trying to find some kind of a path somewhere.

"Ssssst!" said a voice suddenly, and Roderick almost fell over in fright. Then, to his enormous delight a wet nose was thrust into his hand, and something licked him. Was it – *could* it be – Crackers?

No – it wasn't. But it was somebody almost as good. It was the golden spaniel belonging to the old poacher, Mr Twigg. He called his spaniel by the ridiculous name of Mr Potts, after the village policeman.

"Mr Potts! It's *you*!" said Roderick, in delight, fondling the excited dog. Then Twigg himself loomed up in the darkness beside him.

"Why, it can't be *you*, Master Roderick!" said Twigg, in an amazed voice. "What's brought you out in these here fields this December evening? You're miles from home."

"Oh Twigg – I'm *so* glad to see you," said Roderick, in rather a shaky voice. "I'm afraid I'm lost. I set out to go to tea at Mistletoe Farm – and I suppose I didn't know the way."

"I reckon you didn't," said Twigg, and he took the boy by the arm. "Now you hang on to old Twigg, and he'll take you a short way home."

"Do you mean – to Holly Farm, or to Mistletoe Farm?" asked Roderick.

Twigg chuckled. "I reckon I mean Mistletoe Farm?" he said. "That suit you?"

"Oh *yes*," said Roderick, relieved. And he and Twigg set off in the frosty evening together, and were soon treading a path through a field, with Mr Potts trotting at their heels, his nose almost touching them. Twigg talked away as usual, and Roderick listened. Twigg was a bad old poacher, but he was very good company, and had a

243

heart of gold where animals and children were concerned – and what he didn't know about the countryside wasn't worth knowing!

"Your pa got his stock yet?" he asked after a bit. "That's a tidy little farm he's got – Holly Farm. Mebbe I'll come and call on you one day and get you to show me all the corners."

"Oh Twigg, *do*! Please do!" begged Roderick, delighted. "Dad hasn't got any stock yet, though, not even a hen. And we haven't got a dog, think of that – though Dad's having two sent down from Scotland. Punch and Pouncer. But they won't be as nice as Crackers or Mr Potts. Spaniels are the very nicest dogs, I think."

"Why don't you get one of your own?" asked Twigg. "Them that loves dogs are the ones to have them – good for them and good for the dogs too. How'd it be if I got you a pup one day – there's Tommy Lane's dog will have a litter soon – and a good little spaniel she is too, as golden as mine."

Roderick was so overjoyed at this idea that he came to a standstill and Mr Potts bumped his nose against the back of his legs. "Twigg! *Could* you get me one? I'd like it better than anything in the world." Then his face fell. "But Mother wouldn't let me. She hates dogs."

"You ask your Dad then," said Twigg. "If he says yes, I'll tell Tommy Lane and he'll save you the best little dog of the lot."

In a dream of joy Roderick stumbled along with Twigg, wondering how he could ever repay him for such a wonderful gift. He was amazed when he suddenly found himself at Mistletoe Farm, and the farmdogs came barking joyfully up to him.

"We're here!" he said, and tore up to the door he knew so well. Twigg grinned to himself and went round to the kitchen door to see if old Dorcas was in a good enough mood to give him a cup of tea and a slice of home-made cake with a bit of cheese to go with it.

Mr Potts, the spaniel, went with him, looking forward to a bone and a chat with Crackers. He liked Mistletoe Farm. It was a friendly, welcoming sort of place!

CHAPTER 9

Roddy Gets Into Trouble

It was just a quarter to six when Roderick opened the door and ran up the passage to the sitting room. He sniffed the familiar smell of Mistletoe Farm – a smell of log-fires, and stored apples, baking, and farm coats and boots stored in the hall cupboard. He burst open the door, and looked in.

Everyone was sitting round the table at high tea. They had just begun. The oil-lamp was set in the middle, giving off its usual mellow light. The log fire crackled and flamed. Crackers gave a sudden loud bark and leapt on Roderick, licking him from head to foot.

"Why – *Roddy*!" said his aunt, amazed. "Roddy! Are the others here too? I though you weren't coming. Your mother said no, when I asked you all to tea."

"There's only me," said Roderick, holding on to Crackers, and beaming round at everyone. "I wanted to come. So I came. What a lovely tea you've got."

"Come and sit down," said Susan, pulling up a chair for him. "We missed you, Crackers and I. And I think Boodi did too. How did you know the way?"

"I didn't," said Roddy, and told Susan and the others

how he lost his way and Twigg had found him. His Aunt Linnie cut him a slice of spicy ham and set it on his plate. She wondered if his mother knew he had come. Fancy starting out all by himself across the fields when he didn't really knew the way!

The telephone bell rang loudly and everyone jumped. Crackers barked. Jack got up to answer it. It was his Aunt Rose, of course.

"Is that you, Jack? Tell me, do you know where Roderick is? He didn't turn up for tea at half-past four, and we can't find him anywhere. I don't think he'd have been naughty enough to come over to you, but . . ."

"He *is* here," said Jack. "He's just arrived. And he's about to have a jolly good tuck-in, Aunt Rose!"

There was an angry silence. "How *very* naughty of him," said his aunt, in a most annoyed tone. "Not to say a word to any of us, either. He's to come home immediately Jack – immediately!"

"But how?" said Jack. "There's no bus till seven o'clock, and that's always crammed full with people coming back from the next village. He'd better stay the night."

Aunt Rose nearly had a fit. "Certainly *not*," she said. "He's a very naughty boy. He's not to stay to high tea – which is what you're having now, I suppose – and he's to come home at once."

Jack's mother took the receiver out of his hand. Jack was thankful. He didn't like dealing with Aunt Rose when she was in that kind of mood. His mother spoke soothingly into the telephone.

"It's all right, Rose. The child meant no harm – he probably wanted to see us all again, and that was very nice of him. I expect he missed Susan and Crackers a bit. We'll give him a good meal and keep him for the night."

"You'll do no such thing!" cried Rose, in anger. "I tell you, he's a naughty boy, and I won't have him fussed and

246

pampered by you – slipping off like that so deceitfully – causing me all this worry. He never used to be like that – he's quite changed since he lived with you."

"Rose," said Mrs Longfield, warningly, "I can't have you speaking like that. Roddy's all right. And I shall most certainly give the child a meal – he's starving with hunger! But we'll send him back afterwards if you insist."

"I do insist," said Rose, in a trembling voice and slammed down the receiver. Mrs Longfield stood by the telephone, troubled. Silly, jealous, selfish Rose. She would have a lot of trouble with Roddy if she didn't handle him properly. Certainly he had changed – changed a lot, from a namby-pamby, scared little mother's boy, to somebody sensible and trustable, who knew his own mind, and was loyal to the people who had loved him and cared for him at Mistletoe Farm. Mrs Longfield hardly knew what to say when she went back to the sitting room.

Jack had shut the door so that Roddy and the others had heard very little. Roddy was looking rather scared now, but he was tucking in fast, all the same, afraid that he would be made to go before he had satisfied his hunger.

"Your mother was worried about you, Roddy," said his aunt, coming in. "You mustn't slip off without telling her another time. You must tell her you're sorry when you get back, and make things right again." She turned to her husband. "Could you run Roddy back in the car after his meal?" she asked. "I hate to turn you out on a Sunday evening – but would you?"

"Why can't David get out *his* car and come and fetch Roderick?" said her husband.

"Because Aunt Rose wouldn't *let* him!" said Susan, in her clear voice. "You know she wouldn't, Daddy."

"Be quiet, Susan," said her mother, exasperated by Susan's unerring habit of knocking unpleasant nails well and truly on the head. Roderick looked thoroughly miserable. He stopped eating.

"Pass Roderick a sausage roll," said Mrs Longfield, wondering how to manage a pert Susan, a miserable Roderick, and a scowling husband at one and the same time. She too thought that Roddy's father should get his own car and fetch him, instead of Mr Longfield bothering to do so on his precious Sunday evening. But what a fuss Rose would make!

Jane was sorry for Roddy, but she was glad he wasn't going to stay the night. After all, they'd only just got *rid* of their cousins – Jane didn't want any of them back again so soon. Susan wouldn't have minded, of course. She was fond of Roddy, and so was Crackers.

Roddy couldn't enjoy his meal after the telephone call. He dreaded going back home now. He couldn't make up his mind if Mother would reproach him and almost cry – or-whether she would be cold and angry, as she knew so well how to be. She might tell his father to whip him. And his father always did everything Mother told him, then that would happen too. Roddy hardly tasted the delicious sausage roll, and even said no to a slice of ginger cake.

"Well, if you won't have it now, you must take it home with you," said his aunt, and wrapped up a large slice in a piece of paper. "Dorcas said yesterday when she was making it that she hoped you'd have a piece."

"Oh – thanks, Aunt Linnie," said Roderick, and put it in his pocket. He sat back and looked round. He hadn't known how fond he had got of this untidy cosy room. He looked at the picture of horses over the mantlepiece. He looked at the big basket of logs by the fireplace. He looked at the rosy face of his aunt, and for the hundredth time told himself that nobody else in the world had such kind eyes.

He looked at stolid Jack, munching away, and at Jane

with her mop of swinging hair. He looked at his uncle who had now retired behind a newspaper, holding it well up in front of his face because he was half afraid his wife was going to say something about the car again. He did *not* see why he should turn out. Let the boy stay the night!

Susan squeezed close to Roddy, and Crackers licked the two bare knees near his nose, one belonging to Susan, and one belonging to Roddy. "Did you miss Crackers?" whispered Susan.

Roddy nodded. "I wish you'd lend him to me sometime," he said beseechingly. "Just for one night – or perhaps two. Till I get used to Holly Farm."

"I couldn't," said Susan, at once. "You know I couldn't. I wouldn't lend him to the King of England."

"*He* wouldn't want him," argued Roddy. "But I do. I . . ."

Dorcas appeared at the door to clear away. Jane got up to help her. "I'll help too," said Roddy. "To pay for my lovely tea! Hello, Dorcas!"

"Well, here's a surprise!" said Dorcas, and ruffled his hair with her big hand. "And no wonder half the food's gone from the table, with *you* here again! How's my niece Sally getting on over at Holly Farm?"

"I don't know. All right, I think," said Roddy. "She's nice, Dorcas. I like her. She's like you a bit, I think, But she doesn't like Ellen. She told me so. I don't like her either."

Dorcas gave a sniff as she led the way into the kitchen, Roddy behind her with a laden tray. "Stuck-up piece she is!" she said. "I heard about her from the grocer."

Dorcas always heard about everything and everyone from the grocer, the laundry-man, and the postman. As soon as anything happened, old Dorcas knew it. She sniffed again and then rummaged about in the larder and produced two sausage rolls.

249

"You take these home with you," she said. "Sally's a good enough cook, but she don't make rolls like these."

"Oh thanks," said Roddy, thinking he was really doing very well. He put the paper bag of rolls beside the slice of ginger cake in his pocket.

In the sitting room an argument was going on. "You *must* take him home, dear," Mrs Longfield was saying to Roddy's uncle. "I'd love him to stay the night but Rose doesn't want him to."

"I don't care what Rose wants," said her husband, who had no love for his sister-in-law. "Why should I get out the . . ."

Goodness knows how the argument would have ended if there hadn't suddenly been an outbreak of hooting outside the house – it was Roddy's father who had got his own car out and come to fetch Roddy! Thank goodness! thought Mrs Longfield and ran to open the door and let him in.

"Couldn't let you bother to run him over," Roddy's father said to his brother. "Where's the little idiot? He's upset his mother properly. She didn't even want me to come and fetch him – said you were to bring him over. It's a pity this had to happen our first weekend."

Mrs Longfield thought secretly that before many weeks had passed many more things of a similar kind would happen, but she didn't say so. She called Roddy, kissed him goodbye and sent him out to the car. His father wouldn't stay a minute.

Roddy was very silent in the car. His father spoke gruffly but not unkindly to him. "You're to apologize to your mother. You're to have no supper. And you're to go straight up to bed. And remember, Roddy – Holly Farm is your home now, and you belong there and not to Mistletoe Farm."

"Yes, Dad," said Roddy, in a low voice. He did exactly

250

as his father said when he got home. He told his mother he was sorry, and listened to her reproaches without a word. He said nothing about supper, but went up to bed at once. He undressed and got into bed. Then he turned out his light.

He lay there for a while and then, when he heard the others at supper, he got out his two sausage rolls and his slice of ginger cake. Whatever anyone said, he was going to have *his* supper too. "And I bet it's a nicer one than they're having downstairs!" he said fiercely. But all the same poor Roddy didn't really enjoy it very much!

CHAPTER 10

Christmas Comes

The next day was Monday – school again. Roddy was very thankful and tore off immediately after breakfast to wait for the bus. His mother had her breakfast in bed, and he had tiptoed in whilst she was still half-asleep, given her a half-hearted morning kiss, and gone.

Cyril and Melisande had been very scornful about his little escapade. "Making us go hunting all over the place for you!" said Cyril. "And Mother thinking you'd been kidnapped or something. Pity you weren't!"

"I met Twigg," said Roddy, trying to change the subject.

"Pooh – that horrid, smelly old poacher," said Melisande at once. "You be careful of him. He'd better not start coming to *our* kitchen door. Ellen would soon tell him to clear off."

"Sally wouldn't," said Roderick.

"Sally's only a silly girl," said Melisande. "She's not very polite to Ellen, either. Ellen complained to Mother."

"*I* don't feel very polite to Ellen somehow, do you?" said Roderick. "She looks at me as if I was a bit of mud, or something. I daren't go into the kitchen when she's there."

Cyril came back to the subject of Roderick's escapade. He had very much resented having to turn out into the dark, frosty farmyard and hunt about for a Roderick who wasn't there. He said quite a lot about it to Roderick, who rapidly got bored and annoyed.

"Twigg says he can get me a spaniel like Mr Potts," he said, trying once more to change the subject.

"Mother'd never let you have a dog!" said Melisande at once. "*I* don't want one in the house either."

"What – not one like that lovely golden spaniel Twigg's got – Mr Potts?" said Roderick, amazed. He was sorry now that he had mentioned it. Melisande might go and tell his mother before he, Roderick, had sounded his father. He debated how to change the subject again. Fortunately for him the bus arrived at that moment and they all got in.

Melisande met Jane and Susan at school that morning. Susan ran up to her, pleased to see her again. "Hello! How are you getting on at Holly Farm? Do you like it? How's everybody?"

"We like it all very much," said Melisande. "You should see my bedroom, Jane and Susan – it's perfect. The towels have even got my intials on, and match the bedspread. And it's heaven to wash in a proper basin with running water. You really *must* see my bedroom."

"You ought to see mine now, too," said Jane, a little snappily. "I've got room to move about!"

"I don't have to wash up any more," went on Melisande, "or even lay the table. And even when the

252

hens come I shan't bother with them. As for cleaning them out – ugh – I'll never do that again!"

"Who's going to do them then?" demanded Jane. "I bet your father won't have time. And no farmer ever spares a man for silly work like feeding hens."

"Oh, something will be arranged," said Melisande airily. "Anyway, the thing is – you've just no idea what it means to be in a place like Holly Farm with running water and electric light and everything nice."

Jane and Susan soon got tired of all this. They left the excited Melisande and went off to their own friends. Melisande, although about the same age as Jane, was in a class below her, and soon she was regaling her own particular friends there with details of the model farmhouse she had now moved to.

"I hope she gets over it soon," said Jane to Marilyn, her own friend. "I sort of feel she's making more of it then she otherwise would just so as to make me feel that my own home, Mistletoe Farm, is down-at-heel and old-fashioned and shabby."

"Yes. That's rather like Melisande," said Marilyn. "Never mind – it's holidays soon, and maybe you won't need to see her much. I never did like her, anyway, though I tried to, because she was your cousin."

The holidays soon came, and then there was Christmas to look forward to. Mrs Longfield, at Mistletoe Farm, asked all the Holly Farm folk over to Christmas Day. At first Rose hadn't wanted to accept, because she wanted Christmas in her new house.

But Ellen didn't seem at all keen on doing anything extra for Christmas. Sally was willing enough, but Ellen told her mistress that, what with the move, and the new country air, she didn't really feel up to coping with big Christmas parties, so if Madam felt she would like to accept the invitation from Mistletoe Farm, she, Ellen, would be very glad.

"And seeing that Sally and I are both asked too, I'd be willing to give a hand there," she said, as if it was a tremendous favour.

Melisande and Cyril were disappointed, because they too had looked forward to Christmas Day at Holly Farm. But Roddy could have shouted with delight. He didn't, of course, because he had sensed his mother's jealousy of Mistletoe Farm, and said very little about it now. But his heart filled with joy when he thought of Christmas Day over at Mistletoe Farm.

"I bet Dorcas does wonders!" he thought. "I bet there'll be the biggest plum pudding in the world, and the finest mince pies. Gosh, it will be grand!"

It certainly was grand. Everyone went to church on Christmas Day, then they all met together at Mistletoe Farm. It looked beautiful, decorated with mistletoe from the old oak trees, and red-berried holly from many of the holly trees around. Old Man's Beard was twined everywhere too, like wool from grey sheep, and Susan had made strings and strings of tiny cardboard lanterns and paper-chains.

"It's lovely, Sue," said Roderick, admiringly. "Much better than ours. Mother doesn't like decorations much because she says they make such a mess. I say – what a wonderful smell from the kitchen. Do you think we could go out there? I've got a present for Dorkie."

Dorcas was bending over the enormous oven, her face as red as the berries on the holly round her big kitchen. She was basting the turkey. She slammed the oven door shut and beamed at the children.

"What's that? You've got a present for me, Master Roderick? Well, I never. What do you want to go and bother with old Dorcas for?"

"Because you're a very nice person," said Roddy, promptly. "I made it myself for you, Dorcas."

"It was a little carved figure that Roddy had made out of a piece of wood. He had carved a bird because Dorcas was fond of birds, and fed them every day. She admired it very much and put it up on the mantelpiece in a place of honour.

"I hope you'll enjoy the plum pudding, Master Roderick," she said. "You helped to stir it – do you remember?"

They remembered all right. "When I stirred it I was afraid Daddy was going to buy Holly Farm for *us*," said Susan, "and then we'd have had to leave dear old Mistletoe Farm. So when I stirred I wished and I wished we'd never leave Mistletoe Farm – and I made Crackers stir and wish too, didn't I, Crackers – and our wish came true."

"Now you go back to the others and leave me to getting the dinner for you," said Dorcas. "And could you take the old cat with you, because she does keep getting under my feet so. Put her down by the fire in the sitting room, and she'll purr away there like a happy kettle."

Roderick picked up the cat, and he and Susan and Crackers went back to the others. Roddy's mother was looking very young and pretty as she sat talking to some people who had called in. Mrs Longfield looked at her admiringly. How did she manage to keep so pretty and attractive? Mrs Longfield caught sight of herself in a mirror and sighed. Oh dear – her hair was ruffled again, and her face was red with hurrying to see to this, that and the other.

The Christmas dinner was magnificent "And no wonder," said Mr Longfield, beaming at his wife "You and Dorcas are the best cooks in the world! Goodness knows what you do with a turkey to make it taste like this. Isn't she a marvellous cook?"

"Rather!" said his brother. He turned jovially to his wife. "It a pity *you* can't cook like this, Rose," he said.

"The plum pudding was the biggest Roderick had ever seen."

"I've never needed to," said Rose, in a rather a cold voice. "And I hope I never shall."

"I shouldn't think you could boil an egg, could you, Aunt Rose?" asked Susan, in an interested voice. "*I* can boil an egg, and fry bacon, and make toffee and . . ."

"Really?" said Aunt Rose, in such a bored voice that Susan fell silent.

The plum pudding was the biggest Roderick and the others had ever seen. It came in surrounded by purple and yellow flames, all on fire. It was full of money – or so it seemed! Roderick got a sixpenny bit and a threepenny bit, Susan got a shilling, Melisande got a thimble, much to her digust, and Cyril got a threepenny bit. Roderick offered Jane his sixpence, but she wouldn't take it.

"Thanks awfully, all the same," she said. "But you have to keep what you find in puddings, you know."

"Well, I'll *buy* you something with the sixpence then," said Roderick.

Crackers, fruit, nuts, jokes – everything was just right for Christmas. Mrs Longfield was a good housewife and had forgotten nothing. Mr Longfield glanced proudly at her. His Linnie certainly worked hard every day – but whatever she did was very successful.

"She makes the best jam, the best pickles, bottles the fruit perfectly – and she's cheerful all the time!" he thought. He raised his glass and called out a toast.

"To Linnie – all our love – we couldn't do without her!"

The children raised their glasses of orangeade and lime-juice, and shouted at the tops of their voices.

"Mummy! My love!"

"Aunt Linnie – all the best!"

"Best mother in the world!"

"Best aunt too!"

"God bless you, Linnie," said Uncle David – and the only one who found it difficult to join in with pleasure was Aunt Rose. Would anyone ever toast her like that, with delight and joy and love? She couldn't help feeling just a little bit doubtful.

CHAPTER 11

Work At Holly Farm

"Can't *we* give a party, Mother?" asked Melisande, a little while after Christmas. She had very much enjoyed all the jollity at Mistletoe Farm. Everyone had, in fact, except Aunt Rose – and Ellen.

Ellen had not been a success in Dorcas's kitchen. Dorcas couldn't bear her "sourpuss ways," as she called them. She and Sally worked hard, joking and laughing, managing the old-fashioned range well. But Ellen turned up her nose at everything.

"What a place!" she said. "I couldn't stay here a week. That awful stove!"

"Maybe you wouldn't be wanted to stay for more than a week," said Dorcas. "Now, just hand me those tea cloths – land-sakes, can't you even wash up without being told? Sally, don't gape, child. Put another kettle on the stove."

No – Ellen had certainly not enjoyed herself. Dorcas hadn't been impressed by her fine, high-and-mighty ways, and Sally had giggled. Ellen had been very glad to get back to Holly Farm with all its trim neatness and plentiful hot water.

Now Melisande wanted a party. Well, why not? Her mother thought for a moment and then said yes, they would have one in February, when it was her birthday.

"Oh yes – it would be nice to have a party on your birthday, Mother," said Melisande. "Daddy would like that too."

"We'll show your Aunt Linnie that we can put up a much better party than she does!" said her mother. "We'll ask them all over here – and we'll ask all the neighbours too, and you can ask that nice boy – what's his name – the one whose party you and Jane went to in the summer."

"Oh yes – Richard Lawson," said Melisande, pleased. "He's got that wonderful horse, Lordly-One. Perhaps he will ride over on it and show it to Daddy. We'll ask his mother too. She's awfully nice."

Mrs Longfield was pleased to have a party to work for. She began to make all kinds of plans, though it was still a long way ahead. She would have this door taken off and that one – and so join up two rooms nicely. She would turn Cyril's room into a coat-room. She would have this food and that food, and order all kinds of things.

258

She told her husband about her plans. He nodded but didn't smile very much over the idea. "You'll remember, Rose, won't you, that we're not well-off now?" he said. "You can't give extravagant parties like the ones you used to give. You mustn't order this food and that from the London stores – it must all be done at home, just like Linnie does it."

"I didn't think you'd grudge me a birthday party," said his wife, looking like a spoilt little girl.

"I don't," said Mr Longfield, putting his arm round her. "But you know that our new cows and hens and ducks and sheep are coming soon, Rose, and they've got to be paid for – and wages have got to be paid too. I shall have a shepherd to pay and a stockman and an odd man too, you know – and there are Ellen's wages and Sally's. It's a lot to come out of a little farm like this."

"All right. I'll manage everything I can at home," said Rose. "I expect Sally and Ellen can get down to the cooking and baking. I'll have things like sausage rolls and ham – a sort of cold buffet."

Whilst Rose went ahead with her plans, Mr Longfield went ahead with the buying of his stock. His brother Peter, from Mistletoe Farm, gave him all the help he could. Together they chose the best animals in the market, and bought pedigree hens and ducks, and a fine healthy sow.

His brother sold him ewes about to lamb, and there came a day when at last Holly Farm seemed a real farm! Cows mooed in the meadow across the lane, sheep trotted over the grass, and the great sow stretched herself out in the pigsty in the yard.

"Have we *got* to have her there?" asked Mrs Longfield, wrinkling up her nose in disgust. "I'm sure I can smell pig-smell already."

"Well, you can't, Mother," said Roderick, earnestly.

"Pigs only smell when their sties are foul and dirty. Our sow has a tiled sty, and it's washed down every day. You'll never, never smell Martha."

"Martha?" said his mother, startled.

"Yes – I've called her that," said Roderick. "It suits her somehow. I like her."

The hens rushed about the yard all day long, clucking. The ducks, white Aylesburys, swam vigorously on the little pond off the yard. Every creature looked healthy and bonny, especially Martha the sow – and everything seemed to Melisande and her mother to be very very noisy indeed!

"Surely our ducks quack more loudly than any others?" groaned Mrs Longfield, early in the morning. "And *need* we keep that cock? He wakes me up regularly at dawn."

"Yes. He's as good as an alarm clock," said her husband. "I get up as soon as I hear him. *You* needn't worry, Rose – you're always off to sleep again in a few seconds!"

The cows mooed, the sheep baaed. The stockman whistled, the door of the milkshed banged in the wind. Mrs Longfield complained all day long, and her husband tried to be as patient with her as he could.

"If you live on a farm, you must expect this kind of life," he said. "Cheer up, Rose – you'll soon be so used to it that you'll never hear the noises except as a sort of soothing background. And by the way, dear – now that one of the cows has calved, and we have plenty of milk, what about the butter? Pat, the stockman, says his wife can't do it any more, and to tell you the truth, I can't afford to have her either. It's easy to make butter. I'd like you to take on the job."

Rose stared at him in horror. "Make butter? I couldn't possibly! It's heavy work, swinging that churn over and over. I've watched Mrs Lacy, and I know I couldn't do it."

"Don't be silly, Rose," said her husband. "It's only a knack. You've hardly anything to do, and, you know, a farmer can't afford to have a wife who's idle. Most farmers' wives love to help. You must help too. And you must take on the chickens as well. I want you to feed them, collect the eggs, grade them and wash them for market."

"And clean out the henhouse three times a week too, I suppose?" said Rose, bitterly.

"No. I'll do that – or one of the boys," said her husband. "You know, you persuaded me to send Cyril back to school again, didn't you – or he could have done these jobs and many others. Do you want me to take him away after all?"

Rose resented all these jobs bitterly. She resented being told she had nothing to do. Didn't she do the dusting, make some of the beds with Ellen, do all the flowers, and most of the mending? What else did David expect?

"I suppose he expects the same of me as Peter gets out of Linnie," she thought, angrily. "Why did I ever come here? There's Linnie washing and cooking and doing a hundred jobs on the farm and in the house, and David thinks I ought to do the same. And he'll go on thinking it as long as he has Linnie under his nose at Mistletoe Farm, bragging about her pickles, and jams, and fruit!"

Linnie never did brag or boast. She merely took it for granted that these things were her job, to be done well and lovingly for her husband and children, and she did them, and was happy in the doing. She would have given Rose plenty of advice and help if her sister-in-law had asked her – but Rose would never ask anyone for advice!

With a very bad grace Rose took on a few jobs. She said she couldn't possibly carry the heavy chicken pails of food to the chickens and ducks in the morning, so Cyril offered to do it. It meant that he had to run to catch his bus every day, and sometimes missed half his breakfast – but his mother, lying in bed with her own breakfast, didn't even know that.

The poultry had to be fed again in the afternoon before darkness set in, but that was easy – merely corn that could be scattered. Rose did that all right – but once or twice she left it too late and all the hens had gone to roost.

Her husband came along and found her scattering corn in the hen yard, almost in the darkness. He felt annoyed.

"Rose! What's the good of that? The hens have gone to roost. They won't come out in the dark."

"Well, they can eat it early in the morning, then," said Rose.

"They won't. The rats will have had it long before then," said her husband. "We don't want to encourage *them*!"

"Rats!" said Rose, and shuddered. "Oh, are there rats about here? I don't think I shall be able to feed the chickens if there are."

In the end, Sally fed the chickens in the afternoon, and collected the eggs. And when Roddy came home from school he washed them and graded them. Rose said it spoilt her hands to keep them in water so long, these cold days.

"Well, I *like* doing it," said Roddy. "But it will mean I'm in late for tea each day, Mother. You tell Ellen to leave me mine on a tray."

So after that Roddy didn't go in to the dainty afternoon tea, but had it on a tray anywhere he liked. And it wasn't Ellen who got his tray ready, either – it was Sally, and she saw to it that Roderick got a first rate tea, fit for a hungry boy. His mother would have been most astonished if she had seen Roderick devouring ham sandwiches, hard boiled eggs and a great slices of kitchen cake every day at half-past five, after he had done his "egg-job" as he called it.

He liked doing jobs by himself – but nowadays he pretended that he had someone with him – a dog of his own. He talked to his imaginary dog all the time.

"Here's a fine egg, Tinker – as brown as an acorn almost. Down, sir, down – you'll break the egg. And here's another. Nice clean lot today, Tinker. We'll soon be done and then we'll see what's on our tray. Down, dog, down – you're as licky as Crackers! I'll give you a whole ham sandwich to yourself, you're such a good dog."

Nobody heard him except the sleepy hens and one of the stable cats. Sometimes Punch and Pouncer, the two farm dogs safely in their kennels for the night, caught a sound of his murmuring voice and pricked up their ears. But nobody ever disturbed Roderick and his pretend-dog, Tinker.

CHAPTER 12

What Happened One Saturday

One Saturday a dreadful thing happened. An Alsatian dog, half-wild, got into the field where the ewes were, and chased two of them round and round the field. The shepherd had gone off for the day to see his sick mother, and Mr Longfield was at the market. So it was only Roderick who saw what was happening.

He got a stick and ran shouting at the dog. It turned, leapt over the hedge and disappeared. But the damage had been done. Before an hour had gone by both the ewes had lambed – and one ewe was dead beside her two tiny lambs, and the other was alive, with one hardly-breathing lamb.

Roderick was so full of pity and horror that he didn't

know what to do. Where was the stockman? He was nowhere to be seen! Where was the odd-job man – miles away mending a fence somewhere probably. Cyril was playing in a football match.

He rushed off to find Melisande or his mother. But when he had blurted out his story of the dead sheep and the half-dead lamb belonging to the other ewe, his mother turned white.

"I think I'm going to faint," she said. "Oh, the poor things. No, no – don't ask me to come, Roderick. I couldn't, I couldn't."

Roddy left Melisande to see to his mother, and went flying off again, sick with fear. He must do something, he must! Those little twin lambs would die if he didn't do something – and the third lamb was hardly alive.

He bumped into Sally, coming home from her Saturday shopping. He clutched at her.

"Sally! Come quickly! What are we to do? An Alsatian chased the sheep – and now they've got lambs and one sheep's dead. Oh, Sally, what do we do to save the lambs?"

Sally was startled. Then she began to run at top speed down a path. "I'll be back!" she cried. "Don't you fret. I'm fetching somebody."

She disappeared round a hedge and then Roderick heard her shouting and yelling at the top of her voice.

"Sam Twigg! Hey, Sam Twigg! SAM TWIGG!"

"Twigg!" thought Roderick, and his heart lifted. "If only Twigg can come, it'll be all right."

And round the corner with Sally came the short bent figure of Sam Twigg the poacher, limping a little as usual, with Mr Potts, his golden spaniel at his heels.

"Where be they ewes?" he called. Roderick tore up to him. "Here – up in the field," he panted, and the three of them went together through the gate and into the big field.

"Bad enough to lose a fine ewe like that, let alone a little new lamb," muttered Twigg, as he stood looking down at the dead sheep. Her twin lambs were wriggling, and were alive – but the tiny lamb belonging to the other mother had died.

"Can we bottle-feed these?" asked Roderick, almost in tears.

"No," said Twigg. "They'm too small. Come too soon into the world they have. Drat that Alsatian. This isn't the first mischief he've done by a long way. Sally, girl, we'll try the old trick to save these younguns. I'll skin the little dead one, and wrap the two live ones in the dead skin. Then we'll see if the mammy of the dead one will take to them and feed them. It's their only chance."

Twigg was wonderfully deft and quick. In a trice, with Sally solemnly and sadly helping him, he skinned the dead lamb as if it were a rabbit.

The mother had sniffed at it many, many times, wondering why it did not move. Twigg went to the other two lambs, lying by their dead mother, and wrapped the skin of the dead one right over them.

Roderick watched in wonder and astonishment. Whatever was Twigg doing?

But Twigg knew what he was doing all right. He carried the two wriggling new-born lambs to the mother of the dead one, and laid them down beside her, holding the skin tightly over them.

The mother turned away. They were not her lambs. But soon she caught the smell of the skin that lay over the lambs. It had the smell of her own lamb!

She turned her head round and sniffed. She sniffed again. Yes, that was the smell of her own lamb – and yet there was another smell with it too, that wasn't her lamb at all.

She sniffed more closely. One of the tiny creatures wriggled against her, and nuzzled into her soft wool. The ewe bleated very softly. "Ba-aaa!"

"She've taken to them," said Twigg, in delight. "See that? She's licking them now. Another minute and she'll have them for good. You watch."

Holding their breath, Sally and Roderick watched. The big ewe was nuzzling the little lambs lovingly. Carefully Twigg pulled away the skin, so that she could smell the two lambs more strongly. Soon their smell and the smell of the skin were so intermingled that the ewe could not tell one from the other. She didn't even notice when Twigg pulled the skin away and put it into one of his baggy pockets.

They watched the ewe with the two lambs. "She've taken them for hers," said Twigg. "Well, Master Roderick, it's a sad business this – and I'm right down sorry for your Pa – but at least we've saved him two of his lambs."

"Oh Twigg – thank you," said Roderick. "What do we do now? Anything?"

"When's Shepherd coming back?" said Twigg. "He'll need to put hurdles round this ewe and her lambs. I'll wait for him, Master Roderick. You go on in with Sally. I'll give Shepherd a hand with the dead ewe too. Don't you fret. Farming's a toss-up, always was. Got to take the rough with the smooth, though there's some as gets more of the rough than they deserve."

Roderick was quite glad to go into the warm kitchen with Sally. Ellen pounced on her at once. "And where have you been all this time, Miss, I'd like to know. The bus has been and gone this hour since."

"Ellen, it's not Sally's fault," said Roderick. "There's been an – an accident with the sheep. Sally's been helping me."

Sally took not the slightest notice of Ellen. She might not have been there at all. She went to the larder and got a hunk of bread and a bit of cheese and a glass of milk. She set them on a tray and spoke to Roderick.

"You set to and get those down, Master Roddy. You've

266

seen bad things this morning and you're upset-like. You get those down you and you'll feel better."

Roddy did feel better after he had eaten and drunk. He wondered if his father was back yet. He thought he had heard the car. He went out to see.

Yes – it was his father. Roderick wished he hadn't got to tell him the bad news. But then he saw Twigg going up to him. Thank goodness Twigg would tell him.

Mr Longfield looked grim and shocked. It was a serious thing to lose a valuable ewe and a lamb in such a way. Twigg pointed to Roddy, and then beckoned him.

"Roddy," said his father. "This is an awful thing for you to have been mixed up in. But Twigg tells me you were a great help, and you did all you could between you. Thanks, Roddy."

He went off to the field to see the ewe and the twin lambs, and to mourn over his dead ewe too. This really was a bit of bad luck. He had only had the ewe a few weeks too. He built a hurdle round the live ewe and the two lambs she was now very pleased with.

"Why didn't you tell your mother?" he asked, when he had finished. "She would have come and helped."

"I did tell her," said Roderick, turning away. "She said she felt faint. She couldn't come."

"I see," said his father, and then the two of them looked at one another. They didn't say any more, but each was thinking the same thing.

"Sally didn't faint. Sally's only seventeen, but she came and helped." And Mr Longfield was ashamed of his wife, and alas, Roddy was ashamed of his mother.

Mrs Longfield was amazed when she heard what Twigg had done to save the two new-born lambs. "That fellow Twigg!" she said. "That poacher fellow! I've forbidden Ellen to let him come to the back door. Fancy *him* doing all that."

"Rose – Twigg is no longer forbidden to come to the back door," said Mr Longfield. "You will please tell Ellen he is to have a cup of tea whenever he's round this way."

"But she'll leave if she has to give tea to all the poachers in the district!" cried Rose.

"Let her," said her husband and went out of the room. He actually banged the door. Melisande and her mother looked at one another.

"Oh dear – I do hope Daddy isn't going to lose all his nice manners now he's a farmer," sighed Mrs Longfield. "He's never slammed a door like that before."

"He's upset about the ewe," said Melisande. "It *is* a loss, you know, Mother. Perhaps we'd better not have that party."

But before they could say any more, the door opened and Ellen came in with a message. Then she went out again. Melisande looked at her mother.

"You didn't give her Daddy's message," she said. "About Twigg. Aren't you going to?"

"No, I'm not," said her mother. "What good is Twigg to us? Ellen's worth more to us than Twigg! We'd be lost without her. Daddy can have his way in some things – but *we* must have our way sometimes, too, Melisande, mustn't we?"

And Melisande nodded her head. *She* wouldn't give the message to Ellen either. Twigg should still be forbidden to come to the back door – nasty little poacher! What would it matter anyway?

But it did matter. Melisande and her mother had ranged themselves against her father – they were disloyal to him. The family was splitting up into ones and twos. It was no longer united as the Mistletoe Farm family was.

Meantime, because of Twigg, the ewe up in the field was happy, and two motherless lambs had a mother. And

Roderick was talking to his pretend-dog, Tinker, as usual.

"It was marvellous, Tinker. It's a pity you weren't really there. You should just have seen what Sally and I and Twigg did. It was like a miracle!"

CHAPTER 13

Of Gypsies And Other Things

The next thing that happened was the coming of the gypsies. One day the bit of common away on the nearby hill showed nothing but gorse bushes with a little golden blossom flaming here and there – and the next there were gaily-coloured caravans – three of them.

"There are caravans on the common, Dad," said Cyril. He had seen them from his bedroom window as he dressed. His mother looked from the sitting room window saw them too. They looked very gay and picturesque that fine morning.

"How pretty they look!" said his mother. "Quite a picture!"

"Dad won't like them," said Roddy. It was a Sunday morning, and the children were not at school. Roddy was preparing to walk round the farm with his father. It was small enough to walk round – though Mistletoe Farm had to be ridden round, it was so much larger.

Mr Longfield was certainly not at all pleased to see the gypsies. "This means we shall have to keep a watch on the hens and the ducks," he said. "Rose, give orders to the kitchen that any gypsy coming to the back door must be sent away at once and warned of the dogs."

269

"We shall get muddled soon," said Melisande, pertly. "We have to welcome Twigg – and warn off the gypsies."

"Melisande, I don't like that kind of pert talk," said her father, shortly. Melisande looked at her mother and slightly shrugged her shoulders. Really, Daddy was getting quite bad-tempered lately!

He wasn't – but he was already a little worried about the farm. The loss of the ewe was hard – and in the many little ways that he had expected to make ready money to help to keep the ordinary expenses of the farm down, very little was coming in. The butter was not being made properly. The hens were not laying well – and surely they were using far far too many eggs in the house? Mr Longfield had expected to sell double the amount he was able to.

He hated to talk over these things with Rose. She was impatient of such details – but surely, surely she could at least see to the butter-making?

The spotless dairy was no longer spotless. Where before the farmers' wives had put out their big bowls of cream to set for skimming, there were none. The butter-churn was hated, and Rose only went to see if she could make the butter when she had to have some for the house!

And now the thieving gypsies had come! Mr Longfield had been warned of them by his brother over at Mistletoe Farm. They slid into the farmyard at night and stole hens and ducks and eggs. They threw doped meat to the dogs to quieten them. They would even milk the cows at night in the field if they could get them to stand.

"All barns and outhouses are to be kept locked at night whilst the gypsies are camped near," Mr Longfield told Pat the stockman, and George the odd-job man. They nodded. They were good men and knew their jobs on the farm. They liked the trim little farm too – but they didn't like the "Folks up at the house." Particularly Ellen. Ellen looked down on them, and would not let them even enter her kitchen.

"Smelly fellows!" she said to Sally, her nose in the air. "And just look at their boots – do they never clean them?"

As George was Sally's uncle, this was a silly thing to say. Sally flared up at once and there was a loud quarrel between the two of them. Mrs Longfield, sitting in her pretty room across the hall, heard it and frowned. Really, country life was more than she had bargained for. Sally oughtn't to answer back Ellen like that.

She spoke to Sally and Sally sulked. Sally was a first-class little worker, quick and clean and cheerful, and a good cook for her age. She was punctual in the mornings and never minded what she did. She felt sorry for her master when she saw how little Rose helped him.

Cream went sour in the dairy. There never seemed enough butter for the hungry household, let alone to take to sell at the market. There was no bottled fruit, home-made jam or pickles in the store cupboard to draw on, as there was in other farmhouses. That was nobody's fault, of course, because the Longfields had come so recently to Holly Farm.

Still, all this meant added expense, and loss of money. Sally saw it and it worried her straightforward country-mind. "A trim little farm like this ought to be selling two hundred eggs a week and more – and half its butter, with that cow in milk – and keeping itself grand!" she thought.

So one day she went to Mr Longfield, when she saw him gloomily looking at three bowls of sour milk in the dairy.

"If you like, sir, I'll manage the dairy for you," she said. "Miss Melisande could give me a hand on Saturdays. I can't bear to see good things wasted sir – I'll set the cream and make the butter gladly."

"You're a good girl, Sally," said Mr Longfield gratefully. Then he hesitated. "But what about your wages? I doubt if I can raise them any more. My wages bill is pretty big already."

"I'm not asking for a rise," said Sally. "You let me have a little cream to take to my mother, sir, and that's enough for me!"

So Sally took on the dairy. Mrs Longfield was really very relieved. Now she needn't mess about any more in that horrid cold place. The butter never *would* come for her anyway, however much she swung that churn!

It was marvellous how it came for Sally. She hummed as she made the butter in the diary, and emptied the skim milk for the little calf, and set the cream for the next lot of butter. "This is right good work," thought Sally, marvelling that her mistress hated it so much.

Melisande helped her the first Saturday, and then went no more to the dairy. Let that strong hefty Sally manage it all! She wasn't going to wear herself out with that churn. Sally didn't say anything, but she thought very little of Melisande.

Mr Longfield sometimes wondered what his wife did with her days. He often thought of busy, bustling, happy Linnie – her days were full enough. What a pity Rose wouldn't take a few lessons from Linnie on how to run a farmhouse and do the hundred and one jobs that went with a farm-life.

One day Mr Longfield thought he saw a gypsy woman slinking away from the back-door. He questioned his wife.

"Did you tell Ellen not to allow any gypsy round the farmhouse?" he asked.

"Yes, yes, yes," said Rose, crossly. "I'm always telling her things from you. Why?"

"Only because I thought I saw a gypsy woman round at the back," said her husband, and said no more.

The gypsy woman came often, especially at night when Sally had gone home. She could tell fortunes and Ellen was very silly about that kind of thing.

She would stand at the back door whilst the gypsy read

272

her hand and told her wonderful things about herself. She would let her into the scullery and watch her whilst she "read" the tea-leaves at the bottom of a cup. She would remember all her dreams and ask the gypsy to tell her what they meant.

Rose had told her not to let the gypsies come to the door, but Ellen disobeyed her in this. Soon the gypsy knew exactly where the larder was, where the store-cupboard was, and even where the keys of the different places were kept. That big one was the dairy key. That small one was the henhouse key.

Things began to disappear. Sally's tea-cloths went. Kitchen knives and forks disappeared. One or two plates were missing.

Sally asked Ellen about them. "Well, scullery things are *your* look-out," said Ellen. "You should keep your eye on them. If anyone knows where they are, you do!"

Sally flared up immediately. "Do you think I take them home?" she demanded.

Ellen didn't answer. She put on her "sourpuss" face and walked into the hall. But Sally followed her.

"If you start saying them kind of things to me, I'll give my notice in," she threatened. "I'll tell my aunt Dorcas too! She'll come over here and give you a piece of her mind!"

So Ellen didn't say any more. But when Rose asked her what in the world Sally was shouting about, she said in a few spiteful words.

"A few things are missing from the kitchen, Madam, and I was just telling Sally I couldn't have that – and she shouted at me."

"Oh dear," said Rose. "I do so hope Sally isn't taking things home. Do you think she is?"

"I wouldn't like to say, Madam," said Ellen primly, which made Rose feel quite certain that poor Sally was a pilferer.

273

She turned her thoughts to more pleasant things. Her birthday was coming nearer. She must send out the party invitations soon. She turned and spoke to Ellen of the proposed party.

Ellen seemed quite pleased. It would be a change anyway – things were so dreadfully quiet in the country!

"The master says that we must try and make everything ourselves," said Rose with a sigh. "I suppose Sally can prepare a kind of cold supper or buffet, can she, Ellen?"

Ellen looked very doubtful. She didn't like that idea at all. It would mean that she would have to turn to and help in the preparing of the supper. "Well – I don't know, Madam," she said. "She's only a young country girl after all. You've been used to much better things than Sally can do – couldn't you persuade the master to let you have a load of ready-prepared dishes down from London? Like you used to, Madam. After all, it's your birthday."

Rose was weak. If Ellen said Sally couldn't do the meal, then Rose wasn't going to bother to find out if she could. She would order the things from London – so much easier – and oh, how much nicer they would be!

CHAPTER 14

The Days Go By

The invitations went out. Melisande herself wrote out the cards for her three cousins and for Richard Lawson and two of her own school friends. Cyril told her which of his friends to ask too.

"We're going to have a cold buffet in the dining room, and take up the carpet from the parquet floor in the other room," said Melisande. "And dance there. We'll show everyone how these things ought to be done!"

"What about the food?" asked Cyril. Melisande was evasive about this. Rose had told her that she was ordering it from town by van – and Melisande had agreed to say nothing to her father. She decided to say nothing to Cyril either.

"Oh, we shall manage!" was all she said.

Roddy wasn't very thrilled about the party. "It's not the kind I like," he complained. "All this dancing business! I don't see anything in it. Susan and I would much rather have a proper sit-down meal, and games afterwards, like we do at Mistletoe Farm."

"We're not considering what you and Susan like," said Melisande. "You don't need to come if you don't want to. In fact, I'd rather you didn't. You always look such a mess."

"Is Richard coming on Lordly-One?" asked Roddy.

"Yes. It will be full-moon that night, so quite a lot of people are riding over," said Melisande. "Five, I think. What about you stabling their horses for them?"

"Well – I wouldn't mind doing that at all," said Roddy, pleased. "Yes, I'll stable the horses and look after them."

"I bet you'll be at the buffet all evening, gobbling away," said Cyril.

"I don't really know what a buffet is," said Roderick. "Is it what Mother used to have at her parties at Three Towers – a sort of long table loaded with all kinds of cold dishes – and you helped yourself, or asked for what you wanted? If it's that – well, I daresay I might visit it once or twice. I'm always so hungry nowadays."

"You shouldn't be!" said Melisande. "*I* saw the tray Sally got ready for you yesterday – supposed to be for your *tea* – sausage rolls and cheese and cake! I call that high tea – just like we used to have at Mistletoe Farm "

275

"That's why I like it," said Roderick. "I wish this farm was run like Mistletoe Farm. Our house is like an ordinary house, not like a farmhouse. Why, at Mistletoe Farm the hens used to look in at the kitchen door, and sometimes Dorcas would have a little lamb peeping in – one she used to bottle-feed – and she's often had baby chicks there. I'd like Holly Farm to be like that."

"Well, *I* wouldn't," said Melisande. "Go on out, Roderick – and do wash your face and hands before you come in again. You look as dirty as old Twigg."

"Ellen turned Twigg away from the kitchen door last week," said Roderick, remembering. "And this week too. He told me. He said she looked at him as if he was a worm she'd like to cut in half. He said he'd pay her out someday."

"Ellen can look after herself," said Melisande. "She's not afraid of old poachers! I bet Twigg helps himself to eggs if nobody's about near the henhouse!"

"That's a beastly thing to say!" said Roderick, amazed. "What's the matter with this family now? There's no kindness in it!"

He stamped out, holding out his hand to an imaginary Tinker to lick. Tinker was really a great comfort to him. He even slept on his bed at night. Roddy told Tinker everything, and by now his pretend-dog was almost real.

Roderick had settled down at Holly Farm now but he wasn't very happy. His father always looked worried. His mother still treated him as a rather silly little baby boy, when she wasn't being cross with him. Cyril took no notice of him, and Melisande had gone back to being snappy and high-and-mighty – a bit like Ellen, he thought. They hardly saw the Mistletoe Farm folk now, which disappointed Roddy very much.

"After all, we're not so *very* far away," thought Roddy. "But except for seeing Jane and Susan in the bus, and Jack at school, I never see anybody from there. I keep asking Mother if I can go over, but she always find some excuse to keep me away."

The Mistletoe Farm folk were being cautious about asking the Holly Farm folk over. Linnie knew that Rose didn't want to come, and she was sorry that Melisande now looked down on the happy home she had had at Mistletoe Farm. Holly Farm with all its little luxuries had turned her head. "And she had grown to be such a nice, sensible girl," thought her aunt, sadly. "Well, well – she hadn't learnt her lesson quite long enough, I suppose."

Susan would very much have liked to have Roddy over as often as possible. He and she thought the same about so many things – about Boodi, for instance and Crackers, and about young chicks just out of the egg, and skippitty lambs.

Susan, in fact, was the only one who went over to Holly Farm at all. She rode there on Boodi, and was always hailed with delight by Roderick. Crackers fell on him and licked him till his hands, knees and face were dripping wet.

Susan never went to say how-do-you-do to her Aunt Rose. She avoided Cyril and Melisande. "You see, they don't *really* want to see me," she explained to Roddy. "We should only just say something polite to one another, and that's all. So it would really be a waste of time to bother. After all, it's you I've come to see."

Roderick told Susan about his imaginary dog Tinker. He told her carefully, rather fearful that she might laugh at him. But she didn't. She listened, her face solemn and serious. She seemed to think that Tinker was as real as Roddy thought him.

"Where is he now?" she asked, looking round.

"He's lying on my feet," said Roddy. "And if you hold your hand out, he'll lick it."

"Susan rode there on Boodi."

Susan promptly held out her hand. "Yes," she said. "He's licking it. Oh dear – now Crackers is licking it too. Do you suppose Tinker and Crackers will be friends, Roddy?"

And, strangely enough, Crackers suddenly got up and began to roll about on the ground and bark and behave altogether quite madly. "There you are!" said Susan. "He's playing with your Tinker!"

Except when Susan came over on Boodi, Roderick was a very lonely little boy. No boys of his own age lived near. Cyril and Melisande thought him a baby. He liked Punch and Pouncer but they were too staid and serious to play with.

"They're so grown-up," he said to Susan. "They look at me as if I was a puppy, and they never want to play, like Crackers does. Anyway they're always with Daddy or Pat or George."

"The only *satisfactory* dog to have is a dog of your own," said Susan, patting Crackers, and fondling his drooping ears. "You'll have to make do with Tinker till you get a real one. Isn't Twigg ever going to give you one?"

"Yes," said Roddy. "He told me last week that Tommy Lane's spaniel's got a litter of pups now, and they're beautiful. He says I can choose one when they're old enough to leave their mother."

"You *are* lucky!" said Susan. "How did you get your mother to say you could have one?"

Roddy looked gloomy. "I keep mentioning puppies and how I'd like one," he said, "but Mother simply takes no notice. I'm going to ask Daddy straight out – no hinting like I have to do with Mother."

"I shouldn't like a mother you have to hint things at," said Susan. "I like one you can say things straight out to."

"Oh well – I suppose all mothers are different," said Roddy, loyally, though secretly he agreed with Susan. It really was a nuisance to have to keep hinting about a dog, instead of asking plainly.

The invitations to the party were all sent off. The replies soon came back. Everyone seemed delighted to come. Richard sent a very nice note, and so did his mother. Richard added a P.S.

"Coming on Lordly-One, specially to show you how beautiful he still is!"

Melisande laughed and thought of the lovely new frilly frock her mother had promised her. It was to be quite a long one, almost to her ankles.

"If only you weren't so *fat* still, Melisande!" her mother said. "Those eight months at Mistletoe Farm didn't do you any good in that way – another few months and you'd have turned in a country clod like Jane – or Sally!"

Melisande hated to hear her mother say she was fat. She looked at herself in the glass. Certainly her face was now plump and well-rounded, and her body had grown so that not one of her last winter's dresses fitted her at all.

"I don't think I'm *too* bad, Mother," she said. "I'm not half as fat as some of the girls at school."

"I should hope not," said her mother. "Big shapeless lumps most of them are! I wish you'd slim down a bit – and I wish your face wasn't so plump. I'd like you to take after *me*, not your father, Melisande. I've always been slim and I can't ever recall having a fat face."

"Oh well," said Melisande, "you'll just have to put up with me as I am, Mother. Anyway, I do look a bit better than Jane!"

"Oh *Jane*!" said her mother, with scorn in her voice. "I'm surprised she's even been able to stop biting her nails. I don't believe that child *ever* washes her neck! I only hope she'll turn up looking decent at the party."

"It'll soon be here!" said Melisande, with excitement in her voice. "Oh Mother – I *am* so looking forward to it. It'll be the greatest success that ever was!"

CHAPTER 15

A Little Plain Speaking

A week or two went by. It was February, a bright clear February with quite a bit of warmth in the sunshine that flooded Holly Farm and Mistletoe Farm each day. At each farm the ewes had their lambs and the air was full of the baaing of the mothers and maa-aa-aaing of the frisky little lambs. Susan and Roderick loved to watch them skipping about, their long tails wriggling.

On the hedges wriggled the catkins of the hazels, and Roddy thought "lambs" tails was really a very good name for them. A few more blossoms were out on the gorse, though it would not blaze with rich yellow until April. The birds were singing madly everywhere.

Susan's father, at Mistletoe Farm, was happy. He loved the spring. There was a tremendous lot to do on the farm at that time, but it was worth it. Young calves, lambs, piglets, chicks, ducklings – all these came in the spring. Then there was the drilling and planting, the joy of seeing the first faint lines of green in the corn-fields. Then the tree-buds began to swell, the first early primroses could be looked for – oh, spring on the farm was a time to sing and whistle about!

Linnie was always busy then too. She saw to the bottle-fed lambs, feeding them with Dorcas in the kitchen. The calves had to be taught to drink milk from the big farm-pail. Piglets had to be seen to. Hens were laying eggs at top speed every day, and these had to be collected, washed and graded. Butter had to be made. Linnie took charge of all these things, and Susan and Jane helped her splendidly.

281

But Linnie did not force them to do too much. They had their jobs, and unless she had to she wouldn't make them do anything extra.

"You're right about that, Ma'am," said old Dorcas, approvingly. "It's bad to put old heads on young shoulders. That never did do any good that I can see. Children have got to be children before they're men and women. They must walk before they can run."

"You and your sayings!" said Linnie, laughing. "I'm sure that long before you were Susan's age you could practically run a dairy, a kitchen, and poultry on your own."

"Maybe I could," said Dorcas. "But that don't make it right for other children to do."

So Susan and Jane had plenty of time to themselves, once they had done their jobs. They went for long rides on Boodi and Merrylegs together, because they both loved the country round about. Crackers loped along behind, panting.

"Getting his fat down nicely," said Susan, looking down at him. "I put him on the bathroom scales last night, Jane, and he's lost three pounds since we've been taking him with us on our rides."

"Good gracious! He'll soon be as slim as Aunt Rose!" said Jane, and they both laughed.

"Daddy says Holly Farm isn't doing too well," said Susan. "Did you know?"

"No, I didn't. How did *you* know? Daddy wouldn't go and tell *you* that!" said Jane. "You're always hearing things you're not supposed to hear."

"I couldn't help it," said Susan. "I was playing snap with myself under the table, and they didn't know I was there. I crawled out immediately."

"It's a funny thing how often you're under the table or behind curtains or in the corner," said Jane. "If I want to say anything private to Mummy I always look everywhere round the room first to see if you're anywhere about."

"Well, you've only got to say "Are you there, Susan?" and I'll say yes, if I am," said Susan, quite hurt. "Anyway – it's a pity about Holly Farm, isn't it? What's happened, I wonder?"

It was true that Holly Farm was not doing as well as everyone had hoped. Bad luck comes to every farm sooner or later, of course – but it did seem as if Holly Farm was getting more than its fair share just at present.

A cow had fallen into a ditch and broken her leg. One of the horses was mysteriously ill and could not work. Two other cows hung their heads and would not eat. Martha the sow didn't seem happy, and David Longfield was afraid that when the piglets came they would be puny, and no good at all.

The tractor had broken down, and drilling and planting had been held up. When David had told his brother all this, the two men had looked at one another in dismay. "I'll give you all the help I can," said Peter Longfield at last. "But it's a busy time with me, as with you, David. You'll have to make out the best you can with what bit of help I can give. I'll come and see the two cows, anyway."

David Longfield hadn't told his wife Rose any of his troubles. She wasn't the kind of wife you could tell bad news to – only good news. She wasn't like Linnie, whose husband knew that bad, or good, she would always want to hear all the news – to rejoice at the good, and comfort him when it was bad.

The Holly Farm children didn't know of the bad things, either, though Roddy had noticed that the two cows didn't eat. He had noticed too that one of the horses wasn't at work. He liked the three horses on the farm, though he didn't know them very well yet. He liked the cows fairly well but he still wished they didn't have horns.

At Mistletoe Farm the farm and the house were one united whole. Linnie knew every cow, every horse, and so her husband declared, almost every sheep! She knew which fields were to be planted, and which were to be pasture. She kept her eye on everything, and belonged to the farm almost as much as to the house.

She took her share of the farm produce and used it or sold it or stored it. She pickled eggs, and bottled fruit, and had jars of delicious pickled onions on her shelves and pickled cabbage. Her sheets were scented with the lavender bushes that grew round the little courtyard near the goldfish pond. House and farm were all one, and Linnie and her husband shared them both together.

But at Holly Farm the farm and the house were two separate things. Only Roddy in the house knew of anything that went on in the farm, and Sally knew a little. The others knew nothing – not even the name of a cow, or what was planted in any field. A row of blue-purple cabbage would not mean jars of delicious pickled cabbage to Rose – and the lavender bushes would not make Melisande think of bags of lavender to be made in the late summer and stored in the linen cupboard.

Holly Farm, and the buying of it, had been such a slice of good luck to the Longfield family – or so it seemed to them at the time. But good luck has to be held on to, and encouraged and deserved, or it will slip away un-noticed. Now the Holly Farm luck had slipped away, and soon everyone would have to notice it! Mr Longfield had seen it already.

Things were not right at Holly Farm. Rose was not loyal to her husband. She was ignoring his wishes and doing things he would disapprove of. She was disapproving of him too!

"You always fall asleep at night, just as Peter does at Mistletoe Farm!" she complained. "And you're never in to tea at half-past four. And I do think you could remember to scrape your boots well before you come in. Ellen keeps complaining of the state of the hall."

"Let her!" said her husband, sitting down heavily. "All right, Rose, all right – I know I'm cross and touchy and tired. I get up so early, I feel sleepy long before you do at night. And as for coming in to tea at half-past four, that's ridiculous of you. Whoever heard of a farmer who had time for fiddling about with afternoon tea? Why don't we have a proper high-tea at six, like Linnie does? I'm in then, and hungry."

"You're forever talking about Linnie and her wonderful ways," said Rose, in a bitter voice. "She's nothing but a shapeless, red-faced farmer's wife."

"And aren't *you* a farmer's wife?" asked her husband. "Come, come, Rose – you were pleased to get here and have a home together again – or so you said. But you don't do a thing to help. Not a thing. And when a man's tired and comes in wanting a bite and a bit of comfort, all you say is – scrape my boots well when I come in! PAH!"

Rose stared at him, shocked. He so rarely talked like that to anyone – and he was talking to *her*! She dissolved into tears. But for once in a way her husband didn't put his arms round her and pet her like a spoilt child.

"You don't back me up, Rose," he said. "That's what's the matter here. We don't all pull together. How many times have I said those gypsies are to be kept away from the house – and yet George tells me he sees one or other of them at the back door two or three times a week? And how many times have I said old Twigg is to be made welcome – and now I hear he won't come near the place because of our high-and-mighty ways. It won't do."

Melisande and Cyril came in at this moment. They were horrified to find their mother in tears. They had heard their father's angry voice as they came down the hall, but they hadn't for one moment thought that it was with their mother he was so cross.

"Oh Melisande, oh Cyril!" wept their mother. "Daddy's so cross with me. I do my best, don't I! He wants me to be like your Aunt Linnie – and I'm so *different*!"

Her husband got up and walked out of the room. For the second time since they had come to Holly Farm he slammed the door. There was a startled silence after he had gone.

"Don't cry, Mother," said Melisande, putting her arms round the slender, elegant figure with its crown of shining hair. "Dad will get over it. He's always so cross lately, isn't he? He was even cross when I told him about my new party frock."

"And he's getting just like Uncle Peter over at Mistletoe Farm," said Cyril. "He yelled at me last night because I put the radio on to hear a concert – and he said he wanted to read. But actually he was asleep. It's all right, Mother. We're on your side. If Dad wants to turn us all into clods and stupid lumps we won't let him do it!"

He didn't want to, of course. All he wanted was a little help and comfort from a family he loved and longed to do his best for. He went up to his bedroom and sat down heavily in a chair.

He meant to think things out – but he didn't. He had been up since six o'clock that morning and he was tired out. In two minutes he was fast asleep – and Rose was going to be very cross indeed when she came up and found him there!

CHAPTER 16

The Day Of The Party At Last

The day of the party came at last. It was on a Saturday, so the three children were able to help in the preparations. Rose was at her most gracious, because it was her birthday.

Everyone gave her presents. Her husband gave her a beautiful little brooch which he could ill afford – but he had felt sorry for his outburst of temper a few nights before, and was now trying to make up for it. He kissed Rose and told her that instead of looking a year older she looked five years younger.

She was very pleased with that. She loved being fussed and made much of. She felt a little guilty when she remembered the pretty dresses she had bought for herself and Melisande – and all the good things that were being sent down from a London store by van. But still – it was her birthday and David would probably only scold a little!

The sun shone brightly. Everything seemed set for a very successful day. Over at Mistletoe Farm Jane and Susan were trying on new dresses too, and Jack was trying his best to slip away before his mother insisted on seeing if his new suit looked nice.

"*You* ought to have a new frock as well, Mummy," said Susan. "Whenever did you have a new one last? I simply can't remember. Before I was born, I should think!"

"You're about right, darling!" said her mother, laughing. "Well – I might have a new one this spring. Now do stand still while I alter this button. Fancy you going to an evening party."

"I'd rather go in my jodhpurs really," said Susan. "It

would be much more sensible, because Roddy and I are going to stable the horses of the people who ride over. Richard Lawson is coming on his horse Lordly-One."

"Susan! You are *not* going to stable horses in your new party frock!" said her mother, firmly. "You quite understand that, don't you? I don't care what Roddy says. He must do without your help."

Susan looked very gloomy. What a pity! That would have been the best part of the party, stabling the horses and seeing to them – and the cold supper, of course. Roddy had told her of the wonderful supper they were going to have.

"Smoked salmon! Lobster mayonnaise! Caviare sandwiches! All kinds of oddments with things on I don't know the names of – and trifles and jellies and éclairs and meringues! I shall have at least six éclairs, Sue. You can go for the meringues."

Susan told her mother of the list of delicious supper-things. Linnie stared in wonder. "But – I thought Sally and Ellen were doing all the food!" she said. "They can't possibly make things like that – good gracious, Sally's never made a meringue in her life. I doubt if she knows what it is!"

"Sounds to me as if they're getting everything from some outside shop or store," said Jane. "I bet they are! Melisande wouldn't tell me a thing about the party when I asked her. I bet it's all bought stuff."

"Don't keep saying 'I bet,' Jane," said her mother, thinking hard. She felt worried. Goodness, if Rose was ordering things like that, what kind of a bill would David have? Really, Rose was too bad.

Over at Holly Farm there was much excitement at that moment, because Melisande and her mother were also trying on dresses. Rose looked beautiful in hers. She couldn't resist going down and showing herself to her husband.

But when she got downstairs, she heard angry voices in the kitchen. Ellen and Sally were quarrelling again.

288

"I tell you, I left that pile of washing in that pail there," said Ellen's scolding voice. "And when I go to it this morning to get one of my aprons to iron out, it's gone! And what's more, my stockings are gone too, my best ones – *and* that blouse you admired so much the other day, Miss. Now just you tell me – how do things walk off by themselves?"

"If you mean – did I take them – well, you know as well as I do, I didn't," said Sally, in a shaking voice. "How do *I* know where they are? You're always hinting that this is gone and that is gone. I never take nothing that isn't mine, and never have. And what's more, if you repeat what you've said again, I'll walk out, Miss Sourpuss!"

"Oh, you bad, rude girl!" cried Ellen, beside herself with rage. "Calling me names now, are you? Well, let me tell you this – I wouldn't be surprised if all those missing things are in your chest of drawers at home this very minute!"

Mrs Longfield walked into the kitchen, a startling vision in her new party dress. It was pale blue and had little sequins all over it. Ellen and Sally stared at her in surprise.

"Now Ellen," said Mrs Longfield, "don't quarrel like this, please. There's so much to be done on a party day. Sally, get on with your work."

"I'm going, Ma'am," said Sally, sullenly. "I can't work with anyone that calls me a thief."

"Oh Sally! You can't walk out like this on the day of a party!" cried Mrs Longfield, her heart sinking. "You must give me proper notice, anyway."

"I'll refund you my last week's wages, Mam, but I won't stop with Ellen," said Sally. "Unless you tell *her* to go. Then I'll stop."

"Very well, *I'll* go!" said Ellen looking very white and angry. Mrs Longfield could have cried. She took Ellen's arm.

"Ellen, Ellen – you know we can't do without you!" she said. "Or without Sally either."

"Madam – I tell you straight – things have been stolen – my things and your thngs," said Ellen, in a trembling voice. "And I stick by what I've said. It's more likely Sally took them than anyone else. Who else *is* there to take them, anyway!"

A knock came at the back door at this moment, and someone outside gave it a push. Twigg's brown, leathery face looked in. He looked surprised when he saw Mrs Longfield in her party dress, and the angry Ellen and Sally.

"Beg pardon," he said. "I just came to ask if Master Roderick was anywheres around. Been looking for him everywhere!"

An idea flashed into Mrs Longfield's mind. Twigg! Of course, *Twigg* might have taken the things! He was a wicked old poacher, everyone knew that – and if he poached and stole hares and pheasants and trout, he'd steal household things too. It wasn't Sally – it must be Twigg!

"Twigg! You've been told not to come to the house at all!" she called angrily. "How dare you disobey my orders?"

"Because them's not the master's orders," said Twigg, contemptuously. "Where there's a master I don't take no notice of what the missus says. I don't do no harm anyways."

"Were you hanging about last night?" demanded Mrs Longfield. "Did you come sneaking in at the back door then?"

"No, that I didn't," said Twigg. "I were up with old Tommy Lane. And for why do you ask, Mam? You thinking I sneaked in here and took your best silver away? For shame on you!"

His scornful voice and the words he said roused Mrs Longfield to rage. She said things she should never have said.

"You didn't take the best silver – but you look other things, didn't you, Twigg? You sneaked this and that –

whatever you could find. I've a good mind to turn you over to the police."

"If so be Mester Longfield wants to do that to me, well Mester Longfield's welcome to," said Twigg. "But not you, Missus. And now I'll be going. Good day to you, Mam, good day to you all."

Sally was sobbing as Twigg went. She began gathering together the few things she kept at Holly Farm – an overall and one or two aprons.

"Don't go, Sally," said Mr Longfield, alarmed. "I'm sure it's Twigg who took anything that's missing."

"Oh Mam, you don't know any more than Ellen there if it was Twigg or me or anyone else," wept Sally. "You shouldn't ought to have said it was him, Mam. You didn't know who it was, and nor do I. Nor does Ellen for all she says it's me. And you shouldn't ought to fall foul of Sam Twigg. He's a good friend, but he's a bad enemy. Now nothing'll go right with the farm."

"Oh, don't be so silly, Sally," said Mrs Longfield, angry and desperate. "You've no right to leave in a hurry like this. Ellen, tell her to stay."

But Ellen was dumb. Ellen was sure Sally had taken her things, and she glared at her in hate. And Sally went, still sniffing. She bumped into Roderick outside the back door and he ran after her in surprise.

"Sally, Sally! What's the matter? What are you crying for?"

"You ask your Ma," sniffed Sally, and set off at top speed to her home a mile away.

Roderick went indoors to find his mother, feeling puzzled and anxious. She had gone, half-crying, to the sitting room, and Ellen had followed her.

"What's happened?" said Roddy, his head round the door.

"Nothing to do with you," said his mother. "Go and find your father and tell him I want him."

Roddy disappeared again, feeling suddenly gloomy.

"The gypsies fled with the dogs bounding after them."

Whatever could have happened? Where was his father?
Up by the cowsheds, probably.

As he came near the sheds he saw a figure slinking
round the corner. Who was it?

Then he heard a shout. It was his father. "Hey you – what are you doing here? I've turned you off my land six times already!"

Roddy ran to see who it was – surely, surely not old Twigg! No – of course not. It was a gypsy in a shawl, bright gold earrings swinging from her ears. Her bold black eyes stared brazenly at the farmer.

"I came to bring something to Miss Ellen, down at the farmhouse," said the gypsy in a lazy drawl. "I've got something for her. She said to come today."

"Don't lie," said the farmer. "You're forbidden the house, and you know it. Clear off!"

Another figure rose up out of the nearby hedge. It was a second gypsy, a man this time, a dirty-looking rogue who also had gold earrings in his ears.

"We ain't done no harm, Mister," he whined.

"What – another of you!" shouted the farmer in a rage. "I'll set the dogs on you! Hey, Punch, Pouncer – chase 'em off my land!"

The gypsies fled, with the dogs bounding after them. The man shook his fist and shouted out something Roddy couldn't hear.

"Will Punch and Pouncer bite them?" he asked, anxiously.

"Oh no – but they'll give them a good fright," said his father. "Your mother wants me, you say? All right. I'll come this very minute."

CHAPTER 17

From Bad To Worse

Roddy went with his father, feeling upset and worried. What with Sally and Ellen and his mother – and now the gypsies and the dogs – things were certainly getting rather worrying.

They left the cowsheds and went down towards the farmhouse. As they came near a van drew up at the gate. It had a name sprawled across the side. "Harridges, London."

"Now, what do *they* want?" said Mr Longfield. "Go and see, Roddy."

Roddy went. The man was unloading big trays on which were packed the most delicious-looking things. This must be the food for tonight! Roddy's eyes brightened. It certainly looked good. He ran back to his father.

"It's the food for thought," he said. "A whole vanful, Daddy! Shall we really eat all that?"

His father stopped as if he was suddenly struck by lightning. "A vanful of *food*! What on earth do you mean?"

Then he strode to the gate himself and called to the man. "Wait a minute. What's all this?"

The man looked surprised. "Snacks and so on ordered for a cold buffet here tonight, sir," he said. "I was told to deliver this morning."

Mr Longfield looked at the great trays of expensive looking food. He couldn't believe his eyes. Surely, *surely* Rose couldn't have ordered all this when he had expressly told her that everything must be made and cooked at home?

"Got the bill?" he asked, curtly. The man handed him an envelope. Mr Longfield tore it open.

It was for thirty-seven pounds!

Thirty-seven pounds! Food for a party. And he couldn't even buy himself a new water-trough for his cattle! Mr Longfield felt sick.

"I'm sorry," he said to the man. "Take it all back. My wife made a mistake. I can't possibly pay for all that food."

"But sir – I can't take it back," said the man, puzzled. "You see . . ."

"TAKE IT BACK!" shouted Mr Longfield. "I tell you I can't pay for it. Take it back and sell it to some other idiot. You can't sell it to me."

"Sorry, sir," said the man, and loaded the tray back into the van. He got in, backed the van, and drove off without another word. Roddy was terrified. Whatever was going to happen?

"You still there, Roddy?" said his father, and put his hand on the boy's shoulder. "I'm sorry about this, very sorry. But it was the only thing to be done."

"What about Mother? And the party? What will happen?" faltered Roddy feeling as if the world was turning suddenly upside down.

"We'll go and see," said his father, in a grim voice. He turned on his heel and strode off towards the front door. Roddy went too, half fearful.

His mother, Ellen, and now Melisande too, were all in the sitting room. His mother was still in tears, and Melisande was trying to comfort her.

"Oh, David!" she wept, as her husband came into the room. "Sally's gone. And Twigg's been to the back door and I'm sure he's been stealing things – and he said dreadful things to me – threatened he'd be our enemy, and. . . ."

"Rose," said her husband, not noticing Ellen was there, "did you order food from Harridges, after I'd said we were to have it all prepared at home?"

"Oh David – don't talk to me in that voice, *please*," sobbed Rose. "I can't bear it."

"Answer me, Rose," said her husband. He thrust a piece of paper at her. "Look – thirty-seven pounds for food for a party! Are you mad? It came in a van just now and I've sent it all back."

"Oh *Daddy*!" said Melisande, miserably.

"So you knew too, did you?" said her father, turning on her. "What sort of family have I got – paying no heed to my wishes, doing things behind my back – getting me in debt when I'm trying to make my way!"

He suddenly noticed Ellen was there. He turned on her too. "Yes, and I've got something to say to you too, Ellen! Those gypsies – they say you've been having them at the house – one was coming to bring you something this morning. How dare you disobey my orders?"

"What orders?" said Ellen, in fright. "I've disobeyed nobody. I. . . ."

"Pah!" said her master, in disgust. "You're all alike, the whole lot of you – can't be trusted in any way. I tell you this, Ellen – if you disobey my orders once more, you can go. I'm not having anybody I can't trust in *this* house. Now go to the kitchen. I want to talk to my wife without you glowering there."

Ellen fled out of the room and shut the door. She was trembling. What a terrible morning. And that party coming tonight – with no food prepared now – and no Sally to help!

She stood in the deserted kitchen for a minute or two, thinking. Then she ran upstairs quickly. Ellen wasn't staying to help with any party – no, not she. She'd teach the master to talk to her like that! She'd give them all the slip, catch the bus, and then the train – and go off to her sister's. She never did like a country life, anyway. Why, they'd expect her to churn the butter next, now Sally was gone. Let them do the jobs themselves!

Mr Longfield hadn't many more words to say. He was feeling sad and sick at heart. He spoke a little more kindly to the sobbing Rose.

"Do what you like about your party. If you like to call up Linnie, no doubt she'd bring over some food and help you out. But don't expect me to come and dance and make merry, Rose. It's not in my heart to be glad over anything today."

"You're cruel, you're unkind," wept Rose.

Her husband looked sadly at her. Then he noticed that she was wearing a new and beautiful frock – and so was Melisande too. His face hardened.

"I suppose you're going to present me with a bill for those frocks too?" he said bitterly. "Well, you can send them back. I've no money to pay for them. If you'd done what every farmer's wife likes to do, and made money out of your hens and your butter, you'd have had plenty to pay for your finery yourself, Rose. In future, it's no work, no pay, for both of us. We shall have to learn to go without nearly all the things we want!"

He went out – but this time he didn't slam the door, though he would have liked to. Slamming doors wasn't going to be any help now. If he didn't look out, he would be the cause of making his brother Peter lose money on the farm. If only those cows would pull round – and that horse. And if only the sow would have a litter of fine little piglets! If only – if only. . . . Yes, and if only Rose were like Linnie, somebody who pulled with him all the time, instead of against him. And there was Melisande going the same way too.

Inside the house Melisande and her mother were trying

to think what was best to do about the party. "We *must* make up our minds at once, Mother," Melisande kept saying to the distraught Rose. "We must, we must."

"For all this to happen on my birthday too!" wept Rose.

"Let's telephone to Aunt Linnie," said Roderick. "She always knows what to do."

"Yes. Mother, perhaps she would help us with the food – bring a lot over," said Melisande. "She's always got such a store. And Ellen would help, I'm sure she would. Oh, what a pity Sally's gone!"

"Go and ask Ellen if she'll help," said Rose, after they had discussed the whole thing for about twenty minutes, feeling more and more disconsolate.

Melisande went out into the kitchen. Ellen wasn't there. Melisande called her. "Ellen! Where are you?"

There was no answer. Melisande ran upstairs and knocked on Ellen's door. "Ellen, are you here? Mother wants to speak to you."

All was silence in the bedroom. Melisande knocked again and then opened the door. The bedroom looked very bare and tidy. No brush and comb on the dressing-table. No photographs of her sister on the mantelpiece. No nightdress case on the bed. In panic Melisande looked in the hanging cupboard. It was empty.

Ellen had gone – gone without a word, without even saying goodbye. Sally gone – Ellen gone. What a terrible, terrible day! Melisande ran downstairs and broke the news to the horrified Rose.

"But whatever shall we *do*?" said Rose, wringing her hands. "Both of them gone! Oh, we can't possibly have the party then. Ring your Aunt Linnie, Melisande and tell her what has happened. I shall be ill, I know I shall."

Melisande rang her aunt. Linnie listened, shocked. Melisande poured out everything – how her father had sent back the food – how cross he was about the dresses –

298

how he had spoken so sharply to Ellen that she had gone –
oh, wasn't he unkind, and wasn't it all dreadful? On the
day of the party too!

Linnie listened in silence. She saw at once what had
happened. The house had been divided against itself – and
as always happens, it couldn't stand. The household had
collapsed, Ellen and Sally had deserted it – and now hard
times were coming for Holly Farm.

"I'm sorry about all this, dear," Linnie said at last in her
warm, clear voice. "You can't have the party of course.
You must ring everyone up and put them off. Say your
mother is not feeling very well. I am sure she can't be,
with all these things happening. I'll be over tonight to see
your mother and we must plan what we can do."

She rang off and went to find her husband. What a to-
do! Would it break the little family at Holly Farm? Or
make them? Linnie didn't know. It all depended on Rose
– and Rose wasn't much of a staff to lean on!

Susan as usual heard what was said on the telephone.
She was horrified. She ran to saddle Boodi. She would go
over to Roddy at once. He might want a bit of help. She
might even leave Crackers with him for the weekend if he
wanted him. That was the very biggest piece of help she
could think of!

CHAPTER 18

A Dreadful Day

It took Melisande a long time to ring up all the guests and
cancel the party. By the time she had finished it was
almost one o'clock. Her father came into the hall, dirty
and tired.

"Anything for dinner?" he asked.

"Oh *dear*!" said Melisande. "Is it dinner-time. Perhaps Mother has got something ready. I've been simply ages on the phone."

She ran to see – but not even the cloth was spread on the table. She called loudly "Mother! Mother! Where are you? What about dinner?"

A voice answered her from the kitchen. "I'm here, Melisande. I simply can't find out where anything is. And there seems hardly any food in the house."

"Well, we meant to finish up all the bits tomorrow – what was left from the party," said Melisande. "And Sally would have cooked a chicken too, and made a pie. So naturally there won't be much in the larder now. Daddy wants his dinner. I'd better get it, if you can find something to put on the table."

"But where *is* everything?" said her mother, who had now changed out of her beautiful dress, and was in a morning one. "I can't even find a kitchen knife to do potatoes."

"Let's put them in the oven in their jackets then," said Melisande. "You scrub them, Mother."

"But where are the *potatoes*?" said Rose. She sounded quite helpless.

"They must be somewhere about," said Melisande. "Hello, here's Roddy. Roddy, do *you* know where anything is in this kitchen? Potatoes, for instance?"

"Oh yes," said Roddy, "they're in the outhouse off the scullery. I'll get some. I know where everything is. I come and poke about out here when Ellen's out. I say – has she really gone?"

"Yes," said Melisande. "And we shall be in a fine old mess now."

"Well, I'm glad she's gone," said Roddy. "Old Sourpuss! Now perhaps Sally will come back."

"Oh – I *wish* she would!" said Melisande, at once. "She's so sensible!"

It was quite incredible, but it took Melisande and her mother over an hour to get the meal. The potatoes took ages to do in their jackets, and finally they had to be taken out of the oven, cut open and mashed, or they would never have been ready. Rose opened a tin of cold meat and cut herself. It took five minutes to bandage her finger, and she sat down for another five minutes because the sight of blood upset her.

Melisande began to despair of ever getting the meal ready. Cyril banged in and out impatiently, but he didn't try to help. Roddy whistled aggravatingly all the time. Everyone was hungry and cross.

"If I don't get something to eat soon I shall have to go out without anything," said Mr Longfield, appearing in the kitchen. "For goodness sake – does it take an hour to get a bit of meat and potato and bread and cheese on the table?"

In the end he got a hunk of bread and cheese for himself and marched off angrily. What a household! But as soon as he was outside the house he forgot his household worries and thought about a whole lot of farm anxieties. He was glad that his brother was coming over that evening with Linnie. He could talk over his worries with him.

It really was a dreadful day. There were so many many things to be done that Ellen and Sally did easily and quickly, but which Melisande and her mother couldn't seem to tackle at all. Melisande was better than Rose because at least she had had to help a good bit when she stayed at Mistletoe Farm. But still it was like a nightmare – this to be done, and that, and then a dozen more things, and then oh dear, who was to make the butter?

"And there's the hens to feed – Sally always did that in the afternoons," said Melisande. "Roddy, will you do them? And do the eggs?"

"Of course. I always do the eggs anyway," said Roddy,

calmly? "Why can't Cyril do the butter? You've got heaps to do in the house."

So Cyril was turned firmly into the dairy and found out that butter wouldn't come any more quickly or easily for him than for his mother or Melisande!

Susan turned up on Boodi, of course, complete with a pile of sandwiches and slices of cake. "We'll picnic somewhere," she said to Roddy. "I expect Melisande and your mother will be glad not to have to bother about us for dinner this morning."

Roddy told Susan all about the upsets of the morning. "And when Twigg came, Mother accused him of stealing the missing things," he said. "So now Twigg's an enemy instead of a friend. Maybe he'll put spells on our horses and cows and they'll die."

"Twigg wouldn't. He likes animals too much," said Susan. "But I don't expect he'll come to help you any more. And I don't expect he'll give you that spaniel puppy now, Roddy."

"No. I thought of that," said Roddy, gloomily. "I shall have to make do with Tinker. He turned and patted his imaginary dog and then patted Crackers.

Susan was really a great help. She cleaned the hen-house with Roddy, and helped to mend a gap in the wire. She took the calf its pail of skim milk and let it drink. She saw that Pouncer was limping and turned up his paw and took out a thorn. In fact, she was her usual, sensible self, and Roddy felt a great deal better after about two hours of her company.

"Mummy said I could stay with you till she comes over this evening," said Susan. "You can have a ride on Boodi if you like. But I warn you, he's not very good today. He might rub your leg against the hedge, or something."

"I'll watch out," said Roddy and mounted the barrel-like pony. Sure enough, Boodi played his tricks that afternoon, but Roddy was more than a match for him. As soon as Boodi pressed near the hedge to squeeze Roddy's leg against it, Roddy threw his leg over the saddle and yelled "Bad Boodi! Bad Boodi!"

"I do wish I had a pony of my own," said Roddy, regretfully, as he leapt down again. "But it seems that things are not going very well here – so I don't expect any of us will have ponies this year, anyway."

"Which would you rather have – a pony or a dog?" asked Susan, tickling Crackers.

"Oh, a *dog*," said Roddy, promptly.

"I thought perhaps I might have lent you Crackers over the weekend if you felt upself about things," said Susan. "But you don't seem too bad."

"I feel much better since you came," said Roddy. "I'd love to have him – but Mother would have a fit, and I couldn't make her more worried than she is."

"No. I suppose you couldn't," said Susan, very glad that she hadn't got to leave Crackers behind after all. "Who's going to do all the housework and cooking, Roddy, now that Ellen and Sally have both gone?"

"I don't know. Somebody, I suppose," said Roddy, vaguely. "Perhaps your mother would lend us Dorcas."

"She jolly well wouldn't!" said Susan, with a snort. "Why should she? It won't do your mother or Melisande any harm to do their own work for a bit."

"But they don't know how to," said Roddy. "I could clean the boots and shoes, I suppose," he said hopefully. "I like doing that sort of thing. I could do them before I go to bed. And I could bring in the logs for the fires and the coal for the kitchen."

"Aunt Rose won't enjoy washing up and scrubbing the kitchen floor and getting meals, will she?" said Susan, a little maliciously. Roddy said nothing. He found himself wishing that his mother was more like Susan's mother. His

"Bad Boodi! Bad Boodi!"

Aunt Linnie wouldn't groan and moan and sit around in tears, and say what a pity all this had happened on her birthday – she would know exactly what to do and set to work to do it. So would Jane. Would Melisande? Perhaps.

What about Cyril? Would he do much to help? Cyril

had been rather silly, lately, Roddy considered – spouting poetry again, and going on about the wonderful music on the Third Programme. Roddy didn't care about the Third Programme. There was never anything funny or anything exciting on it at all, and he couldn't think why Cyril was always raving about it.

"Do you remember how your father used to shout at Cyril in the evenings, when he wanted to turn on the radio?" asked Roddy, remembering. "When we were all at Mistletoe Farm, I mean. Well, Daddy does it too now – he made me jump out of my skin the other night, he yelled at Cyril so. I must say I rather like Daddy when he yells."

"Yes, I do too," said Susan. She was just about to say that the person he ought to yell at most of all was her Aunt Rose, when she stopped herself in time. Roddy was always loyal to his mother, whatever fault he might find in her himself.

"What time is it?" asked Susan, when they had finished feeding the hens, collecting the eggs and washing them. "Goodness – quarter to five! I'm beginning to feel a bit hungry, aren't you? When do you have high tea?"

"We don't have it," said Roddy, gloomily. "We have a dreadful sort of dainty afternoon tea – all mats and cloths and things, with hardly anything to eat. Usually Sally lets me have a tray with something decent on it all to myself – but now she's gone I suppose I won't have it – unless I get it myself."

"Well, get it yourself then," said Susan. "Let's wait till we're a bit hungrier and we'll go and collect something out of the larder."

There was no afternoon tea that afternoon. Rose had gone to lie down at three o'clock, and had fallen fast asleep. Melisande was struggling with things in the dairy, doing her best to help Cyril. Neither of them had any idea of the time.

When they at last went to look at the clock in the kitchen

it said half-past five! "No wonder we're hungry!" said Melisande. "Goodness – wouldn't I like to tuck in at one of Aunt Linnie's high teas today!"

Her father came into the kitchen too, at that moment and heard what she said. "I agree with you," he said. "High tea at this time's just right on a farm – and my word, look here – there's your Aunt Linnie coming along with her hands full of food. Bless her! She knew we'd welcome something to eat over the weekend!"

And, before ten minutes was up, everyone except Rose, who was still dozing, was sitting round the table tucking into ham and sausage rolls and cheese and cake – and drinking scalding hot tea made the way Linnie always made it – better than anyone else, so everyone declared.

Rose came down, half asleep – and stared in silence at the party round the table, and the obvious high tea that was going on.

"Come on, Mother!" said Roddy, making room for her. "This is just as good as being back at Mistletoe Farm – everybody round the table, plenty of decent food to eat, and lots of talk going on!"

CHAPTER 19

Holly Farm In A Muddle

Linnie left a good deal of food at Holly Farm for the weekend – half a ham, an enormous cake that Dorcas had baked specially for them that afternoon, some jam tarts and a cold roast chicken.

Her brother-in-law, David, was grateful. He took her hand

in his and pressed it. "You're good and kind, Linnie. I'm afraid we're in for rather a bad time now – no help in the house, unless the stockman's wife can give a hand – and Rose isn't really capable of tackling things."

"Well, she must try, David," said Linnie. "I will give her any advice or help that I can, you know that. Your three children can help a lot too – they *had* to help when they lived with me!"

Sunday was a muddle, and Rose was in despair most of the day, when she realised all the things there were to do. Melisande began to feel rather impatient with her mother. Fancy taking twenty minutes to make one bed!

Cyril said he didn't mind helping on the farm, but he wasn't going to mess about the house. "You might at least help with the washing-up," said Melisande, crossly.

"*I'll* do that," said Roddy. "And look – I've cleaned all the boots and shoes. There they are on the scullery floor."

So *that's* what you've been doing all this time!" said Melisande. "I wondered where you were. Oh Roddy – you *have* done them nicely! It's such a horrid job too – cleaning shoes."

"I like it," said Roddy. "I'll do what I can to help you, Melisande, so long as it isn't things like making beds or dusting. You can give me things like *cleaning* to do. I wouldn't even mind scrubbing this scullery floor for you, like Sally used to do. I like making things clean."

"That's funny –seeing you always look such a little grub yourself!" said Melisande. "Mother – look how well Roddy's cleaned the shoes! Really, he's a great help isn't he?"

"Dear little Roddy!" said her mother, drifting into the scullery, looking harassed and pale. "I don't know what we should do without him. You want to help Mother all you can, don't you?"

Roddy didn't like it when his mother talked to him in this baby way. He nodded and went out.

"Funny, solemn boy!" said Mrs Longfield, looking vaguely round the scullery. "Oh Melisande – isn't this awful? I simply don't know where to begin, do you?"

"Daddy's gone to see if Mrs Johns, the stockman's wife, will come and give a bit of help," said Melisande. "I only hope she can! And Aunt Linnie is going to get Dorcas to ask Sally to come back, now Ellen's gone. But even if she does, we'll have to do most of the housework ourselves, Mother – and as I shall have to be at school all day, I don't know how you're going to manage!"

Tears came into Rose's eyes. Melisande looked at her in exasperation. Then she remembered how she herself had always been able to "turn on the tap" at any moment, as Jack used to call it, when they stayed at Mistletoe Farm. Still, she, Melisande, had grown out of it – Mother never had.

She took no notice of her mother's tears, and piled the breakfast things into the steaming water. She was thankful to have plenty of hot water. There was none at Mistletoe Farm. Every drop had to be boiled on the kitchen stove. Here, at Holly Farm she had only to turn the tap and out came the water, steaming hot.

Aunt Linnie telephoned during the day. "Is that you, Melisande? I've got bad news, I'm afraid, dear. Sally has just been in to see Dorcas – and she's already got herself another job and is starting tomorrow. What a pity!"

"Oh *dear*!" said Melisande, in despair. "Can't she possibly cancel that and come back here?"

There was a slight pause at the other end. "I don't think she wants to," said her aunt's voice. "It's this business about those missing things, Melisande. Ellen thought it was Sally who stole them – and apparently your mother accused old Twigg. Sally's as honest as the day, of course – and she says old Twigg wouldn't steal from any Longfield, whoever else he might steal from! If only we could find the

308

real culprit and clear up this unpleasant business! Even so, I doubt it Sally would come back. She seems to have taken a real dislike to your mother."

Rose was amazed when Melisande repeated this conversation to her. "Sally doesn't like me – when I was so kind to her!" she kept repeating. "I suppose she adores your Aunt Linnie, though!"

Her husband came in, stamping the mud off his boots at the door. He called out to them. "Mrs Johns can give you one or two hours each day, that's all. But it's something!"

He went away, calling Roddy to come with him round the farm. Roddy clicked to his imaginary Tinker and followed his father, pleased. He liked this Sunday walk round the farm.

"I hate that Mrs Johns!" said Rose, taking up a tea-cloth to dry the breakfast things. "Surly and rude! She picks her teeth too."

"Oh Mother – what does that matter if she scrubs the floor well, and can cook a joint or something?" said Melisande. "Roddy likes her – and I've noticed that the people Roddy likes are usually all right."

"Roddy's only a baby," said her mother. "He likes the oddest people."

"Mother, Roddy's *not* a baby," said Melisande, thinking of the rows of cleaned boots and shoes, and the way Roddy had come to fetch the chicken food and mixed it and boiled it up that morning. "I do think you should stop thinking he is – he really doesn't like the baby way you speak to him sometimes."

"Melisande! Surely *you* are not going to turn against me too," said Rose, pathetically, and Melisande was sure that she would see tears in her eyes again if she looked at her mother. So she didn't look.

"Nobody's turned against you," she said, beginning to

sound impatient. "But Mother – couldn't you be a bit
more like – well, like Aunt Linnie? She sort of holds the
family together – and when bad things happen, they
don't seem as bad as they are, because we all know Aunt
Linnie's there to lean on."

Her mother threw down the tea cloth and went out of
the room. *Linnie!* Everyone quoted Linnie to her! Linnie
was the last person in the world she wanted to be like.
Linnie was too good to be true – she knew how to do
everything, she was a paragon of all the virtues! She was
sure though, that Linnie never read a book, never
listened to good music, never had a thought outside her
eternal cooking and washing and her hens and butter.

"Well – I will *not* grow into a cabbage like Linnie!"
said Rose, out loud. "I will *not!*"

Cyril, passing at that moment, heard her and was
astonished.

"What did you say, Mother?" he asked. "What's all
this about cabbages?"

"Everyone seems to expect me to behave like your
Aunt Linnie!" said his mother, miserably. "And she's
just a cabbage – or a – a turnip, Cyril. She's got
absolutely no interests beyond her house and her horrible hens and their dreary eggs. I *can't* be like her! I
must have music and poetry and books, and pretty
clothes. Linnie's just a country clod."

"She's not, Mother," said Cyril. "You're quite wrong.
She's as fond of poetry as I am. She *loves* good music
too. Do you know, last summer when I got my radio
(which by the way Aunt Linnie helped me to get) she
used to come out into the old barn with me when there
was a symphony concert on – and we'd listen to it together – with the hens clucking all round us!"

Rose looked at him in astonishment. He went on
earnestly. "She knows far more poetry than I do – she

310

reads all she can, though she's hardly a minute to spare. But none of these things *show* because she puts her family and the farm first – that's all. But she's not a clod or a cabbage or a turnip – or anything you've called her! I bet she could be far cleverer than anyone in our family, if she had more time."

"You never told me this before, Cyril," said his mother. "Nobody ever tells me anything!"

"Well – I didn't think you'd be interested," said Cyril. "And I knew you didn't like Aunt Linnie. It's a pity you don't, Mother. She could really give you lots of advice now!"

Once more Rose turned away in angry annoyance, her pretty face sullen and frowning. She went upstairs and fiddled about, straightening this and that.

"I'd rather leave this place altogether than stay on like this – and have Linnie thrust down my throat by everyone, even my own children!" she thought. "I wonder if David would give it up. I'm not fitted for a farm life. I'll wait till things have settled down a bit and then I'll ask him. If he really loves me he'll give it up and we'll find a nice little house in a town."

She looked out of the window and saw Roddy solemnly marching along with his father. "What a funny little boy he is!" she thought. "I don't understand him. He never tells me anything he thinks. He just seems to lead his own life – quite one on his own. But he's a good little boy really. It's his birthday soon – I'll buy him a really nice present."

She watched the two of them pass into the yard, talking very earnestly together. "What *can* they be talking about?" she wondered. "Roddy never talks like that to *me*!"

Roddy was talking about something most important. In fact, at the moment, it was the thing that loomed biggest in his life. He was actually talking about the spaniel pup that Twigg had offered to give him out of Tommy Lane's litter!

And his father was listening with interest and pleasure! Would he say yes? Would he say that Roddy *might* have a dog of his own?

CHAPTER 20

Roddy Has A Wonderful Afternoon

Roddy hadn't meant to say anything about the pup at all. It all happened in rather an odd way.

He was walking with his father, and Punch and Pouncer were running with them. Roddy, conscious of his imaginary dog Tinker, who went with him everywhere, of course, wondered if Tinker liked Punch and Pouncer.

He decided that Tinker didn't. Tinker was like Crackers – a dog that knew his own worth, and although he said good morning and wagged his tail to the other farm dogs, he kept to the house and family. Tinker was the same.

"Come to heel, Tinker," muttered Roddy, below his breath, and turned to see it Tinker had obeyed. He had, of course. He was a most obedient dog. Roddy forgot that he was with his father and bent down and patted him.

Mr Longfield was puzzled. What was Roddy doing, patting the air like that? Then, a few minutes later, he noticed that Roddy was holding out his hand as if he was giving it to a dog to lick.

"Roddy – what are you doing that for?" asked his

312

father. Roddy put his hand down and went very red. He said nothing.

"It's almost as if you've got a dog with you that I can't see," said his father, sounding puzzled. "A dog that keeps to your heels, and that you pat – and then he comes and jumps up at you, and you hold out your hand for him to lick. What's it all about?"

Roddy looked up at his father, delighted. "Oh Daddy – *you* can almost see him too then! That's Tinker – my imaginary dog. I've missed Crackers so much, you know. So now I've got Tinker."

Mr Longfield didn't know what to say. He thought hard. How much Roddy must have wanted a real dog, if he had created an imaginary one! But an imaginary dog was no good to anyone. Roddy must have a real dog, that was certain.

"We must see about getting you a real dog, Roddy," he said. "You can call him Tinker too. But he must be real."

Roddy gave a gasp. After all his hints and worries and wonderings about asking for a dog – here was his father saying straight out that he could have one!

He immediately poured out all that Twigg had suggested about a golden spaniel pup.

"One of Tommy Lane's," said Roddy, happily. "His golden spaniel has a lovely litter – and Twigg said I could choose one. He'd fix it with Tommy Lane. But oh, Dad – Mother's offended him – he's our enemy now, isn't he? She said he's stolen things from Holly Farm. He's never coming again – so it's no good going to Tommy Lane's about the pup. He wouldn't give me one."

"Twigg won't bear *you* any malice," said his father, sad and angry to hear again how Rose had sent away Twigg in such a manner. "He'll not come near us again, I don't doubt – but he won't hold all this against *you*, Roddy. He's a kindly fellow at heart. Go and see him today, if you like."

313

"I could catch the bus," said Roddy, eagerly. "I could take my dinner with me in a packet. I'd be back before it was time to feed the hens. Oh Daddy – I never, never thought you'd say yes so easily!"

He darted off to the kitchen. Nobody was there. He made himself some badly cut sandwiches of bread and ham and cut a piece of cake. He wrapped them up in paper and set off to catch the bus, his heart singing. There was no time to tell his mother where he was going. He mustn't miss the bus!

His father went to see the horse who was ill. The animal was pleased to see him. It wanted company, and it liked this big, burly farmer who stroked it and talked to it comfortingly. The vet, had been already and had shaken his head. "Not too good," he had said. "But we must just hope for the best. There's nothing more I can do."

Mr Longfield sensed that the horse wanted company. He decided to sit with him for an hour. He looked at his watch. If he did that he wouldn't be able to be in time for lunch – and Rose would be cross. So he did just what Roddy had done – went to get sandwiches. He too, got his own, so as not to bother his wife or Melisande. He called up the stairs to where he heard them at work in the bedrooms.

"I shan't be in for lunch. I'm taking sandwiches." And out he went to his big shire horse. Animals were funny things. They wanted something else beside food and shelter, work and rest. They wanted comfort sometimes, because when they felt ill, they were frightened, though they didn't know why. They wanted friendship – and they responded to love and understanding more than to anything else. Mr Longfield knew that. Well – if this big old horse wanted anything of that kind now that he was ill, he should have it!

Roddy was in the bus, wishing it would go as fast as an

314

aeroplane. His eyes shone. He forgot about his imaginary dog for the first time for weeks. He was thinking of the pup that he would have – that *perhaps* he would have, he thought, correcting himself. If only Twigg was still friendly to him!

He came to Twigg's cottage at about two o'clock, for he had had to walk a good way from the bus. He knocked at the door. A dog's bark sounded at once.

"Come in!" called Twigg's voice and Roddy opened the door. Twigg was sitting in a ramshackle old armchair, rocking himself to and fro, Mr Potts at his feet. The dog ran joyfully to Roddy and fawned on him, slobbering all over him.

"Well! Here's a welcome visitor, Mr Potts!" said Twigg, and he twinkled at Roddy. "Come you in, Master Roddy. And what have *you* come for this Sunday afternoon – to see me or to see Mr Potts?"

Roddy laughed, delighted that Twigg was still friendly to him. "Twigg, do you remember you said you'd ask Tommy Lane for a pup for me?" he said. "Well – Dad says I can have it, so I've come over. But Twigg – do you still feel like getting me a pup, after what happened yesterday? I'm very very sorry about that."

Twigg gave him a gentle punch in the chest. "That's got nought to do with you and me, son," he said. "Women and their tongues is one thing, you and me's another. I won't say aught against your mother to you – but I'll not be coming to Holly Farm again this long year. As for the pup, we'll go straight-along and have a look at he!"

Roddy could have thrown his arms round the dirty old poacher. It was a puzzle how a man could be so bad and yet so good – how he could do such wrong things and such kindly ones! Still, Roddy wasn't going to bother his head about that – all he wanted was to see his pup!

They went up to Tommy Lane's little cottage. Crocuses

315

bloomed, and one or two early daffodils, but Roddy never even noticed them. He could hear tiny little yaps coming from somewhere!

Tommy Lane had heard them coming and he opened the door. "Come you in!" he said. "Mebbe I know what you've come for, young sir!"

A lovely golden spaniel was lying in a pile of old rugs. With her were four tiny pups, nuzzling round and rolling in the rugs with yappy squeaks. Roddy knelt down beside the mother dog and fondled her, his eyes on the squirming yellow pups.

One crawled toward hm, and he felt a tiny tongue licking his hand. He lifted the puppy up gently. It was the tiniest, dearest little thing, its ears already beginning to droop beside its beautifully shaped head.

"Mr Lane! Twigg! Could I have this one?" he asked, beseechingly. "I like it best of all. It came over to me and licked me."

"You have he, then," said Tommy Lane, nodding his untidy old head, and winking at Twigg. "You have he, young master – and train he well. He'll follow like a shadow at your heels, same as Mr Potts with Sam Twigg. Ah – you can't beat they spaniels."

Roddy was too overjoyed to speak. He fondled the tiny puppy, while the big mother watched him out of her beautiful eyes.

He found his tongue at last. "Can I take him home with me today? Is he ready to leave his mother?"

"Yes, he's ready," said Tommy Lane. "The first pup went yesterday, and he's all right. Give him plenty of milk at first – and let him feel his teeth on something as soon as he wants to. Fine little dog he be."

A thought struck Roddy suddenly. "Oughtn't I to pay for him?" he said. "I've got some money in my money-box still – Christmas money."

"Mr Lane! Twigg! Could I have this one?"

"I reckon four of these pups will be paid for," said
Tommy Lane, "so I can give away one for nothing if I
wants to. You keep your money, young sir, and spend it

on your new dog – he'll want a collar soon, and a lead – and mebbe you want to bring him up in luxury like, and give him a basket!"

"You're *kind*, Mr Lane," said Roddy, burying his nose in the silky coat of the tiny spaniel. He smelt nice. "Someday I hope I'll be able to do *you* a good turn!"

"Well – me and Sam Twigg owes the Longfields at Mistletoe Farm for a-many kindnesses," said Tommy Lane, scratching the mother spaniel's soft head. "This here pup is a bit in return, like."

Roddy was very happy. He sat in Tommy Lane's cottage and ate his sandwiches there, listening to the talk of the two old countrymen. He could have listened for hours. The talk was of badgers and owls and hares and pheasants and foxes and weasels and otters and moles – fascinating talk for a young boy to hear. What a wonderful afternoon! Sitting there with his new pup pressed into his neck, and listening to the country wisdom of the two old men was a memory that was to remain with Roddy for the rest of his life.

He got up reluctantly at last. "There's no bus," he said to Twigg. "Could you please tell me the best way to get back across the fields – without losing myself!"

Twigg twinkled at him. "Me and Tommy will take you part of the way," he said. "We'll tell you the rest. It's quite easy, really."

They took him part of the way and left him to walk the rest by himself. As they said, it was really quite easy. He walked in a dream, his puppy in his arms.

"Tinker!" he said. "You're real now! You aren't just a little imaginary dog – you're a real one. I can feel you, warm and soft. I can hear you. I can even smell you! You're my very own Tinker-dog, and you'll belong to me and nobody else for ever and ever."

318

CHAPTER 21

A Shock For Roddy

Poor Roddy! He was met by cross looks and hard words when at last he arrived home just before dark.

"You naughty boy! Where have you been? You didn't come in for lunch, and you weren't at Mistletoe Farm!" scolded his mother. "We telephoned to see."

"Didn't Daddy tell you where I'd gone?" asked Roddy, surprised.

"We haven't even *seen* Daddy," said Melisande, also cross. "I've had to feed the hens too, and collect the eggs – just when there's so much to be done."

"Oh gosh!" said Roddy, remembering suddenly that he had promised his father to be back in time. He had utterly and completely forgotten. "I'm sorry, Melisande. I really am."

"But where have you *been*?" said his mother. "And what's that you've got there, wrapped in your scarf?"

Roddy uncovered the spaniel puppy, who was now fast asleep. "Tommy Lane gave him to me," he said. "Isn't he beautiful?"

His mother stared at the puppy as if she couldn't believe her eyes. She was very angry indeed. "A *puppy* – when you know I won't have a dog in the house! You can take it back. I forbid you to have it – without even *asking* me, too!"

Roddy went white. "He's mine," he said. "And Daddy said I might have him. I asked him."

"What's the good of asking *Daddy*!" said his mother, her voice rising high. "*He's* not got to look after him, and clean up after him, and feed him! You're to take him back."

"I shall look after him myself," said Roddy. "And feed him and everything."

"And what about when you're at school all day?" said his mother. "How can you look after him then?"

Roddy hadn't thought of that. All his happiness went. The pupy woke up at the moment and yawned a little spaniel yawn. Roddy set him gently down on the floor. Here was a perfect little picture.

"Look, Mother," said Roddy. "He's such a darling. Don't you like him now you see him properly?"

"Horrid little thing!" said Rose, obstinately. "Here's your father. I shall tell him you're to take it back."

But Roddy's father said no – Roddy could keep the pup, and the boy's heart lifted. But it sank again when his mother spoke bitterly.

Well, *I* shan't look after it when Roddy's at school!" said Rose. "If you think I'm going to bother to feed it and clean up after it, and have it under my feet all the time, I'm not. If *I've* got to train it, it won't enjoy its training!"

"You're cruel, Mother!" said Roddy, almost in tears. He could picture so well what might happen. His mother wouldn't give it food every few hours. She might smack it every time it got under her feet or made a puppy-mess. She would cow it and frighten it, and it would be unhappy. He looked at her with scornful dislike, and for a moment Rose was frightened at his look.

He picked up the tiny creature and wrapped it in his scarf again. He turned and went out, without heeding the calls of his father.

"I love you and you're my dog – but I'd rather you were someone else's dog and happy, than mine and miserable," said poor Roddy. He walked all the way back to Tommy Lane's, and opened the door. Nobody was there except the spaniel with her little family. Tommy wasn't back yet. He had probably gone poaching with Twigg!

Roddy put the puppy back gently on the pile of rugs. He felt in his pocket and took out a notebook. He scribbled a

320

few words, and put the note on the table, where Tommy Lane found it a few hours later. Twigg read it to him, for Tommy couldn't read.

"I've brought back my pup. I mustn't have it, Mother says. But thank you, Mr Lane. Roddy."

He got back home about eight o'clock, tired and miserable. The family were anxiously waiting for him. They had put a meal ready for him on a tray, for they had had high tea long ago. It had been decided by everyone – except Rose – that high-tea would be more sensible now there was no one but themselves to get the meal. Rose could always get herself an afternoon tea if she liked to!

"Come here, Roddy," said his father, struck by the boy's tired and miserale face. "Where have you been? We've been worried about you? Where's the pup?"

"I took him back," said Roddy. "That's what Mother wanted, wasn't it? But – I don't think I'll ever be able to forgive you, Mother!"

He went out of the room and upstairs without touching the food set ready for him.

"How *unkind*!" said Rose, the easy tears coming. "Just because I objected to the dog. Why, Roddy looked at me as if he almost hated me then!"

"Do you wonder, Rose?" said her husband, wearily. "Hatred is so much easier to win than love – and so much harder to get rid of. Hadn't you better be careful?"

Roddy didn't say a word to anyone about the puppy he had had for such a short time. He didn't even have his imaginary dog any more. He got up as usual next morning and did his jobs well and thoroughly and caught the bus for school with Cyril and Melisande. But he didn't go and say goodbye to his mother – who, astonishingly enough, was still in bed! She complained of a bad night, and the others had left her to sleep.

"Though if she thinks Mrs Johns will get her her

breakfast when she comes, she'll be mistaken," said Melisande, tired already with getting the breakfast and making the beds before catching the bus. "Oh dear – I do so wish we had Sally. She was so sensible and nice."

Mrs Johns didn't take up Rose's breakfast. She had no intention of doing so. She banged about in the kitchen and scullery and woke up Rose completely. Rose rang the bell.

But Mrs Johns took no notice of bells. She just went on banging round. In the end Rose had to get up and get her own breakfast. Mrs Johns watched her grimly. She was a dour and surly woman.

"I've done round the kitchen and the scullery. Now I'm off," she said. Rose was dismayed.

"Oh, but I wanted you to do the other rooms too," she said, "and cook a joint for us."

"Ma'm, I've got my husband and six children to see to," said Mrs Johns, "to say naught of hens and ducks and goats and a pig. Think shame on yourself for lying in bed till this time of day, and not getting a bit ready for your man when he comes in. *I'm* not getting his dinner – I'm off to get dinner for the eight of us back home."

She banged her way out and slammed the door. Rose was angry and depressed. How dare Mrs Johns speak to her like that? But she wouldn't dare now to tick her off. If she did, Mrs Johns wouldn't come again – and then things would be worse than ever.

They were bad enough as it was. The next few days were uncomfortable and miserable for everyone. Rose didn't really try to cope with things, she felt much too sorry for herself. Melisande had to turn to before breakfast and do what she could – and after school she worked hard in the house and dairy too. Otherwise the house would have been a pigsty.

Roddy did his bit too. He didn't seem to mind what jobs

322

he took on. Melisande found that she was depending on him more and more. He *always* did what he said he would. Once, when Mrs Johns didn't come, he even scrubbed the scullery floor, which had got unbelievably filthy. He felt quite proud when he saw how nice it looked.

His father was worried about him. Roddy avoided his mother whenever he could and hardly spoke to her. He said very little to his father either. In fact, he looked a miserable, obstinate little boy, although he worked hard before and after school, and could be completely trusted with the hens and ducks and eggs.

One evening Linnie telephoned. "She wants to speak to you, Daddy," said Melisande, holding out the receiver to her father.

"David!" said Linnie's voice. "We've been thinking it might be a bit of help to you if we had Roddy to stay with us for a bit – till you get someone living in to help you. Susan would so love to have him."

Roddy's father turned from the telephone and spoke to Roddy. "Roddy – it's Aunt Linnie. She says they want you to go and stay with them. Would you like to go, old chap?"

Roddy's face lighted up. Misteltoe Farm – that place of warmth and friendship and love where he had been so happy! Aunt Linnie and her cheerful kindness – Dorcas in the kitchen – Jack and Jane to tease him – and dear old Susan and Crackers. Crackers! He could share him.

His father waited. "Well, Roddy? When would you like to go? Tomorrow?"

Then Roddy said a most surprising thing. "No, Daddy. Who'll do my jobs here if I go? It would be awfully hard for Melisande to have to do the things I do, as well as what she does now. Tell Aunt Linnie I'd *love* to come – oh, I really would – but I don't see how I can leave Holly Farm *now*."

His father gave him a long look. Then he turned to the telephone. "Linnie? He'd *love* to come – I can see he wants to with all his heart – but he's not deserting us, Linnie. He's standing by us!"

He clicked the receiver back into place. He went to the surprised Roddy and gave him a bear-like hug. "You've done me good!" he said. "Thanks, Roddy – I *do* want your help. You're a brick!"

He went out to make sure the henhouse and barns were locked. Such a lot of thieving had been going on. Melisande and Cyril, left in the sitting room with Roddy, looked at one another. They could guess what an effort it had been for him to say no to Aunt Linnie's offer. He did so love Mistletoe Farm – and Susan and Crackers!

"Thanks, Roddy," said Melisande. "As a matter of fact – *I* couldn't do without your help either!"

"You're a sport, Roddy," said Cyril. And for the first time that week Roddy beamed. His family wasn't so bad after all!

CHAPTER 22

An Enemy At Work

Three weeks somehow dragged along. Holly Farm was no longer a nice comfortable home to live in. It was dirty and untidy, meals were not good, and very often tempers were short.

Melisande had far too much to do, and she soon looked thin in the face, and lost some of her plumpness. She grew resentful because she thought that her mother, with all the day in front of her, seemed to achieve so little. She snapped at Rose, and Rose either snapped back or cried. Roddy and Cyril couldn't bear it. They cleared off out-of-doors as much as they could.

Mrs Johns still came in for two hours in the mornings, grim and surly, noisy as ever. Rose was so afraid of her that she never went near when Mrs Johns was in the kitchen. Which was a pity because the grim woman had a kind heart underneath her rough ways, and would have taught Rose many a useful tip.

Cyril found that suddenly he had a great deal to do on the farm. The odd-job man fell ill with a bad chill, and was away a week. When he came back he was not fit to do a full day's work, so when Cyril came home from school he had to turn to and do many jobs. He didn't grumble, but he didn't do them willingly, or in a friendly manner, which was a pity.

Roddy pegged away at his own jobs as usual, slow, but sure, and was always there when Melisande was in difficulties. If the clothes line broke he mended it. If the sink got blocked he miraculously unblocked it. If the boiler fire went out he could light it more quickly than anyone.

"Honestly, you're a marvel, Roddy," Melisande said, warmly. "You're more grown-up than any of us, sometimes! Roddy –listen – I *do* wish you'd had that puppy. I'm very sorry about that."

"I don't want to talk about it," said Roddy, and changed the subject abruptly.

Aunt Linnie came over twice with Dorcas. How Dorcas worked away in the kitchens, and how spotless and shining they looked when she left! How Aunt Linnie cooked and baked, and what a fine sight the larder was when she had done!

Rose hovered round, no help at all. Linnie spoke kindly but firmly to her.

"Rose – wouldn't you like me to show you how to do

some simple cooking and baking? There was hardly anything fit to eat in the larder when I came. Food is so important to a growing family – and what about poor David? He looks quite thin."

"I don't feel well," said Rose. "I'm hoping to get somebody in to look after the house. Then I can rest. I need rest. This is a very dreadful time for me."

Linnie sighed. As long as Rose thought only of herself, they would never get anywhere! She said no more, but was pleased to see Melisande's face when the girl came home and saw the full larder and shining kitchens.

"Oh *look* Mother! Isn't Aunt Linnie wonderful – and Dorcas too!" said Melisande, giving them both a hug. "It's the first time for weeks I've felt happy to come home."

"You've had some bad luck, no doubt about that," said Linnie. "It's time it went!"

But instead of going, it suddenly got worse! Roddy came flying indoors the next morning with very bad news.

"Dad! The ducks have gone – and half the hens!"

Everyone ran out to see. It was true. Only one solitary duck swam on the pond – and it was plain there were only half the usual number of hens.

"Who's done that?" said Cyril, angrily. "Who's been along and stolen them all?"

"It must be Twigg!" said his mother. "He said he'd be our enemy. It's Twigg!"

"It can't be," said her husband. "Twigg wouldn't do a mean thing like that to us."

"He would! He would!" said Rose. "He's not forgiven me for accusing him in front of Sally and Ellen of stealing those things!"

Mr Potts the policeman was sent for. He too was inclined to think it was Twigg. He pointed out some small footprints in the mud round the henhouse.

"Everyone ran out to see . . . only one solitary duck swam . . ."

"Sam Twigg's got small feet," he said. "So has Tommy Lane."

Mr Potts had no love for Sam Twigg. Too often Twigg had met Mr Potts the policeman in the street, and had at once turned round and shouted to Mr Potts his spaniel – so that everyone imagined he was talking to the policeman.

"Hey, Mr Potts, come here, you! Potts by name and Potty by nature! Urrrrrr! Wicked Mr Potts!"

And the policeman had had to bear all the delighted winks and grins and chuckles that the village people gave when they heard Twigg's cheeky shouts. He was really very glad indeed to make Twigg the culprit in this business of stolen poultry.

"Well, I'll go and talk to Sam Twigg," he said, shutting his notebook. "Frighten the life out of him, I will. Ah, he's a slippery one that – but I'll get him some day."

And off he marched to give Twigg a most unpleasant half-hour indeed, and to make the old poacher very angry and resentful.

That afternoon the stockman had bad news too. He reported that about six of the cows were sick, besides the two already ill.

Mr Longfield hurried off to see them. As soon as he had examined them he telephoned the vet. This was serious. He was a very worried man indeed when the vet, came.

The vet examined the cows carefully. Then he stood up and looked gravely at Mr Longfield. "Have you any enemies about here, Mr Longfield? Someone's been doing something to damage these cows of yours – I can't tell you what, but something in the poisoning line."

Twigg's name came to Mr Longfield's lips but he did not say it. He could not bring himself to think that the old poacher would do a thing like this to him – even though Rose had mortally insulted him!

"Now that I've seen these cows I wouldn't be surprised if that horse of yours, and the other two cows, haven't been doped in the same way as these," he said. "See here, sir – see those little holes in this cow's neck? Well, something has been injected there – something that's made the cow sicken."

Mr Longfield felt sick himself. How could anyone do these things to helpless animals, just to revenge themselves on the owner? He turned at the sound of footsteps and saw Mr Potts the policeman again. He had come to report on his interview with Twigg.

"Afternoon, sir," said Mr Potts in a voice as ponderous as his walk. "About this here matter of Sam Twigg and your poultry, sir. I saw him and I saw Tommy Lane too. They were both out last night, but they both deny they were over this way. But you can't believe a word they say, sir."

"Who's this you're talking about? Twigg?" said the vet. He turned to Mr Longfield. "Well, Twigg *could* have done this all right, Mr Longfield, if he's an enemy of yours. He was in a racing-stable at one time, and he knew a lot about doping horses. I don't suppose he has forgotten his knowledge. He was always a twister, was Sam Twigg. Mind you, he's a marvel with animals. I admit it myself. Twigg can often do what I can't – but if he's your enemy, beware! He's a good friend – but I wouldn't like to have him for *my* enemy."

"There you are!" said Mr Potts, pleased with this long speech. "That's it, sir – Twigg was along here last night with old Tommy Lane – and the two of them took your ducks and hens, and worked mischief to your cows. No doubt about it, sir. I'll arrest him and put him in the cells – and Tommy Lane too!"

"What about the cows?" asked Mr Longfield, turning to the vet. "Will they live?"

"I doubt it," said the vet. "It's a big loss to you. They're fine cows, I know. Look, take these pills. Sit up with the cows tonight, and if any of them groan, give them these. It'll ease their pain, poor creatures."

He went over to where he had tied his horse, leapt on its back and rode off. "Poor Longfield!" he thought. "He's in a sad mess now. Those cows look like dying tonight. They're worse than the others were."

Mr Potts went off gleefully to Twigg's cottage again, pedalling away on his bicycle happily. Ah – now he'd got him, the old rogue, the pest, the toad! That was a very serious business – doping valuable cows like that.

Twigg listened, looking astounded. Tommy Lane was with him. Twigg took the policeman to a shed outside, lifted up some sacking, and showed the policeman four fine pheasants, still in their feathers.

"I *were* on Mester Longfield's land last night," said Twigg. "And them's what I got. But I weren't on Holly Farm land, I were on Mistletoe Farm land. And if you go and tell Mester Peter Longfield that, mebbe he'll send for me and dress me down hisself – but he won't go for to send me off to the cells with *you*, Mr Potts."

"You can't prove you got those pheasants on Mistletoe Farm," said the policeman, triumphantly. "I'll take you along to the police station for questioning, Sam Twigg. And you too, Tommy Lane. Come along, both of you!"

"I'll just get me coat," said Twigg, looking very subdued. He and Tommy went in at the back door of the cottage. The policeman bent over the pheasants, counted them, and made a few entries in his notebook about them. Then he stood up and called.

"Twigg! Lane! I'm waiting!"

There was no answer. All was quiet in the cottage. A sudden thought struck Mr Potts. He ran in at the back door and gazed round the tiny scullery. Then into the parlour. The cottage was empty!

330

"Drat him!" shouted Mr Potts, angrily. "He went in at the back – and out at the front. Just as I'd nicely got my hands on him too. I'll make him feel sorry for himself when I catch him!"

But it was difficult to know where he was going to catch Twigg. There wasn't a sign of him anywhere. In fact, it wasn't worth while bothering to look for him. Mr Potts knew that quite well. He went scowling back to the police-station. You wait, Twigg, that's all! You just wait!

CHAPTER 23

The Choice

That evening Linnie and her husband both went over to Holly Farm, deeply troubled. There seemed no end to the bad luck that had overtaken the farm. This last business of the cows was very serious indeed.

Cyril and Melisande were out in the dark dairy, lit by one small electric light, trying to churn the butter, which, as usual, refused to come till long after it should. Melisande was tired out. She had been up at half-past six that morning and had had a long day at school. Cyril too was tired. He had been up with his father at six, and out on the farm to help the odd-job man, who was still only doing half-time work.

They were cross and snappy. "I feel I'd almost sooner never eat butter again than have to get it like this," said Melisande. "Sally always got the butter to come much more quickly. We don't do it properly."

"Dorcas said butter came quicker for good tempered

people than for bad," said Cyril. "You temper's been so bad lately that no wonder the butter doesn't come."

"What about yours?" retorted Melisande. "Listen – is that someone's car I can hear? Yes – it must be Aunt Linnie and Uncle Peter. They're coming over for a serious talk to-night."

Roddy was in the kitchen, cleaning all the dirty boots and shoes again – and some of them were very dirty indeed, especially his father's and Cyril's. He had spread a news-paper on the floor so that he shouldn't make too much mess.

There was only Rose in the sitting room when Linnie and Peter went in. David was washing his hands, still worrying about his cows.

"Well, Rose dear," said Linnie, kindly, as she went into the room. "This is sad news again. You certainly are having a run of bad luck."

"It's too long a run," said Rose. "We shall be ruined – and all your money will be lost too, Peter."

"Oh, we're not ruined yet by a long way," said her brother-in-law, cheerfully – more cheerfully than he really felt. "It means harder work for a longer time – and maybe Cyril *will* have to leave school now, to help – because in my opinion that odd-job man isn't fit to work on a farm with that tummy trouble of his – and if Cyril takes his place, why, there's one wage saved!"

"I don't *wish* Cyril to leave school," said Rose, in her coldest voice. "It was a mistake coming here – a mistake coming into the country at all. I think we should leave and get a house in town somewhere – and David can get a job in some business. It seems quite obvious that we can't make this farm pay, and . . ."

"My *dear* Rose! You've only been here a few months!" said Peter. "What nonsense you talk! Wait till you've been here for five years before you say you can't make a farm pay."

332

"I don't intend to be here for even five months!" said Rose. "I hate it! It wasn't so bad when we had Ellen and Sally – but I can't seem to get anyone except that hateful Mrs Johns."

"Rose – Peter certainly can't afford to pay *two* women to run this little farmhouse," said Linnie. "I manage our big one with Dorcas alone – and you know how old and awkward it is, compared with yours. You'll have to make do with one, if you can get her."

"That decides me," said Rose, her voice shaking. "How could I ever manage with one – and only a country girl at that! What sort of life would it be for the children? What . . ."

"It would be exactly the same life as for *our* children!" said Linnie, getting cross. "They're happy enough – and so were yours when they lived with us. Shame on you, Rose! As soon as a little trouble comes, all you want to do is to run away, instead of facing it!"

"Have you ever *tried* facing troubles, Rose?" asked her brother-in-law, dryly. "No – you haven't. Well, I'll tell you what happens when you do – what *always* happens! They fade away – they get smaller and smaller – and then one day they're gone. But you have to face up to them and fight them. And that's what you never have done – and never will do it seems to me."

His brother David came into the room. "Hello, Linnie – well, Peter. It's good of you to come. Bad business this – ducks and hens nearly all gone – horse dying and six or eight cows going the same way!"

"To say nothing of Rose being no help to you at all!" said Peter. "Has she told you what *she* proposes?"

"No. What?" asked David, and turned to his wife.

"David, we're going to give up the farm, find a house – quite a little one, in town – and give up this dreadful life," said Rose, trying to speak calmly. "Cyril is not to leave

333

school and work on the farm. I wouldn't hear of it. Melisande can go to a nice school in town and so can Roderick. I don't like the schools here."

Her husband was too astonished to say a word. Rose went on, speaking quickly.

"I hate all this! I know we'll never do any good with Holly Farm. Why, we've failed already! We'll throw our hand in and leave while we can!"

"*We*?" said her husband. "And who do you mean by *we*, Rose?"

"All of us," said Rose. "You, me – the children."

"Count me out," said David, grimly. "I've got this farm and I'm keeping it. A bit of bad luck isn't going to knock *me* out! I've got Peter behind me too. And listen to this, Rose, because it's my last word – I'm a farmer, I'm going to remain one, and I'm sticking here!"

"Well – I'm *not*!" said Rose, her face going an angry red. "I shall leave you and take the children and go into town. I won't have them brought up like this."

"Oh Rose, Rose!" said Linnie, distressed. "These are dreadful things you are saying!"

"Be quiet!" said Rose, fiercely. "You think I ought to stay and slave like you do, don't you? Well . . ."

"That's enough, Rose," said David, looking suddenly angry. "If you had half the stuff in you that Linnie has, I wouldn't be sitting here feeling more ashamed of you tonight than I've ever felt ashamed of anyone in my life. You a wife! You a mother! You don't know how to be. You're neither wife nor mother – you're only Rose, pretty, spoilt Rose, who can't stick by her man, or look after her children!"

Rose flared up again. "How dare you talk to me like that! Where are the children? You'll soon see they prefer to go with me, than stay here on this horrible farm!"

"We'll fetch them," said Linnie, in a troubled voice. "I saw Cyril and Melisande in the dairy, as I came by."

They went to the dairy. Cyril and Melisande were still there, thankfully making the butter, which had come at last, into big pats. Melisande's face was thin and white, and her body was no longer plump. "Poor child!" thought Linnie, with a pang. "She's been doing all Rose's work as well as her own jobs. And Cyril looks worn out too. School and farmwork combined are too much for him."

"See how my pretty Melisande looks now, with all these things to do!" said Rose, angrily. "She's losing all her looks. I won't have it!"

They found Roddy in the kitchen, solemnly setting out the shoes he had cleaned. "What a good little boy!" thought Linnie. "And what a shame he couldn't have had that pup."

Susan had told her all about this, and she had felt angry. Roddy asked so little, and did so much. How could his mother have refused him such a little thing?

"And look at Roddy – slaving himself to death over jobs like this!" said his mother. Roddy looked up, surprised.

"Hello, Aunnt Linnie!" he said, pleased. "Look at the boots and shoes! I clean them just as well as Jack cleans them at Mistletoe Farm, don't I?"

Soon all three children were in the sitting room with their parents and their aunt and uncle. They looked in surprise at the grown ups. Why were they all so solemn?

"Children," said their father. "Your mother has put forward an idea. I want you to hear it and choose for yourselves what you want to do about it. Tell them, Rose."

"Well, my dears," said Rose, "I feel we can't go on with Holly Farm. I'm sure we shall always have bad luck. And it's much too hard work for me, and for all of you. Daddy wants Cyril to leave school and take the odd-job man's place. I don't want him to. Nor do I want you, Melisande, or you, Roddy, to slave as hard as you do – you,

335

Melisande, in the house, and you, Roddy, with the hens and other things. It's not fair."

She paused. All three children were listening intently. "So what I propose is this," said Rose. "I propose that we give up Holly Farm, and go back to the town life we know. Cyril will still go to school. We shall all have a much more comfortable and happy life, and we shall have learnt our lesson – the country is not for us!"

She stopped. Roddy stared solemnly at her. Then he looked at his father.

"Are you *really* thinking of leaving the farm already, Daddy?" he asked. "We've hardly come."

"No. I'm not leaving," said his father, steadily. "It's my farm and I'm stopping here to farm it. But if your mother wants a town-life she can have it, of course – without me. And I want you children to go with her, if you would like to. You can make your own free choice, and I shall respect it. You can always come here for weekends, of course."

Roddy went over to his father at once. "I'm staying here," he said. "You'll want *one* of us, won't you? I'm staying. I like the farm and all the jobs. Anyway I wouldn't run away from you like that, when things are bad!"

Linnie felt the tears come into her eyes. Was this the silly little mother's boy she had known nearly a year ago? How grown-up he sounded now.

"Very well. You shall stay with me on the farm," said his father, and put his arm round Roddy. He looked at Cyril.

"I expect you'd like to go with your mother," he said. "She'll need you."

Cyril hesitated. "She won't need me as much as you will, Dad," he said. "I don't like running away – and that's what it comes to. I'll be glad to leave school and come and work on the farm till things get better. I'd be a coward to desert the ship. I'll stay here."

And now it was Melisande's turn. She was torn in two. She felt sorry for her mother – but how much sorrier for her troubled father. "Who would look after you all and make Holly Farm a home for you, if Mother wasn't here?" she said. "I – I couldn't bear you just to have a housekeeper person. She couldn't make it home Mother, oh Mother – I'll *have* to stay with the others – you do see that, don't you? *Somebody's* got to look after them and make a home – and I can't bear a stranger to do that. I must stay – and I'll leave school as soon as I'm sixteen and stay home altogether. Things will be easier then."

An urgent knock sounded on the door just as Melisande finished speaking. Then the stockman's voice came.

"Mester Longfield, sir – come on up to the cows. They be right bad tonight!"

CHAPTER 24

Unexpected Friends

The two brothers rushed out of the house at once. Cyril followed. Linnie looked at Rose, who was crying pitfully in her chair. Melisande was trying to comfort her.

"Leave her alone, Melisande," said her aunt, wearily. "Nobody is stopping her from leaving, and living the life she longs for. She can see you all whenever she wants to. She has got her own way."

"I haven't, I haven't!" wept Rose. "I've lost my

husband and my children – nobody wants to come with me. I'm all alone."

"Well, don't go, then," said Roddy, sensibly and calmly. "I simply can't think what all the fuss is about, Mother. If you really want us all, stay with us. But you *don't* want us, actually, we're too much of a bother. I think it would be a very good idea if you had a lovely time in town and came to see us sometimes, like you used to do at Mistletoe Farm."

He went out of the room. "He doesn't love me a tiny bit," sobbed Rose." "And he used to be such a loving little boy."

"You shouldn't have sent that puppy of his away," said Linnie. "You spoilt his love for you then. He's a funny little boy. He'll never forgive you for that. Come, Rose, stop crying and go up to bed. I'll tidy round the kitchen a bit before I go. You go to bed too, Melisande, child – you look tired out."

"I am rather," said Melisande. She took Rose firmly up to bed and left her. She felt too tired to comfort her mother and listen to her grumbles that night.

Outside in the cowshed, the two Longfield brothers, the stockman and Cyril stood looking down at a moaning cow. Roddy peeped in at the half-open door, afraid to go any further in case he was sent out.

"If Twigg did that, he deserves to get imprisonment for life!" said David Longfield, between his teeth. "Poor creature – even those pills don't seem to have eased her."

"I don't believe Twigg could do this to animals," said his brother. "No, not even if he felt he had to revenge himself for a bitter insult. He might steal the hens and the ducks – I wouldn't put that past him – but he wouldn't damage stock."

Roddy listened in horror. However could *anyone* think Twigg would make the cows ill like that? They didn't know Twigg as he did, or they would never say such a thing.

His father suddenly saw him standing there, and, not wanting him to see the cow dying, sent him off at once.

Roddy obeyed. But he didn't want to go back to the house. It was a lovely night. He'd go for a walk – and for the first time for days he would take the imaginary Tinker with him for company!

He set off over the fields. He knew a hill where rabbits played at night. There would be enough moon to watch them by.

"Come on!" he said to Tinker. "Heel, now heel! No rabbit-hunting yet!"

When he got to the hillside he sat down, and the imaginary Tinker sat down too. Roddy could almost hear him panting. Then he very nearly jumped out of his skin!

It was *real* panting he heard. And it was real pattering feet he heard too. And now there was hot breath on the back of his neck, and a delighted wuff in his ear!

Roddy could hardly breathe. Surely – surely it wasn't his imaginary dog coming alive! A wet tongue licked his ear and two paws weighed down his shoulder. Roddy looked at this suddenly-materialised dog in wonder – yes – it was a golden spaniel, just as he had imagined Tinker to be.

Then a voice came from the bushes. "Mr Potts. Where are you?"

Roddy leapt up a if he had been shot. Why – it was Twigg – and this dog was not his imaginary Tinker come alive, it was Mr Potts, Twigg's own golden spaniel.

"Twigg! Twigg! Where are you? It's me, Roddy."

Two shadows detached themselves from the blackness of the hedge. They were Twigg and Tommy Lane. "What you doing here this time of night?" demanded Twigg.

"Never mind that. Twigg – did you know Daddy's cows were dying?" said Roddy.

"I did," said Twigg, grimly. "And seemingly, 'cording to old Potts, I'm the one that killed them."

"That's silly, Twigg," said Roddy. "You couldn't

339

possibly harm a cow. *I* know that. But I know something else too."

"What's that, young sir?" said Twigg.

"I know that if anyone in this world could keep them alive, you could keep them alive, you could, Twigg," said Roddy, earnestly. "Please, Twigg – come and see them. One's groaning dreadfully."

"Well – mebbe I know what's wrong with your cows," said Twigg, in a suddenly grim voice. "Mebbe me and Tommy Lane have been after them what did the damage – and mebbe we've got out of them what it was . . ."

"And mebbe we knows as how to cure 'em," chimed in Tommy Lane's voice. "But we won't. Folks as send the police after us don't deserve no help."

"Perhaps we don't," said Roddy, desperately. "But the *cows* deserve it. They're good cows, Twigg – you've seen them."

"Ay. I've seen them," said Twigg. "Here, Mr Potts, to heel. We've got work to do tonight. We're going along to undeserving folks and we're going to do them a right good turn – all alonga this here pest of a boy!"

"Oh Twigg – thank you," said Roddy, and hung on to Twigg's arm in sudden heartfelt gratitude.

They didn't say much as they made their way, the four of them (counting Mr Potts the spaniel), over the fields to Holly Farm. They came to the cowsheds, which were still lighted by a lantern. A groaning noise came to their ears.

"Now you go back to the house, Master Roddy," said Twigg, stopping outside the cowshed door. "There's things to be done as isn't fit for young eyes to see – t'would only worrit you, and get into your dreams. You go to bed – and if things go well, you'll know it soon enough."

Roddy squeezed Twigg's arm and set off obediently. Twigg and Lane went into the shed, much to the amazement of the Longfield brothers and of the stockman there.

Many hours later five very tired men stumbled out of the sheds. One cow had died – but all the rest were saved. The horse was all right too – it would soon take a turn for the better and be fit for work in a week.

"I don't know exactly what you did, Twigg," said David Longfield. "Your hands are as quick and deft as the paws of a cat – but all I can say is, you've worked miracles. God bless you, man – you've got the free run of my land for all the time I farm it – and Tommy Lane too. I'll never forgot tonight."

"Thank you kindly sir," said Twigg, a grin stretching his leathery face. "That's young Master Roddy got me here tonight. Pity about that pup, sir – he were right down pleased with it. Tommy Lane here has kep' it, just in case. Does your heart good to see a young-un like Master Roddy."

"Yes. Chip of the old block – like your son Master Jack, sir," said Tommy Lane to Peter Longfield. "Well goodnight, and the best of luck, sir – and if you want some of your hens and ducks, you'll find them with the gypsies over to Whortleberry Hill – if they're still there tomorrow!"

"What!" cried David Longfield, in astonishment. "How do you know?"

"Well, me and Tommy here, we didn't like old Potts the policeman coming after us with tales of stolen hens and ducks, like," said Twigg. "Nor didn't we like them tales of damaging cows and horses, sir. So we ups and goes to find them what does do these rascally things – the gypsies who lived on your bit of common till the day afore yesterday."

"The gypsies!" said David and Peter together and the stockman grunted. "But they've gone," said David.

"Yes – I told you, they're over to Whortleberry Hill," said Twigg. "You turned 'em off you land, sir, and you miscalled them and set the dogs on them – quite right too,

341

they'm rascally folks, not like us honest poachers. Well, they're spiteful, sir, – and before they went, they took your ducks and hens – and damaged your cows. They damaged that horse of yourn too, and the other cows, no doubt of that. You set that bossy old policeman after them gypsies, sir. They've got your ducks and hens running about still, under their caravans. And mebbe you'll find other things belonging to you *inside* the vans. You set old Potts after them gypsies!"

"I will," said David Longfield, grimly.

"And tell that policeman I'll be waiting at home all tomorrow to accept his apologies," said Twigg, maliciously. "You tell him that from old Twigg. Goodnight to you, sirs."

He and Tommy Lane and Mr Potts the spaniel melted into the shadows. David gave a sigh. "Well – he's done a good night's work for me, has old Twigg. I wonder what's happened to poor old Linnie all this time!"

They went back to Holly Farm. There was a light burning in the sittingroom but otherwise the house was in darkness. The men got themselves something to eat and drink. The door opened softly as they sat silently at the table.

It was Rose. Rose with swollen cheeks and swollen eyes – a very subdued and miserable Rose.

"I waited up for you," she whispered. "Linnie went home in the car. Are the cows better?"

"Yes. They'll be all right now," said David, wearily. "Peter, will you sleep on the sofa?"

"I've made up the bed in Ellen's room for him," said Rose, and she took him up. He said a curt goodnight to her and shut the door. She went down to David.

"Well, Rose, you made a poor show of yourself tonight," said her husband, "but we'll say no more now. Go to bed. I'm going to sleep down here. I'm too tired to undress."

"I just want to say one thing," said Rose. "I'm not going to leave Holly Farm either, David. I'm sticking by you too. I

342

can never be as good a wife and mother as Linnie – but I'll be a second-best, if you can put up with that."

"Bless you, Rose," said David, smiling for the first time that day. "That's the best news I've had for a long time – and I'm too tired to talk about it! Too tired even to tell you I love you just as much, and we'll begin all over again!"

Rose kissed him and went upstairs by herself. David was asleep before she had got to her bedroom door! In Ellen's room Peter was fast asleep too.

Rose got into bed. She had heard a lot of things from Linnie that night after the men had gone out to the cows – hard things, straight things, terrible things. And then Linnie had got into the car and driven away and left Rose to her own thoughts.

She had gone to Melisande, but Melisande had not changed her mind about sticking to the farm. Neither had Cyril. She had not attempted to go to Roddy.

She couldn't bear to be alone, in a town house all by herself! She knew that. But sticking to Holly Farm meant discomfort and unpleasant things and hard work. She had given her children the choice and they had chosen the hard way. She was the only weak one of the family – and they could quite well do without her.

But Rose, staring into the darkness, knew that she couldn't do without *them*. She couldn't. And now she would somehow have to make them feel they couldn't do without her either, and that would be very hard. David loved her – she would soon win him back. Cyril thought the world of her – it wouldn't be very difficult to get *his* love back once more.

And she would win back Melisande too – she would even get up at half-past six every morning, so that her children shouldn't have to come down and get their own breakfasts! What a tremendous resolve for poor Rose.

She would ask advice from Linnie and Dorcas and follow it. And what about Roddy?

Roddy didn't like her any more. She knew that he didn't. He was cold to her – all the lovely warmth of feeling he had once had for her was gone. It would be very very difficult to win Roddy back.

Yes – that certainly would be difficult, the most impossible task of all – and there was only one sure way of doing it. *David* knew what it was, but he wasn't going to tell Rose. She would have to think it out for herself!

CHAPTER 25

A Proper Family Again

The next day dawned bright and clear. The cock crowed loudly as he always did. David Longfield awoke with a jump, stiff and tired after his night on the sofa. He glanced at the clock. Half-past six!

He heard his brother coming down the stairs – and then he heard somebody in the kitchen. "Surely not Melisande down already!" he thought.

"No – it wasn't – it was actually Rose! Rose with eyes still red, and a very tired face, but an astonishingly cheerful Rose. "I'm just getting you something to eat," she said. "The kettle's almost boiling. Don't go out till you've had something."

Peter was astonished. He didn't know that Rose had completely changed her mind. "What a pity she isn't always like this!" he thought.

The men went out to the cowshed. Rose rushed round

344

doing this and that. She was very tired, but she was no longer miserable.

Melisande was astonished beyond words when she came down. So was Cyril.

"Don't look so surprised," said Rose. "I've changed my mind about leaving you and the farm. *I'm* staying too. It seems as if you could all have done without *me* – but I find I can't do without *you*!"

The children were more touched than they showed. They gave her a hug, and Cyril whispered in her ear. "I'm glad, Mother, awfully glad!"

They told Roddy when he came down a little later. "Mother's not leaving us, after all. She's sticking to the farm."

"Oh," said Roddy, not sounding in the least interested. He was much more interested in wondering how the cows were!

They caught the bus to school as usual. It had been arranged that Cyril should finish his week out and then go on to the farm – at least till this bad spell had passed.

They came home at tea time, wondering what news there was. The bus was late and it was a quarter-past five before they stepped off it at the bottom of the lane. They ran up to the farm.

They passed the farmhouse window, and peered inside. "My goodness!" said Melisande, startled, "someone's laid hightea – cheese and ham and all! I could do with it too – we're so late."

"Well, if it's high tea I'll come in too," said Roddy, who usually collected his tray and shot off to the henhouse by himself.

Melisande went to find her mother. She was in the kitchen, making the tea. Melisande stared at her in surprise, for she was wearing something she had never seen her in before!

"Mother! You've got my overall on!" she said. "Oh Mother, it's so *peculiar* to see you in that – but you look nice and homey. I like it. Let me help you."

"No. It's all done," said Rose, looking flushed and young again. "We'll all have tea together. I can hear Daddy coming in too."

In five minutes time the family were sitting down to a really good high tea, "just like Mistletoe Farm" as Roddy noticed with satisfaction. Melisande and Cyril were very happy, and their father laughed at their jokes. Only Roddy was stolid and silent as usual, and barely said thank you to his mother for passing him his tea.

"You know that we're *all* sticking together at Holly Farm, don't you?" his father said, wondering if Roddy knew. "You know that, don't you, Roddy? Mother too."

"Yes. Cyril told me this morning," said Roddy, not looking up.

"Roddy! Aren't you *glad* Mother's not going away to town?" said Melisande.

"Well – it wouldn't have made much difference," said Roddy. "Not to me, I mean. Mother didn't really bother much about me or what I wanted – did you. Mother?"

"Don't talk like that, Roddy," said his father, ashamed of him.

"Sorry," said Roddy, and munched at his bread and cheese.

The telephone rang. Melisande went to it and came back glowing. "Oh Mother! That was Dorcas – and what do you think – she says Sally's just been to see her and she doesn't like her new place, and Dorcas has told her to come back to Holly Farm!"

"Good!" said Cyril, Roddy and their father together. Rose beamed. "Is that really true, Melisande! Oh, I must tell Dorcas how glad I am!"

Dorcas was cautious over the telephone. She knew that

346

Mrs David, as she called her, had turned over a new leaf and was going to try and be sensible – but she wasn't going to be too friendly to her till she knew if she was going to keep it up!

"Yes, Ma'am," she said. "Sally's here now. She can't come for two weeks, Ma"m, but you'll manage till then, I don't doubt. Yes, Ma'am, I'll tell Sally you're very pleased. Yes, she's not a bad girl, Sally Goodbye, Ma'am."

Then the table talk turned to the cows. Except for that one that had died, all of them were now on the mend. The shire horse had actually stood on his feet. Mr Longfield looked a different man that evening.

"Well, well!" he said. "Cows on the mend, old Blackie getting better, Sally coming back – what more do we want? Seems as if our luck is turning at last!"

Rose suddenly thought of what her brother-in-law, Peter, had said the night before. "Face up to troubles, and they'll melt away – but you've got to face up to them first."

There was the sound of footsteps coming up to the front door and then a peremptory rat-a-tat-tat. Melisande went to answer it. It was Mr Potts.

"Your father in, Miss?" he said. "Ah, good evening to you, sir. Er – acting on advice from Mr Sam Twigg, I went over to them gypsies at Whortleberry Hill, sir – the ones that camped on your common some time back – and there I found the hens and ducks, I've set down on this list, sir."

He presented Mr Longfield with a neatly written list. "Mr Twigg, sir, he tells me they belong to you – the ones that were reported stolen."

"The ones you thought he stole," said Roddy's disapproving voice. "I always knew he didn't."

"I have – er – apprehended these here poultry, sir," went on the ponderous Mr Potts. "They're at the police-station, along with a few other things of yours, and on your recognizing the same as your property I should be pleased if you would remove them forthwith."

"And I should be more than pleased to do so, Potts," said Mr Longfield, delighted. "I never thought I'd get any of those back."

"Well, sir," you were lucky," said the policeman. "I reckon the gypsies have eaten about eight of the hens and ducks sir, – but they couldn't manage the lot. Probably they meant to sell them."

Mr Potts departed. Mr Longfield went back to the table, rubbing his hands. "Another bit of luck I didn't expect," he said. "Well, Rose dear, I must get the car out and 'remove my property from the police station forthwith' as Mr Potts puts it."

"I bet he was wild when he found that it was the gypsies who stole the hens and damaged the cows and not Twigg," said Roddy. "And he'll be wilder still when Twigg tells him he can poach all he likes on Mistletoe Farm and on Holly Farm too!"

"David! I just want to ask you to bring something back for me in the car," suddenly said Rose, and she slipped out after him. She looked back to see if any of the children were listening, and then whispered in his ear.

He caught her to him and gave her a hug. "Bless you, Rose – that was the last lovely thing left that could happen. I'll bring it, don't you fear."

He drove off in the car. Soon the tea was being cleared. Roddy went out to grade and wash the eggs as usual. He whistled to his imaginary Tinker.

"Everybody's happy," he informed Tinker. "Everything's come right. Wag your tail, Tinker. But let me whisper something to you. I still can't forgive Mother for what she did about that pup!"

He finished the eggs and went indoors to wash. He

heard his father's voice in the kitchen. "Did you bring back the hens, Dad?" called Roddy.

"Yes," called back his father. "Only seven ducks and hens are missing. One of them laid an egg in the car coming back – and two of them laid eggs for Mr Potts in the police station."

"Come out here, Roddy!" called his mother. "Something else came with the hens."

Roddy went out to the kitchen. He went in at the door and then stood transfixed. His mother was holding something in her hands – something that cuddled against her and squealed.

"Mother," said Roddy, and took a step forward. He could hardly believe his eyes. It was his pup – the little spaniel pup he had taken back to Tommy Lane – the very same one.

"Here you are, Roddy – it's yours," said his mother, in a warm voice. "I was silly to think I wouldn't like it. It's perfectly sweet. I shall love to look after it when you're at school. It's just as nice as Crackers."

"Nicer," said Roddy. He took the tiny squirming creature and held it against his neck. It tried to get down his shirt. "Tinker!" said Roddy, happily, squeezing it gently. "You really *are* a tinker!"

"Mother told me to bring it back for you," said his father. "I was so pleased."

"You're a darling, Mother, and I love you!" said Roddy, his heart overflowing with joy. He gave his mother such a hug that she squealed like the puppy. "It's the nicest present in the world."

"The best bit of luck you've had for a long time, Roddy!" said his father. "But you deserve it."

Roddy beamed at his father and mother as he fondled the squirming pup. "Looks as if we're a proper family again, doesn't it, Dad?" he said.

It does indeed, Roddy – and long may you be happy with Tinker and all the rest at Holly Farm!